The Road Back

'You step over that threshold and you needn't bother coming back,' Tom said.

'I don't intend coming back, unless of course you get all the mod cons fitted, then I might think about it.' But she found herself talking to the door. Tom had shut it in her face.

But Milly did go back, some forty-odd years later, under the sentence of death and determined, before it was too late, on a reconciliation with her husband, travelling to Norwich by Intercity and sitting opposite a young woman with unhappy but stunning violet eyes.

Elizabeth Tettmar has written numerous short stories for women's magazines, and children's books. She lives in Harwich.

Also by Elizabeth Tettmar
and available in Mandarin

House of Birds
The Years Between
The Scarlet Landscape

Elizabeth Tettmar

The Road Back

Mandarin

A Mandarin Paperback
THE ROAD BACK

First published in Great Britain 1997
by Mandarin Paperbacks
and William Heinemann
imprints of Reed International Books Ltd
Michelin House, 81 Fulham Road, London SW3 6RB
and Auckland, Melbourne, Singapore and Toronto

A CIP catalogue record for this title
is available from the British Library
ISBN 0 7493 1943 7

Typeset in 10 on 13.5 point Meridien
by Deltatype Ltd, Birkenhead, Merseyside
Printed and bound in Great Britain
by Cox & Wyman Ltd, Reading, Berks

To Jane *with love*

Prologue

It was September 1946 and most of those who had been in service overseas were back home and out of uniform.

There were exceptions. Milly Stevens woke suddenly on that particular Saturday morning to find her husband standing over her and gave a tiny squeal of surprise, for she had thought him still in Palestine. He seemed even bigger than she remembered and the desert sun had bleached his fair hair white. His skin, on the other hand, was the colour of old leather.

It was unfortunate, she thought, for Tom to have surprised her, after three years' absence, with her hair in curlers and even more unfortunate that he should find her with a man in her bed, now dead to the world with his mouth open, and snoring. Not for long, however. Tom had him out of bed and by the scruff of his neck before he had time to utter Jack Robinson.

Milly held her breath as she listened to the sounds that heralded Sid's precipitant ejection into the street. Tom had snatched up a bundle of clothing from the bedside chair as he passed and that, by the sound of it, had followed Sid's undignified exit. The front door banged, then came the heavy tread of army boots on linoed stairs. Milly hastily removed her curlers.

What would Tom do next? Turn on her? She doubted it. He was a gentle man for all his size, and she was fully confident of her ability to twist him round her little finger. But now he was back again and looking down at her with an expression in his eyes that produced a queasy feeling in the pit of her stomach, not entirely unsatisfactory. She made to get out of bed but he stopped her.

'Stay you there,' he said. 'But have a good look at the pattern on the lino first 'cos you'll not be going to see it again for another week.'

Tom was aroused by the sound of heavy traffic: the whine of trams going past the window, of footfalls and carrying voices. It took a minute or two for him to become orientated to his surroundings, then he looked at his watch. Twelve o'clock – midday! He had been asleep for an hour. He rose from the bed, drew the curtains and was about to open the window, for the small and over-furnished room smelled stale, when he remembered that this was London and the air outside would be no fresher than that in. He began to dress.

Milly stirred, then opened her eyes and blinked at him. 'I thought we were going to stay in bed for a week,' she said drowsily.

'I've changed my mind. I can't stay in London. I can't stand the noise, or the smell, or the crowds.'

Three years in the army had not stamped out his Norfolk accent or flattened the burr of his gentle vowels.

'Can I get you some breakfast?' Half-heartedly she made another attempt to get out of bed.

'I had my breakfast hours ago.'

Impassively he studied her, his eyes a startling blue against his thick white lashes. In the brighter light his skin looked more like bronze than old leather. 'How long you been carrying on?' he said.

'I haven't been carrying on the way you think. Sid's been a good friend to me. Besides he was company, and everyone needs company during an air raid.'

'You love him?'

'Course I don't. I only ever loved you.'

'You reckon.' His expression remained impassive. He picked up his kitbag and slung it over his shoulder.

'Where're you going?' Panic assailed her. She could deal with blows, but this calm acceptance was something she couldn't understand.

'I'm going home. If you want me you know where to find me.'

'We ought to talk things over first,' she said, out of bed and by his side in a flash. With shoes on she came up to his shoulder, barefooted she was just about on a level with his breast pocket.

He looked down at her. 'There's nothing to talk out and I'm not staying in London a day longer than necessary. As I said, I'm heading for home.'

Home to Thomas Stevens was a gamekeeper's cottage in a small hamlet adjoining Thornmere known as Thornmere Green, though there had been no green since the National Enclosure Act of 1801. There he had been born and bred, and there he had taken his bride after their marriage in the parish church. Their honeymoon had been short and sweet, and immediately afterwards he had sailed for the Middle East and Milly, homesick for London, had left her in-laws' cottage and returned to Islington and her old job as a machinist at the clothing factory which, since the outbreak of war, had produced in vast quantities uniforms for members of His Majesty's forces.

She spent her free time, when not working or out enjoying herself with her workmates, writing him chatty letters, filling the flimsy pages with descriptions about her job and how boring it was, or of the little house she was renting. But she kept quiet about the dashing Polish soldiers or the willing GI's who escorted her about town. She thought there was no point in rubbing it in about her life of pleasure when his life as an infantryman was anything but pleasurable.

Tom was not a natural letter writer. His scant and irregular missives were of the 'hope you are as well as this leaves me at present' variety. Still she treasured them and wept sentimental tears over them, before filing them away in an old shoe box and changing out of her overalls into a dress more suitable to go dancing in.

It was on a dance floor that Tom had first spotted her. He was not a dancing man, he had never been to a dance until the night a buddy from his company had inveigled him into coming to this canteen in Soho, where good food was on offer and dancing went on until two o'clock in the morning.

'It's run by a countrywoman of yours – a Lottie Foster, good-looker in her time. Ever heard of her?'

'Nope.'

'You should have, she's from your part of Norfolk – a place called Thornmere. Lived, when she was young, at the level-crossing cottage there.'

'Oh ah,' said Tom without interest. The word Thornmere had conjured up for him not the railway cottage or the railway track it served, but a lonely gamekeeper's cottage amid a landscape of flat fields and isolated spinneys. Thornmere itself, with its rows of cottages, its pub and

Memorial Hall and one or two important houses, held no attraction for him.

The canteen when he entered it even less so. It was difficult at first to get one's bearings, coming straight from the black-out into the light obscured by a haze of cigarette smoke, but as his eyes became accustomed to his surroundings they settled on a diminutive figure in red, jitterbugging with an American airman as if her life depended on it.

If it wasn't exactly love at first sight, it was something akin to the pleasure he felt when watching a freshly hatched clutch of pheasant chicks darting about their mother, or the sun rising above Eastern Acres on a winter's morning. He experienced the same catch at his throat which those who knew him well recognised as a stirring of deep emotional feelings. Lennie Ashe, sitting across from him, lowered his glass and said, 'Go on, go an' ask her for a dance.'

'I don't know her.'

'An' you never will get to know her just sitting there. It's every man for hisself these days. I've been watching you watching her for the last ten minutes. You fancy her, don't you?'

'I can't dance.'

'I can't either, but it don't stop me smooching around the floor when I've got the chance. The music's stopping; go on, before someone else grabs her. Me, for instance.'

Tom didn't grab her – far from it. Hesitantly he asked for a dance, then gingerly took her into his arms, fearful as if he might snap her in half.

'Tighter than that,' she said laughingly, drawing his arm more securely around her tiny waist. 'Otherwise we'll lose each other in the crush.'

She had a face that reminded him of a wild pansy, soft

and velvety, with enormous dark eyes that smiled confidently up into his. Because his great uncertain feet were constantly tripping over hers, he lifted her clear of the floor and walked with her in time to the music.

'You great loony,' she said. 'Put me down.' But she was laughing as she said it. She was a rare one for laughing, he discovered later, the slightest thing could set her off. Before the night was out they were both in love and talking marriage.

Milly, though not twenty-one, had no one to ask permission of. Tom was twenty-six and had never been so bowled over before. He was still pinching himself to make sure he wasn't dreaming when orders came through about an overseas posting. Things moved with incredible speed after that.

They were married in a church the size of a cathedral, a legacy from the Flemish weavers who had settled in that part of Norfolk in the Middle Ages. It was a neglected church, for the parish had long since vanished, some said because of the Black Death, others that the labourers had left their homes in the late-eighteenth century for the cotton and woollen mills of the North, where work was plentiful. It was rarely used, this great old church, having now only one service a month when the vicar of Thornmere came riding out on his bicycle with an attaché case of prayerbooks strapped to the carrier, and celebrated Holy Communion with a handful of scattered parishioners.

Milly and Tom made history by being the last couple to get married there. Six months later, a bomb dropped at random gutted it.

Milly was not there to join the few who went to gaze mournfully at the ruins. Two weeks after Tom had sailed away she shook the dust of Norfolk from her feet. She could have put up with her silent and hostile in-laws (she thought); she could have got used in time to the earth closet at the end of a very long garden (she hoped); but never in her life would she get used to the silence, the loneliness and the isolation.

The Stevenses did not possess a wireless. They had no need of one they said, they got all the news they needed from the postman when he called, which was not very often. They did take a newspaper once a week, which fulfilled a dual purpose: keeping Mr Stevens entertained on Sunday and supplying them with toilet paper for the rest of the week. It was a task allotted to Milly to cut the sheets of newspaper into suitable sized squares and thread them on a length of string, an undertaking she considered was adding insult to injury.

Being back in Islington was like coming back to life. The sound of traffic all around her was sweet music to her ears. The cries of the vendors in the markets, the jostle of the queues at the stalls, the familiar London voices of friends and neighbours were for her a renewed delight. She vowed then that she would never leave London again, yet now, just a week after Tom's abrupt appearance and even more abrupt departure, she was contemplating following him back to Norfolk.

She hadn't set eyes on Sid since the morning he'd been thrown out on his ear. She missed him, but she felt she had no right to cohabit with another man now that her husband was in the same country. She would be sorry to give up the little house in Grant Street, for she had never had a home of her own before, but even the memory of the earth closet paled at the thought of Tom's muscular arms around her.

Her mother-in-law had died the previous year, but her father-in-law was still thriving, though retired now. She didn't think he would be much of a problem. Of the two, she had liked him best, for it was he who had always answered her letters the few times she had written. She'd have two men to look after, she mused. She rather liked the idea of that, it was a challenge and she always welcomed a challenge, also she wanted to make Tom proud of her. She wanted him to see what she could really do when she put her mind to it.

She wrote to him to tell him she was coming. He wrote back and said he would meet her at Thornmere Halt station. The following week she closed the front door of number 22 Grant Street and sent up a fervent and silent prayer. Please dear Lord, help me to stick it out this time. In her present frame of mind, given the choice of staying in London or being with Tom, Tom won hands down.

'Nice bit o' bunny you got on there,' remarked her next door neighbour, staring rheumy-eyed at her jaunty little fur jacket. He had just returned from the jug and bottle department of their local, with a bottle of liquid lunch sticking out of his pocket.

'Coney, Mr Richards,' she corrected him.

The old man chuckled. 'That's just a fancy name for rabbit. I've got a hearthrug just like your coat. Lovely and warm on me bed in winter. Leslie 'Eath bin busy again, then? That's the third rabbit coat I've seen walking down this street this week.'

Leslie Heath ran a second-hand clothes shop in Feather Lane, where at times rich pickings could be had for the looking, especially after one of his trips to a dealer in the West End. He had no truck with clothing coupons, preferring to deal with second-hand clothes which were not on ration. Neither, according to Leslie, were his little coney jackets which he sold on the side.

'Stands to reason they must be second-hand. They were first-hand on the bunnies, weren't they!'

They were smart little garments to look at, but extremely uncomfortable to wear as, being unlined, the seams of the pelts scratched one's skin. All right, Milly thought, as she studied her reflection in the glass, so they were only rabbit, but that was better than going to make her peace with Tom in her only other coat, two years old and made from an army blanket. In her opinion there were just as many army blankets as there were rabbits walking along Grant Street.

She was glad of the jacket when she got down from the train at Thornmere Halt, for an east wind came tearing across the fields and nearly took her off her feet. Apart from the porter, Tom was the only other person in sight and she the only passenger to alight. By the time the train steamed off again they had exchanged perfunctory greetings and Tom had relieved her of her case.

When she had come to him as a bride he had arranged for a hired car to meet her at the station, now she was only a wife he expected her to walk. So ran Milly's thoughts as he eyed her speculatively, from her hat made of three narrow strips of felt and some veiling, down to her three-inch heels.

'D'you think you can make it? It's across two fields, over a stile and down a lane.'

'I walk miles in London. I'm not frightened of walking.'

'In those clackers? On wet ground?' His doubt was a challenge to her. I'll show him, she thought.

And she did. But the stile was her undoing – her skirt proved too tight. 'I'll have to hitch it up,' she said. 'Look the other way.'

Instead of which he lifted her bodily over, and as he put her down again he kissed her. 'Do you ever bolt again,' he said, 'you needn't worry about coming back.'

In spite of her good intentions, there were many times Milly felt like bolting in the following weeks, for conditions in the gamekeeper's cottage had deteriorated since the demise of Mrs Stevens. Neglect showed everywhere, especially in matters of cleanliness and tidiness, and never more noticeably than in the dreaded outhouse at the end of the garden. Mrs Stevens had scrubbed the stone floor of the closet every other day and was most liberal in her use of disinfectant, but neither scrubbing nor disinfectant was much in evidence now.

Still, in the first days of what Milly looked upon as her second honeymoon she was in such a state of blissful anticipation that she overlooked minor matters such as cooking on an ancient stove and washing clothes encrusted with mud and as stiff as boards.

Tom's love-making technique had improved considerably since his time overseas and she guessed she had some black-eyed Middle Eastern beauty to thank for that, but after the first week his performance fell off somewhat. She tried to make allowances for him; he was up every morning at six o'clock, out in the open all day organising the shoots and ready for bed by nine o'clock, and once in bed, he fell quickly asleep. She too was ready for bed by nine o'clock, but not to sleep. She lay there listening to Tom's deep breathing, and on the other side of the wall her father-in-law's heavy snores, and felt more and more dissatisfied with her lot. She hadn't realised that the transition from bride to wife could be so painful.

She thought often of her little house in Grant Street with its gas lighting and running water and though the lavatory was outside it shared the same roof as the house and was on main drainage. She had only to walk up the street for the cinema or the music hall and Feather Lane with its well-stocked stalls, and within easy distance were a variety of eating houses that served meals all day. There was nothing approaching that at Thornmere Green. Just field after field fading into the horizon and pheasants strutting about crowing, just asking to be shot, stupid things.

The first time Tom brought home a brace of pheasants she nearly had a fit. 'What am I supposed to do with them?' she wailed.

'You pluck 'em and draw 'em, then roast 'em,' he said patiently.

It was old Mr Stevens who plucked and and drew them for her. His rheumatism prevented him doing any outside work, or even following the guns, so he was glad of something to do, and especially glad to show this little ignorant London miss the facts of country life. He also showed her how to cook the pheasants the way his wife had done, but either the oven was too hot or not hot enough, for Milly never got the hang of using the damper properly. They were as tough as old boots when the time came to eat them.

'They should 'ave bin hung,' grumbled her father-in-law. At first she thought he was referring to her, and though she would have been the first to admit she was no cook, being hanged for it was a bit much. Wistfully she thought of the sausage and pie shop near the Angel, but doubted whether either of the Stevenses, father or son, had even heard of such a heaven.

But finally two events, one on top of the other, precipitated her second hasty retreat to London.

The first was Mr Stevens's cold. When Mr Stevens had a cold they all suffered. He sat by the kitchen fire all day with his feet in a mustard bath, hawking and spitting. He looked upon a cold as a personal affront. He rarely caught one, but when he did he considered he had been singled out on purpose. He needed constant commiseration.

Milly also needed commiseration. Today Tom was delivering a truckload of pheasants to the butcher's at Beckton Market and had promised to take her with him. She hadn't been outside the door, except for the punishing trips to the end of the garden, for over a week. A visit to the market town, a chance to do some window shopping, even buy something, perhaps, couldn't be missed. She needed some more face-cream and she could stock up with some up-to-date magazines. She was childlike in her pleasure and expectation until Tom brought her down to earth by saying he felt she should stay at home with the old man.

'He'll need you to top up his mustard bath,' he said. 'Mother used to do it whenever the water got cool. Tha's the only thing that do him any good.'

Her outburst followed a short period of speechlessness. Tom listened to all the things she'd like to do to him, to his father and to the mustard bath in particular, with his habitual impassivity. When silence fell, he said in his usual unhurried manner, 'Anything you'd like me to bring you back?'

'Yes, a rope,' she screamed. 'So that I can hang myself.'

A slow smile spread across his face. 'Oo ah,' he said.

She got some relief from a storm of tears. She went to the back door and, opening it, looked out at the dreary landscape. A mist was rolling up over the big field Tom called Eastern Acres. The black bare branches of the hedgerow trees traced a lacelike pattern against a milk coloured sky, the beauty of which was lost on her. A pheasant crowed forlornly, as if aware that his day of reckoning had come. There was no answering sorrow in her heart, only a deep hatred of the countryside and all that went with it. As far as she was concerned the sooner it was all covered over with concrete the better.

'Shut that door, you great slummicking mawther,' came

an ear-splitting yell from behind her. 'Thass making a bloody draught.'

Tom came back in mid-afternoon. First he had to return the truck he had borrowed earlier. Afterwards, taking a short cut through a spinney, he found a rabbit in one of his traps. He put it out of its misery and took it back to Milly.

She stared at it wide-eyed. 'And what am I supposed to do with that?'

'I'll show you how to skin it, then you'll know another time. You know how to make rabbit stoo, don't you?'

'I've never made rabbit stew in me life.'

'There's nothing to it. You just stick it in a pot and stoo it.' Tom didn't waste time when talking. In his capable hands the rabbit lost its skin before Milly's stomach stopped heaving.

'Now all you got t' do is to gut it. While you're doing that I'll go and dig you up some vegetables.' He looked at the rabbit with relish. 'I'm partial to rabbit stoo,' he said. 'It'll go down well for supper on a cold day like this. Put in a bit o' bacon as a taster, Mother always did, and thicken it up too. I can't abide watery stoos.'

Milly looked at the pathetic carcase dripping blood on the table top. She looked at the window which framed Tom's tall figure making purposefully for the vegetable plot. She looked at her father-in-law dozing over the fire, with dribble running down his chin and saw in him a replica of Tom as he would be in fifty years' time. At last she steeled herself to look at the pelt, that sad little bundle of fur, and wondered how many rabbit stews did it take to make a coat like hers, and at that thought tears flooded her eyes and rolled unchecked down her cheeks.

She hated this wretched country. She hated its smells and mud and dirt and cruelty. She hated its lack of essentials like gas and electricity and water, and more than anything else she hated her life as a skivvy.

She looked at the floor that she had to scrape every morning before she could scrub it. She looked at her father-in-law who took everything she did for granted, and she looked once more at the makings of a rabbit stew with the pelt neatly spread out beside them and imagined them whole and skipping about in the buttercup meadow; and she vowed to herself that as soon as she was able to replace it she'd never wear her rabbit-skin jacket again.

'I'll go now,' she vowed. 'And I'm damned if I'll ever come back again.'

Tom had lingered in the garden to see the sun sink beyond Follet's Dyke. He watched the sky turn from red to saffron to mauve; he watched as the last few skeins of sunset-coloured cloud drifted and merged into an opaque sky. Satisfied with the day that was fading around him, appreciative of his lot and looking forward to a good meal to finish off with, he turned towards the house with a handful of what his mother had called pot herbs – 'Goo down to garden and dig me up a handful of pot herbs, bor' – pot herbs in this case being a turnip, onion, carrot and parsnip. He went indoors, whistling. He had a surprise for Milly. He had bought her a frilly little apron, the kind waitresses wore, in the market. She had no lack of aprons for his mother's still had plenty of wear in them, but they were the big, old-fashioned, wrap-around kind and Milly, bless her heart, deserved something prettier.

He had not been unaware of the efforts she had made in the past few weeks, it just had not occurred to him to mention it. He'd make it up to her some day, he thought. For a starter he would borrow the truck again on Saturday and take her to the cinema at Beckton Market. She'd like that.

Milly, bless her heart, was wearing her little fur jacket, her short, tight skirt, her wisp of a hat and her three-inch heels.

'What's the meaning of this?' he said, dumping the vegetables down on the table.

'The meaning of this is that I'm going home! And what's more, I'm not coming back, not to this – this pigsty.'

Milly was horrified – the word had slipped out. She had intended to say labour camp; labour camp was already voiced in her mind, but she heard herself say pigsty instead. She saw Tom's face harden, his mouth set. 'I'm sorry,' she said. 'I meant to say labour camp.'

'What d'you mean by labour camp?'

'A place to labour in, that's what it means to me. Work – work – work and no let up. I never go out – I never see anybody, all I do is clean and cook and wash clothes, and before I can do that I have to pump water up from the well. It's not human what you expect from me and I don't intend to go on doing it any longer. I'm going home – back to my own people!'

He went over to the door and barred the way with his arm. 'How d'you reckon getting to the station?'

'I'll walk like I did last time.'

'In those shoes – in the dark!'

'I'll crawl on my hands and knees if necessary.'

Their raised voices disturbed old Mr Stevens. He sat up, coughing violently. 'What's all this then?' he said. His voice rose to a howl, 'Me water's gone stone cold!'

They ignored him, intent only on each other.

'You step over that threshold and you needn't bother coming back,' Tom said.

'I don't intend coming back, unless of course you get all mod cons fitted, then I might think about it.' But she found herself talking to the door. Tom had shut it in her face.

But Milly did go back, some forty-odd years later, under sentence of death and determined, before it was too late, on a reconciliation with her husband, travelling to Norwich by Intercity and sitting opposite a young woman with unhappy but stunning violet eyes.

One

Carla, lost in uncomfortable memories, was jolted back to the present when the train came to an unexpected halt at a station. She glanced out at the name board. Diss. So they were now in Norfolk. Once the very thought of Norfolk would have sent a quiver of pleasure coursing through her veins, would have set her off calculating how much longer before stepping out on to Norfolk soil. Now, as the train, starting up again, gathered speed, she stared out at the gentle landscape bathed in the cool, pale sunshine of early spring with hostile eyes. It was all such a far cry from the purple hills of Tuscany that she could have wept.

Tears did start to her eyes, but she blinked them back. She had done enough crying in the past six months to last her a lifetime. More to the point, she felt she was under scrutiny by the woman sitting opposite. She felt a growing antipathy towards her, who, instead of putting her case in the space between the backs of seats reserved for luggage, had wedged it beneath the table that separated their two seats. She had strewn the table itself with several bulging carrier bags, a distended handbag and a hat the shape and colour of a button mushroom. Carla more than once had tried to move her legs but found herself fenced in by the suitcase and the table. She needed leg-room more than most people, for her legs were exceptionally long.

It was her legs, she felt sure, that had first attracted Tony's attention, bringing him across the Piazzale Michelangelo to where she was sitting, dreaming over the view. Her flatmates complained of having their bottoms pinched when they went abroad at night-time; that indignity had never happened to her, perhaps, as Sophie suggested, because she hadn't much of a bottom to pinch. But she had plenty of leg and this brought forth many cries and whistles of admiration until she stopped wearing short skirts, which looked ridiculous on her, like a crane wearing a frill, and took to trousers instead. Ah, those happy carefree days at the beginning of her love affair with Florence, as heady as wine and as sweet.

Another rush of unbidden tears threatened to overwhelm her. She concentrated on present miseries instead, allowing her irritation to grow out of all proportion against the woman opposite. She knew there was nothing to stop her getting up and finding another seat if she wanted, except for the apathy that wrapped itself around her like a wet cloak. Looking round, she saw that the compartment was practically empty, and she and her fellow passenger sat crammed together in splendid isolation. Suddenly she saw the funny side of it and smiled in spite of herself.

The woman took advantage of this and, leaning forward pushed the barrier of carrier bags out of the way. 'Excuse me,' she said, 'but do you know Norfolk well?' She spoke in a peculiar mixture of assumed gentility and cockney vowels.

Carla's knowledge of Norfolk was exceedingly small, resting almost entirely on an old level-crossing cottage in a quiet corner of Broadland, but she saw no reason for imparting that information to a stranger.

'Not really,' she said non-committally. She had no intention of getting into a conversation with one who she sensed had been itching to talk ever since the compartment emptied. She looked the gossipy type. Given the opportunity, Carla thought, she would start embarking on her life history.

And yet . . . There was something heart-warming about the other's expansive smile and her dark-brown eyes were brimming with friendliness. She was one of those women who in youth, Carla surmised, are like pocket Venuses, but who in middle age expand to a size out of all proportion to their tiny feet. This one was well past middle age; she must be somewhere between sixty-five and seventy-five. She bore her years well. Her face was too plump for wrinkles to get a hold and her hair was unstreaked with grey, though that was probably due to her hairdresser's skill rather than to nature. Her suit was stylish, not couturier class exactly, but certainly off an expensive peg. Carla found her irritation fading.

The woman's next question came like a bolt from the blue. 'I don't suppose you've heard of a place called Thornmere, have you?'

Carla's heart skipped a beat. Of all the little-known villages in Norfolk, why had this person picked on Thornmere? Like a wounded animal she was stealing back to Thornmere, unknown to friends or family, to find comfort and consolation in her own particular lair. She craved the isolation of the gatehouse, the only place she knew of that could afford her the privacy she needed, and now this stranger with her probing questions was in danger of undermining it.

Perhaps her dismay showed in her expression for the woman added hastily, 'I only asked because when I last went to Thornmere a long time ago – long before you were born – 1946, in fact – I got out at a station called Thornmere Halt. But today, when I bought my ticket at Liverpool Street, I was told Thornmere Halt was shut down years ago. That the whole of that line from Norwich to the coast had been axed in the Sixties and even the rails taken up. Then how do they expect people to get to Thornmere now, I ask myself?'

'I don't think there is a bus to Thornmere itself,' Carla said. 'But you can catch one from Norwich to Beckton Market. That's a little town about three miles' distance from Thornmere, and from there you could get a taxi to the village.' She said this with some reservations, not knowing the other's financial situation. Never mind that her suit looked expensive, that was nothing to go by. It could quite easily have come from one of the charity shops.

The train began to slow down as it approached the terminus. The woman put on her hat, stuffing most of her hair out of sight. Carla lifted her holdall and a portfolio from the rack. The main bulk of her belongings she had left in Florence. When one makes a sudden decision to run away there is no time to think of packing.

The train came to a stop. The woman collected her bits and pieces together. 'Would you be going to Thornmere yourself?' she asked hopefully.

Carla could not lie, and what did it matter anyway? Once this journey was over their paths would diverge. She nodded.

'I suppose you wouldn't share a taxi with me?' came the next quick-fired question.

'From Beckton Market?'

'No, all the way to Thornmere. Save messing about with buses.'

Carla had intended doing this herself, so could not now refuse this offer. It would seem odd them both lining up for separate taxis when they had got this far in their acquaintanceship. She supposed she could pretend she was staying in Norwich, but she was tired of pretence. There had been enough of that in Florence.

'Now for a porter,' said the other, 'Or is it trolleys?'

'I'm afraid it's trolleys.'

A deep sigh. 'Worse thing they ever did was to get rid of porters. How do the old and infirm manage, or mothers with young babies? Seems to me the only people who are catered for on the railways these days are the young and able. I don't know how I would have got on at Liverpool Street if it hadn't been for a very gallant Polish gentleman. He helped me on with my case and then sat next to me as far as Manningtree. I don't suppose you noticed?'

Carla hadn't noticed anything about her fellow passengers until the case obstructing the movement of her legs made its presence felt and that was two-thirds into the journey.

'He was with the Free Polish forces during the war, so we found a lot to talk about. He never went back to Poland but married an English girl and settled down at Upminster. I was ever so sorry when he got off at Manningtree, but he had to change for the Harwich line. He said he was meeting some relatives off the ferry. Fancy coming all the way from Upminster to meet someone off the ferry at Harwich, but the Poles are like that. So gallant. I met an awful lot of nice Poles during the war,' she added reminiscently, then more briskly, 'If you could push and I pulled, dear, I think we could get this case off the train between us, don't you?'

They not only got it off the train but also on to a trolley. Afterwards the woman straightened up, panting a little. She took her compact out of her bag and dabbed at her face. She smiled as if they were old friends. 'I reckon it's about time we exchanged names – mine's Milly, Milly Stevens.' She held out a small and dimpled hand.

A worn gold band was embedded in her ring finger. She wore no jewellery. Carla gave her name.

'Carla – that's unusual.'

'It's short for Charlotte.'

'That's a name you don't hear much of these days. I like the old-fashioned names, myself. Milly isn't short for anything. My mother had the good sense not to have me christened Millicent. I don't suppose I looked a Millicent even in them days.' Now and then she made a grammatical slip, which Carla found endearing. She loved the way Milly said 'innit' in her refined accent, and wondered who had tutored her and why.

It was well-nigh impossible for Milly to talk and walk at the same time but she did not seem to realise this. She tottered at Carla's side, puffing like a grampus. 'Nobody uses surnames these days – it's first names right from the word go. I blame it all on the telly. Everybody gets called by their first name on the telly – except politicians. They're always addressed as Right Honourables. Honourables, that's a laugh. Have you noticed that nobody seems to say yes, either? It's always right. "Is that the way to the Ladies?" "Right." "Do I change here for Edmonton?" "Right." Another saying that gets on my wick is "There you go then." I hear it at my supermarket all the time. "Go where?" I says to the check-out girl one time and she goggled at me – didn't know what I meant.' Milly tittered.

'Mind you, we had some silly expressions in my day too,' she continued. 'I was always saying "Oh my godfathers", whenever I was taken by surprise. One day my husband says to me, "Who are these godfathers you are always talking about. Did you ever meet them?" That made me laugh. He could always make me laugh, Tom could, he had such a dry way of saying things.'

They were the last passengers to leave the platform and there was already a small queue waiting for taxis. When their turn came the driver made short work of transferring Milly's luggage from the trolley to the boot of his car. He looked enquiringly at Carla. 'And yours, miss?'

She indicated the holdall slung over her shoulder, the portfolio under one arm. 'I travel light.'

He grinned. 'Sensible girl.'

He had no idea the way his use of that word girl lifted Carla's spirits. With the ominous figure of thirty on the not too distant horizon, and the thought of Vanessa's youthful freshness constantly on her mind, the term was more than a compliment, it was an ego booster, and oh, how her ego needed boosting.

She slipped into the back of the car beside Milly and it wasn't until she leant back against the upholstery that she realised just how tired she was. She had slept little last night and had not made up for it on the plane as she had hoped. It seemed to her that she had been travelling for a lifetime.

A longing for the gatehouse, for its unique tranquility, stole over her again. More than anything she craved solitude, but first there was another half-hour or so in Milly's company. She dredged up the remains of her fortitude to sustain her for another barrage of inconsequential chatter, but this time Milly remained perversely silent, absorbed in staring out of the window at the passing scene. She didn't speak until Norwich was well behind them and there was nothing in sight but field after field of growing barley. Then she said with a trace of sourness in her voice, 'I see there's still plenty of space to be had up here.'

Quick as a flash the driver came back at her. 'Not so

much as there used to be. Take Thornmere, for instance, the place you're heading for. We used to call any job that way going out to the sticks – now we say going out to the bricks. That's progress!'

This was not what Carla wanted to hear at all. 'D'you mean there's been a lot of building in the past three years?'

'Soon there won't be any open road left between Thornmere and Beckton Market. It'll be houses, houses all the way.'

But they soon discovered that the driver had taken a jaundiced view, for once they came off the dual carriageway that linked Beckton Market with the coast they were back in deep countryside and once again drove alongside fields of growing crops. Carla began to look out for landmarks and the first soon came into view – the old stone bridge that crossed the river by the Ferry Inn, and the inn itself squatting on the further bank as it had done for nearly two hundred years.

Milly sat up. 'Does that place do bed and breakfast?'

'It does and I can recommend it. Cost you half of what it would in Norwich.'

'I'd like to have a closer look at it.'

They crossed the river and stopped at the car-park by the side of the inn. Two boats were tied up at the staithe and from the bows of one of them a young woman was laughingly throwing bread to a noisy gaggle of ducks. It looked an idyllic scene – the ancient hostelry, the languid river, the sweeping willows just breaking into leaf.

Milly, however, seemed unimpressed. 'Yes, it looks pretty enough,' she conceded. 'But I bet the toilet is an earth closet down the bottom of the garden.'

The driver grinned at them via the mirror. 'Better than that, ma'am. Nothing less than a family three-holer. It saves a lot of queuing in the rain.'

Milly knew she was being ribbed. She liked anybody who could give as good as they got. She laughed. 'Thank's very much but my queuing days are over. I had enough of that during the war. Can't you find me something a little more modern? You know the sort of thing – tea-making things in the bedroom, *en-suite* bathroom and remote-control television.' She said this with her tongue firmly in her cheek, for nothing she had seen so far – empty fields, an old inn and a windmill converted into a private residence – led her to expect much in the way of amenities. Even the approaching housing estate, followed by terraces of gentrified cottages, failed to bolster her expectations.

'There's the Thornmere Hall Country Club,' said the driver. 'That meets all your requirements, and it's not so out of the way, either.'

Carla, who had stayed at the country club three years ago, was tempted to break in here. The comfort and food had been beyond compare. She had slept in a king size bed with silk hangings and the bath taps had the appearance of plated gold, but it hadn't come cheap. She wondered if she should whisper a word of warning in the woman's ear to save her any embarrassment later. While she dithered, Milly said, 'Sounds just the place I'm looking for.'

In Milly's eyes it was an imposing old house with tall brick chimneys and the promise, if one could go by outward appearances, of a highly civilised standard of living. In Carla's eyes it was the place where she had made the momentous decision to go ahead and have the derelict level-cottage renovated, and from there to go off in search of her unknown father. That alone had made the long and costly venture worthwhile.

'Who'd expect to find a place like this out here in the wilds. Does it pay?' Milly enquired as they turned into the drive.

'It ought to. It's busy all the year round, what with weddings and functions and conferences. It's booked up weeks ahead in the summer, but I think early in the season like this you should be all right.'

The lodge was occupied, washing was blowing on the line. Carla thought fleetingly of her stay there with Jessie Stoneham. They had been good friends once. She supposed she would have to look Jessie up some time, but not yet. There was nobody she wanted to see just now, not even her father. Milly said, 'Thornmere looks a lot better off than it did last time I saw it. I noticed the church roof has been re-thatched. Done recently, was it?'

'Last year. Not before it needed it, it was last re-thatched in 1922. That church is worth a visit if you're staying any time. It was mentioned in the Domesday Book.'

Milly had no interest in the Domesday Book and did not intend to spend her time looking at churches anyway. She had quite a different quest in mind. 'Them cottages we just passed. They've had money spent on them too, by the looks of it. More money about these days, I suppose?'

'It's all down to the incomers. They're the ones with the money. Bought up all the old properties and had them modernised to use as holiday homes. Some have retired here too, and yes, I suppose they have brought money into the village. It was mostly the incomers who got up a subscription for the repair of the church roof. Still, I can't help feeling sorry for the young ones when they want to set up home together. They can't afford to buy any of the cottages if they fall empty, even if it's one of those that haven't been done up. What we could do with now are a few more shops. But everybody's got cars these days and off they go for their out-of-town shopping, excepting the local OAPs of course, and there isn't even a bus for them.'

By now he had drawn up at the entrance to Thornmere

Hall. He got out and walked round and opened the door for Milly. Carla followed her.

Milly said, 'There's no need for you to get out here, ducky. The taxi'll take you on. You'll take her on, won't you, driver? It's only a few yards further up the lane.'

'Of course I'll take her on. I won't keep you waiting long, miss, I'll just see this lady settled in first.'

'I really would rather walk,' said Carla.

Something about her tone convinced the other two and they said no more. Milly kissed her goodbye. 'Thank you for your help, luv, I couldn't have managed without you at Norwich. I'm not going to say goodbye. I expect I shall be staying here for a little while and I'm sure to bump into you sooner or later. Thornmere isn't all that big, is it?'

Carla waited, watching their entry into the Hall, Milly puffing from the climb up the steep steps to the entrance, the laden driver close on her heels. He looked surprised to see Carla waiting when he returned to his cab.

'You've changed your mind? You want me to take you on after all?'

'No, I just want to settle up my share of the fare.'

He grinned. 'That's all been taken care of. I don't think you'll have much joy there, miss.'

'But I can't let her do this, I hardly know her.'

'None of my business, miss, but that lady has a mind of her own and I don't think you'll have much luck changing it.'

'This puts me in a very awkward position.'

'I wouldn't mind being in such an awkward position, myself. I'd call it providential. Can I give you a lift to the end of the drive?'

'Thank you, but I would still prefer to walk.'

'Suit yourself.'

*

It was still standing, the old gatehouse, a pale-washed monument to the nineteenth-century railway age; a legacy from her great-grandmother whose childhood home it once had been. She had almost convinced herself, during her stay in Florence, that it was all a dream – that short busy period in her life when she had put all her time and energy and a good part of her capital into bringing this old house back to life.

She recalled as if it were yesterday the occasion when she first set eyes on the gatehouse, not the solid railway cottage that had housed several generations of Fosters, but a ruin, a vandalised relic left over from the Beeching era, empty, derelict, left to rot. She had come upon it in the gloom of a November afternoon amidst a bleak and inhospitable landscape. A flock of starlings returning home from a day's foraging in the fields had come swooping out of the sky, swirling around the slated roof like a moving black cloud. She had dubbed it the house of birds for there was evidence of birds everywhere, and in the crumbling bedrooms, the remains of house-martins' nests.

There had been more evidence of neglect and dilapidation inside the house. Broken window glass and rotting matter had strewn the floors, mats of cobwebs clung to the walls, the hearths were full of fallen soot and overall was the throat-catching smell of damp and decay. The place looked fit only for demolition and the site to be sold off as a building plot, an idea she had in mind when she first set eyes on it.

It was the house-martins' nests which changed her mind. Lottie, her great-grandmother, had always set great store in superstitions relating to birds, and house-martins and swallows were sacrosanct to her – birds of good fortune, bringing luck to those houses they chose as nesting sites. Could she afford to throw away all this good fortune? Carla had asked herself at the time, and decided then and there to use her inheritance to rebuild Lottie's old home. By so doing, she had developed a deep and lasting love for Norfolk, a love that was tested very severely when she arrived in Florence.

What had happened to the gatehouse since her absence? she now wondered. There was certainly an improvement in the garden which when she left had been little more than a wilderness. Larry, her father, had kept his promise to her and had had it laid out in lawns and flower beds now ablaze with daffodils. He had also gone ahead with converting the old outhouses at the end of the garden into a studio. She was longing to see that, for she had never had a studio before – but first things first. She was tired. She wanted a cup of tea, a shower and a change of clothes in that order. She let herself into the kitchen.

There was no change here, it was exactly as she had left it. Though her father had told her he would camp out here occasionally to keep the house aired during her absence, there was no evidence of his presence, except, and she smiled at this, all her little ornaments and knick-knacks in the sitting-room had been put away for safe-keeping. She knew he had always been fearful of causing damage in what he called her doll's house.

The sun's rays slanted through the tall windows, dappling the carpet with a shifting pattern of light. The clock was ticking softly, the heartbeat of that sleeping house. It was an eight-day clock in a delicate china case that she had discovered in an antique shop in Norwich. The very fact that it was running and keeping good time showed that her father was regularly visiting the gatehouse. Someone, too, was keeping the place clean, for there was not a speck of dust to be seen. Irina her step-mother's work she guessed, for housework was not something she could imagine her father putting his hand to. Mowing the lawn yes, but housework no.

She went upstairs, first to the middle bedroom, which she had taken as her own. This was the room which Lottie had shared with her little sister Violet; the one where she, Carla, had painted a fresco of sweetpeas all round the walls. Some of the flowers had faded and others had obviously been recently touched up. Larry's work? A real labour of love if so, for he hated what he called 'a finicky job'. Dear Larry.

She went downstairs again and into the kitchen and raided the fridge. She found a carton of long-life milk unopened, a tin of ham and a loaf in the freezing compartment. She soon thawed that in the microwave. It was two o'clock and she hadn't eaten since a snack on the plane that morning. While she waited for the water in the tank to heat up she went out to have a look at the studio. A blackbird followed her, scolding furiously, no doubt on duty guarding a nest in one of the shrubs. A neat brick path had been laid the length of the garden curving from the kitchen door to the studio, but not in a straight line. Larry would never have countenanced that.

Her father's promise that he would have the outbuildings converted during her absence had been more than fulfilled. The ruins of the old pigsties, the outside loo, the woodshed and wash-house had all been swept away, and instead there was now a roomy and workmanlike structure made from the flint blocks and Welsh slates of the original buildings. Inside, the sense of space was even greater, the light augmented by the pale-washed walls. It had a large north-facing window of course, and another by the stable-door entrance. That was Larry's idea, Carla guessed, picturing him leaning over the bottom half of the door, musing over the garden with his inevitable cigarette.

He had not been idle while she had been away. On the walls there were views of the gatehouse from every angle, one a long shot of the cottage that he must have painted from the far side of a neighbouring field. It was such a change from his earlier phase of paintings of dereliction, that these latter works could well stand for resurrection. The mere fact that he had hung them on the walls showed he had no intention of selling them. She wondered if she could wheedle one out of him to hang in her bedroom.

The familiar smell of oil paints, turpentine and cigarette smoke transported her back to the attic studio of Tony's villa in Florence, with its large skylight and panoramic views over the city. For a moment or two she felt off balance, torn between an anguished longing and a relief that she had escaped in time. She had come away to forget, so what was the point of dwelling on the past, but the sudden scalding tears that filled her eyes proved that she had no control yet over her feelings.

She shivered, not from any ghost that might have walked over her grave but because she suddenly felt chilled. It was cold in the studio. Little sun penetrated its thick walls. Electric space heaters had been installed and she switched one on now, knowing that it would take an hour or two before the studio warmed up. By then she might feel like putting the finishing touches to the sketches in her portfolio. She had to do something, the day would be intolerably long otherwise. She had craved for solitude and now that she had it, she didn't know what to do with it. She half-wished that Larry would put in a sudden appearance, even though it might mean facing an explosion of wrath when he discovered she had sneaked home without informing him first.

For the first twenty-five years of her life her father had been an enigma, never mentioned in the old Wenley house which had been her home until her great-grandmother died. Now, for more than three years he had been a powerful factor in her life and it seemed inconceivable that there had ever been a time when she had not known him.

Again that night she slept fitfully and consequently awoke the following morning with a rampaging headache. She searched everywhere for some aspirins; she turned her holdall inside out, but with no success. She must have taken her last tablet on the plane from Siena.

She showered and searched out some old clothes she had left in her bedroom cupboard. Did it matter that they were three years out of date? Jeans and T-shirts change little, if at all. She pulled a mustard-coloured sweat-shirt over a cotton top and tied back her chestnut-coloured hair with a piece of black tape she found in her dressing-table drawer. She'd need the sweater if she were going out.

She looked at herself critically in the mirror. Normally pale, three years under an Italian sun had given her skin a healthy golden glow, but many nights without sleep had left dusky smudges under her lower lids which, however, unnoticed by her enhanced the violet tints in her eyes. All she could see – and she had to look for them – were a few lines at the corner of her eyes, which Sophie, like the good friend she was, assured her were laughter lines, but which Carla knew were a reminder that thirty was just a year and a few weeks away.

It was fresher this morning; the sun had not yet pierced the early morning cloud and there was even a faint dusting of frost on the grass. She hoped the post office stores stocked aspirin or something similar – she felt she could not hold out much longer. These blinding, stultifying headaches had only started six months previously. She refused to connect them with Vanessa, a small, spirited and dainty little creature with long blonde hair who appeared at Tony's workshop one morning and enquired sweetly if this was Senor Antonio Conway's masterclass? If it had not been before, it became so from that moment, thought Carla, noting the sudden intent that flickered in and out of Tony's discerning black eyes.

Masterclass, she had repeated bitterly to herself. Mistress-class more like it, for by then she had lost any illusions that she had the sole tenancy of Tony's bed. It had been a hard pill to swallow, knowing that she was only one of many, but it hadn't lessened her love for him.

They had met, she and Tony, at the beginning of her second week in Florence and during that short spell she had feasted so much on what beauty the city had to offer in the way of art and achitecture that she was suffering from a bad case of cultural indigestion. She had 'done' the Duomo and the Baptistery. She had climbed Giotto's bell-tower and posted a card to her father from the café at the top. She had admired, with a thousand others, Ghiberti's Gate of Paradise, and finally that morning she had visited the Academy of Fine Arts to see Michelangelo's David. She was not experienced enough to tell it from the copy in the Piazza Signoria, but she could appreciate the importance of the original. She had bought a poster of the statue and later hung it on the wall of her bedroom which had called forth many ribald remarks from her flatmates. She ignored them all. For her the David was a work of art. It put into perspective her own small talent, but it also gave her something to strive for. Perfection.

And then, at the beginning of her second week, she had crossed the river by the Ponte San Niccolò and climbed the Hill of San Miniato, drinking in the scent of lilac from walled gardens, to the Piazzale Michelangelo just for the pleasure of the magnificent views over the red roofs of Florence and beyond to the dreaming hills of Tuscany.

She was out of breath and her feet were aching, and when she spotted a vacant seat she made for it with an audible sigh of relief. She was not long left in peace. Florence, she discovered, abounded in beggars, most of them gypsies. One approached her now, an old woman with a basket of roses. She gave one to Carla then held out her palm. Carla, not yet familiar with the Italian coinage, had fallen into the habit of holding out a handful of loose change and allowing the shop assistants or stall holders to help themselves. She did this now and without hesitation the woman gleefully snatched up a few of the coins and made off, chuckling.

'You know that you have just been outrageously cheated, or are you so stinking rich you don't care?' came a voice from slightly above her. She looked up at a slight, trim, swarthy figure, whom she would have taken for an Italian but for his very English accent.

She melted in the warmth of his smile. 'How did you know I was English?' she said.

'By your clothes.'

'Oh dear, are they so awful?'

'Not awful at all. You look charming.' He was no stranger to charm himself and she dropped her eyes, out of practice with this kind of dalliance. Without asking permission he seated himself by her side. 'Do you know that with what that old crone took from you you could have bought a dozen such roses in the market?'

'It was my fault. I was never any good at maths.'

He laughed softly. 'Then may one enquire what you are good at?'

'Sightseeing.' She reeled off descriptions of all the amazing sights that had inspired her with such emotional delight, finishing with her heroic climb up all 414 steps of Giotto's bell-tower. A group of young Italian students had urged her on with cries of *'Uno piano', 'Uno piano.'*

'And you made it?'

'Indeed yes, and was rewarded with a delicious cup of coffee and a glorious view from the terrace.'

He gave another low chuckle. 'And you've done all that in just over a week? You're better at it than the Americans. I wish I were your age, seeing Florence again for the first time. I'm a little sad too, because you have left me so little to show you. However, there are still some quaint little corners to poke in. But first, some refreshment.'

He took her to the nearby Boboli Gardens, where over refreshing cups of lemon tea, they exchanged names and potted life histories. Carla's amazement grew as she listened to him, because his life seemed to parallel so much of her own. She broke in to tell him so. He looked amused and sceptical at the same time.

'Your mother was deceived by a man who abandoned her when she was pregnant?' His voice rose.

'He loved her, but he just could not face the responsibility of marriage. And then, would you believe, he went on to marry no less than three times and had children by all three wives.'

This time Tony could not hold back his laughter. 'That was rather overdoing it, wasn't it? My father never countenanced marriage either, he just liked having affairs, especially with susceptible little English misses who came to Florence to learn how to paint.'

Carla gave an embarrassed little giggle. 'I am also an English miss who has come to Florence to learn to paint . . .'

'Are you susceptible?'

She chose to misunderstand him. 'If you mean am I

susceptible to Florence, yes I am. But what happened to your mother?'

'She returned to England to face *her* mother with the news that she was pregnant. I don't think it was a very happy time for her then. She lived long enough to name me after my father and then she gently expired, leaving me to the tender mercies of my formidable grandmother.'

'I was also brought up by my grandmother and great-grandmother,' cried Carla excitedly. 'But they weren't at all formidable, at least my great-grandmother wasn't. This is most extraordinary.'

'I went to college. I studied art. Did you?'

'No, I gave up college to stay home to look after my great-grandmother, because my grandmother by then had died. I suppose I am more or less self-taught, though I did inherit some of my father's talent. Did you ever meet your father?'

'As soon as I left college I came to Florence with the express purpose of seeking him out and kicking him down the length of Italy and into the Mediterranean Sea.'

'And did you?'

'Alas, no. The miserable bastard did me out of that pleasure. He died the year previously.'

There was a short silence, whether out of respect for the dead or because neither of them could think of what to say, Carla could not be sure.

She was the first to break it. 'And you stayed on in Florence?'

'Not immediately, but long enough to get bitten by the Renaissance bug. I returned home, obtained a place at an academy of art for a couple of years, then returned to Florence to continue my studies.' He stared dreamily into the middle distance. 'I returned to England on and off while my grandmother was still alive, but once she died there was nothing to keep me there. She left me a small legacy and my father's people, as if in propitiation for his sins, gave me the lease of a clapped-out old villa. With that and what I make on my classes, I have enough to keep the wolf from the door.' And a little more, thought Carla, noting his silk shirt and gold watch. 'Now, tell me more about this Bluebeard of a father of yours,' Tony was saying. 'He paints. May I know his name?'

'Laurence Marsh . . . Larry.'

He was impressed. 'I know of him. I know his work. He has quite a following.'

'He has in quite another sense – all female, and sitting at his feet and adoring him. Irina, his wife, refers to them as his disciples.'

He chuckled at this. 'Did you ever want to kick him down the boot of Italy, metaphorically speaking, I mean?'

'I did once, but when I got to know him better I couldn't help but like him. I like him very much. I owe being here to my father. It was he who pushed me out of the cosy little nest I had built for myself and sent me off on my travels. He thought I was too insular. He said I was socially deprived. He said it was the result of being brought up by two old biddies.'

'Two old biddies?'

'My grandmother and my great-grandmother. My mother was killed in a motoring accident when I was little more than a toddler.'

'I see what you mean by our lives running on parallel lines. I agree it is odd, but I would challenge your father on the assumption that you are socially deprived. I would rather say that you are just an old-fashioned girl and I find that very refreshing.'

She looked away from him, across at the far vista of the misty Tuscan landscape and forced herself to say what she felt must be stated, and with conviction. 'Larry gave me another piece of advice, He told me to fall in love. He said sex is good for art – that it enhances the emotions and that works of art lacking in emotion are just lifeless.'

She was determined to scotch at birth any idea that she was just an old-fashioned girl.

The post office luckily stocked aspirins. She bought two bottles while she was about it, anticipating more restless nights followed by devastating headaches. She also bought a newspaper and a carton of fresh milk. On her walk home she stopped to visit the church, ashamed that when she had passed it yesterday she had barely noticed it. It wasn't only the roof that had been renewed, the churchyard had undergone a transformation too. The old overgrown graveyard that she remembered, with tombstones rising out of the grass like crooked teeth, had been replaced by neat areas of well-cut grass. The tombstones had been removed and were were now stacked side by side along the boundary fence.

That was sad in one way, for she could not now seek out the graves of her forebears without referring to the parish records, but she could at least look for their headstones, which she did, two of them, one bearing the names of Lottie's mother and father, and baby brother; the other of Lottie's youngest sister, her eldest brother who had been cremated, that other brother whose remains had been left on a Flanders field and that of Lottie herself.

Carla stared at the newly carved lettering, biting her lip, remembering all too well that cold November day when she had scattered Lottie's ashes in the garden of the derelict gatehouse. That had been the start of it all, she thought. The start of the gatehouse's rejuvenation and of the long road that had eventually led her to Florence and Tony. She turned away.

There was nothing grand about Thornmere church. It was a far cry from the magnificent churches she had visited in Florence, which in themselves were each a museum or a work of art. But as she sat there in the pew nearest the door, a feeling of peace stole over her and she was able to remember with equilibrium the last church service which she had attended.

It was her first springtime in Florence when Tony had taken her on Holy Saturday to the Easter Vigil in the Duomo. It started at 11 p.m. and would, Tony told her, go on until about one o'clock in the morning. She was subdued by the size of the congregation, and by the solemnity of the occasion. Nervously she held on to Tony's hand as they followed the usher along the aisle, wondering if she was trespassing where she had no right to be. She could not follow the service of course, but she copied Tony, kneeling when he did and rising with him. Not that anybody would have noticed if she had erred, the Cathedral was packed. They were each given a candle to hold and at a certain part in the service the candles were lighted by sidesmen, and in that flickering candlelight, against the grandeur of their surroundings and with the intoning like an anthem in the background, she had what she could only think of as a religious awakening and made all sorts of fervent vows to God, which, being the weak sinner that she was, she found difficult to keep.

As an antidote (Tony's words) he took her, the following morning, to Communion at the Anglican Church. It was nothing like as grand as the Cathedral, or any of the churches she had as yet visited, but it had a certain fame in as much as it had once been the home of Machiavelli, though Carla could not be sure if that added to its prestige or not.

When they arrived they found the door locked. The previous service had not yet finished. Except for the period of the siesta and closing time at night, the Duomo was never locked, the services went on against the hubbub of sightseers. That's the difference between the Italians and the English, Carla thought, that's the difference between Tony and me, because in spite of his English upbringing, he was in some ways more Italian than English.

Her headache had gone. The few minutes spent quietly in the village church had been more effective than the two aspirins she had swallowed in the post office. Outside she found the sun shining, it promised to be a glorious day. The frost had melted, the bare branches of the trees were festooned with tiny droplets of moisture. On her walk back along the lane she saw signs of renewed life in the hedgerows. The blackthorns were white with blossom, the pussy willow was plumping out with little caterpillar-like cushions and the last of the primroses made pale splashes of gold in the grass verges. She had come home at the right time of the year. There was no place in the world that could compare with England in the spring, she thought, closing her mind to a vision of the fragrant daphnes scenting the avenues and gardens of Florence.

As she passed Thornmere Hall her thoughts reverted to her companion of yesterday, Milly Stevens. A real little busybody, and yet there was something about her that Carla found very likeable. Her outspokenness and honesty perhaps. She hoped she would see her again soon because there was the matter of the taxi fare to be settled.

Two

Her father's car was parked in the lane outside the cottage. She recognised it immediately – the old Rover he had bought when he had his first success with his paintings, and even then it was second-hand because cars like that were no longer being made in the Sixties. It had had several new engines since, but its bodywork was still in spanking condition owing much to his loving care and enormous bills at the garage. He refused to replace it. He despised the idea of driving around in a machine made by other machines. The Rover had been made during the days of skilled panel beaters and in his opinion the woodwork and leather upholstery, though beginning to show their age, put plastic and man-made fabrics to shame. It had its disadvantages, the little rear window being one of them, but that was a small price to pay, compared with his pride in such ownership.

The back door opened and he stood there staring at her, his heavy brows drawn together in a frown. The three and a half years since their last meeting had not aged him, his hair was as thick as ever, though somewhat whiter. He was dressed in cords and a hairy tweed jacket and, with his hands in his pockets, glowered at her. 'So you came sneaking back like a thief in the night,' he said.

This is how we started off, she thought, at odds with each other. She jutted her chin. 'I came sneaking back, yes, but not in the night, and not like a thief.'

'You stole my peace of mind. I call that theft, don't you? You haven't written to me in weeks. I came down here this morning to cut the grass and what do I find? Signs of you all over the place.' His face suddenly crumpled like a deflated balloon; he flung out his arms. 'Oh, my darling girl, you don't know what it means to me to see you again. Come here and give me a hug.'

She didn't hesitate. She ran to him, burying her face in his shoulder and inhaling the odour peculiar to him, a mixture of tweed and tobacco smoke and the eau de Cologne with which he liberally laced his bath water.

He knew she was fighting against tears, he himself was having the same difficulty. He waited until his vision cleared, then held her at arm's length, scrutinising her with his penetrating blue gaze. 'You're far too thin and you look ill, but my God, I'm damn glad to have you back. Why the secrecy? Why do me out of the pleasure of meeting you at the airport? Why do Irina out of the fun of planning a family get-together? What went wrong, Carla? What happened to your plans to circumnavigate the world? I had cards from you from all over Europe – then Florence and everything came to a stop. What happened? Did you fall in love?'

'You could say that.'

'With Florence?'

'With a man . . . but with Florence too. They were interchangeable . . .' Her voice fell away to a whisper, then a deep sigh.

He studied her, taking in the heartache evident in her eyes, the weary droop of her shoulders as if life were too hard to bear. 'D'you want to tell me about it?' he said soberly.

'Not particularly – not at this moment. Please Larry, give me time.'

There was a crunch of footsteps in the lane. They both looked round. A tall, fair-bearded man came strolling past the cottage with a sleek-haired honey-coloured dog padding at his heels. The man raised a hand in greeting, before turning into what was once the old railway track.

'You won't find it so quiet at the cottage now that that track has been turned into a nature trail,' Larry said. 'Especially at weekends.'

'That man seemed to know you. What will he think, seeing you with your arm around a woman?'

'Not so surprised as he would have been if he had seen it around a man. But not to worry. The only time I come in contact with Dr Blood is once a month when he takes my blood pressure and that doesn't take longer than five minutes. If he did feel anything at all by seeing me with my arm around you, it would be envy.'

She heard only the first part of his sentence. Her expression changed to one of concern. 'I didn't know you had high blood pressure.'

'Yes, thanks to you. Never writing, never fully explaining why you decided against following my itinerary and setting out to conquer the world. Of course I worried about you, I couldn't sleep some nights thinking about you and wondering what you were up to, and blaming myself for having sent you on such a hare-brained scheme. You don't know how many times I nearly booked a flight to Florence. It was Irina who stopped me. She said I had no right to pry into your private life. That you weren't a child but a woman and had no obligation to me whatsoever. That didn't help my blood pressure either.'

Carla's eyes were so expressive of her anxiety he had the grace to look shamefaced. 'Sorry kiddo, I was laying it on a bit thick. There's nothing wrong with my old ticker, as the doc will verify. He's more worried about my lungs than my heart. He says I'm digging a grave for myself every time I buy a packet of cigarettes. I'm trying to give it up but my willpower doesn't come up to Dr Blood's estimation.'

'Did you say Dr Blood? That's a rather unsuitable name for a doctor . . .'

'Very suitable in my opinion, but it's just a quirk on my part, calling him Blood. His name is Brooke actually.'

'You don't call him Dr Blood to his face!'

'I'm not the sort who goes round saying things behind anyone's back I wouldn't say to his face.'

'And he doesn't mind?'

Larry's eyes gleamed with quiet humour. 'Not coming from me, he doesn't. He's an affable chap – popular with his lady patients. You couldn't do better than register with him, Carla, that is if you intend making this your permanent abode.'

The implied question in the last part of that sentence was not lost on Carla. She had no idea when or where she might finally settle, and as for men who were popular with the ladies, she had had her fill of them. She shied away from a subject that could cause her embarrassment and asked her father whether he had already breakfasted.

'I brought it with me. I was going to have a fry-up after I had cut the grass, but let's have breakfast first. I want to talk.'

'As long as you don't ask me any questions about Florence.'

'I won't ask you any questions at all. I'll leave you to do all the questioning.'

They ate in the kitchen at a table by the window looking

through a screen of montana, prolific just now with small pink buds.

Her father did the cooking – bacon, tomatoes and scrambled eggs – all in the microwave. The microwave was an innovation. He followed her gaze. 'I treated you to that. I couldn't be bothered to wait for the oven to heat up – and all that frying and grilling. I had more important fish to fry.' He paused. 'Something of everything for you, too?'

'Just eggs.'

She looked at her plate and then at his, piled with the bacon and tomatoes that she had rejected. 'So this is what you call a fry-up.'

'Stop quibbling and eat. You'll find it excellent.'

It *was* excellent and, surprisingly, she found herself enjoying it for just recently she had had no appetite at all. 'I won't want any lunch after this,' she said.

'You need feeding up. I don't like to see those hollows in your collar bones. Have you . . .' He was about to enquire if she had been seriously ill but her warning glance stopped him. He changed his tone to a lighter one. 'Notice any other improvements since you were here last?'

'You mean the phone? Yes, I noticed that; one in the hall and another in my bedroom.'

'A phone is essential, especially living out in the wilds like this. I could never understand your objection to it. I had to be able to tell Irina when to expect me home so that she could have my lunch ready.'

She smiled to herself. He hadn't changed, her father. His self-interest was still as intrusive as ever, only his charm kept it from being objectionable. 'Tell me about Irina,' she said. 'Tell me about the children. You never gave me much information in your letters.'

He scoffed. 'A lot more information than you ever gave

me. And beware of calling them children. Even the two little ones would grind their teeth over that.'

'They take after you, then.'

'They all take after me. You are the only one who "du different", as they say here in Norfolk.'

It was on the tip of her tongue to retort that she had never had the chance to be anything else but such a reminder would be out of place in their new-found relationship. 'Tell me about them,' she begged.

There was nothing he liked better than to expand on his family. He leaned back in his chair, replete and at ease. There was Andrew, his elder son, mothered by a little Greek girl called Marie who had died so tragically young. Andrew, whom Carla had never met was now working for his doctorate at St Andrews. Of the two children by his second wife, an American now living with her second husband in Philadelphia, Timothy, the eldest, was in his second year at Cambridge and Victoria in her last year at school; and Irina's two 'babies' – Hannah, now seven, and Emma, six, were attending the primary school only ten minutes' walk from their home at Beckton Market.

'So now you have it,' he said, reaching over for the coffee pot to replenish his cup. 'And you must come and see them as soon as possible. They'll be as cross with you as I am to think you sneaked home without any warning. They were planning to have a home-coming party for you.'

'Then don't tell them,' she pleaded. 'Wait until the bulk of my luggage arrives. I have some gifts for them in my case. I wouldn't want to come to the Thatched House empty-handed.'

'I must tell Irina. I keep nothing from Irina.'

'I don't mind Irina knowing,' said Carla musingly. 'Irina is what the Italians call *simpatica*.'

Her father smiled. 'You picked up some of the lingo, then.'

'The more important words.'

'Such as *amore*?'

They exchanged glances, Larry's falling before hers. 'Sorry, that slipped out.' He rose, gathered the dirty dishes together and put them into the sink. 'We've been sitting here talking quite long enough. Now let's give the garden an airing.'

A thrush was singing in an apple tree. Overhead, a lark soared. The sky was the translucent blue of midsummer rather than April, but the wind had that touch of Norfolk freshness about it that Carla had missed in Florence.

'Thank you for my garden,' she said feelingly. 'When I remember how it was and see how it is now, I can hardly believe it's the same. I love the flower beds, but I thought you had an objection to flower beds.'

'I have, I hate the tiresome things, always having to be watered or weeded. These were Irina's idea. She said I had planted so many evergreens in your garden it made it look like a cemetery. I like evergreens, they can look after themselves.'

In Larry's garden they were obliged to look after themselves for there was no one else to do it for them. It was Larry's contention that a garden was a place to relax in not to slave in. Sometimes, at Irina's insistence, he ran the mower over the lawn, but only haphazardly. He had once been known to mow around a table and deck-chairs rather than move them out of the way. He liked a wild garden, he said, it attracted wildlife. He could certainly claim to house the best colony of butterflies in Station Road. That he had kept her small plot in such good order while she was away said much for his sense of duty.

They lingered for the rest of the morning in the studio,

becoming re-acquainted with each other and with their muse. Carla admired each of his paintings of the gatehouse, but the one painted from a distance held her entranced.

'I love this one the best,' she said. 'It's hardly recognisable as the gatehouse, it's just a white blob in a corner of a cornfield, but it's Norfolk – it couldn't be anywhere but Norfolk. You've got the atmosphere and that lovely indefinable quality of light that we get here on a fine day. I hope it's for sale.'

'None of them are for sale. I did them for you – welcoming you home, not knowing it was going to be so soon.'

She stood transfixed. 'You can't just give them away. They're worth pots of money. I could buy them from you. Please let me buy them from you.'

'Have you got pots of money?'

Unaccountably she blushed. 'Not as much as I had before I went to Florence. I was rather extravagant in Florence.'

She had gone mad among the tempting shops around the Duomo, buying gifts to send to the Thatched House, particularly on birthdays and at Christmases. Gifts, too, for her friend Sophie who spent so little on herself, and the most expensive of all for Tony, from the jewellery shops on the Ponte Vecchio, which he accepted with such grace and without embarrassment. If, in moments of doubt, she wondered if she was not in fact buying his love, she quickly dismissed them. He asked her for nothing. She gave spontaneously because she loved giving – her time, her trust and her love.

Her father was saying, 'I forfeited twenty-five years of your life, so don't now begrudge me trying to make up for it in the only way I know.'

'But there were other expenses – having the garden laid out, erecting the tombstones for the Foster family and the building of this studio. The money I left couldn't have covered all that.'

'Let's get off the subject of money,' he said testily. 'The time has come to have a serious discussion about those paintings I found in your portfolio.'

The sun had moved westwards, shining now not through the main windows of the sitting-room to which they had moved as there were no comfortable chairs in the studio, but through the smaller, narrower one that faced down the lane. Carla, looking over her father's shoulder, saw a car approaching. 'I think I'm about to have a visitor,' she said apprehensively.

Her father turned his head. 'It's young Smithson, driving his old Sierra – the village taxi. Yes, Thornmere has a garage now, an off-shoot from the one at Beckton that has lavished such tender care on my old bus. Good, I don't think he's stopping here after all. I hope not, I haven't said all I want to say about your canvases.'

Her father was right – the taxi did not stop. It made a left-hand turn across the planking where the level-crossing had once been and continued up the lane that Carla always thought of as leading to nowhere. She caught a momentary glimpse of the passenger, a small dumpy figure in the back, and had a pretty shrewd idea who she was.

'What was I saying?' said her father.

'Some rather unpleasant things about my paintings.'

He crossed over and sat beside her. 'You wouldn't want me to be otherwise than honest, would you? I couldn't help comparing them to the exquisite little water-colours you showed me on my first visit here. I told you then, I remember, that water-colouring was your *métier*. What made you change to oils?'

'The class I joined worked only in oils . . .'

'To produce feeble copies of the great Renaissance

masters, if yours are anything to go by. Did you spend three years in Florence doing only that?'

She had started with water-colours. She remembered catching a bus to Fiesole. It was just a short drive climbing up between cultivated fields and olive groves, and when she alighted she had made straight for the Roman amphitheatre where she had sat and eaten her lunch of cheese rolls and grapes. She had brought her camera with her and had wandered afar that afternoon taking shots of the rolling Tuscan landscape. Later, in her room, she had started on the series of water-colours with which she had hoped to impress Tony, longing to hear his delightful 'Bravo, my dear, bravo', with which others, more successful with oils than she, had been rewarded. She had painted line-and-wash studies, relying on her memory for the subtle blends of colour, and on her camera for the tricks of light and shade.

One in particular she had prized above the others, a simple compilation of cypress and olive trees highlighting in a subtle blending the different shades of green and silver. She had allowed herself one other colour, a splash of gold where the sun lit up a clump of dandelions. She hadn't seen any dandelions – she did not even know whether they grew in Tuscany or not – but she thought that a little poetic licence would do no harm.

Tony thought differently. For some reason the painting aroused in him a passionate reaction. 'You waste your time on something like this. You paint weeds when you have the whole of Florence's magnificent gardens to choose from. Don't bring me trumpety little things like this. I have no time to comment on pretty little water-colours. There is no emotion in water-colours, no depth of feeling. Pale wishy-washy things. Leave them for the children with their paintboxes.'

She told Larry only the bare facts of Tony's criticism, but it was more than enough. 'The man's a bloody fool,' he said angrily. 'A mountebank. Who recommended him to you, this self-styled tutor?'

'I met him in the Piazzale Michelangelo . . .'

Her father looked at her as if she were beyond hope. 'And took him at his word that he could teach you to paint. . . ?'

'He seemed very knowledgeable. He had been instructing would-be hopefuls for years . . .'

'God help them.' He went on staring at her as if seeing her for the first time. 'I can't believe this. A daughter of mine taken in by a charlatan. Leave water-colours to children, indeed! The man condemns himself out of his own mouth. It takes skill to paint a water-colour successfully. It takes an artist – something that obviously he is not . . .'

She put up a hand as if to stop his flow of words. 'Larry, please, don't . . . it hurts.'

His voice softened at once. He took her hand, patting it as if she were a child needing comfort. 'Where are these water-colours? Let me be the judge, let me tell you what I think of them.'

'I can't.' She looked away to hide the lies her eyes might reveal. 'I left them in Florence. I expect they'll be sent on with the rest of my things.'

She had destroyed them, tearing them up into tiny pieces and burning them in an empty fireplace.

'Well, start again. You have plenty of inspiration at hand. You need look no further than the garden. Stick to flowers. You're good at flowers.' He rose, looking at his watch.

'D'you mind if I give Irina a tinkle? She was only expecting me to be an hour. I came to mow the lawn, remember.'

'I'll do that. I'll be glad of something to do.'

'I've left you the washing-up, but domestic affairs are not important. Your painting comes first – remember that. Your work must always come first. If you haven't got your paints with you pop into Norwich and get some. But get started; and that's not a suggestion, it's an order.'

'I could do with a wife,' she said, as she walked arm-in-arm with him to his car. 'You know, one of those marvellous innovations that does all the work around the house.' She was speaking with irony, but he took her seriously.

'I'll tell Irina. Irina will know of someone who'll come and clean for you.'

'No – not yet. Let me get myself sorted out first, Larry. Let me have some time to myself.'

Again came the sound of an approaching car. Kevin Smithson in his Sierra came rumbling over the planking. He waved to them, turned and drove on towards the village. This time he had no passenger with him.

Milly stared, as if unseeing, at the roughly turned soil, the whitish bare patch overlying the brown, at the stunted tree she remembered as a full-berried holly. 'It don't seem possible,' she said incredulously.

Kevin shifted his weight from one foot to the other. There was a car waiting in the yard jacked up ready for a complete overhaul, and an MOT coming in at two o'clock, but he couldn't leave the old girl looking like this.

'Are you sure this is where the cottage was? You say this is your first time back in over forty years. This might not even be the same lane.'

There were lots of nameless lanes in Thornmere, or if

they had once had names they were no longer remembered.

'It's the right lane. I ought to know, I walked it twice. Besides, that ruin of a church we passed, that's where I got married. No, I remember Thornmere Green all right and where we're standing now used to be the gamekeeper's cottage.'

It was obvious even to Kevin Smithson's untutored eyes that a building of sorts had once been here. There were give-away signs like broken bits of slate and bricks and the uncultivated state of the soil compared to the fine tilth of the land that surrounded it.

'It's changed though,' said his passenger in the same bewildered tone of voice. 'Everything has changed. I'm sure the fields were smaller in them days and there were hedges both sides of the road. It wasn't all open like this. Why were they done away with?'

'So that the farmers would have more land for growing corn.'

Milly considered this. 'Didn't we have some grain mountains a few years back?'

'I think we did.' He had an uneasy conviction that he was being led down a blind alley. This little woman had given him more than one surprise already.

'So now I suppose they're going to put the hedges back again.'

'Well, yes, they are. They've already started on it in some parts of the county . . .'

'And the hens are all shut up in barns and battery houses, and sows penned in concrete sties, and calves in crates. Seems to me the farmers don't need any land at all these days. They might just as well concrete the whole bally lot over.'

Milly's cheeks had gone a mottled red. She looked

belligerent and tearful in turn. Kevin glanced at her with concern. 'You're tired, Mrs Stevens.'

'No, I'm not tired, I'm just mad. I'm bloody mad. Coming all this way to see my husband and not as much as a brick left to show where he once lived. Not even a plank from the earth closet, either. I hated that earth closet, but God what wouldn't I give to see it now.' She blew her nose into a man-sized tissue.

'Let me take you back to Thornmere Hall.'

'No, I don't want to go back there – not just yet, not until I decide what to do. You run along. I know you've got other jobs to see to. I'll be all right.'

But still he lingered, loath to leave her like this out in the wilds. 'I can't possibly leave you on your own out here . . .' The idea worried him more than it did his passenger.

'I'll enjoy poking about a bit,' she assured him. 'And when I get tired of that I'll start walking back. I know the way.'

He looked at her flimsy high-heeled shoes. 'You'll never do it, Mrs Stevens, it's over two miles.'

'I've done it before and I'll do it again. You'd be surprised what I can do when I put my mind to it.'

He did not doubt her, but he still felt unhappy at leaving her stranded. 'I'll give you an hour and if there's no sign of you by then, I'll come looking for you.' They settled for that. Milly paid what she owed him and watched him drive away. It was as she had told him. She wanted to be on her own. She wanted to think.

She did most of her thinking in the old church where she had been married, with the war on and knowing she had Tom on loan only. They had decided on the church where Tom's own parents had been married as Mrs Stevens had offered to provide the reception. It was very much a Utility wedding for everything then was strictly rationed, including the guests, for Tom had few relatives and hers were all scattered around the outskirts of London and none of them willing to make the journey up to Norfolk.

She had worn a forget-me-not-blue dress that she had designed and made herself with cap sleeves and a half-belt that tied at the back, and with it she wore a navy-blue halo hat and carried a navy-blue bag.

Tom was in uniform of course, and his father had worn the twill knee breeches and the velveteen jacket of a gamekeeper, and his mother had dressed all in black as if she were attending a funeral, which, to judge by her expression, she was. But she did them proud with the breakfast later. It was a meal such as they had not seen in years – ox-tonguc, providentially supplied by the local butcher, which Mrs Stevens had boiled, skinned, coiled into a cake tin, covered, then pressed by standing it under one of the legs of the sofa and leaving it all night.

'Du that look a real treat,' said her husband appreciatively, when she turned it out on to a dinner plate the following morning. It certainly went down a treat after Spam, supplemented by a chicken too old to serve any other purpose than to be roasted in a slow oven. To follow the cold meats, home-grown beetroot and potatoes, came an immense pumpkin pie. Nobody got up hungry from that table and even trim little Milly had had to loosen her belt.

And now the church was just a ruin, hardly noticeable under the ivy that screened it. Nature had taken over. In one or two places the trees in the churchyard thrust spectral branches through the broken windows as if seeking a stranglehold on what was left of the interior. As she sat in what remained of one of the old pews, birds flew in and out with nesting material in their beaks. She had no doubt that bats hung upside down above her head. Most of the roof had gone. She could see a patch of blue above, the only means of light there was, for the door, blown off its iron hinges when the bomb fell, had been supplanted by dense vegetation. She got up, after saying a silent prayer, and went out into the sunshine.

She walked on a few more yards, then turned to have one last look. She conjured up an image of the church as it had been and saw it as it was now. Just like our marriage, she thought, grand to begin with, but a right ole cock-up at the end.

Carla had washed up the breakfast dishes, mown the lawn and raked out the moss. She was reluctant to go back into the house because there was nothing more to do there and staying busy helped to keep troubled thoughts at bay. As hard as she tried not to dwell on Tony, he would persist in creeping back to mind. His sloe-black eyes, irises indistinguishable from the pupils, were forever appearing in her inner vision, his soft, teasing voice ringing in her ears. That was the Tony she had loved a year ago, even seven or eight months ago. The Tony she loved now would not even meet her gaze and his caressing voice was for other ears.

She was weeding one of the flower beds that had been completely taken over by wild violets. She hated pulling them up, for they were one of her favourite flowers, but they were in danger of smothering the tender shoots of lily-of-the-valley that were just beginning to show. She wondered why violets were thought of as modest flowers. They were anything but. Their tenacity exceeded even that of couch grass. No matter how many times they were weeded out, they returned. There was a saying in Norfolk for plants that refused to grow: 'Come you up or up you come.' There was no need to say that to violets.

She sat back on her heels to rest a moment and in doing so spotted a figure, a mere speck, a long way up the lane. Instinctively she guessed who it was and got to her feet.

What should she do – go and meet her or wait in case she was mistaken? She hesitated until the figure became recognisable, then set off at a trot. Even from this distance Milly looked a pitiful sight and was limping badly, quite unlike the cheerful little woman on the train.

'You've lost one of your heels,' Carla said when they were within speaking distance.

'Yes. Serves me right for wearing high heels at my age. Than's what vanity does for you.' Milly produced another man-sized tissue and dabbed her face, and by doing so smeared dust and perspiration together, unintentionally making a kind of mud-pack.

Carla took her arm. 'Can you manage as far as my cottage?'

'I'll do it even if it kills me.'

They made it step by painful step and at last, and with great relief, Carla helped her guest into the most comfortable chair in the sitting-room and switched on the electric fire. With its flames licking around the artificial logs it added a cheerful touch to the room. She left Milly in order to fetch a bowl of warm water to bathe her feet and a damp flannel for her face.

'Stay there and soak your feet while I make you a cup of tea.'

Milly made mild protesting noises. Such treatment, she said, should take place in the kitchen, not in such a pretty room as this. She might splash the carpet – worse still, she could knock the bowl over and then what a mess. Her father-in-law used to soak his feet in a mustard bath and he made more mess than a pig wallowing in a mud bath. But her protests petered out as if the mere effort of using her voice was beyond her; Carla could see that she was so overcome with fatigue that she would be asleep before the kettle boiled.

She was, but she awoke the minute Carla touched her. Tea revived her. She straightened her hat and tucked a strand of loose hair back into place. 'I hope I haven't made too much mess.'

'I can't see any mess.' Carla didn't say so but the state of Milly's feet appalled her. One was bleeding and both were badly swollen. 'Do you think I ought to call a doctor?'

'No.' Milly was very decided about that. 'I'll be as right as rain as soon as I've rested. You got such a thing as a plaster?'

Carla found a first-aid kit in the kitchen. Thoughtful Larry – or more likely, Irina. She ministered to the swollen feet as gently as she could. Caring for her great-grandmother for seven long years had taught her much in the nursing line. She had a few words of warning. 'You're never going to get into those shoes again, Mrs Stevens.'

Milly tittered behind her hand. 'You don't have to tell me that. Aren't I a silly ole fool wearing such shoes at my age. My husband used to call them my clackers. I don't think I'll be doing much clacking after this.'

Carefully Carla lifted Milly's feet out of the bowl and dried them, and left them resting on a beaded footstool she had bought at a flea market in Norwich. She had never allowed it to be used before for the fabric was so old the merest touch could turn it into dust, but now, as a support for Milly's feet, she didn't give it a second thought.

'Would I be poking my nose into something that doesn't concern me if I were to enquire what you were doing at Thornmere Green? As far as I know there's nothing there except the ruins of an old church,' she said.

Milly regarded her with mildly wistful eyes. 'I was

reliving old memories – I was married in that church – in 1943 it were.'

'Married in that old church! I thought it had been destroyed centuries ago; that it was one of the ruins Oliver Cromwell knocked about a bit. What happened to it?'

'What happened to it was one of the things that usually happen to me. Bad luck follows me round like a shadow. It got bombed a few weeks after I got married. I suppose I was lucky I wasn't in it at the time. Looking back now, I think it was an omen.'

'An omen?'

'My husband was posted overseas,' Milly said. 'I didn't see him again for three years. He was living with his father in a gamekeeper's cottage about a mile from the church. I tried to fit in, God knows I did, but things got me down. The loneliness, the hard work, the lack of mod cons. I left him in the end. I thought he'd come after me, or write even, but he didn't and I was too obstinate to make the first move. Then my life changed and I met someone else – and well, things just drifted. Then, not long ago, I had a sudden urge to see Tom again. I wrote but didn't get any answer and thought that was just like Tom, being perverse, so I came up here to see him, and guess what?'

'What?' said Carla mustering her thoughts. Milly's breathless account had got to the point without her.

'It's gone. The cottage – it's just vanished and nothing there to show for it except a patch of chalky soil.' Milly sniffed and reached for another tissue and in doing so caught Carla's eye. She gave her a watery smile.

'Don't look so sad, dear. It's all past history and it's got its funny side too if you think about it. The last thing I expected was to find that the cottage had vanished into thin air. I dreaded the idea of finding that Tom had moved, or shacked up with another woman, or even died. I'd geared myself up to face any one of them possibilities – but to find the cottage gone, that was the last thing I bargained for. It's taken all the wind out of my sails, if you know what I mean.'

Carla had no ready words of comfort. For one thing, she had assumed that Mrs Stevens was a widow. Now she found she was seeking a reconciliation with a husband she had not seen for more than forty years. Any reply she made to that, she thought, would sound hollow.

Finally, she came up with what she thought was a sensible suggestion. 'You say your husband was a gamekeeper? Would it be any good trying to contact the farmer or landowner he worked for?' She remembered then that she was referring to someone who worked in the district a long time ago. 'Or the employer's descendents,' she added.

'He worked for a syndicate of businessmen. They rented the shooting rights, but I don't know who from. Tom never told me. He could see I wasn't interested in that side of his life. Some of the syndicate came from Norwich and the rest from the Midlands somewhere. When the shooting season was over he used to raise pheasant chicks and help out on neighbouring farms. He knew a lot about trees, too. I know he was responsible for the coppicing of the trees in the spinney but I never knew what that meant. I wish I had taken more interest at the time.' Milly's voice faded away as sleep once more threatened to overtake her.

The silence was shattered by somebody knocking on the back door. It was Kevin Smithson, looking the picture of anxiety. 'Would you have seen a plump little old lady going past here? I was supposed to have collected her along the lane. I've been backwards and forwards umpteen times keeping my eyes peeled, but she's vanished into thin air. I don't see how I could have missed her.'

'She's here,' said Carla. 'She's in the other room soaking

her feet. She's walked them down to the bone, by the look of them.'

'Thank God, I was beginning to wonder what had happened to her. She's such nice old thing, too. I wouldn't have had her come to harm for anything.'

'Watch it,' called Milly from the front room. 'Not so much of the old if you don't mind. The only thing that's old about me at present is my feet.'

Kevin grinned and lowered his voice. 'Nothing wrong with her vocal cords, either, or her hearing.'

'Wait here,' Carla said, 'I'll get her ready for you.'

There was the question of shoes. Carla tried one of hers, size six, on to Milly's size-two foot. The effect was ludicrous. 'You could try a pair of my sports socks,' she suggested. 'They'd be better than nothing, though I expect they'll come up to your knees.'

They did, which Milly thought hilarious. 'Everybody will think I'm wearing bedsocks,' she said. 'You haven't got a pair of plain white, have you? I don't like all them flashy colours.'

'It's only to get you out to the car, hardly anybody comes past here – not on weekdays, anyway.'

Reassured, Milly allowed Kevin and Carla to give her an arm each and help her along the path. Once seated in the passenger seat she wound down the window to thank Carla again for all she had done.

'Don't forget what I suggested,' Carla said. 'Make enquiries around. There's the people at the post office, and the vicar, and the police at Beckton Market. Even the council. A cottage just can't disappear without someone knowing something about it, especially in Thornmere.'

'It's not the cottage I'm worried about, I don't care two hoots about the cottage. It's what's happened to Tom that matters. How am I ever going to get in touch with him again?'

'Put an advert in the paper?' suggested Kevin tentatively. He was not quite sure what they were on about but he felt it was up to him to make a contribution. 'Or ask to see the electoral roll.'

Three

Jessie Stoneham, normally referred to as the housekeeper at Thornmere Hall but in practice more its chatelaine, was very concerned about her guest in room 16. She had been brought back earlier that day in an exhausted condition with both feet badly blistered and one bleeding. On discovering the reason for these injuries, Jessie clicked her tongue reprovingly.

'You at your age, walking all that distance and in Hangman's Lane of all places. I can't remember when it was last made up. It's not safe even for a much younger person.'

Milly compressed her lips. She was getting weary of this constant reference to her age. She didn't look that old, did she? she asked herself. She didn't feel old, except just at present. Now she felt more like ninety.

She liked the housekeeper, they had much in common and there was a natural empathy between them. Both were liberal in their outlook, but not inclined to take fools lightly.

Miss Stoneham was apt to fuss a bit, but that was the norm, at least in Milly's experience. The older she got the more she was treated like a child, and she resented it for it made her feel that she was no longer considered capable of thinking for herself. But the housekeeper's kindly concern caused her no offence. Rather, it filled Milly with the conviction that she was in safe hands.

Jessie happened to be in the foyer, giving instructions to the receptionist, when Kevin, with the help of the gardener, had carried Milly bandy-chair fashion into the hotel.

'I'm sorry,' Milly apologised. 'But I couldn't manage the steps.'

The housekeeper instantly went into action, giving orders, taking command, and in no time at all, Milly found herself tucked up in bed with her feet rebandaged. The housekeeper's exasperation when Milly refused to allow her to send for a doctor was very marked. 'What have you got against doctors? Are you a Christian Scientist?'

'No, I'm not a Christian Scientist, I'm not anything, but the less I have to do with doctors the better I like it.'

All Milly wanted now was to be left alone so that she could rest in peace. She had given Miss Stoneham a satisfactory explanation of why she was taking a walk along that particular lane – for sentimental reasons, there was no need to say more – but it was when she told of Carla's part in her escapade that the housekeeper's manner changed.

'You mean Miss Foster of the old gatehouse?' she said sharply.

'Yes. We happened to meet on the train yesterday and shared a taxi to Thornmere.'

The other frowned. 'That's odd, I didn't know she was home. I didn't know she intended coming home, she said nothing about it in her last letter. I would have thought she'd have got in touch with me before this. But there, I suppose she's got more important things to do.' She looked and sounded affronted.

Though her eyelids were drooping with sleep, Milly's curiosity was aroused. 'Did you know her well, then?'

'She stayed with me at the lodge for several months

while she was having that old gatehouse restored. We became very close. More than just friends – she was like a daughter to me. Ah well, different times, different needs.' Miss Stoneham looked pointedly at Milly's untouched tray as if to take out her feelings on that. 'You haven't even made an attempt to eat and I went to such trouble. I cooked that myself.'

'I'm sorry, but I'm just too tired to eat,' Milly said apologetically, feeling that she had done nothing else that morning but apologise. 'I'll have something later on. Please don't think I don't appreciate the way you're looking after me.'

Miss Stoneham took up the tray and made, straight-faced and straight-backed, for the door. 'Anyone walking along Hangman's Lane in shoes like yours needs looking after, in my opinion.'

'Hangman's Lane? Is that really its name?'

'It was when I was a girl but hardly anybody calls it that these days. Hardly anybody goes that way any more, not since the trains ceased running. My father told me that there used to be a gibbet at the far end in the old days. His grandfather or great-grandfather, I can't remember which, actually saw the last man to be hanged there. He was only a lad at the time and nothing could get him past that gibbet ever again. It was taken away soon after.'

Hangman's Lane, said Milly to herself when the door finally closed on the housekeeper. A gibbet and a bombed-out church! No wonder her marriage had been jinxed from the start. It hadn't stood an earthly.

The sleep she craved for was long in coming. Her body ached all over and her feet were pulsating with pain, but her mind was alive and kicking. She had no control over her thoughts and they wandered at will.

I wonder, she thought, did things begin to go wrong for

me when I discovered about sex? She was about eight and a half at the time of the discovery. She was never able to take sex seriously after that.

She was living then with her mother in a small terraced house in Plaistow. She had no father, but she had a lot of uncles who visited on a regular basis. She looked forward to their visits for they never left without giving her a tip. She soon discovered that those who looked as if they could least afford it were the most generous with their sixpences. The better-off uncles never went above tuppence and the wealthiest one of all, Uncle Wagstaffe, the one who proudly wore a gold watch chain with a sovereign dangling from it, only ever gave her a pat on the head.

Uncle Clem, by far her favourite, was a sailor in the Royal Navy and never came to see them without bringing gifts from foreign lands. She liked him best, not because of his exciting presents – like on one occasion a canary in a bamboo cage – but because he showed her how to do press-ups and handstands and cartwheels in a tiny yard behind the house they called the garden. The last two accomplishments she quickly mastered, but she could never get on with press-ups. Just two, then she was out of breath and lying flat on her stomach. Uncle Clem, however, seemed to be able to go on for ever – or at least until her mother called them in for tea.

Then came the night when she awoke suddenly and heard moaning noises coming from her mother's room. Her mother sometimes got very bad cramp and it was then Milly's job to massage her legs until the pain went away. Yawning, she slipped out of bed and went to see if her help was needed.

A strip of candlelight showed from beneath the door of her mother's bedroom. She softly turned the handle and peered in, and there was Uncle Clem doing press-ups in her mother's bed. She had never been so surprised in all her life.

Some native wit, some primeval sense of caution, warned her that it was best if she made herself scarce. She went scurrying back to her own room. It took her a long time to get back to sleep for her mind was going like clockwork.

The following day was Saturday. She got up later than usual, dressed and went down the stairs and through the door that opened straight into the kitchen. Her mother sat alone at the table, smoking a cigarette and reading the paper. She squinted at Milly through her cigarette smoke but said nothing.

Milly looked around the room. 'Where's Uncle Clem?'

'He had to rejoin his ship.' Her mother returned to her paper. Milly sidled up to the table. 'Mum . . .'

'Eh. . . ?'

'I saw Uncle Clem doing press-ups in your bed last night and,' Milly sniggered behind her hand, 'I saw his bare botty.'

Her mother eyed her speculatively. 'Did you, now?' She put her paper aside. 'What would you say, pet, if we left this dingy little house and went and lived in a bus?'

Live in a bus! Milly had never heard of anyone living in a bus but the idea held her in thrall.

'A real bus, like the ones that go along the street, you mean?'

'One that's retired and up on chocks, with a stove-pipe sticking through its roof and its own little garden, somewhere in the country. It will be like living in a cottage. A lot of people are living in buses and trams these days, either because they haven't got homes or can't afford to keep them. I know of a bus for sale and I know someone who'll help me buy it.'

'Uncle Clem?'

'No, not Uncle Clem. Now go and put the kettle on and make me a fresh pot of tea.'

They had heard the muffled giggles outside the door last night and the patter of feet across the narrow landing. Clem had said, 'I'm going to make myself scarce tomorrow. I'm not staying around to answer her questions. She's as sharp as a needle, your Milly.'

She'd be sorry not to see Clem again, thought Milly's mother, stubbing out her cigarette in the saucer, but she'd be sorrier still to have to stay on in Carlin Street. Nosy lot of old cats around here. Spiteful looks and wagging tongues. A fresh start, in fresh surroundings and no more uncles. Here, a deep sigh escaped her. Well, just one, anyway. She couldn't very well keep Sam Wagstaffe out of his own bus.

Oh that bus – all these years later Milly could still smell that bus. A smell compounded of damp, and cigarette smoke, and stale cooking. Living on a bus had not turned out to be the adventure she had expected. For one thing the staircase was out in the open and it had been jolly cold in winter, going up to bed and coming down in the morning. The bus had been draughty too. No cupboards for their clothes. No shelves to keep the presents Uncle Clem had given her.

'Just be thankful you have a roof over your head,' said her mother. 'There's many haven't, these days.' It wasn't much of a roof either. It let in the rain on wet days, and on windy nights the branches of a nearby tree scraped relentlessly against its top and kept her awake.

Now Milly turned with difficulty on to her other side, preferring to stare at a blank wall rather than at the group of trees she could see outside the window. She failed to see the beauty of the sunlight sifting through their fresh young leaves, for to her trees were a menace. The elm tree that had loomed over their temporary home had changed the course of her life.

The country, she found, could be lonely. She missed the sound of traffic and popping up to the corner shop for sweets, and she had a mile and a half to walk to school along a narrow lane beneath an archway of trees which shut out the light and muffled all sound. She wasn't used to silence.

The other children often took a short cut across the fields, but there were cows in the fields and Milly would have walked an extra mile rather than confront a cow. She wasn't happy at school either. She was lumped with the others from the bus and tram community, referred to by the local children as 'that gypsy lot from the chicken farmer's field'. She missed the games she had played in the playground of her old school. Hopscotch and 'The Farmer's in his Den', skipping ropes and sorbo rubber balls, and tops when in season. The local children played different games, usually choosing sides and competing against each other in energetic ways, like running races or leap-frog. She was never chosen to take sides, she was too puny.

Her mother was wise in country lore. She had been the only daughter of a farm-worker and had gone into service when she was fourteen. Milly supposed she had had a father, because everybody else she knew at school had fathers, but knew better than ask her mother about him, for that was the one thing certain to bring on one of her bad turns.

Milly hated her mother having bad turns: she was always frightened she might not get over one. Polly would stay in bed all day with the curtains drawn, a handkerchief soaked in vinegar on her brow and a bucket nearby, ready for when she felt sick. When finally, late in the afternoon, she called down for a cup of weak tea and a slice of dry toast,

Milly knew that the bad turn had taken a turn for the better and her mother would soon be her old unruffled self again.

It was very strange, but all the time they lived on the bus her mother did not succumb to a single bad turn. Not even the visit from the woman living with her husband and three small children in the tram opposite had brought one on. The woman had called to borrow half a cup of sugar and stayed to gossip. Milly sat on the step and listened.

'I suppose, Mrs Wagstaffe, your husband must work away from home, as he only manages to get down weekends. But there, you're only too glad that they've got a job at all these days, aren't you? Wish my ole man could find something . . .'

'My name is not Wagstaffe, it's Nickson – Polly Nickson – and I haven't got a husband, Mrs – er.' Polly proffered an open packet of cigarettes.

The neighbour readily helped herself and lit her cigarette from Polly's. 'Watson, Edith Watson. I suppose you lost your husband in the war . . .'

'I didn't lose him, Mrs Watson. He kind of lost me . . .'

Milly, sensing from the tone of her mother's voice that they were approaching forbidden ground, piped up, 'Mr Wagstaffe is my uncle. I've got lots of uncles. My favourite one is Uncle Clem – he's a sailor, but I haven't seen Uncle Clem since . . .'

'Milly,' said her mother quietly. 'We're out of water. Take the bucket and get some for me, will you.'

That was another thing Milly had against the country, it didn't have running water, not where they lived anyway. To fetch water meant having to trudge across a field to the chicken farm where a stand-pipe had been erected in the yard. She hoped Mr Apsey would be around, for he always gave her an apple from the store, or a handful of small, hard hazel pears.

He had, he told her mother the first week he called to collect the ground rent (five shillings a week, inclusive of water), been a violinist in the orchestra of a West End cinema, but had lost his job when the talkies came in. There were thousands of musicians thrown out of work when talking pictures superseded the old silent films. At first he had tried busking with a friend of his who was a pianist. They had pooled their resources and bought an old open van, and with a piano aboard had toured the streets of the City and central London. The pennies mounted and they did well until the Depression deepened and more and more buskers appeared on the streets. When the Welsh miners arrived, marching in slow time in an orderly group along the pavements of High Holborn, filling the space around with their harmony, they knew it was time to throw in their hand.

With the help of a government grant they had invested in a farmhouse with six acres of land and started up a chicken farm, letting off what land they did not require to squatters. 'No offence, ma'am, that's just what we call our tenants.'

'Ma-am' became 'Polly' in no time, and 'Mr Apsey' just as naturally gave way to 'Jack'. But they were never on such familiar terms with the piano player. To them and to other members of their community he was known simply as the Egg-man, for he it was who peddled the eggs around the surrounding towns and villages as far east as Southend-on-Sea, driving the old van that had once peddled a piano around the streets of London.

They weren't such bad old days really, Milly reflected drowsily. They had their moments. She had never been entirely happy, had always been homesick for London, but she hadn't been that unhappy either. Just pined, as did the canary in his bamboo cage until he finally pined himself to death. But death was not something Milly now cared to dwell upon.

When some two hours later Miss Stoneham looked in to see how her patient was getting on, she found Milly sitting up in bed, staring with some misgiving at her left leg. 'Look at the size of it,' she said. 'It's come up like a balloon.'

Miss Stoneham looked and did not like what she saw. 'I feel obliged to call a doctor, Mrs Stevens. After all, you are my responsibility.'

'My philosophy', said Milly, 'has always been that if you ever get anything wrong with you, you wait and see if it gets better. If it gets better, all to the good. It is doesn't, then is the time to get a doctor.' It was a philosophy that a neglected lump in her breast had refuted, but she saw no point in telling the housekeeper that.

Dr Brooke – known in the village by the uncomplimentary title of the 'Old doctor', for he looked much younger than his seventy-odd years, whereas his son Nicholas was flatteringly referred to as the 'Young doctor', though well into his forties – was a tall, well-set-up man with a full head of snow-white hair, clear hazel eyes and a ready smile. His smile disappeared, however, when he saw the state of Milly's leg. 'What brought this on?'

She told him about her walk along Hangman's Lane to the old gatehouse, but not the reason why. He seemed unsurprised, as if nothing the public did could surprise him any more. He examined the blister around the nail bed of the large toe on her left foot and pitted her swollen ankles with his thumb. Finally he asked her to sit up so that he could sound her chest and listen to her heart.

It was during her struggle to haul herself up to a sitting position that her night-gown slipped and revealed the scars of a recent mastectomy. Their eyes met.

Dr Brooke pulled a chair to the bedside and straddled it. 'I think a little heart to heart is called for, don't you?' he said quietly.

Later he accosted Miss Stoneham in her office. 'Mrs Stevens has no living relations, no close friends either, I understand. When I enquired the name of her next of kin, she said she didn't know. When I asked who could I get in touch with to discuss her problem, she said you. Do you want that responsibility?'

Easter was near at hand. Jessie had plenty on her mind, juggling rooms and deciding whether or not to take on extra staff. She was Thornmere born, she had worked at Thornmere Hall most of her life, first as a matron when it was a girls' school, then as housekeeper when it became a country hotel. She was used to making decisions, but could she, she asked herself, find the time to take on another responsibility? Could she have the heart to turn Mrs Stevens away? The answer was no.

'It would be a temporary measure only?' she asked.

'Until she is on her feet again, which may not be for a week or two. She needs rest. It is not a thrombosis, which was my first thought when you phoned me and which would have meant getting her into hospital straight away. It's not serious, but not something to be taken lightly, at her age. She'll still need to get up for a short while each day to exercise her leg, but no more walks along rutted lanes. I'll need someone to keep an eye on her and you are excellent at that, Jessie. I'll pop in again tomorrow with some tablets for that toe infection and a diuretic to get rid of the fluid in her legs. She's retaining too much fluid.'

'She's carrying too much weight,' said Miss Stoneham, who was not noticeably short of upholstery herself. 'For her height, I mean. That can cause the legs to swell.' She was not averse to teaching the doctor his own job.

'Oh, I don't know, I think she's just comfortable. I expect she was a petite little thing when she was young.' The doctor prepared to leave. 'She has other health problems too, but I don't feel at liberty to talk about those. Of course, if she feels like confiding in you that's a different matter. I think she's a very strong-minded lady with plenty of grit, so you two should hit it off famously. Will there be any problem about keeping her on?'

'She only booked that room for two nights and every bed is taken for Easter. I don't know where I'll put her . . .'

'You'll find a way, Jessie, you always do,' he said with conviction.

Thank goodness Easter was over, thought Carla, as she hung her washing out to dry. It was a good drying day – blue skies and scudding clouds, and since her cases had arrived from Florence she had been washing every day, for her need to cleanse the past, even symbolically, had become imperative.

So much for solitude, she thought, so much for shutting herself away to get on with her misery in peace. Hardly a day had gone by since she had arrived back at the gatehouse without someone calling. First her father and then Mrs Stevens, who had been much on her conscience. Oh dear, she thought, John Donne was right with his 'No man is an Island'. Small chance for anyone with friends and relations to be an island. Her own particular island set amid its fields of barley was not unassailable. When I'm ready, she thought, when I can face it, I'll return the calls.

She took out the last item in her basket, a henna-coloured tunic dress she had bought at the San Lorenzo market. Most of her Italian clothes had come from that market. There were other markets just as enticing, but San Lorenzo was her favourite. It had an atmosphere that exhilarated and challenged her and she loved nothing better than to become one with the throng of visitors who picked their way between the stalls, seeking bargains in fabrics, clothes, or leatherware.

Her delight in her purchases caused both Sophie and Tony much surprise, for they thought of her as a woman of means and could not understand why she did not buy her clothes at the via de'Tornabuoni, but she had no burning desire to possess designer suits or dresses or shoes. She wore that which she felt most at home in and if she could buy what she wanted in a market, so much the better. She dressed to please herself, not to impress others, so she liked to believe, knowing that in fact she dressed to please Tony more than anyone, though he had once said to her, 'With a figure like yours you could wear a sack and get away with it.' But his eyes as he said it had followed a women in a Pucci dress.

Her tastes, she suspected, sprang from her peasant stock: her great-grandmother rooting around the stalls of Beckton Market before the First World War, her grandmother on the look-out for bargains in Berwick Market during the Second World War. And Charley, her mother, breezing along Carnegie Street during the Swinging Sixties. They have all left their mark on me, she thought.

That Sophie and Tony both thought her wealthier than she actually was was due to the hotel at which she was staying when they had first met her. Renovating the old gatehouse had made a considerable hole in her great-grandmother's legacy, yet when she arrived in Florence she had allowed the taxi driver to recommend one of the most exclusive hotels in the city, and there she had languished until rescued first by Tony and then Sophie.

Tony introduced her to Sophie Phillips, a girl with long dark hair and candid dark eyes, who helped in a café Tony often frequented. An English girl, he said, who, half-way through studying for a science degree, had dropped everything, come to Florence and found work with the Offredis.

'I don't know why,' he said. 'She's a bit touchy on the subject. She already knew the Offredis, as she had worked for them during her long vacations. She lives on the job, you might say. She rents the flat above the café and shares it at present with two English graduates, both working for their doctorates, both on Italian art. They have lively discussions from which poor Sophie is excluded, so she may be glad of your company. Shall we see?'

But Sophie was reluctant at first to commit herself. 'Yes, there is a vacant room on the top floor, not very large and it gets no sun which some people think might be an advantage. You won't like it after the Bellovista.'

'I was lonely there and bored, and rather overwhelmed by the opulence,' Carla had explained. In fact she was out of her depth, frightened of putting a foot wrong, more intimidated by the waiters than she was by the other guests. She had led a sheltered life for the last seven years, in service to her great-grandmother. She had sacrificed her youth to someone she loved very dearly and had no regrets, except that her years of purdah, as she sometimes thought of them, had left her somewhat self-conscious.

She had said to Sophie, 'I'd much rather stay among English-speaking people. I'm a dud at languages.'

'I know of a small, friendly *pensione* where the proprietor speaks excellent English.'

'I stayed in small friendly hotels in Prague and Dresden, but I still didn't feel particularly at home.'

Sophie laughed. 'The idea of travelling to other countries is not to feel at home.' She did not miss the entreating look that Carla cast at her. Why not, she thought, the extra money would help towards expenses. 'Come up and see the room before you come to any decision,' she said. 'You might not like what you see.'

At this point Tony, after saying he had an appointment to keep, left them.

Sophie stared thoughtfully after him. 'Have you known him long?'

'I only met him for the first time yesterday in the Piazzale Michelangelo. He picked me up in the most chivalrous way.'

'Nobody could accuse Tony of lacking chivalry. Did you tell him you were rich?'

'Good gracious, I'm not rich.'

'Anyone who can afford to stay at the Bellovista is rich in my book. In Tony's book too, I shouldn't wonder.'

'He could see I was lonely. He thought I would fit into private rooms better. He gave a very good account of you.'

'This is not the most fashionable part of the city. You won't see many tourists around here.'

'Which would suit me fine.'

Still Sophie lingered, one foot on the staircase that led to the apartment above. 'Tony said you had enrolled with one of his classes. Do you paint?'

'A little, but not professionally – as yet. I came to Florence hoping to find a tutor to help me improve my technique. I think Tony can help me there.'

'Nobody could accuse Tony of lacking technique,' said Sophie dryly. She took Carla's arm. 'But come on upstairs and see the room for yourself.'

It was about the same size as the middle bedroom at the gatehouse. Carla felt she could live with that. From the window there was an unlimited view of the sienna-coloured roofs of Florence. She could live with that too. 'I could be as snug as a bug in a rug up here,' she said.

'I hope I'm not supposed to take that literally.'

They shared a sense of satisfaction in each other. They felt they had been acquainted all their lives. All they had to do now was to come to some financial arrangement.

'Young' Dr Brooke with his dog came into sight along the nature trail as Carla finished pegging out the last of her washing. He raised his hand in greeting. Hardly a day passed when she did not see him going past the gatehouse, often while she was working in the garden. He always gave her a wave, but had not yet addressed her, and she had no wish to make the first move.

Now he said, 'That's a sight one doesn't see very often these days – washing blowing on the line. Another old custom wiped out by high technology.'

She supposed he was referring to tumble driers. It surprised her that such a manly-looking man should take such an old-fashioned point of view. He didn't look much like her idea of a doctor, with his bushy fair beard and a tweed jacket that had seen better days. The dog that padded obediently at heel was far better groomed than his master.

Both dog and man came to a halt by the fence that separated her garden from the one-time railway track. He held out his hand. 'Nicholas Brooke, and this is Ranger. Shake hands, Ranger.' Ranger obliged by thrusting a paw through the railings.

'A very well-trained dog,' she said.

Now that she was close up to him she could see that Dr Brooke was younger than he had looked at a distance. In his early or middle forties, she guessed. The beard made him look older. He had a direct, observant gaze she found herself incapable of returning. His eyes, large, grey and widely spaced, were his best feature. He topped her by several inches and having to look up to him was an unusual experience for her, for she was unused to facing men on her own level. Even wearing flat heels she had had to look down at Tony, not that that dented his ego in any way. As Sophie would say, 'Nobody could accuse Tony of lacking egotism.' For Carla that was part of his charm. She had fallen in love with him not because of his faults, but in spite of them.

It was as a doctor that Nicholas Brooke observed Carla, not as a man admiring a pretty woman, though there was that in it too. The pallor beneath the faint tan, her thinness, the dark rings under her eyes, and those eyes, otherwise beautiful, so lack-lustre and sad. Had she been ill, this violet-eyed woman, had she suffered a bereavement? Her father had said nothing about that, only that she had gone to Florence to brush up on her art work. Nicholas knew far more about Carla than Carla did about him.

She was looking at him now without focusing on him. He could tell she did not see him, but was looking through him at some inner image. He felt that if he snapped his fingers in her face she still would not come to. He said, raising his voice a little, 'Your father has told me a lot about you.'

She did come to. She blinked. 'Eh?'

'I said, your father has told me a lot about you. About your plans to circumnavigate the globe. I was interested. I had trodden that path myself.'

He had her full attention now, though not her interest. 'I hope you went further than I did. I only got as far as Florence. When did you do your travelling?'

He pulled a wry face. 'More years ago than I care to remember – as soon as I left school, actually. The world was a different place in those days – the Sixties. We didn't take life so seriously as the young do today. I saw most of the countries I set out to see, including a long spell in the

United States, then I returned to England and fulfiled my father's ambition for me; I studied medicine.'

'No regrets?'

The smile left his eyes, his face clouded over. 'Yes, I have my regrets. Can anybody go through life without regrets?'

She could not answer that. She too had her regrets, of course, but they were all centred around Tony. But no Tony and no regrets? The idea was inconceivable.

Dr Brooke continued on his way, taking long strides as if to make up for lost time. It was Ranger who turned to look back at her, waving his tail. She waved back at him and felt foolish for doing so. She wondered if she should get herself a dog, or a little cat. It would be company. Impatiently she again picked up the washing basket. Only a few minutes ago she had been bemoaning the fact that she did not get enough solitude, now she was considering lumbering herself with a pet who would have to be trained, fed and looked after. You don't know what you want, she complained, but she did. She wanted to put back the clock to the day she had sat in the Piazzalle Michelangelo and an old gypsy woman had proffered her a rose.

Larry had come early on the morning of Good Friday and had taken her off in spite of her protests to the Thatched House. 'You are not going to spend Easter on your own,' he said. 'You're going to spend it with your family.' For the first time, to his great satisfaction, he had his family, all of them, under the same roof at the same time.

It was only a short-lived gratification for him, for later that day they were dispersing – Andrew to an obscure Greek island to become re-acquainted with his mother's people, and Tim and Victoria off to Philadelphia to join their mother for the Easter holidays. Carla had felt apprehensive about meeting this assortment of half-sisters and brothers, but she had worried unnecessarily, for like their father they did not know what it was like to feel embarrassed and could see nothing awkward about being confronted with a sister they barely knew. She was one of them and that clinched the matter.

Andrew, the eldest, was short and swarthy and reminded Carla of what Larry had said about his first wife: 'She had eyes like pools of ink.' Andrew too had ink-black eyes which smiled favourably on his unknown sister. 'Welcome to the club,' he said.

Tim looked much as she remembered, except that he was taller now than she. Victoria hovered at his shoulder as she had at their first meeting, less self-assured than her older brother, for whereas Tim shook Carla's hand up and down as if it were a pump handle, Victoria gently placed hers in Carla's palm. The girl who had been a born-again Christian at fourteen, now had the look of a saint, which she certainly did not inherit from their father.

Irina's two chicks jostled to be noticed. Emma, the younger, pushed herself forward. 'We're going to have an Easter egg hunt on Sunday after Sunday school,' she said in a high singsong voice. Her eyes, large, round and dark like her mother's, fastened on the bag Carla was carrying. 'Do they have Easter eggs in Florence?'

Yes, they had Easter eggs in Florence. Last Easter Tony had taken her on Easter Day to Santa Maria del Carmine, one of the least spectacular of Florence's churches, but containing Masaccio's magnificent frescoes in the Brancacci chapel. By now Carla knew Tony well enough to be slightly cynical about his emotional reactions to works of art, but he stood before the famous scene of Adam and Eve being banished from Paradise with tears in his eyes and she knew they were genuine. Embarrassed, she walked away.

There was a constant stream of children attended by their mothers taking their Easter eggs up to the altar to be blessed. An old woman, dressed all in black, came in with a basket of fresh eggs covered with a snow-white napkin and they too were blessed. Again feeling like an intruder, Carla walked away.

When Tony came looking for her she was in the act of lighting a candle she had set among other lighted candles in a side aisle. 'Why are you doing that?' he said sharply.

Why had she done it? She did not rightly know. On a sudden impulse? – a form of prayer? – begging for guidance? 'Because I felt like it,' she answered vaguely.

He was angry. 'Lighting a candle is a significant gesture, not one to be taken lightly.'

'I did not light it lightly,' she said. It was the last time they went together to any of Florence's churches.

'Yes,' Carla said now, 'they do have Easter eggs in Florence, but I didn't bring any as I wasn't sure how they would travel. I'll buy you Easter eggs when I go to Norwich tomorrow.'

She had not come empty-handed, however. There was a doll each for Hannah and Emma, dressed in Florentine national costume with the word 'Firenze' stitched on the skirts. Silk scarves in bold colours for Irina and Victoria and leather-bound desk diaries for the men.

'Just souvenirs,' she said. She had bought them in a mad rush around the shops on the eve of her departure from Florence.

The three travellers left soon after lunch, Larry taking them to Norwich to see them onto the train to London. Irina busied herself in the kitchen. Carla couldn't remember a time when Irina was not busying herself in the kitchen. Irina's girls took it upon themselves to entertain her.

Later, having supper at the large pine table in the kitchen, Carla said during a lull in the conversation, 'I understand you had a plague of mice over Christmas?'

Irina smiled. 'The girls won't forget that in a hurry. Did they tell you about my box of Belgian chocolates?'

'That the mice ate the whole top layer?'

'I'd left it in the sideboard in the dining-room. I didn't remember it until weeks after Christmas, then I found the top layer completely demolished. The silver papers around the chocolates were still intact, but the chocolates inside had vanished. I admit to my shame I suspected the girls at first, then I saw the droppings.'

'Need we have this conversation at the supper table?' said Larry, as he reached over to spear another pickled gherkin. 'It puts me off my food.'

'Nothing could put you off your food, darling,' said Irina serenely.

'Mummy threw the chocolates in the dustbin, and there were still lots of them the mice hadn't eaten,' said Hannah in a doom-laden voice.

'What did you do?' asked Carla. Mice to her were no problem. They were a way of life in the apartment in Florence.

'I called the pest officer in and he put down poison in strategic places, and . . .'

'Their tinkies all turned blue,' finished Emma triumphantly.

Irina ignored this. 'That was the end of the mice except for one persistent one. He really took the place over, kept popping up and trotting across the floor whenever he felt like it. I bought a trap and baited it with cheese, but he didn't go near it, so then I tried chocolate. I knew by this time they liked it. Chocolate isn't safe from mice.'

'And you caught it?'

'Yes, I caught it,' said Irina with regret. 'It was one of those break-backed traps and I was really quite choked when I saw the poor little thing lying there, looking so utterly dead . . .'

'It was very flat,' said Emma solemnly.

'Shall we change the subject?' said Larry, spearing another gherkin.

On Saturday Larry took Carla into Norwich to buy Easter eggs, and on the way back they stopped off at Beckton Market to buy a car.

There had been much discussion about cars the previous evening. The little girls had gone to bed and Irina, Carla and Larry relaxed with martinis before a fire in the drawing-room.

Carla needed a car and Larry claimed he knew just the one for her, a three-year-old Fiesta, one lady owner, only seven thousand miles on the clock. It was a snip.

'Don't let him bully you into it,' said Irina, putting down her glass and taking up some knitting. 'If you want a new car, Carla, you have it.'

'I just want something with four wheels that will go,' said Carla.

She bought it from Smithson's, the garage that serviced Larry's Rover, and as Larry had said, it was a snip. The lady owner had taken good care of it, using it only to go shopping, to church on Sunday and the occasional outing. It was taxed and ready to drive away, it would be hers as soon as Easter was over and she could make the necessary arrangements with the bank.

And Sunday brought the great egg hunt. Four little friends from the Sunday school joined in.

'We couldn't do this in one of those pernickety little gardens, all neat beds and manicured lawns,' said Larry with glee, watching as the excited children trampled through the wilderness he called his garden.

'Those children are going to get very grubby,' said Carla, watching one little boy digging into the soft soil with his bare hands. 'Did you bury the eggs, Larry?'

'No, I tried that one year and it wasn't a success – the mothers complained. This time they are hidden in the bushes.'

Most of the bushes bore thorns or prickles. Carla envisaged snagged clothes, scratched hands and legs, and decided not to stay for what she thought of as a tearful conclusion. She joined Irina in the kitchen and took over making the sandwiches for tea.

'He doesn't change, does he?' she said.

Irina looked at Carla over her glasses. 'He has changed considerably. I no longer have to console the poor females I called his disciples, nor to mop their tears when he hurts their feelings . . .'

'You mean he doesn't hurt their feelings any more? That he has grown mellow with old age?'

'I mean there are no longer disciples to console. Larry no longer needs admirers to feed his ego. He has grown up, Carla, he has grown up.'

Carla listened to the cries of disappointment and joy, frustration and rhapsody, coming from the garden. The umpire, in a booming voice, was instructing the players, demanding to know whether they were hot or cold. 'I detect no signs of it,' she said.

The gatehouse, she found, was cold, dark and silent after the Thatched House. She solved the first problem by switching on the central heating and lighting the fire in the sitting-room, and the rooms grew lighter as threatening clouds dispersed. But she could do nothing about the silence. It followed her about like an evil spirit. 'You wanted solitude and now you've got it,' she said. She had no pity on herself.

Whenever she felt like this she wrote to Tony. It released her tension to pour out her feelings on paper. She wrote letters she had no intention of posting and, if through a lapse of sanity she were tempted, she knew he would just ignore them. She imagined herself as Charlotte Brontë pouring out her hungry soul to her beloved M. Heger. She knew one of Charlotte's letters by heart and walked about quoting it to herself:

> Monsieur, the poor have not need of much to sustain them – they ask only for the crumbs that fall from the rich man's table. But if they are refused they die of hunger. Nor do I, either, need much affection from those I love. But you showed me of yore a little interest – I hold on to it as I would hold on to life.

Heart-breaking words, painful in their supplication. No, she thought, even I who am not a feminist by any means could not demean myself to that extent. Yet she knew if she were to see Tony coming down the lane at this moment she would run to meet him.

She had given him her home address. He could easily get in touch if he wanted to. On her arrival back at Thornmere she had sent him a picture postcard of Norwich Castle and had written on the back a message to the effect that she had arrived safely, and thanking him for giving her the benefit of his expertise during the past few years. She had written it in such a way that its subtlety would not be lost on him. She could hear him now, giving a little snort of annoyance as he read it, see him tearing the card into pieces before throwing it into the wastepaper basket. He could put up with a woman's tears better than he could her mockery. He had no time for women who distanced themselves from him, as she had when she had first sensed his interest was waning. Flattery would have got her everywhere, but even she, besotted as she was, had her price.

And when she did, a few days later, see a familiar figure coming down the lane, it was not Tony she ran to meet but Jessie Stoneham.

'So why', said Jessie, releasing herself from Carla's embrace, 'have you not been to see me? Is it a question of off with the old friends and on with the new?'

Carla bit back a smile. The same old Jessie, having her little grumble first before allowing the full warmth of her feelings to come through. 'I kept phoning, you know, even though I was so busy over Easter I didn't know which way to turn, and all I got was that horrible mechanical voice that didn't sound a bit like you. I hate talking to machines.'

Carla had no excuses and made none. She had always been honest with Jessie, who had given her shelter and moral support during the period of the gatehouse's renovation. She had not heard the phone, she must either have been working in the garden or the studio. The oppressive silence of the house had sometimes been too much. Outside, she could at least listen to the birds.

'It's two weeks since I heard you were back at Thornmere,' said Jessie, more now in sorrow than in umbrage. 'I've been waiting for you to get in touch, but no such luck. Why are you avoiding me, Carla?'

'I wasn't avoiding you, you are the last person I should want to avoid. But things haven't been easy for me lately, Jessie. I just wanted a breathing space to pull myself together.'

They were inside the house by now, in the pretty little sun-filled sitting-room. Carla fussed over her guest, plumping up the cushions on the sofa for her, switching on the fire before seating herself beside her. In spite of the sun the room felt chilly. 'It's good to see you again, Jessie.'

'You know where I live. You've got my phone number.' But it was Jessie's last snipe and a half-hearted one at that. She was not one to bear a grudge, or to score points off someone who looked so cast down. 'We had grown so close, Carla. I used to love chewing over old times with you. I really missed you when you went away. I kept your room just as it was, but I've got another lodger now, your friend Mrs Stevens. I've put her in your old room. I had to move her because her room in the hotel was booked and there was no other available. She's like you, prefers staying with me rather than at the Hall. Doesn't say much for all that splendour, does it?'

'It says much more for your hospitality,' Carla replied with feeling. 'Those few months that I stayed with you, the way that you mothered me, helped me with plans for the gatehouse. Do you think that they meant nothing to me? They did – they still do. It's just – Jessie, look at me . . . I've been ill.'

'I can see that; you still look ill. I noticed it as soon as I saw you. Is that why you came home?'

'Yes, but I didn't want to advertise the fact. I'll tell you something, Jessie, that I haven't even told my father. I was on the edge of a nervous breakdown. I even tried to commit suicide. I swallowed a bottle of aspirins, but it wasn't enough. A friend found me in time and it was all hushed up. I'm so ashamed now when I think of it. I always thought I was a clear-headed sort of person.'

Carla had been speaking in short, broken sentences. She

buried her face in her hands, but lifted her head when she felt Jessie's arm go round her shoulders.

'Was it a man?' Jessie's voice was vibrant with emotion. She blamed all the troubles of the world on men. With the exception of a few, like the two doctors and Carla's father, she couldn't see any use for them. She eased herself nearer to Carla and the warmth of her body was a comfort in itself.

In little above a whisper, Carla said, 'It always is a man, isn't it?'

'Not always. I tried to commit suicide once and it certainly wasn't over a man – I was only fifteen and a half at the time.'

'Jessie! – you of all people. I don't believe it. You're just saying that to make me feel better . . .'

'I don't just say things and I don't tell lies either. I have never told anyone what I am about to tell you. The story died with my mother. It was during my first job – in an office. I was so proud of working in an office – nobody in my family had ever aspired to that before. My mother was ambitious for me and sent me to evening classes to learn shorthand and typing, and after only a few months I landed this job with an engineering firm in Norwich.

'Everything was fine at first, but I wasn't very good at shorthand and made a lot of mistakes in my typing. Finally I was told that they would have to replace me with an experienced shorthand-typist. I didn't know what to do. I couldn't go home and tell my folks I had lost my job, I couldn't face them. They were so proud of me and had boasted so much about me to friends and relations . . .'

'Didn't you offer to go back to evening classes if the firm kept you on?'

Jessie stared absently at the flames licking the artificial logs. 'I knew it would be no good. I knew I'd never master shorthand . . . those long technical words they used. I'd never be able to cope. I didn't say anything to my parents. I finished my week at Crow's and still didn't let on. I kind of hoped a miracle would happen. I caught the train to Norwich the following Monday as usual and spent the day looking for work. At my age, without experience, I didn't stand a chance. I had a little money in my post office account and I eked that out to pay for my fare. I tried to do without lunch because my mother always had a good meal waiting for me, but I used to get so hungry walking about the city all day. Friday was coming nearer and I wouldn't have the money to give my mother. I always gave her my pay packet unopened and she would give me a few shillings back for pocket money. I was so proud the first week I did that, I really thought I was paying my way. I had a gold chain bracelet that one of my better-off aunts had given me. She always said it was given her by one of her followers. It was the only thing of value I had and I tried to pawn it. I can't tell you what it cost me going into that pawnbroker's. My mother would have died of shame had she seen me. It was all for nothing. The bracelet wasn't even gold. That was the end. I thought the only way out was to commit suicide. I just couldn't go home without a pay packet.'

Jessie once again lapsed into silence. Carla waited.

'I had no money to buy poison with – whether you could buy poison over the counter I didn't know. I didn't fancy throwing myself under a tram or a bus – I didn't want to get hurt. I thought the best way would be to die of pneumonia, then everybody would be sorry for me and the only way I could think of to get pneumonia was to get my clothes wet. My mother was always saying when I got caught in the rain: "Don't let those clothes dry on you or you'll get pneumonia." So I went into the Ladies on Thorpe station and thoroughly wetted all my underclothes – just dribbled water from my hand down my neck until everything was soaked – and I travelled back to Thornmere Halt like that, standing up all the way as it was too uncomfortable to sit down. It was winter and got dark at four o'clock. I didn't go home. I wandered about the lanes getting colder and colder, and when I finally decided that I must be on the verge of pneumonia I gave up. I had a key but I knocked on the door and my mother and father fell on me. They had imagined all sorts of things happening to me. They had worked themselves into a right panic. When I told them the reason why I was wet they made more of a fuss of me than ever. They couldn't do enough for me, Carla.' Jessie's voice trembled slightly. 'They wrapped me in blankets and sat me down by the fire and gave me my supper on a tray. Bacon and two eggs I remember, and didn't that go down a treat. I hadn't had anything to eat all day.'

'And did you get pneumonia?' said Carla, her emotions so mixed she wasn't sure whether to laugh or cry and ended up doing a little of both.

'Did I, heck! I didn't even get a cold. But I'll tell you what I did get – another job, keeping books this time. I soon picked that up. I was always good at figures.'

'I think', said Carla, 'you made that up just to make me feel better.'

'Every word of it was true,' declared Jessie. She heaved herself with difficulty to her feet, for the soft cushions of the sofa had wrapped themselves around her like a billowing vice. 'Now, what about a nice cup of tea?'

And it was over tea she brought Carla up to date with the latest news on Milly Stevens.

Four

Milly lay wakeful in bed listening to the noise the birds made outside. One kept on repeating itself. Worse than a bally alarm clock she thought – it had awakened her as soon as it got light. It was now seven o'clock and she was gasping for a cup of tea.

If she were still at the hotel she would have been out of bed and made herself one before this, but staying with Jessie (they were on first-name terms by this time) had certain disadvantages and not having tea-making things in the bedroom was one. Having to go down a step into the bathroom was another. She always remembered the step going down, but her mind was on other things when coming out and consequently she tripped and went plunging through space and came down with a thwack that shook the landing.

'One more fall and I'm supplying you with a gozunder,' Jessie threatened. 'I've got one with a crest on it you can have. It came from the Massingham family and my mother bought it at an auction when the estate was broken up – she said she felt she had a right to it as she'd emptied it enough times when she was a housemaid up at the Hall.'

But Milly could not be tempted with a crest. She had

given up that sort of thing, now she could afford to stay in hotels with *en-suite* facilities, she said.

Eight o'clock, and Jessie came in with the tea.

'There's a bird out there driving me potty,' said Milly. 'Isn't there any way you can shut him up.'

Jessie listened with her head on one side. 'That's a thrush! Fancy anyone wanting to shut up a song-thrush.'

'I'd shut up anything that wakes me up at five o'clock in the morning.' Milly looked hopefully at her landlady. 'Please let me get up today. I'm sick and tired of staying in bed with nothing to do but think. There are so many things I want to get on with.'

'Name me one.'

'Get my hair washed and set for a start.' It worried Milly that her parting had been getting wider by the day. It was over three weeks since she had had her last tint.

'You'll have to go to Beckton Market for that. We have a visiting hairdresser in Thornmere, but she doesn't . . .'

'Doesn't what?' said Milly sharply.

'Do anything fancy. Just a shampoo and set – not even a blow dry . . .'

'I don't see why I can't get up. My leg's gone down.'

'The doctor is coming this afternoon, we'll see what he says – until then you stay put.'

An hour later the front door closed behind Jessie Stoneham and her footsteps could be heard crunching along the drive. Milly lifted her breakfast tray from her lap and placed it on the bedside table. She went along to the bathroom, showered and put on a clean night-gown, then, mindful of Jessie's threat, lifted her foot clear of the trap for the unwary.

She did not return to bed but in her dressing-gown sat by the window, looking out on the broad sweep of grass that spread either side of the drive. Jessie had told her that she could remember as a child seeing a grand avenue of elms that led from the main gates to the entrance to the Hall. At the beginning of the war the Hall was requisitioned by the War Office and very soon afterwards four anti-aircraft guns appeared in the grounds.

'I was told the soldiers took down some of the trees to make room for their ack-ack guns,' she said. 'I expect some went for fuel too. Everybody was short of fuel during the war. But what a sacrilege – those beautiful old elms.'

Milly saw nothing beautiful about trees, especially not an elm tree. An elm tree had, for her, shattered a dream and killed her mother. She had been delighted, when she read many years later, that Dutch Elm disease had decimated most of the elm trees left in the country. Rough justice, she considered it.

She remembered only too well the day the tree blew down. That day would have been one of the highlights of her life if it hadn't been for the manner in which it ended. Mr Ansley had suggested a run out to Southend. Just he, her mother and herself.

'Not the Egg-man?' Polly queried.

'No, it's his day for cleaning out the hen-houses, that's how I managed a loan of the truck.'

It was September and the day promised fine when they arrived at Southend. Her mother had kept her away from school for the occasion. 'We won't get many more days like this, so best make the most of it,' she said.

Jack told them that the wireless had forecast gale force winds later in the day, but there was no sign of the wind rising yet. The sea was only slightly turbulent, sending spray splashing against the breakers. Milly tucked her dress into her knickers and paddled out as far as her knees.

They called her in when it was time to eat and they had

their dinner at a fish-and-chip café under some arches. Milly didn't like fish so she had chips on their own, a whole plateful of crinkled chips. She had never seen crinkled chips before. In her estimation they tasted much nicer than straight ones.

'I wouldn't mind living here,' said her mother, looking dreamily out at the sparkling water and the trippers queuing up for a ride on one of the pleasure boats. 'I really could settle down in a place like this.'

'So could I,' said Jack, looking not at the sea but at her mother.

'An' so could I,' said Milly, seeing her existence expanding as one long holiday, where sticks of rock, rides on the train along the pier, and paddling in the sea were a way of life.

They paid a brief visit to the Kursaal, brief because after her first ride on the scenic railway Milly was sick and brought up all her chips. After that she didn't feel much like joining in anything and could hardly raise any enthusiasm for a tram ride to Old Leigh.

They thought a walk alongside the ozone might bring colour back into her cheeks, and making their way westwards along a track that connected Old Leigh with the new railway station built out in the marshes, they came to the first of the many boats moored side by side, each with a gangplank connecting it to land.

'People must use them as houseboats,' said Polly. 'Look, each boat has its own little letter-box. The postman must deliver along here. What a trek for him.'

'More comfortable than living in a bus,' said Jack thoughtfully.

She looked sharply at him. 'What does that mean?'

'Just an observation. Look, there's one for sale. Shall we make enquiries?'

The man in the boat next door had all the information. The owner had moved away, leaving his address with his neighbour.

'I'll write it down for you, if you're interested.' He took them into his own boat in order to do this. His wife was sitting in the main saloon, crocheting what she called a 'dolly'. There was not a single object in that room, be it a book, pipe, vase, or ashtray, that did not have a lace doily snugly placed beneath it.

The saloon appeared enormous compared with the living-room in the bus. There were lace curtains up at the window and a bowl of dahlias on the table.

'Does it rock much when the tide's in?' asked Polly.

'Not that you'd notice. Mind you, this is an old cockle bawley, steady as a rock.'

'The one for sale looks smaller.'

'It is. It was someone's fancy yacht in the good old days, got lovely lines to her. She's been stripped down and you wouldn't know her from any other tub, except for her brasswork. She's got some lovely brasswork and Mrs Edwards used to keep it a treat. Would you like to look over her? I've got the key. Mother, put the kettle on, it won't take us any longer than two shakes of a lamb's tail.'

The *Wayfarer* was bereft of all personal touches. It was little more than an empty hull; but even so, Milly heard Jack whisper to her mother it had great potential, whatever that was. It had a living-room, two bedrooms, or cabins as their guide, Mr Moore, called them, and a long, narrow galley, equipped with a Calor-gas stove, a great improvement on the Primus they used on the bus.

'Only one drawback,' said Mr Moore. 'Drinking water has to be collected from the large house you can see from the main road. But that's no hardship.'

'We're used to collecting water,' said Milly importantly.

All this time, she noticed, her mother and Jack were holding hands. Now they went into a huddle.

'I reckon I could get work in season, perhaps all the year round. With all these big hotels and dance halls . . . A violinist ought to get a job easily enough in a place like Southend. I don't mind what I do, anything would be better than cleaning out after ruddy chickens.'

'And I could go out cleaning. I'm not too proud to do cleaning.'

'It'll be a fine life for the kid. Soon put some flesh on her bones.'

They continued this conversation on their way home with Milly wedged between them, half asleep. In her hand she was clutching a stick of rock she had bought for the Egg-man.

'I didn't know he was a friend of yours,' said her mother.

'He's not.'

'Then why did you spend your last penny on him?'

Milly found it difficult to answer that because she wasn't quite clear herself.

' 'Cos I thought he might be lonely staying at home by himself all day while we were enjoying ourselves. Besides,' she added in a firmer voice, 'you're supposed to bring back a present of rock from the seaside, everybody does.'

'That kid deserves a better home than a bus,' said Jack, pressing his point. 'She's something special, your Milly.'

'If you say so,' said her mother.

The 'something special' fell asleep. She awoke when the truck gave a sudden shudder. 'What happened – what was that?' she cried in alarm.

Her mother put an arm around her. 'It's the wind, caught us sideways. It won't be long before we're home now, pet. Why don't you try to have another little sleep.'

But further sleep was impossible. The wind had got up

and the noise it made as it whipped against the sides of the truck started Milly quivering.

'Good thing we haven't got a top to this truck – we'd be over,' said Jack, but Milly felt safe within the circle of her mother's arm and with the warm bulk of Uncle Jack on her other side. He was still talking about the *Wayfarer*, He had been talking about the *Wayfarer* ever since they left Old Leigh.

Her mother laughed teasingly at him. 'Do you always go on like this when something takes your fancy?' she said.

'Always.'

'No wonder the Egg-man is always giving me such dirty looks.'

'Forget about him, we've got our own lives to live. I think I can raise half towards the purchase price. How much do you think the bus would fetch?'

'It isn't mine. I told you about my arrangement with Sam Wagstaffe . . .'

Jack growled low in his throat. 'That's another reason I want to get you away from there . . .' He looked sideways at Milly as she stirred. 'What about you, girlie,' he said. 'Would you like to live on a boat?'

'Not half.' Her answer came straight from her heart. She visualised endless days on the beach and endless plates of crinkly chips under the arches.

It was dusk when they arrived back at the encampment. Candles and oil lamps flickered like glow-worms in the windows of the trams and buses. 'It looks cosy at night, doesn't it,' said Polly.

Jack admitted it did. 'Darkness hides a multitude of sins,' he said. He lifted Polly down from the cab and held her tight as he steadied her on her feet. 'I'll just run the kid up to deliver her rock,' Milly heard him say. 'I'll see you later. We've got a lot to discuss.'

The truck was buffeted by the wind all the way along the narrow track to the farmhouse. The trees caught in their headlamps looked in Milly's fancy to be doing a kind of St Vitus's dance. Lights shone in the windows of the farmhouse. 'Bert's getting supper,' Jack said. 'I wish I had thought to bring him something back from Southend too.'

The rock was now limp in Milly's hand. She apologised as she handed it over to the Egg-man. 'I'm afraid it's got a bit bendy. I expect I held it too tight,'

'It'll taste just as good,' the Egg-man said reassuringly. 'Would you like . . .' but Milly did not learn what it was she might like for a noise like a crack of thunder interrupted their conversation. The air was full of the sound of a tree groaning, then came a crash that sent a shudder through the house.

'Oh, my god,' said Jack running to the door. 'That sounded like that old elm . . .' Milly dashed to follow him, but the Egg-man held her back.

'You stay with me, he said. 'Perhaps you could help me eat some of this rock.'

A lot of uncles she had never met before came to her mother's funeral and these, unlike the ones that had visited Carlin Street, brought aunts with them. Milly, pale, tearful and looking smaller than ever in a skimpy black dress Mrs Watson had hurriedly run up for her, felt herself under close scrutiny.

They were sitting in the best room of the farmhouse and the Egg-man had made them all a cup of tea. Milly went off to find Uncle Jack and there he was, sitting behind one of the hen-houses, blowing his nose. He pulled her down on to his lap.

'What are the old busybodies saying now?'

'They're choosing who will have me.'

'Has anyone volunteered?'

Milly did not understand what he meant. He blew his nose again. He had been blowing his nose a lot since he found her mother in the rubble of the bus. 'That stick of rock saved your life, girlie,' he said, but she didn't understand that either.

'I wish I could stay with you and the Egg-man,' said Milly, laying her head on his shoulder.

'So do I, dear, but we haven't got any claim on you and tongues would wag.' Her mother used to complain about tongues wagging in Carlin Street. Milly did not rightly know what it meant, but could only suppose it was something rather unpleasant.

It was finally decided among the brothers that Milly would be shared between them, three months at a time with each household.

'Won't do much for her schooling,' said Jack.

'At least she'll be living in a respectable home for the first time in her life,' retorted the aunt with the sharpest nose.

They left that afternoon, taking Milly and two dozen eggs between them.

They weren't such a bad bunch, thought Milly, her opinion mellowed by the distance of sixty-odd years. They had done their duty by her and she suspected she had been a right little puss at times.

She was surprised when Jessie ushered in Dr Brooke, for it wasn't the same Dr Brooke she had seen before. This man was younger and bearded and she did not feel so much at home with him, though he shared with his father a reassuring bedside manner. He was far more thorough in his examination, taking her blood pressure and temperature and pulse, sounding her chest and her back and heart. He was pleased with her condition and said she could now manage the stairs, but stressed the need to rest if her leg showed any sign of swelling again. His final piece of advice, which she had no intention of taking, was to buy herself a pair of flat-heeled shoes.

'There's a good shoe shop at Beckton Market,' said Jessie after showing young Dr Brooke to the door. 'We could get Kevin Smithson to take us in one afternoon.'

'I've never worn flat-heeled shoes in all my adult life,' said Milly stubbornly. 'And I don't intend to start at my age.'

'All right, be like that, but next time you find yourself walking behind a short, fat person in three-inch heels take a good look. You might learn something.'

Jessie was half-way down the stairs when Milly called her back. 'When is your next free afternoon?' she said contritely.

Carla was pleased with her latest purchase. The Fiesta was indeed a snip. She tried it out on a trip to Norwich to buy artist's materials. She had done no serious painting since her return to the gatehouse, telling herself it was because she lacked the materials. Such was not the case. What she really lacked was enthusiasm; and she doubted that she had, any longer, the ability to paint anything worthwhile. Tony had undermined all her faith in herself as a painter, chiefly because of his criticisms of her water-colours.

She got what she required in an artist's shop near the market-place: cartridge paper, tubes of paint, a palette and some sable brushes. She had learned one thing from Tony: not to leave her brushes on their points in a jar of water for any length of time, for then they acquired a permanent curve. A simple precaution like that, she thought, and she had had to be told. She hadn't even had the nous to think of it herself.

'You'll never make a artist,' her grandmother had once

said when as a schoolgirl she first voiced that ambition. 'All you'll ever be able to draw is a breath.'

That memory still had power to hurt. I'll show them, I'll show them all, she had thought at the time. 'I'll show them,' she said to herself now. Them, in this case, meaning Tony.

But not you, Lottie, she thought, you always had faith in me. There was a time when she believed that Lottie haunted the gatehouse; she could sense her nearness as an intangible yet positive presence. But once the gatehouse was restored and became a living home again the spirit of Lottie left her as if her part in the restoration was over.

Carla had tried to express this idea to Larry, but his reaction had verged on anger. 'Get away from here, Carla. For God's sake get away. There is a different world waiting for you out there. You have a gift – a talent – don't bury it here in this remote corner of Norfolk. Take it out and air it.'

So she had aired it in Dresden and Prague and Florence and finally to Tony. He had carried on where her father had left off – taking over her life and telling her how to live it

Am I one of those submissive sorts of woman who have to have a man to tell them what to do, a left-over from the Victorian age? she asked herself. But she thought her submissiveness was more because she had been brought up entirely by women. Men, to her, were a different species, with whom she had never felt at home.

She had had a brief crush on a boy her own age during her last year at school, and she had met a man at art classes during her Wenley days who had taken her to bed, but she hadn't really enjoyed the experience. She felt that sex without love was not for her and knew it for certain when she fell helplessly in love with Tony, for he had aroused in her a passion that both delighted and shamed her at the same time.

It was always a disappointment to her that during those first few memorable months together he had never invited her to move in with him, for there was plenty of space in the shabby old villa that was both his home and his place of work.

An Italian family occupied the ground floor and Pia, the wife, did all the things for Tony that Carla would have given her eye-teeth to do, such as his washing and shopping and cooking and cleaning. As she got to know him better, some of that enthusiasm wore off, for there were better ways of serving him besides slaving for him. He was a man who valued his privacy and who also had a very low boredom threshold, which she did her best to alleviate.

She had entertained him greatly at first with tales of her two grandmothers; the beautiful and tragic model who had been her mother; the talented vagabond who was her father and, frequently, the gatehouse she had rescued from extinction. In fact she raved about the gatehouse so much he soon lost interest.

'A level-crossing cottage,' he had said once, when she had gone on about it longer than was necessary. 'What is so marvellous about a level-crossing cottage? It has no architectural value, it is no thing of beauty – it's just a functional building. Now this, this villa is a different matter altogether.'

They were sitting in his apartment at the time. The first and second floors were his 'living space', the attic his studio. All were in a state of grim disrepair.

'Look around you,' he said, waving a hand at the peeling walls and flaking ceiling. 'Sniff hard. Do you know what that smell is? It's dry rot. The place is riddled with dry rot This villa was the home of a wealthy silk merchant when your potty little gatehouse was only a potty little idea in some railway magnate's mind.'

His vehemence surprised and perturbed her. 'Won't your Italian grandparents help you out?'

He shrugged his shoulders. 'They bought me off with this dilapidated villa.'

'Your allowance. . . ?'

'It wouldn't even replace the window frames.'

'The bank. . . ?'

He laughed mirthlessly. 'What collateral could I offer them?'

Then she heard herself making a suggestion that had been far from her mind a moment before. '*I* could lend you the money to have the villa repaired.'

A flash of furious black eyes. A voice that cut like a lash. 'I don't borrow money from women.'

'I'm not just "women". I'm a woman who happens to love you very dearly, and I also love this old house and don't want to see it crumble away.' Her sincerity broke down his resistance. A few moments of doubt, then he concurred. At his insistence it was done through an *avvocato*: a short-term loan with high interest.

It was all settled within a few weeks and then the workmen moved in. The art class at the top of the house worked to the sound of hammering and chiselling, scraping and sawing. Pia went about in a state of woeful melancholy. When, several months later, Carla decided to flee, the repairs were still not completed and the interest had mounted alarmingly.

She spread out her new purchases on the working table in her studio. She worked better on a table than an easel, especially when painting water-colours. Painting with oils on a large canvas was a different matter. She sketched out in pencil some red and yellow tulips she had bought in the market, then went over them in wash. She worked with one eye on the clock. The two letters she had received from Florence so far had come by the second post. In neither had Sophie made any mention of Tony.

She lived on the forlorn hope that Tony would write to her, knowing she was setting herself up like an Aunt Sally just to be knocked down again. Since the day last autumn when Vanessa had walked into the studio, Carla had known instinctively that here was her replacement. Tony had been restless for months, often impatient with her for no apparent reason. She had recognised the signs, she had been warned of them by Angelica, a cynical, dark-eyed beauty a lot older than herself, who said if it were any comfort to her she was to be congratulated for staying the course longer than any of his other conquests. Eighteen months was the record so far, before his interest began to wane.

Carla had taken this remark for what it was, a defamation by a jealous woman to revenge herself for past slights. She was not ignorant of the fact that Vanessa had a wealthy father, for she *did* purchase her clothes at the via de'Tornabuoni and drove around the streets of Florence in a Lamborghini. And yet, though all the evidence showed that Tony was attracted by wealth, Carla had refused to believe that he could be bought.

She had convinced herself that his lessening interest in her coincided with the decision over the loan. She felt it hurt Tony's pride to have to be beholden to a woman. He liked his women to be beholden to him. He bathed in the warmth of their gratitude. For him to feel gratitude in return undermined the good opinion he had of himself. All this she told herself as a sop to her own pride. It hurt to have to acknowledge that a younger and more beautiful woman had supplanted her, that she had unwittingly severed their relationship with her cheque-book.

She had known that the only thing left for her to do was to withdraw her presence with her dignity intact, but had stayed and suffered, and when the day came that she could take no more humiliation, had made her exit unnoticed.

She had waited for Tony to phone her at the flat or for delivery of one of his untidily scrawled notes. Neither had been forthcoming. She had wondered if he had even noticed her absence from the class. At length one day she'd found the strength to break the deadlock. She went to a travel agency and booked a flight to London.

She was standing back admiring her morning's work when her father walked in on her. She thought the painting of the tulips was the best thing she had done in months. Satisfaction with her work was a long overdue sensation.

At her elbow, her father stared at her painting in silent speculation.

'Well?' she said.

'I can't fault your draughtsmanship.'

She knew that tone of voice. 'You don't like it!'

'What makes you think that?'

'You damn me with faint praise.' It was a quote from one of L. M. Montgomery's books. She had been an avid reader of the 'Anne' books in her girlhood.

'It has no life in it – no movement.'

'It is *still* life,' she said mordantly.

'You know what I mean.'

Yes, she knew what he meant all right, that was the trouble. But she did not want him to confirm her worst fears – that an essential spark had gone out of her work. She wanted his praise, even if it were dishonest. She wanted his encouragement. She wanted help.

Unaware of her requirements, her father went on with what he thought of as helpful criticism. 'Compare these tulips, technically perfect as they are, with the sweetpeas on the walls of your bedroom. Damn it, Carla, those look so real you can almost smell them. These don't look real, they look dead. Flat. Two dimensional. There's no movement, no *emotion*, that's the word I am looking for – emotion. You painted those sweetpeas upstairs with love. What were you feeling when you painted these?'

'Depression,' she said.

Larry looked hard at his daughter then and saw tears clinging to her lashes. He propelled her to one of the two chairs in the studio and faced her on the other, his hands resting on his knees. 'What happened to you in Florence?'

She answered his question with another. 'When you saw me off on my voyage of self-discovery, as you called it, can you remember the advice you gave me?'

'Let me see . . . To visit all the art centres of the world including those in the Far East?'

'There was that, but on a more personal level, you told me to fall in love while I was about it, as sex is good for art.'

'I don't see anything wrong in that.'

'But you didn't tell me what to do when the one I fell in love with fell out of love with me. What effect that would have on my painting.'

He leaned foward and took her hands in his. 'Carla, oh, my poor Carla. I didn't mean that intense sort of love. I meant some light-hearted little affair . . . a holiday romance . . .'

'I'm not the sort that goes in for light-hearted little affairs,' she said tonelessly. 'It's all or nothing with me, worse luck.'

He wished she were young enough to take her on his knee, as he still did with Emma or Hannah when they needed comforting. He remembered the day he and Irina had seen her off at Heathrow, pretending an assurance she was far from feeling, going blindly off on her travels with an assumed mantle of independence. His heart had ached for her even then.

'I hope she'll be all right,' he remembered saying.

'Of course, she'll be all right. She's like you, she'll land on her feet anywhere.'

But she was more like her mother. With her, it was all or nothing too.

Now he said, 'Are we talking about the chappy who sounds like an ice-cream merchant? Antonio, or some such?'

Carla gave a half-hearted smile. 'Nobody dared call him Antonio, he went off like a rocket if they did.' Except for Vanessa who always addressed him as Antonio, rolling his name round her little pointed tongue and daring him with a mischievous smile to rebuke her in front of others.

If I could have made light-hearted fun of him like that, I might not have lost him, Carla thought. There was nothing light-hearted in their relationship on her part. For her it was deadly serious. 'What shall I do, Larry. Tell me what to do,' she said. 'If I can't paint any more, how shall I fill my days?'

He would have liked to have suggested that she found herself a job, but he knew that she had had no formal training except looking after an elderly relative and he hardly liked to suggest she should go and work in an old folks' home.

He got up and went off to study the tulips again. 'I was too critical,' he said. 'I gave a snap judgement when I should have taken my time. Your draughtsmanship is good and so is your brushwork and I like your method of letting the white of the paper grin through in places. The fact is, I know you can do better. Your technique is vastly improved, but it lacks . . . Damnation, I can't find the right word. Freshness for want of a better – yes, that's it, freshness. That's what it lacks. The flowers look tired. They look as if they need to be put in a bucket of water to be revived.'

Carla laughed in spite of herself. 'I need to be put in a bucket of water to revive,' she said ruefully. 'I feel so tired. I wake up feeling tired.'

'What you need is a good medico. You should go and see my Dr Blood.'

'Larry, please . . .'

'All right, Dr Brooke then, the Young Dr Brooke. Go and see him. I can highly recommend him.'

'I have no wish to see him,' she said. 'What is wrong with me no doctor can heal.'

But she did see him, a few days later when she took Milly off to the hairdressing salon at Beckton Market. It wasn't her first meeting with Milly since the episode of the painful feet. Carla's conscience had been plaguing her that she not been to see her fellow passenger before this, then on the morning of the twenty-first of April, which happened to be her birthay, she was struck by a sudden idea and went off to Norwich to buy a bottle of champagne and twenty-nine long-stemmed carnations. Armed with these peace offerings, she knocked at the door of Thornmere Lodge.

Milly's voice came as from a distance. 'The door's on the latch, just come right in and leave the fish in the kitchen.'

Carla went to the foot of the stairs. 'I'm afraid it's not the fishmonger, Mrs Stevens. It's Carla from the old gatehouse.'

'Carla! I was just thinking of you, wondering how you were getting along. Come on up, girl – you know where to find me and the name happens to be Milly.'

Carla stood on the threshold of Milly's room reliving in her memory the time when she had been its tenant nearly four years ago. It hadn't changed. The same mahogany furniture. The same iron bedstead. The fat eiderdown, the crotchet-edged sheets and pillowcases. Only the best was good enough for guests of Jessie Stoneham.

'You are looking much better than the last time I saw you,' said Carla. She suddenly felt rather foolish standing there, clutching the carnations in one hand and the bottle of Bollinger in the other. It had seemed such a good idea this morning, sharing her birthday with another; now it seemed just an affectation. 'I brought you these,' she said in a rush.

Milly's eyes rounded with surprise and delight. 'For *me*? Champagne and flowers! What have I done to deserve this?'

'It's what you're going to do. You are going to help me get through one of the most difficult days of my life.'

They were sitting either side of a little table in the window, Milly in a kimono-style dressing-gown, like its owner past its prime, but still fetching enough to catch the eye. Carla had been downstairs and found glasses in the pantry and a vase tall enough to take the carnations.

'Anybody would think it was my birthday. I can't remember the last time I celebrated my birthday. I don't care to remember them any more.' Milly drank with relish. Champagne was too good to be merely sipped. 'Tell me, Carla, why is today particularly difficult?'

A shadow crossed Carla's face. Her eyes grew vague. 'It's my twenty-ninth birthday. In some ways that's worse than being thirty. Thirty is a nice round figure; twenty-nine is saying farewell to your twenties. The twenties are supposed to be the most productive of one's life – what have I produced? Nothing.'

'It seems to me more like a saddo day than a birthday,' said Milly, helping herself to more champagne. 'Age has nothing to do with years, it has to do with how you feel. I avoid looking in a mirror, if I can help it. I'd be feeling quite young and lively, then I'd catch sight of myself in the glass and heigh presto, the illusion would vanish. I'd say you're feeling pretty down today, aren't you?'

'I was, but I feel better for talking to you.'

'That's the ticket.' Milly held the champagne bottle up to the light. 'There's not much left, not enough to save for Jessie. Shall we finish it off?'

Carla smiled in a foolish, dreamy-eyed way. 'You finish it off, Milly. I feel woozy enough as it is. I'll buy Jessie another bottle when it's her birthday.'

'You'll be so lucky. The date of Jessie Stoneham's birth is on the official secrets list.'

Carla had two hours to whittle away before collecting Milly. Milly was having the full treatment; tint, shampoo and set, and a facial. Carla idled around the stalls, comparing Beckton Market all the time with the exciting markets of Florence. As Sophie might have said, 'Nobody could accuse Beckton Market of being exciting.' Then she spotted a second-hand bookshop. Next to browsing around a street market came the pleasure of browsing around a second-hand bookshop, never knowing what treasures one might unearth. She was always hoping she might find a first edition. She collected first editions.

She had to step down into the shop, which was small and not too well lit. The smell of old leather, mustiness and dust filled her nostrils. There was no sign of a bookseller and the only other potential customer had taken a heavy volume down from the shelf and was studying it.

He was tall and well-built, clean-shaven and smart,

wearing a silver grey suit and dark suede shoes. His bulk looked familiar. She was sure she had seen that broad back before. And while she was racking her brains he turned and saw her, and smiled.

He put the book he was holding under his left arm and came across to her. 'Fellow bibliophile, I presume?' he said in friendly fashion.

She stiffened. She had allowed herself to be picked up once before in this same free and easy manner and look where that had led her. She did not answer. The other's grin broadened. 'You don't know me?'

She took a closer look. Crisp, light brown hair, humorous grey eyes – humorous, until one surprised in them a latent sadness which she had done on the last occasion. The blood rushed to her face. 'Dr Brooke,' she stammered. 'I didn't recognise you without a beard. What have you done with your beard?'

'I shaved it off. I always shave it off for the summer and grow it again in the winter. Don't worry, Miss Foster, I have patients who never notice my beard is missing until I start to grow it again. And may I ask what are you doing here? Browsing or seeking?'

'Passing time, actually, though I'm always on the look-out for a first edition.'

'Aren't we all. Mine isn't a first edition, eleventh in fact. *Gray's Anatomy*, published 1889. A present for my father. He had a more up-to-date edition when he was a student, but that fell to pieces from over-use. He'll be tickled pink to get this.'

'His birthday?' she queried, birthdays being on her mind lately.

'No, just a replacement, rather overdue. It was I who wore out his old one when I was a student. All those fiddling little bones . . . it took me a long time to memorise them. Not so Dad, he can still reel off every bone in the body. He specialised in anaesthetics but still opted for general practice.'

'As you did?' she asked, out of politeness rather than interest.

If he sensed her lack of interest, his friendly manner did not change. 'I opted for psychiatry actually, then changed my mind and joined my father in practice. No, I haven't regretted it,' he said, answering the question she had had no intention of asking. 'I'm on my way to a psychiatrists' conference in Cambridge now. Can I give you a lift as far as Norwich?'

'I have to pick up a friend from the hairdresser's in half an hour.'

He nodded. 'Another time, then.' He lowered his voice. 'The shelf at the back, next to the one where I was standing – there's a first edition of Flora Thompson's *Still Glides the Stream*. 1948, if you're interested. I was nearly tempted to buy it for my mother . . .'

She was gone in a flash. She did not hear his chuckle, or the proprietor coming through from the premises behind the shop, or the transaction that followed. She was too busy on the trail of Flora Thompson.

Five

An accident which could have been calamitous but turned out to be just foolhardy happened to Carla during the first week of June. She fell off a ladder whilst attempting to evict a sparrow from a house-martins' nest.

The house-martins had nested beneath the eaves of the gatehouse ever since they were ousted from inside the house itself. Carla, since early May, had waited impatiently for their return, fearing that the good fortune their presence guaranteed would not be hers this year. She was desperate for some good news, preferably in a letter from Florence.

Like her great-grandmother, Lottie, she was highly superstitious when it came to birds. A single magpie foretold sorrow; a crow, flying in from the left, was bad news. Swallows or martins brought good news. She was foolish enough to mention this to her father.

'What about a duck?'

She stared. 'I've never heard any superstitions regarding a duck.'

'Well, one flew over me the other day and crapped on my head. I call that hard luck.'

The day she saw the first martins swooping above the

gatehouse her spirits soared. If they nest under the eaves, she told herself, it means I'll hear from Tony.

They did nest under the eaves again. They repaired the nest from the previous year, then mated against the wall. All was set for the breeding cycle to turn once more, but then the sparrows arrived.

Being bolder and more pugnacious than the gentle martins, the sparrows soon gained the upper hand. Their beaks were stronger and they could with ease break down some of the mud to widen the opening enough to suit their own requirements. In no time at all they were lining the nest with bits of fluff, or feathers they had collected from the garden. Carla spotted them.

She shouted, she screamed, she waved her arms, but her outburst had no more effect on them than did the frustration of the evicted martins. Tears of rage filled her eyes. She needed that good fortune and she was damned if she was going to let mere sparrows take it away from her.

She had recently received a letter from Sophie with the news that Vanessa had moved out of her hotel and into Tony's villa. And following hard on that came a letter from Tony himself, the first since she had left Florence, containing a cheque for the outstanding interest he owed her. The accompanying note, far from being offhand, was friendly and courteous, though completely lacking in sentiment. It could not have hurt her more if it had been downright vindictive.

But her anger dissolved and a feeling of hopelessness took its place. What had Vanessa got that she hadn't? Youth? Beauty? A millionaire father? All three. But she could not or would not believe that Tony had taken up with Vanessa because of that only. There must be affection too. She could not think uncharitably of Tony for long, try as she might, but that did not mean that she was another

Charlotte Brontë, begging crumbs from a rich man's table. She would rather starve! So his letter remained unanswered, at least for several hours, then, good manners getting the better of her, she wrote a brief acknowledgement of the cheque.

There were other letters she had written to him but never posted, the ones she thought of as her 'dream' letters in which, when her despair became too much to bear, she poured out all her frustrated longings. She kept these in the rosewood bureau she had inherited from Lottie and when at last she received the long-awaited letter from Tony, with its untidy and heart-stopping handwriting, to find that it only referred to business matters, she had promptly taken the unposted letters down to the bottom of the garden and burned them in the incinerator.

The wind whipped up the ashes and one or two bits of the charred pages went flying over the garden. She ran after them, tore them into smaller pieces and stood over them until they turned to ash, finally seeing the fading words imprinted on the last piece of paper – 'Darling, what went wrong?' before that too crumbled before her eyes.

You went wrong, she told herself savagely. You were warned often enough. Pia, with pity in her eyes had told her, 'Signorina, 'e no good for lady like you. 'E too . . . too . . .' But Pia had been lost for English words.

Sophie was never lost for words. She had said, 'Do you want to finish up like Angelica . . . hanging on year after year in the hope that she might win him back? I'm surprised you've hung on so long already. If he finds someone else he'd rather take up with he'll drop Vanessa just the same way he's dropped you.'

It had been the beginning of an ugly quarrel and they did not speak again for several days. Sophie had come to her finally with swollen eyes and begged to 'make up'. Carla was only too glad to comply. Sophie was too good a friend to lose. The present two lodgers, the last of a succession who had replaced the graduates, were poor substitutes.

All this now flashed through Carla's mind as she struggled with the ladder she had taken from the lean-to shed. It was aluminium and light compared with the old wooden ladders much loved by window cleaners, but it was made in two parts, one sliding on top of the other, so extending the ladder to double its length. She managed the extending part without much difficulty, but bringing the hasps over to join the two parts together was not so easy. She did it finally after many tries, and at the cost of two broken finger-nails. All this time the sparrow perched on the guttering above the martins' nest carried on a defiant chirruping.

She was nearly half-way up the ladder when one of the hasps sprang open. It was fortunate for her that she wasn't right at the top. It was even more fortunate that May had been extremely wet, too wet to cut the grass which was now long, lush and as soft as a mattress. When the ladder folded beneath her she fell on her back, winded and unable to move, but still very much alive, and heard, in the near distance, the baying of a dog.

It was Nick Brooke's day off. He had taken Ranger for his usual exercise along the nature trail and was on his way back and nearing the gatehouse when he saw a small piece of white paper caught up in a spray of cow parsley. He picked it up and read what was written there: 'Do you know what love is all about, I wonder?'

Nice question, he thought. The writer was a woman if the phraseology and handwriting were anything to go by. He put the slip of paper back where he found it, thought better of it, picked it up again and put it in his pocket without quite knowing why.

Sadly, he did know what love was all about. For him, it was two years of unalloyed happiness followed by ten years of bitter grieving. Not a fair exchange, but when had life ever been fair? As the intervening years had ground by, his good times had slowly begun to outnumber the bad, but they had taken their toll. He was determined never to commit his happiness into the hands of only one person again. It had been safety in numbers now for some little while.

His reflections were interrupted by a sudden scream. Ranger pricked up his ears, then barking a response, set off at a lope towards the gatehouse. Nick, when he arrived on the scene, took it in at a glance. A ladder in two pieces, Carla spreadeagled on the grass and Ranger, anxious to do his bit, licking her face.

'Please, take your dog off me,' said Carla faintly. 'He's making me so wet and I think my shoulder is broken.'

Nick went down on his knees and ran his hands over her with a sure and careful touch. 'Nothing broken,' he said, 'But to make sure we'd better get you to hospital for an X-ray . . .'

Close to like this, Carla could see that his eyes were not entirely grey, there were tiny golden flecks radiating out from the pupils. He had kind eyes, never kinder, she felt than now. 'Please don't send me to Casualty,' she pleaded. 'I went to Casualty with my grandmother once. She had tripped and broken her wrist. They couldn't give her an anaesthetic because she had just had her lunch. We sat and waited for ages in that place. I've never forgotten it . . .'

'How old were you?'

'Ten.'

'A very impressionable age. But all the same, I'd like you to come and see me tomorrow.'

'As a patient?' she said.

'Of course, as a patient.'

'Does that mean I will have to register with you. . . ?'

'Not especially, but it would be wise if you intend staying for any length of time. Why?' He seemed amused. 'Have you got anything against registering with me?'

She blushed and looked away. 'I'd rather register with your father.'

'I'm afraid my father isn't taking on any new patients. He's semi-retired, but if you have anything against me I can recommend Dr Driver of Beckton Market. With one proviso; he doesn't do night calls.'

She had a feeling he was laughing at her. He was perfectly serious, but his eyes gave him away. 'I can assure you I won't go falling off any ladders at night,' she said.

'Just what were you doing up that ladder, anyway?'

She told him. He looked unsurprised, as if his patients made a habit of falling from ladders whilst ousting sparrows from the nests of house-martins.

'What have you got against sparrows?' he asked. 'They are birds too, with the same urge to feather their nests and raise their young.'

'Sparrows are with us all the year round – they can go anywhere to build their nests. Martins are with us for such a short time and much more graceful to watch.' Not for anything would she have told him the real reason for her preference for house-martins.

He smiled down at her in a quirky sort of way with one side of his mouth raised slightly higher than the other 'And how did you intend to drive the sparrows away?'

'By removing all the nesting material they keep putting in until I wore them out.'

'Using the ladder each time, I presume?'

'There's no alternative.'

He sat back on his heels, appraising her. 'You're a very determined young woman.'

'In some ways I suppose I am.'

'Let me help you up . . .' He slipped his arm around her took her, left hand and lifted her to her feet. 'How do you feel now?'

'A bit dizzy. I'd like to sit down.'

He helped her into the gatehouse and through to the front room which was warm with sunshine and redolent with the scent of clove pinks that Carla had arranged in a vase on the mantelpiece. She was pleased to think that she had put herself out to do some housework that morning, though she would have preferred to get on with her painting. Not that Nick Brooke struck her as the sort of man to notice dust, or worry about it if he did.

Gently, he helped her on to the sofa. 'I'd like you to take off your blouse so that I can have a better look at that shoulder,' he said,

It wasn't a blouse, it was a shirt, and all she had on underneath was a bra. She hesitated. 'You're not my doctor yet.'

'Who is your doctor?'

'He lives in Essex. I haven't been in Norfolk long enough to register with anybody yet.'

'The offer is still open,' he said promptly.

She realised that she was making a fool of herself. He did not see her as a woman, he saw her for what she was, someone who had risked her neck for the sake of a pair of house-martins – in other words, an idiot.

There was no absence of tenderness in his examination of her, yet careful as he was, he could not help but inflict pain. On one occasion she cried aloud.

'No bones broken,' he said. 'But I think you may have pulled a muscle which can be just as painful. Keep it rested for now and I'll call in tomorrow morning with some pain-killing tablets. Have you anything to see you through tonight?'

'Paracetamol?'

'Excellent.'

At this point the kettle on the stove in the kitchen let out a piercing whistle. Ranger, who had been ordered to stay in the garden, came running in. There was nothing he liked more than a saucer of tea.

'So much for my training sessions,' said Nick.

The cup of tea he made for her was strong and sweet. Carla preferred it weak and unsugared. The grimace she made when she tasted it did not go unnoticed.

'Sorry,' he said, 'but that is the prescribed remedy for shock.'

'I'm not in shock, am I?'

'You will be when you get to bed, that shoulder is going to give you hell. A hot-water bottle will help ease the pain.'

The night before the temperature had been up in the 60s. She had slept on top of the duvet and in the nude.

But it was time for him to go. Even on his day off he liked to pop into the surgery to check up on emergency calls, anxious not to leave all to his father. He was very protective towards his father, she sensed. He'd be back, he said, he knew of a gadget guaranteed to ward off sparrows and he'd bring it along later and fit it up for her. He made her comfortable with cushions behind her back and her arm in a sling to ease the pull on the injured muscle, and that was how her father found her some fifteen minutes later.

'What are you doing lying there?' he said, not noticing the sling or perhaps taking it for some fancy way to wear a scarf. 'I thought you'd be in the garden on a fine day like this, or at least in the studio. Anything the matter with you?'

If she expected sympathy she was not going to get it. Her father laughed uproariously at her story. 'Didn't I tell you once that your stupid superstitions would be the death of you? Well, they very nearly were. You could have broken your neck.'

'I've pulled a muscle, that's all.'

'That's all! Irina once took it into her head to borrow Victoria's bike. She said she felt guilty about using the car because of the polution problem. Well, she fell off the bike and wrenched her arm and that gave rise to what the doc called a frozen shoulder. A frozen shoulder is no joke. Irina's gave her gyp for nearly six months, and she tried everything; physio, steroid injections, pain-killers. I'm just warning you in case – just to let you know what you're in for.'

'Larry, did you come to cheer me up?'

'I came to see if you'd taken my advice. Got any new work ready for me?'

She had started on an arrangement of roses in a squat brown jug and was anxious to finish it, for she felt she had recaptured some of her old skill and was painting not just with her fingers but with her heart – the core of her emotion, as her father expressed it. As soon as she mentioned this he was gone and stayed away so long she guessed he had taken the opportunity to have a cigarette. When he returned she could tell by the look on his craggy face that he was reeking with satisfaction.

'You're getting it, kid,' he said. 'It's not quite there yet, but it's coming.'

What did he do to her, this charlatan in Florence, besides quashing her zeal? Larry asked of himself. Broke her heart, dented her self-confidence and destroyed her ability to paint fresh and delightful little water-colours. Well, she was rid of him now and all that was needed was the right chap to come along to take his place.

From the window he saw a car coming down the lane. 'The doc's back,' he said. 'Did you tell me he was bringing you some contraption or other for your shoulder?'

'I said he was bringing me a gadget that would keep the sparrows away.'

'H'mph. I must see this for myself.'

She heard the two greet each other like old friends. She overheard enough of their comments to monitor their movements. They were raising the ladder against the wall.

'How do you fix it to the guttering? You can't nail it on,' she heard Larry say.

'I glue it. I did one for my mother and it stayed put for two seasons.'

Glue it, she thought. Glue a ladder to the wall? I must see this for myself.

Larry came in looking as pleased as a dog with two tails. 'Do you know what he's doing out there? He's made a miniature blind out of strips of plastic ribbon and he's sticking that over the entrance to the martins' nest. Very decorative. The idea is that the martins will be able to swoop under and up to get to the nest, but the sparrows, not being so acrobatic, will be flummoxed. He's ingenious, that Nick, always coming up with some idea or other. Did you know he has a boat down on the river?'

'I know nothing about him.'

'Well, he's got this old tub moored up on the river – a pre-war hire craft that he's converted into a houseboat – roomy old tub it is too. For getting about in he uses a little runabout, or launch to give it its correct name. A spanking little craft – it would go like a bomb if it were allowed. We sometimes take a trip down to Yarmouth together.'

'*We*? I didn't know you were that close.'

'We're old fishing buddies. We fish off Winterton beach in winter. You've got to be tough to withstand that, that's why I like having my personal doctor with me. I'll ask him to take you for a trip up to the mill. You'd enjoy that.'

Her smile was decidedly ironic. 'Have you forgotten about my frozen shoulder, Larry?' she said sweetly. 'Ask me again in about six months' time.'

Having just spent six weeks in a private hotel within sight and sound of the North Circular, Milly was surprised by how much she was looking forward to the peace and quiet of Norfolk.

She was on the train, Norwich bound and, tired of looking through the fashion magazines she had bought on the bookstall at Liverpool Street, she leaned back in her seat, resting her eyes.

As always when she was on the verge of sleep, her mind reverted to the past, in this case, the recent past. As soon as she felt well enough, and with her doctor's blessing, she had gone back to London to resume the quest for her missing husband.

She had visited Somerset House, where no record of his death could be traced. This gave her heart to contact the War Office, where she spoke to a junior member of the staff whose knowledge of the war, she came to realise, was based entirely on *Dad's Army*. She had called on the Salvation Army, who, though extremely helpful, did not hold out much hope after such a lapse of time, and so at last she came to the conclusion that she would be better off making enquiries in Thornmere, for the best help she had had so far had come from Jessie.

That had been when they were having tea in the garden in the shade of a morello cherry tree which then was a froth of white blossom, when Milly, acting on a thought that suddenly occurred to her, asked Jessie if she had ever heard of a local gamekeeper by the name of Stevens.

'D'you mean old Tom or young Tom?' Jessie said. 'I can remember them both very well. I never liked old Mr Tom, not since the day he caught me scrumping his apples. That was during the war and I wasn't very old, but he put the fear of old Nick in me. I kept well away from Hangman's Lane after that.'

Milly, momentarily stunned by the realisation that this information had been hers for the asking since the day she arrived, found her voice. 'A-and young Tom?'

'I never knew much about young Tom. He was a quiet, reserved sort of chap. I know he went in the army when war started, but then so did most of the young lads in the village. He was out in Palestine for some time. I did hear tell he married a London girl, but I don't think anything came of it. She disappeared off the scene soon after the war ended and nothing more was ever heard of her. Tom got even more unsociable then, but he was a good son and took care of his father until he died, and *he* lived to be ninety.'

Milly did not immediately answer. She was doing a quick bit of mental arithmetic. 'What year was that, then?'

'Oh, must have been '71 or '72, I don't remember exactly. Is it important?'

'It is to me.' Tom would have been in his early fifties then. How could a man in his early fifties disappear off the face of the earth? With ease, apparently.

Jessie resumed her narration. 'As soon as the old man died, Tom was off. Nobody really knew where, but some said to London. Someone else said he had it on good authority that he went up to Scotland to try his luck on the oil-rigs . . .'

Milly broke in. 'What did he look like when he got older?'

Stopped in full flow, Jessie's expression went blank. 'I don't believe I ever saw him when he got older. He kept himself to himself and I never had cause to go that way. I remember him best as he was in uniform. All the girls at school had a crush on him, most of the girls in the village too. He had a tall, upright figure, with the bluest eyes you ever saw and hair the colour of corn. Then he had to go off and marry that little minx from London . . .'

'She wasn't a little minx, and she had a bigger crush on him than any of you village girls,' retorted Milly tartly.

Jessie's mouth dropped open. Colour flooded her face. '*Stevens*, I should have realised. But who was to think . . . So you were Tom's wife. Well I never! You've fair taken the wind out of my sails.'

Wind or no wind, Jessie still had breath to ask questions, which she did in rapid succession, but not the sort of questions Milly cared to answer – as yet.

'Yes, it was a wartime wedding – just one of those things and it didn't work out. I couldn't settle in the country, not after London, so I went back. Tom could've found me if he wanted to, he knew my address, but he never made the effort.'

'But what made you come looking for him after all this time?' said Jessie curiously, when Milly again lapsed into silence.

Milly roused herself. 'I'm not getting any younger and nor is Tom, if he's still around. I just thought it would be nice after all these years to make up. I've never borne him any grudge and I don't think Tom is the grudging type either. Mind you, people change. What happened to the cottage?'

'Some lads got in one evening, larking about – you know

what boys are like when they get together. They lit a fire in order to bake some potatoes, so they said. The place was like a tinderbox and it was ablaze in no time. They gave the alarm but by the time the fire engine arrived everything was gone – furniture, clothes, the lot. And what was left of the old place had to be pulled down, it wasn't safe. Apparently Tom had walked out and left everything as it was, and given a spare key to the landlord of the Ferry Inn, the only friend he had, I believe, and him not a close friend, just a drinking companion from time to time. No, it's a mystery what happened to Tom Stevens,' Jessie concluded with a sigh.

'I expect he died,' said Milly dejectedly, but in her bones she felt he was still alive and waiting somewhere, perhaps, for his wife to turn up. And she might have turned up long before this if Fred Lewis hadn't put in an appearance.

Fred. Milly, staring out at the scudding Norfolk landscape, spoke his name softly to herself. She owed a lot to Fred. She owed to him the fact that she now had the means to go looking for her missing husband. She owed him her comfortable life-style. She settled more comfortably in her seat, content to let Fred take over her thoughts, most of which in conjunction with him were pleasant.

As a boy he had worked in the stockroom at Garland's. By the time Milly joined the firm he was in charge of the counting house. He had missed the war: minor ear trouble had exempted him from National Service, and from then on his promotion was rapid. When the war ended he was general manager with a place on the board. The New Look, in a roundabout way, brought Milly to his attention.

For years now Utility clothes had dominated the market. Though made to a high standard, they had to conform to certain rules such as a limitation to the number of pleats and buttonholes and seams. Milly, taking advantage of the discount allowed to staff, took her Utility dresses home and set about redesigning them. With a little ingenuity she converted two pleats into four. She added her own buttonholes if desired, and took out seams or let them in according to taste – anything to make them look just that little bit different.

One morning the girl on the next machine hissed at her, 'Ole Cod's Eyes is watching you.'

Without moving her head Milly glanced sideways and upwards in the direction of the mezzanine floor. Mr Lewis's office was on that floor and he made a habit of leaning on the rail and looking down at the workroom below. It was frightening to Milly to know that she was being singled out for his attention. Surely a handful of hooks and eyes hadn't been missed, and those old brass buttons? Who'd want brass buttons now that the war was over? And that end off a bolt of tartan with a flaw in it. Only good enough for the scrap heap. She thought over other past indiscretions and prayed she wasn't due for the chop.

He sent for her later that day and said without any preamble, 'Is that one of our dresses you're wearing?'

She was at once on the defensive. 'I didn't pinch it, if that's what you think. I bought it fair and square, and I've got the receipt at home to prove it.'

His full lips curved into a half smile. 'I'm not accusing you of stealing it. I'm just intrigued as to why you felt you had to improve on it. Didn't you like it as it was?'

'It was all right, but too plain for my taste. I like something dressy.'

It was certainly dressy in Milly's meaning of the word. She had added a mandarin collar to the plain neckline, shortened the sleeves to bracelet length and converted the pleats to a more flattering flare, alterations that gave the dress a touch of style.

Fred Lewis knew a selling feature when he saw it and wished it were in his province to improve on the whole of that line in the same way. He could double the profits if it were allowed. But Garland's wasn't in the business of high couture; it had built its reputation on cheap and popular styles purchased entirely by mail order. His ambition was to branch out on his own and with the help of a good designer and a few skilled seamstresses build up a reputation at the more expensive end of the market. The same gut feeling that had got him where he was today singled out Milly as a potential accessory. The girl certainly had a flair for design, but had she any practical experience?

He questioned her. She had an aunt, it appeared, who was a self-taught dressmaker. Milly had acquired all she knew from her.

'Aunt Ada could copy a dress just by looking at it,' she said proudly. 'She didn't have to have no patterns or anything.'

'Can you do that?'

Milly looked smug. 'I don't need bought patterns. I make up my own.'

He sat her at his desk and told her to sketch an evening dress, then he left her. When he returned about twenty minutes later he found she had drawn a dress with its hemline about six inches off the ground. Otherwise he couldn't fault it.

'Do you think women will fall for a short dress for evening wear?' he pondered. 'Most women like long dresses. It makes them look graceful.'

'This length will make them look young. I'm too short to wear a long dress gracefully. I make all my party dresses ballerina length. I used to, I mean. I don't go to many parties these days, worse luck.'

Fred Lewis pulled on his lip. 'Ballerina length evening wear, huh? It's certainly an innovation, but it won't catch on. It's neither one thing, nor the other.'

When a few months later the New Look exploded on to the fashion world Fred remembered the little girl from the workroom and sent for her. He had made fulsome promises to her that day which had not materialised. Now he eyed her with renewed interest.

'Christian Dior seems to have beaten you to it,' he said.

Milly grinned. 'He's added a few things I didn't think of, like a nipped-in waist and getting rid of shoulder-pads. I never did like shoulder-pads, I always cut mine out.'

'Do me a few sketches,' he said. 'See if you can improve on Dior.'

When she took them in to him later that afternoon he was noticeably impressed. 'I've got two tickets for a fashion show at the Chamberlain Hotel, Harrogate, for tomorrow evening. Would you like to come with me?'

She was so surprised she heard herself stammering out, 'W-what about your wife?' She didn't care whether he had a wife or not, but she wanted to make sure.

'My wife's away, staying with her sister.'

'Does that mean I'll have the afternoon off?'

'Take the day off; have your hair done or something.'

She hesitated at the door. 'Will we be coming back tomorrow night?'

He pretended to consider this. 'Shouldn't think so,' he said casually. 'Better pack a toothbrush in case. Is there anybody who would mind if you didn't?'

'No. Can't say there is.'

The Chamberlain Hotel had just been completed when war was declared. It was promptly taken over by the War

Office and just as promptly handed back again in 1945. Since then it had had a completely new refit and Milly was impressed by its grandeur and opulence – but then, Milly was easily pleased. She was equally impressed by Lyons Corner House.

Her room was magnificent, spacious and light and overlooking some public gardens in which dogs were walked on leads and babies wheeled in perambulators. Besides that by which she had entered there were two other doors to her room, one into her private bathroom and one into the bedroom next door, she supposed, though, it was locked. She heard someone cough. Never having stayed in a hotel before she accepted communicating doors as the norm. Handy for a family, came a fleeting thought.

She unpacked her overnight case and spread its contents on the bed. A change of underclothing, a change of shoes, her toilet bag and make-up bag, her party dress and, last but not least, her night-gown. It was even shorter than her party dress, because she'd only had a small remnant of parachute silk to make it from, but what it lacked in length it made up for in fancy work. It was really wasted as a night-gown, she reflected. A pity there was no one to see her in it.

By the time she came to put it on that night she had lived through so many experiences she felt life would never be the same. She had eaten roast duckling in orange sauce; she had seen ice-cream encased in a meringue shell brought straight from the oven to the table. She had tasted champagne and watched the soignée women in their ankle-length dresses drink it like water. She thought how sad it was in some ways that with the New Look the long slinky look had come to the end of its era.

And then when Mr Lewis had whispered to her that he wanted her to keep a mental note of any new ideas featured in the dress parade and if possible to jot them down for reference later, and even, providentially, produced a sketch-pad and pencil which he tucked into her programme, she felt she had reached the peak of her experiences, not knowing then that the icing on the cake, as it were, was being left for later.

It had been easy, sitting in the back row unnoticed, to make lightning sketches of anything that took her fancy. She thrilled to the danger of it, for she guessed there must be danger in what they were doing or Mr Lewis would not be taking such precautions. She thrilled to the signs of wealth and grandeur all around her, pinching herself to make sure she was still the same Milly Nickson who used to do cartwheels across the yard at Carlin Street.

At heart she was still that same Milly and now, surfeited with excitement and perhaps one glass of champagne too many, she pirouetted around her room on her toes, then did several cartwheels across the floor with her night-dress flapping about her face.

'I like the view,' said a voice from the direction of the communicating door. 'From here it looks most tantalising.'

She scrambled to her feet, scarlet in the face, and pulled her night-gown over her knees. 'I was just letting off steam,' she said defensively.

Mr Lewis came further into the room, closing the door of the other room behind him. 'I know just what you mean. I feel like letting off steam myself.'

She backed away, holding out her hands as if to fend him off.

'You don't think I'm going to let you sleep by yourself after that little revelation,' he said laughingly.

She considered that thoughtfully. 'No, I suppose not,' she said.

*

'Excuse me,' said the young man sitting opposite. 'But did you want to get out here? We've arrived at Norwich and this train doesn't go any further.'

Milly came to with a start, reluctant to leave the past at such an interesting juncture, for Fred Lewis, in spite of his cod-like eyes, his thinning hair and signs of an incipient paunch, had proved a most satisfying lover.

She sighed. 'Yes,' she said. 'It seems I have come to the end of the line. I suppose you wouldn't be a dear and help me with my case, would you? Old biddies like me are not catered for by British Rail.'

Six

August settled like a moist, warm blanket over Thornmere. In the fields that had not yet been harvested the corn wilted. The house-martins, dotting the telegraph wires like notes on a staff, were clustering in readiness for their long flight back to South Africa. High summer had been fine and clear but now, with autumn just around the corner, mist shrouded the trees and lay in the hollows like pools of still water.

The martins, for whom Carla had put her life at risk, had rewarded her by rearing two successive broods without further interference from the sparrows. She had watched, proprietorially, the fledglings' first tentative flight to try out their wings. She had been delighted when the whole cycle started all over again. She considered a painful shoulder a small price to pay in exchange for weeks of delightful observation of the martins' domestic arrangements.

Jessie, who was a constant visitor throughout Carla's convalescence, could not understand or even share Carla's passion for house-martins. 'It would craze me,' she said, 'having to clean that mess off my kitchen windows every day. I don't know how you put up with it all so calmly.'

'Because I'm not as house-proud as you,' said Carla. She knew it would be impossible to explain to Jessie what it meant to her, watching the bird life in her garden, especially that of the martins. They were constantly tumbling and swooping and gliding above the gatehouse, hawking for insects. Soon they would embark on their long migration and she would not see them again until May, and winter came in between. She loved the autumn with its colourful landscape and mellow days, but she dreaded the winter. She dreaded the short days and long unendurable nights, for it seemed to her then that all colour and all brightness had gone out of the world.

She had first started getting her attacks of depression during the long years as a self-appointed carer to her great-grandmother. Winters then had seemed endless. Winters in Florence had evened the score. She felt freer, more energetic even on cold days – and Florence could indeed be cold in winter, but it was a drier, more healthy cold. The winter after Tony had deserted her had been the exception. She had fought a losing battle against depression, which only Sophie's tact and understanding had helped her through. This winter – what? Well at least, she thought, in an attempt to jolly herself out of her doldrums, she would be spared the sight of seeing Tony and Vanessa walking about hand in hand like a pair of adolescent sweethearts.

She tried to bury such thoughts in her painting. Painting for her now was more of a therapy than a pleasure. Larry had told her of a forthcoming exhibition being held at the Assembly Rooms in Norwich. When she said she had nothing good enough to exhibit he impatiently brushed her excuses aside.

'You need something like this to shake you out of your blues. The trouble is, you've got too much time on your hands and having a goal – something to work towards – might be just the spur you need. Anyway, wouldn't you like to see your work on display? I would, and I know Irina would. Ask Nick Brooke to run you up to the old mill. That would make a likely subject for a water-colour painting.'

There was no need to ask Nick Brooke to take her for a run up to the mill, he had already suggested it. She had refused, thinking her father had put him up to it. She could imagine Larry's approach. 'The poor kid's going down the drain – some love affair or other that went wrong. She's lonely, stuck in that place all on her own, see if you can wheedle her out for a boat-trip – do her the world of good. Homoeopathic treatment, isn't that what you call it?'

'Not in this case. Homoeopathology is treating like with like. You don't want me to give your daughter small doses of depression, do you?'

'Just take her out in your ruddy boat!'

No, she couldn't imagine her father going as far as that, though her suspicions were somewhat aroused when Nick did invite her one evening to go with him for a cruise upriver.

But before that she had started on some paintings to exhibit at the Assembly Rooms. It was, as her father had said, a goal to aim for. She went through some recent sketches and selected three that could be improved upon. One was the bowl of roses she finished with her father more or less breathing down her neck in case she fell back into bad habits and painted with her head rather than her heart. Another, a blackbird's nest just discernible amid some honeysuckle and the third, the derelict church at Thornmere Green.

She had intended this as a present for Milly Stevens but Milly was an elusive person to get hold of these days. Her return from London had occurred unannounced. She had given nobody the opportunity to meet her at the station and now, with the same lack of consideration to Jessie's way of thinking, she had unexpectedly and surprisingly made arrangements to go to Aberdeen and had been there ever since, having found a congenial landlady who was also a superb cook. She tactlessly mentioned this to Jessie in one of her letters.

'Doesn't say much for my cooking, does it,' Jessie grumbled. 'And so much for Dr Brooke's instructions to keep her quiet. She's supposed to be taking things easy. She must be at least ten years older than I am, but she gets about like a two-year-old. She sometimes gives me the impression that she hasn't got enough time to do all the things she wants to do.'

'Why Aberdeen in particular? Has she got relations there?'

Jessie gave a deep sigh. 'I suppose in a way it's my fault. I told her there had been rumours that her husband had gone to Scotland to look for work. I told her about two men from Beckton Market who went up to Scotland to work on the oil-rigs and did so well for themselves that when they came back to Norfolk they were able to pool their resources and start up their own little business. I should have kept my big mouth shut.'

The whole of Thornmere now knew that Jessie Stoneham's lodger had been married to a Norfolk man and was trying to find his whereabouts. If she had tried all the places suggested or hinted at, Milly's feet wouldn't have touched the ground.

'When will she be back?' asked Carla. The art exhibition was billed for the third week in September.

'She doesn't say. So far it seems she's having no more luck in Aberdeen than she had in London, but she's not giving up hope.'

'She didn't strike me as the sort of person who would ever give up hope,' said Carla thoughtfully.

*

Carla made her trip up to the old mill the following week, giving in at last to Nick's blandishments. The original mill had been burned down some years ago, whether through an accident or sabotage was never established. A business-man from Norwich bought the empty shell and converted it into a craft centre with restaurant attached, which became very popular with summer visitors. Nick asked her quite casually one day if she would like a run upriver to the old mill and dinner afterwards. Carla at first declined, then reflected that was only cutting off her nose to spite her face and accepted.

It was a beautiful evening following a humid day. They set off upstream at about six o'clock when a limpid sun cast long shadows across the still waters. It was refreshingly cool on the river, and everything looked so clean in contrast to the lanes where the dust lay thick on the hedgerows and the flowers in the villagers' gardens wilted from thirst.

Travelling by launch, thought Carla, was just like gliding along in a floating car. It had all the comforts of a tourer with all-round vision, but none of the discomforts of traffic jams or impatient drivers honking from behind. There were a few other boats about that evening but not enough to impede their slow but steady progress upstream.

Swallows swooped about them, touching lightly down on the water to snatch at an insect, before swooping away again. She spotted the odd coot or moorhen amid the reeds, but the bolder ducks were everywhere. She might with luck, said Nick, knowing her interest in bird life, see a great crested grebe, though that would be more likely on one of the Broads.

They passed the Ferry Inn where holiday makers sat out at tables in the garden and children fished unsuccessfully for tadpoles, for what tadpoles there were had long turned into froglets. From now on the river narrowed markedly.

'No more pleasure boats,' Nick said with satisfaction. 'Nothing larger than this little runabout. Plenty of water fowl though, especially when we get to the mill pond. By the way, I hope you don't mind me asking you, but have you brought some homework to do?'

He was referring to her dispatch case. She opened it to show him its contents. A sketch-pad, a box of mixed pencils and crayons, a camera and a fine woollen shawl. Though Nick had told her not to dress up to eat at the mill she had changed into a cream silk dress she had bought in the San Lorenzo market. The shawl was a precaution against evening breezes.

Nick knew all about the exhibition at the Assembly Rooms. Larry was so inordinately proud of his daughter's achievements he couldn't stop talking about them, though woe betide anyone who enquired after his own. Carla's one fear about the exhibition was that none of her paintings would sell. She could take it, but she dreaded Larry being disappointed.

Nick said, 'It's a good thing we made an early start. If your aim is to do some sketching you'll need the light. I've booked a table for eight o'clock. Will that give you time?'

'Plenty. I only have to do a few rough sketches. I'll photograph some scenes to give me the colour and how the shadows fall. Half an hour will be plenty.'

'I'll fill in time in the bar and then come to fetch you.'

She was pleased he suggested that. Being watched as she worked put her off. She preferred to make her mistakes in private. She wasn't quite sure in her mind what she would choose as a subject. The mill itself, she felt, would be too big a project for a small water-colour. It cried out for oils and a large canvas. When they arrived at their destination, the mill-pond itself took her eye, neglected, overgrown, but full of wildlife. A heron flapped its large wings and was away, legs trailing, as they approached.

'Look,' said Carla, lowering her voice. 'Is that a rat sniffing around in the reeds?'

'No, it's a water vole. You're not frightened of little hairy objects, are you?'

'No, I'm not, be they mice, or rats, or voles, but I don't think I could say the same of large hairy objects.'

'I am no longer a large hairy object, not since I removed my beard,' he said. 'Surely you weren't frightened of me then?'

'I can't imagine anybody being frightened of you,' she said sincerely.

He tied up the launch and left her sitting there with sketch-pad on her knee and pencil in hand. 'See you in half an hour, then. Sure that's long enough?'

'It will have to be, the light will have gone by then.'

She was utterly alone in a world of silence except for the odd rustlings in the reeds. Occasionally, a coot called and another answered. Far off, she could hear the sound of traffic on the Norwich road but here was peace and quiet and when Nick came to fetch her she was so lost to the world that she gave a slight start when he spoke.

'How can you work in this half-light?'

'I wasn't working, I was dreaming.'

'Of Florence?'

She looked at him. 'What made you say that?'

'You *were* dreaming of Florence.'

'As a matter of fact, I was.' She said it in a voice that precluded further questioning. She took the hand he offered to help her out of the boat.

'You'll find the Ladies on the left as we go in. What will you have to drink?'

'The same as you.'

'A pint of bitter?'

'Anything but that. I'm not a beer drinker.'

'Wine?'

'I'll leave it to you.'

A bottle of Medoc was brought to their table to go with Nick's sirloin steak and Carla's lamb cutlets. The mill was renowned for its good, plain English cooking. One did not go there expecting curries or traditional Continental dishes.

Nick said, 'I'm not conventional about wines. I drink what I like.'

And Carla repeated what she had once said to Tony under similar circumstances, 'I know nothing about wine.'

They had been dining at the time at a small *ristorante* under the shadow of the Duomo, and Tony had toasted her with a glass of Chianti. '*Viva* my little barbarian.'

Being called little both amused and flattered her. 'Why barbarian?' she said.

'Because you drink *cappuccino* after your meal and don't know a good Chianti from a poor one.'

'I know nothing about wines.'

'You know nothing about history either.' His eyes had gleamed softly in the evening light. They brimmed with teasing laughter. 'Two thousand years ago my ancestors, the Romans, referred to your ancestors, the Britons, as barbarians. Nothing has changed much since then.'

'It has always been thought in my family that our ancestors came over with the Vikings,' she responded lightly. 'And I dare you to call the Vikings barbarians. Ravagers and pillagers perhaps, but not barbarians. Great seaman and abductors of women, they could have taught your ancestors a thing or two, especially how to control their wives. So what do you say to that, you half-barbarian.'

'I'd say that if you put your face any closer to mine, I'll kiss it.'

It was the period of their acquaintanceship when slight and teasing exchanges in public were a form of foreplay leading in the privacy of Tony's apartment to an intense and satisfactory denouement. That period hadn't lasted long. Ten – twelve months? It had been followed by a period of slow and heart-breaking stagnation and after the stagnation had come Vanessa, and Carla, helpless, had watched from the sidelines Tony's transformation from a moody and often silent companion back to the animated and charming individual with whom she had fallen love.

'Penny for them,' said Nick suddenly. He had been watching her for the past few seconds, noting the expressions of sadness and pain that had in turn darkened her violet-coloured eyes. Larry had hinted something about an unhappy love affair. Nick had a sudden unexpected urge to punch some unknown person on the jaw.

Carla came to to find his gaze upon her and to her annoyance felt herself blush. 'I was just dreaming,' she said evasively.

'I can recommend the apple pie,' he said. 'The pastry melts in the mouth and the apples come from the mill's own orchard. Bleinham Oranges – delicious! You won't find apples like those on the supermarket shelves.'

'Just coffee, thank you.' Then as a nod to barbarism, 'Do they serve *cappuccino* here?'

'They do. The demand is stronger than their scruples.'

He informed her that she was driving the launch back. He sat her behind the wheel and said there were only two things to remember – to keep to the right and give way to sail.

'What if we meet with one of those huge holiday cruisers?' she wailed.

'You won't find any cruisers or yachts either this far upstream. It's far too narrow; nor any hired craft out after dark, they are not fitted with navigation lights. The moonlight will be bright enough for us to steer by.'

He untied the launch, gave it a push, then jumped easily in beside her. He did not start the engine. The current took over and all Carla had to do was steer.

'It's much nicer drifting like this without the noise of the engine,' she said. 'You can hear the sounds of the night more clearly,' and at that moment an owl hooted as if in agreement.

He rested his arm along the top of the seat behind her shoulders. He sat sideways on, so that he could see her better. Neither spoke. Both were in a quiescent mood, in his case brought on by dining and wining well, in hers, he made a guess, through memories. He had his memories too which he guarded just as secretly. He couldn't expect information from her without giving some in return. He broke the silence. 'What do you know about me?'

She didn't answer at first. The bow wave of some small creature heading for the opposite bank distracted her attention. She steadied the craft. 'That you are a good doctor and very popular with the locals.'

'Not as popular as my father. Anything else?'

She hesitated, feeling uncertain as to the drift of this cross-examination. 'Larry said something about you being a widower, but nothing more than that.'

'Because he knows nothing more than that. I don't talk about it more than I can help. I've been a widower now for twelve years, but the scar still remains. I was married for two years – two blissful years. Not long to last one a lifetime, is it?'

He sounded more philosophical than bitter, more wistful than sad. 'You don't have to tell me this,' she said. 'Not if it hurts.'

'The hurt went years ago, but remnants of guilt remain. It should have been I who was killed that night, not Christine . . .'

'You don't have to tell me this,' she repeated, as he hesitated. She felt uncomfortable. She was no better at listening to confidences than she was at communicating them.

'But I want to tell you,' he persisted. 'I feel in the mood to confide in someone. Would it bore you to listen?'

It would not bore her. She was good at switching off her concentration and substituting her own thoughts and Nick had a pleasant, rather soporific voice, easy to listen to. Very soon, however, she stopped listening with only half her mind and gave him her full attention instead.

Christine was a second-year student at Berkeley University when they met in the autumn of '66, both then aged twenty, just a few months separating their birthdays. He was on his latter-day version of the Grand Tour, hitch-hiking round the world. He had 'done' Europe and parts of India and was now out to conquer the New World; though actually, he said, it was the New World that conquered him. He intended to stay in California for six weeks and stayed on for six months, earning his keep by a series of jobs from packing and stacking in a supermarket to helping at a hot-dog stand on a street corner. Letters from his mother followed him from place to place, entreating him to return home and resume his studies. Now, with a goal in sight, that goal being marriage to Christine, he began thinking seriously of his career.

She came from a professional family who expected her to

marry well. They admired Nick's initiative in 'bumming his way round the world' as they called it. They admired all forms of enterprise as long as it produced money, and the sort of money he was making at present would not keep their daughter in paper handkerchiefs.

'So I came home and took up a place at my father's old teaching hospital. I knew just a bare medical degree wouldn't be good enough for old man Hankin, so I decided to specialise in psychiatry. Psychiatry goes down well in America. Everybody I was introduced to over there had his or her analyst. I could see that second to law – and now, of course, plastic surgery – it was a good little money-spinner.'

'Surely that isn't the right attitude to take towards medicine?' Carla was shocked by his materialist viewpoint. He had never struck her as a man interested in worldly goods.

'It certainly isn't. It's enough to make poor old Hippocrates turn in his grave. But you see, I was in love, and when you're in love you can't think straight – I couldn't, anyway. Chris and I saw as much as we could of each other as possible. I spent all my long vacations with her people; she flew over whenever she could get away. She was a journalist now, working on the paper her father edited. My mother grew very fond of her. She couldn't see why we didn't marry when I qualified. She was longing for grandchildren, especially a granddaughter. She's got this thing about girls. She covets your two little sisters every time she sets eyes on them.'

'When did you finally get married?'

'About ten years after we met. We'd lived together before then, of course. Christine's father had no objection to that. I studied for my psychiatric diploma in America. I intended to practise in the States. I was willing to take out American citizenship, and then Christine died.'

'If you'd rather not go on,' said Carla hesitantly. The lights of the Ferry Inn shone ahead. They would change places then and Nick would switch on the engine, for both banks of the river were lined with cruisers tied up for the night, and drifting in the dark could become more of a hazard.

'There's not much more to tell. One night we were out of Scotch and we had friends coming for dinner. It was my fault, I had promised to restock the bar and I forgot. I offered to go out at once and get some, but Christine insisted on going as she had already changed and I hadn't. She only had to drive two blocks to the liquor store. She didn't even get half-way – some maniac in a stolen car drove straight into her. I killed her, Carla, as sure as fate. I killed her and I killed our child too . . . Christine was three months pregnant.'

It was very quiet after he had stopped speaking. The noise and the laughter from the bar at the Ferry Inn was muted from this distance. Moonlight played on the water and a faint breeze stirred the leaves of the willows. It was an idyllic setting for romance, but romance was the last thing on the minds of the two silent people in the boat.

Nick stirred himself. 'Pull in here. I'll tie up while we change places, it'll be safer.'

It was two miles to the gatehouse from where Nick's houseboat was moored in a narrow cutting off the main river. Nick had had Kevin Smithson drive them down earlier in the evening. Nick never used the car when he had drink in mind. They decided to walk back as the distance to the public phone box to summon a taxi was only a little less than to the gatehouse itself. The evening was warm, though Carla was glad of the shawl she had had the foresight to bring with her. To Nick, she looked like a wraith in the moonlight. He helped her ashore and made fast the launch to the houseboat.

'Thank you for being such a good listener,' he said, adjusting his pace to hers. 'I had no intention of unburdening myself to you when we first set out this evening. It must be something about you, your empathy for want of a better word, that drew me out.'

His words made her feel a fraud. It wasn't that she had been so much a good listener as that she had been a captive listener. Yet his story had made an impact on her. Her own underlying misery seemed nothing by contrast.

'Was it your wife's death that decided you to return to England?' she asked.

Not entirely, as she discovered. He had taken a sudden distaste to his way of life.

'When I took up psychiatry,' he said, 'it was with the idea of working with children. There are a lot of disturbed kids about these days, lacking, as so many do, a stable home life. That was the group I was aiming for, but there was no money in it and the temptation to make money proved too great, so I gave all my time listening to the outpourings of the more pampered members of society. There were some genuine cases among them,' he conceded, 'but mostly the patients I had were just paying me to listen to them talk. I listened, but at the same time I thought of my father, carrying on alone in his country practice, working all hours, yet a contented man. I knew he had always hoped I would go into partnership with him. Financial success did not seem important to me any more, so I threw it all up and came back to England. It was the first step on the road back for me,' he continued reflectively. 'Back to peace of mind, I mean. I came to terms with my guilt, though it still haunts me at times. And I've got my bolt-hole – my old tub – for when, as sometimes happens, the past comes rushing in. I go off there and just idle for an hour or two. It's marvellous therapy. I read, I play music. I sometimes fish. I disturb nobody and nobody disturbs me. It's my refuge.'

'Mine is the gatehouse,' she said.

It was looming up towards them now, solitary against the night sky. They came to a natural stop by the fence.

'You don't get nervous living here all on your own?' he asked.

'I've never thought about it. Who would want to harm me?'

'There are a great many disturbed souls about these days,' he said on a warning note. 'I still keep my hand in with psychiatry, locuming at different hospitals. Not that I have to go far to find psychiatric cases, I find them in general practice too. I sometimes think I'm doing the job that was once done by the parish priest. I think of my surgery as the confessional. Some of my patients get benefit just by talking over their problems with me. It's having time to listen that is the important factor.' Suddenly he said, 'Have you ever considered keeping a dog?'

'I don't think I have the patience to train a dog.'

'You can borrow Ranger any time you like . . .'

She laughed. 'I don't think Ranger would think that much of a deal. Coming in for coffee?' She said it as casually as she could so that he would not think there was an implied invitation in the offer. She hoped he would say no. She had enjoyed his company, but now, more than anything, she wanted her bed and her feet in their tight-fitting shoes were killing her.

'No, I mustn't stay. Dad's been on call all evening and I must get back to relieve him.' In the moonlight Carla's eyes looked like two blank holes. She held her face up to him as if inviting a kiss. She wasn't, he knew, it was just the way she held her head. Yet he wanted to kiss her. He felt a stirring of emotions that had lain dormant since Christine's death. He cursed himself for having persuaded Carla to register with him, for now kissing her was out of the question.

The next day Carla got a postcard from Sophie. It was the ugliest postcard she had ever received and she recognised it immediately. It was of the statue of a dwarf riding a turtle on the Fontano del Bacco in the Boboli Gardens. The dwarf (a favourite of Cosimo the First) was a grotesque and ugly figure, naked of course, not even a fig-leaf to adorn his personal equipment, which, in contrast to the rest of him, was rather small. Carla wondered what the postman made of it.

When she turned the card over, however, her smile broadened to a grin. Surprise and delight took over. Sophie did not waste words. 'Coming home – for good – some time the end of September. Letter following when I have time to write. Busy sorting out and packing. All my love, Sophie. P.S. Thought this might appeal to you.'

One of the many beautiful vistas of Florence would have appealed more, thought Carla as she fixed the card to the fridge with a Pekingese magnet. Her thoughts immediately reverted to Tony. Would Sophie have any up-to-date news of him? She hardly mentioned him in her letters now and Carla wondered if the coolness that normally existed between them had, for some reason, dropped to freezing point.

The day of the exhibition was drawing nearer. Carla was notified that she would be sharing a room with two other painters, who turned out to be two single ladies of uncertain age. She knew she was lucky even to have been allocated that much space. The demand for rooms was heavy and many would-be exhibitors had had to await their turn. She felt she had got by on the strength of her father's name, or perhaps as she had only four pictures to show, space was found for her. She had no other water-colours ready to exhibit and none of her oil paintings was good enough, mainly, she felt, because she had painted them not to please herself but Tony.

Pricing her exhibits was a headache. She left that to her father and was staggered by what he asked for them. 'Nobody will fork out that much,' she exclaimed.

'They will – they are worth every penny. And the frames, don't forget the frames. You didn't get those for nothing.'

Her father went with her to the Assembly Rooms the evening before the exhibition to help her hang her pictures. Not that she needed any help, but being Larry, he had to be in on the act. Besides, he said, he was an old hand at this. The two other exhibitioners, a Ms Watson and a Miss Starling, had about twenty-five pictures between them. Miss Starling had never exhibited before and was rather nervous. Catalogues had been printed and these were already distributed on the seats of the chairs.

'I think your water colours are exquisite,' said Ms Watson to Carla. She was a large woman with two chins, wearing a brightly coloured floral-patterned dress rather on the tight side. 'Personally, I prefer painting in oils.' Then lowering her voice, she said, 'You can get away with murder with oils. Oils hide a lot of imperfections. You have to be so much more skilful when painting with water-colours. Still, you can get such grand effects with oils, can't you.'

Certainly Ms Watson had achieved some grand effects – mostly in fierce, bold shades of orange and red and purple, for she was very fond of sunsets. Miss Starling's paintings, on the other hand, were muted and low-key. Somewhat like their owner in fact, thought Carla uncharitably, for

Miss Starling looked rather anaemic and dressed entirely in grey, the same colour as her hair, which did nothing for her complexion. Carla caught her father's eye and quickly looked away.

'Well, what do you make of those two?' he said, after bearing her off to the restaurant for a cup of their refreshing coffee. 'Odd couple. D'you think they're lesbians?'

'Dad! They didn't even meet until this evening.'

His mouth fell open. 'Dad! – did I actually hear you call me Dad? That's the first time you've ever acknowledged me as your father. I feel like someone out of East Lynne.'

He was grinning from ear to ear, but she could see he was touched, which in turn touched her. 'I called you it in outrage,' she said honestly.

'Then be outraged as often as you like,' he answered smartly.

She did not go to the exhibition for the opening, she was far too nervous. During the night before she had wakened in a cold sweat, following a dream in which her paintings, lost amid Ms Watson's huge canvases and Miss Starling's pale offerings, were bare of the small red stars that adorned each of the exhibits belonging to the other ladies.

She woke up with a headache, quite determined to drive into Norwich, collect her paintings and disappear again before anyone was about. Common sense told her that was not feasible. In any case, dreams always came opposite, didn't they? – so Lottie always said. Ms Watson and Miss Starling were taking the morning and afternoon shifts together. She said she would do the evenings, taking over at five o'clock.

She got there at quarter to and the first thing she saw as she walked into the room was that all four of her water-colours were marked as sold. Her eyes went straight to the other paintings. Not a star among them. She did not feel at all excited, just rather numb.

'All yours were sold within an hour of the opening.' said Ms Watson, sounding jollier than she looked. 'As you see, we haven't been so lucky.'

'It's only the first day, dear,' Miss Starling fluted at her elbow.

'It's all written up in the record book. And the cheque is in the cash-box.'

'Cheque? For all four? Were they all bought by the same person?'

Miss Starling answered, 'A man.'

'What sort of man?'

Miss Starling was vague. 'Just the usual sort of man.'

'I wasn't here,' said Ms Watson, intimating that if she had been affairs would have been conducted in a much more businesslike manner. 'I had just popped to the loo. The whole transaction couldn't have taken longer than ten minutes.'

A terrible suspicion assailed Carla. 'Was it my father?'

'Oh, no, my dear, I would have known your father.'

Another suspicion took its place. She was anxious for the other two to leave, which they did eventually, after entertaining her for some minutes with some of the peccadilloes of the viewing public.

'Some came just to pass the time – no intention of buying; just walking around and looking and not saying anything, taking no notice of us, either.'

'Very unnerving . . .'

'One quite liked my *Sunset over Breydon Water.*'

'And a woman nearly bought my *Mousehold in Winter*. She said she was going to the craft fair at the Castle and would call back later, but she never did,' added Miss Starling wistfully.

'There's plenty of time yet,' said Ms Watson sharply. 'There's another five days.'

'Another five days,' echoed Miss Starling with noticeable lack of enthusiasm.

They went at last and Carla opened the cash-box. It was what she had suspected – a cheque signed, in a firm hand, N. Brooke. Why, she wondered – why? Her cheeks were still burning when her father turned up.

'Sold, all sold. What a triumph,' he said, then with another closer look at her, 'What's up?'

She told him exactly what was up.

'Good for him. Shows you he's got good judgement. There's a feather in your cap.'

'I don't see it that way at all. If four different buyers had come in at different times and bought one each I would have been chuffed. But for someone I know to come early and buy all four means only one thing. He was fearful that they might not sell at all and wanted to save me embarrassment.'

Her father gave her a quizzical look. 'That's rather a high-handed way of looking at it, isn't it? Why should Nick Brooke pay out such a large sum to save your pride? Does he like you that much? Does he like you at all? What went on between you that evening you boated up to the mill?'

'Nothing,' she said, going scarlet. Her father had misinterpreted her meaning. 'I didn't mean he bought the paintings because he felt under any obligation to me, because he doesn't. I wouldn't have minded if he had bought just the one of the mill-pond, because he was there when I sketched it. But why did he buy them all? Why couldn't he have given me the satisfaction of finding out that other prospective buyers might have liked my work enough to buy it? Why such a gesture? Give me one good reason other than philanthropy. And why should he feel philanthropic towards me? He doesn't owe me anything.'

'Perhaps he bought them as a present for his mother. He's very fond of his mother.'

'But all four! I could understand it if it were only two to make a pair. I'm going to tell you something though, I don't intend to cash the cheque. I'd rather tear it up.'

'That would be a very childish gesture. If you really feel that you can't accept Nick's money then give it to charity. Perhaps there's one for destitute artists. If there isn't, there should be. I was a destitute artist once and your mother kept me until I got on my feet, bless her loving little heart. You certainly haven't inherited this pig-headed streak from Charley.'

'No, Dad, I inherited it from you.'

They were distracted by a slight cough from the direction of the doorway from where a smart, elderly lady beamed on them both. She came forward. She got as far as saying, 'I've come to see whether . . .' when her expression changed. 'Oh, I see they're sold – all four of them! Oh, how disappointing. I should have bought the one I wanted this morning while I had the chance. My own stupid fault, I will put things off.' She turned to Larry, taking him to be in charge. 'Do you think C. Foster will be showing again – at the next exhibition, perhaps?'

'I'm sure it's more than likely,' he said. 'She has had such a great success this time.'

'Great success,' Carla muttered when they were alone again. 'One buyer!'

'Two. Possibly more if you had any more paintings up your sleeve.' Larry's eyes suddenly lit up. 'I tell you what, you've got until the end of the week. Why don't you skedaddle off home and paint another couple of pictures? We could just about squeeze another pair in.'

She turned a frosty look upon him. 'I can't turn out pictures like sausages. I can't just turn a handle and, heigh presto, another painting appears. You, of all people, should know that.'

'When I was your age I was a commercial artist and had to work to a deadline. My work wasn't any the less worthy for that.'

But Carla was adamant. 'No more exhibitions for me! My nerves can't take the strain.'

Bemused, Larry shook his head. 'I've had three wives, and I've got four daughters, but still I'll never understand what makes a woman tick,' he declared.

A week went by before Carla had the opportunity to speak to Nick Brooke again. It had been an eventful week. There had been more enquiries about her work from hopeful punters and Ms Watson and Miss Starling had sold enough of their paintings to put the seal of approval on their venture. For the first time Carla realised that the money they made was more important than the boost to their egos. It meant they could afford to put their names down for the next exhibition which was to take place just before Christmas.

'I've just about covered my expenses,' said Ms Watson with satisfaction. 'The frames for these great canvases cost a small fortune.'

'You can sometimes pick them up second-hand at auction sales,' Miss Starling remarked helpfully. 'Most of them need some repairs but it works out much cheaper than buying new.'

'How are you getting yours home?'

'My brother is collecting me . . .'

'Do you think he'd have room. . . ?'

'Of course, dear, he'd be delighted to give you a lift.'

Carla doubted it, seeing the size of Ms Watson's work once it was taken down from the walls. She was pleased, however, that the ill-matched pair had hit it off so well. She felt she was witnessing a friendship in the making.

'See you at Christmas,' said Ms Watson, giving her a hearty handshake. 'Pity you didn't have any more paintings to sell.'

'Yes, it was in a way.'

She had got over her annoyance with Nick Brooke. She realised she had behaved illogically. As her father said, it had been big-headed of her to believe that Nick had bought all four of her exhibits just to save her possible embarrassment. She had dodged him the whole week of the exhibition, hiding in the cottage whenever he went past. But now, with the exhibition behind her, she felt free to accost him, which she did a day or two later.

He usually walked Ranger before surgery, this particular morning he was earlier than usual. She had dressed, but had not brushed her hair or creamed her face when she spotted him from her bedroom window. She ran down the stairs and met him at the gate.

'I haven't had the opportunity to thank you for buying my paintings,' she said.

She thought she saw a trace of mischief in his smile. 'I was under the impression you were avoiding me.'

'I've been busy helping at the exhibition . . .'

'Of course.'

'And tomorrow I have a friend coming to stay.'

He looked rather whimsical. 'No more trips up to the old mill for a while, then.'

'Please, why did you buy my paintings?'

'Because I wanted them. I saw enough of your work that evening to whet my appetite. I went to the exhibition early to make sure nobody else bought the painting of the mill-pond before I had a chance; then when I saw the other three, I liked them all so much I couldn't make up my mind between them, so I bought the lot. That dragon in the floral dress wouldn't let me take possession of them. I had to wait until the end of the week.'

Carla remembered what Larry had said about Nick's mother. 'Did you buy them for anyone in particular?'

'I bought them for my surgery. The walls of my father's surgery are decorated with family photographs, mostly of me. As a baby, as a toddler, with the school rugger team. I find it highly embarrassing. All I had on my walls was a calendar. Your paintings have certainly given my room a touch of class. I'm already getting enquiries about them – I could get you plenty of orders.'

'Thank you, but I don't think I'm up to commissioned work yet.' She hesitated, then with a rush of honesty, 'I was avoiding you. I felt embarrassed about you buying my work – all of it – I thought you did it out of kindness, to prevent me being upset if none of them sold. I realise now how utterly stupid I was.'

She felt that her innermost thoughts were bared to him. Under his searching gaze her eyes fell. He said, 'For you to feel like that means that somewhere along the line somebody has severely dented your self-esteem. Or has destroyed your faith in your own ability. Believing I had bought your paintings purely from altruistic reasons is belittling your own talent. Believe me, Carla, I bought your paintings for one reason only. I coveted them.'

She felt foolish but relieved. She could not think of anything opportune to say but Ranger came to her rescue. He had been sitting patiently at his master's feet, and now gave a little whine.

'He wants his breakfast,' said Nick. 'So, for that matter,

do I. Pay me a visit, professionally if not socially, but do come and see my paintings.'

'I must warn you, I'm a very healthy person. No doctor would get rich on me.'

'I gave up dreams of riches years ago.'

She stayed at the gate until he rounded the bend, gave him a last wave, then went indoors and sought out her cheque book. She made out a cheque to a children's charity for the exact amount that Nick had paid for the paintings. Only then did she feel free to pay his cheque into her account.

What you need is a psychiatrist, she thought.

She set off for Norwich the following morning to meet Sophie at the station, eager to see her old friend again. Unfortunately Sophie could only spare her a few days as she was starting college in October. 'Tell you all about it when I see you,' she had written on one of her cards, this time a respectable view of Buckingham Palace, guaranteed not to shock any postman.

They met as if they had been parted for a lifetime. Sophie shed a few tears. 'Take no notice,' she said, as she blew her nose. 'I've been on an emotional switchback for weeks.'

She loved Norwich, or what she could see of it from the station car park. She loved Carla's car. She loved Carla's Paisley shirt and cord skirt. She herself was dressed in a pair of trousers verging on the tight side and a sweater the size of a tent. Her hair, which was plentiful, was held back by an orange scarf, the same colour as her lipstick. At the Trattoria Offredi she had always dressed soberly and in uniform.

'I have never been so happy in my life,' she said, as they bowled along the Norfolk byroads. 'I feel free from care – I feel young again.'

'You are young. You haven't got thirty breathing down

your neck as I have. Any particular reason for your happiness, Sophie? Are you in love?'

'Better than that. I'm back where I started three years ago. I'm back at my old college at London University.'

'Why did you ever leave?'

Sophie pulled off her scarf and shook her hair free. To Carla, it seemed a gesture, as if throwing off all restraint. Sophie lowered the window and took a deep breath. The wind blew her hair over her face and she parted it with her hands as if parting a curtain.

'I love the smell of the country,' she said. 'It smells so fresh after London. I know nothing about the country. I've always lived in the suburbs. What's all that green stuff growing in that field over there. Cabbages?'

'Sugar beet. They'll start harvesting it in November. Sophie, why are you evading my question?'

'I'm not evading it, I'm just postponing it to a more appropriate moment. Let me just bask in all this uncluttered space. Isn't Norfolk big? Aren't the skies huge? I've never seen such wide skies.'

'That's because they are not shut out by tower blocks or mountains.'

'You must have wonderful sunsets.'

'And sunrises too. We can also get clouds and dull, grey, misty mornings – to say nothing of the winds. Oh, those north-east winds.'

'But you love Norfolk . . .'

'I've always loved Norfolk.'

'And Florence. You loved Florence?'

'That wasn't love, that was adoration.'

Carla pulled in to the side of the road to allow passage for a car towing a caravan. 'Look,' she said. 'Ahead, there's the river and the inn I told you about. Another ten minutes and we're home.'

'I love that word home,' said Sophie softly. 'There's something heart-lifting about it. I've come home.'

'Tell me about it.'

Sophie did, later, when they were having lunch in the garden under an apple tree bearing fruit the size of gourds. Before that, Carla had shown her to the room she had prepared for her, the largest of the three bedrooms, the one where Lottie's parents had slept. It looked over a large tract of arable land where, in the wake of a plough, seagulls and rooks were foraging for grubs.

'Listen,' said Sophie, holding up one finger. 'Just listen.'

'I can't hear anything.'

'That's what I mean. Listen to the silence. It's incredible.'

'Wait until a low flying Jaguar comes streaking over, as they do sometimes. You won't think it so peaceful then.'

'I am too happy to be disturbed by threats. I am savouring every moment as it comes.'

Carla looked at her friend with envy. When had she last felt as joyful as that? Too long ago to remember. With luck some of Sophie's *joie de vivre* might rub off on her. On an impulse she gave the other a hug. 'I'm pleased you're here, so very pleased. You're going to act on me like a tonic. I wish you could stay longer.'

'I start college next week, but I'll be coming up again. Now I know the way, you won't be able to keep me away.'

Although there had been a slight frost that morning it was warm enough now to sit out of doors to have their lunch. Carla had her meals out of doors at every opportunity and consequently had acquired a tan that went well with her chestnut hair and violet eyes. Sophie, on the other hand, being dark-skinned to start with and having lived so long under hotter skies, was as brown as a gypsy. They complemented each other admirably.

Carla had made a bacon and mushroom quiche which

they ate with salad and crisp rolls that she had collected from the local baker's on her way to Norwich that morning. They washed it down with a glass of rough cider that Sophie, later, blamed for the soporific trance that overcame her before she had hardly finished eating.

Carla let her sleep. She quietly removed the remains of their meal, washed the dishes and took her place once more in the garden. In so doing she disturbed Sophie who struggled back into consciousness. 'I wasn't asleep,' she said throatily. 'I was just studying the insides of my eyelids.'

'Would a cup of coffee help to wake you up?'

'Brilliant idea.'

And it was over coffee that Sophie opened her heart and told Carla things she had kept to herself for years.

It all began when her father at the age of fifty, seeing nothing but retirement and old age ahead of him and never having done anything more exciting in his life than place an annual bet on the Derby, suddenly decided to make up for lost time.

'You mean he had an affair,' said Carla as Sophie paused.

'Oh, nothing as ordinary as that. I think my mother could have forgiven him that, but he suddenly announced to us both one day that he was sick of being the bread-winner; sick of working from nine to five, five days a week; sick of mowing the lawn and watering the garden; sick of Saturday morning shopping and walking the dog every evening. To sum it up, I think he was just sick of responsibilities, sick of my mother and sick of me. I think what brought it to a head was when I started college. They had always had to budget carefully. Now they had my expenses to take into consideration.

'You really have to know my father to appreciate the change in him, Carla. He was the most fastidious of men. The first thing he did when he came home of an evening was to change out of what he called his business suit into an old cardigan and slacks. He made a new suit last four years and then it still looked new. He always looked so presentable, so respectable. I don't think he had a single vice. He didn't drink, he didn't smoke. They thought the world of him at the solicitors where he worked. He started there as an office boy and rose to be head clerk before he left.'

'He left?'

'Oh, yes, he left, without giving them any notice. He gave my mother and me just twenty-four hours. He said he had taken exactly half of what was in the bank and transferred it to another branch. He said he was leaving the following morning to fulfil a lifelong ambition. He wanted to be a tramp.'

'A *tramp*!' Carla sounded, Sophie thought, just like Edith Evans in the film she had seen of *The Importance of Being Earnest*.

'A life of no responsibility. Going where he pleased, doing what he pleased. He planned to tramp the whole of the British Isles, doing odd jobs to help pay his way. He said he'd send us a card now and again to let us know he was still alive, but we wouldn't be able to get in touch with him as he wouldn't have a permanent address. He said he'd leave us the house and half of his capital, and that lots of people had to make do on less than that.'

' "What about Sophie. Who's going to pay her expenses at college." ' Sophie mimicked her mother's wails. 'And guess what my father retorted to that? "If she has the guts I credit her with she'll get herself a job and work her way through college." They were the last words he spoke. We watched him go, wearing his oldest clothes, with a knap-sack on his back and carrying a stout walking stick that had belonged to his father. My mother went into hysterics but I just felt numb. My father and I had never been what you'd call close. We were not a demonstrative family. We didn't hug or kiss one another, or even touch. But do you know, Carla, when I watched him walking away down the street without once looking back I felt a rush of affection for him. Poor old Dad, I thought, he had spent the whole of his life pleasing others, now he was doing something to please himself. The best of luck to you, I thought, and then of course I had to see to my mother.'

The afternoon eased away. The sun, like a huge Chinese lantern, sank lower in the sky. The two girls did not notice, nor the fact that a little breeze had sprung up and was raising goose-pimples on their arms. They were too engrossed, one talking and the other listening.

'My mother's biggest worry was what the neighbours would say. Well, I dare say they had plenty to say, but it didn't reach our ears. It didn't worry me, but my mother wouldn't go out for weeks. When she finally accepted the fact that my father wasn't coming back, she pulled herself together and started making plans. First of all she advertised for boarders. She had room to take three and she enjoyed cooking, so that side of it was no problem. Sifting out the enquiries was more of a headache for her, but she was lucky. She was suited almost at once with a middle-aged couple and an elderly bachelor. I waited to see if it would work out and it did, right from the start. My mother isn't the easiest of persons to get on with, but she and Mrs Baxter hit it off right away. Then I felt free to make plans of my own. I knew it was no good thinking I could return to college. Even if I got a grant it wouldn't have been enough to cover expenses and I was determined not to add to my mother's money troubles. I had always loved working for the Offredis, now I wrote and asked them if they would care to take me on on a permanent basis. They said they would and what was more, offered me the flat as part of my wages. I earned that flat, Carla. I worked long hours, seven days a week, but I didn't mind that. I was even able to save a little so that I could go home occasionally to see how my mother was getting on.

'Actually, she was doing all right for herself. The Baxters had a car and often took her out. They were keen bridge players, and my mother and Mr Hetherington both played a little, so now they could make up a foursome. Do you know, Carla, I sometimes got the impression that my mother didn't miss my father at all.'

'And your father?'

'Yes,' said Sophie thoughtfully. 'My father, that's quite a different story.' She shivered and rubbed her arms, which did not go unnoticed.

'Come along, you're getting cold,' said Carla. 'You can finish your story indoors.'

She switched the central heating on that evening. For herself the fire on low would have been sufficient, but Sophie was used to a warmer climate.

'Can you bear to hear any more about my family or am I boring you to tears?' asked Sophie once supper was over. They sat curled up in easy chairs facing each other.

'I shall be very disappointed if I don't hear what became of your father. He didn't suddenly reappear, did he?'

'That's exactly what he did, but how did you guess?'

'It wasn't so difficult. With you returning to college now, and being in such high spirits, I knew something wonderful must have happened.'

Martin Phillips had appeared one evening. He let himself in with his own latchkey, went straight through to the sitting-room where a bridge session was in progress and said, 'Hetty, I'm back.'

Carla had an inclination to laugh. She suppressed it. This

wasn't the moment, she thought, for laughter, yet laughter mixed with tears bubbled up inside her. What pain one human being can inflict upon another, she thought.

'How did your mother react?'

'She screamed, or so she told me later. She didn't recognise Dad at first. He had put on weight and his skin had weathered to the colour of old leather. But it's all right, Carla. Everything has worked out well. The boarders are staying. My mother said right in front of them that if it were a choice between them or my father, she would choose them. She didn't intend to give up her little outings, or her game of bridge. Dad was quite willing for them to stay. In fact, I think he welcomed it. He had already been in touch with his old firm and they had agreed to take him back, but on a much reduced salary. He told us he worked his way right round the coast of Great Britain and that included the Shetlands and the Orkneys, too. He'd had some incredible adventures. He kept the boarders entranced, relating them. And now, would you believe, he wants to write a book about it all and he will too. I'll never discount anything my father says in future.'

Sophie had a need to talk and Carla was only too pleased to listen, anxious now to hear the end of the story. Sophie still had money worries, but no worse than most university students. There was the possibility of a grant and her mother, that most capable of women, had managed to save, and that money she intended for Sophie.

'I'll repay her when I get my degree, and hopefully a job. That will be the first item on my agenda.' They had talked their way through the evening. As Carla had got wearier, so Sophie had grown livelier. She looked as fresh now as when she had first arrived.

Carla stifled a yawn. 'What kind of job?'

'I'd like something in economics, but I don't mind as long

as it's something that will wash Renaissance art out of my hair. I'm up to here with the Renaissance.'

'But you loved Florence.'

'And I loved the Offredis, and I had a soft spot for old Leonardo, for he was a bit of a scientist. But all the rest was way above my head.'

'Sophie, was there ever a man in your life?'

'I had my moments. Sex never bothered me – I could take it or leave it – for the past few years I've mostly left it. I had more important things on my mind.'

Carla could remember once saying practically the same thing to her father and his outraged reaction. She smiled. She had come a long way since then.

'Did Tony ever make a pass at you?' It took some effort to ask that, but it was something she had been wanting to know for years.

Sophie gave a careless shrug. 'He tried but he didn't get very far. He's not my type.'

'What is your type, Sophie?'

'Those hunky man's-man types. Unfortunately they are inclined to fall for the kind of girl who needs protecting. Anyone can see I don't need protection.'

'And here comes the sixty-four-thousand-dollar question. Are Tony and Vanessa as thick as ever?'

Sophie saw in Carla's expression the effort that question had cost her, though she hid it well. She said; 'I haven't seen much of Tony lately. He's been eating at far more exclusive restaurants. Vanessa has taken him off to America to meet her parents and his villa is up for sale. You can read what you like into that. You were well rid of him, Carla.'

'So I keep telling myself. The trouble is, I can't always believe what I say.'

They made the most of their few days together. The next day they spent in Norwich trawling the shops for bargains during the morning and relaxing at the theatre in the afternoon. They had been invited to the Thatched House for an evening meal, where Sophie was at once set upon by the two little ones and claimed as their own. As she said to Carla later, 'If I don't make it as an economist I can always become a children's nanny. I get on well with kids.'

She got on well with Victoria too who was normally reserved with strangers. Victoria had not done well enough at her A levels to get a place at university, which upset her much less than it did her father. Until she decided on her plans for the future she was working at a nursing home in Beckton and loving the work. The boys, Sophie was told, were on a walking tour in the Lake District and due home the following week.

'What a nice family you have,' said Sophie as they motored back to the gatehouse. 'You are lucky. I missed so much not having any brothers or sisters.'

'I only discovered mine a few years ago.'

'A lucky discovery.'

'I think so.'

They spent Sophie's last day idling about Thornmere and in the late afternoon walked down to the river. It was a long walk and they took it slowly as if to stretch out what time they had left together. It was still and silent by the water, but the mosquitoes gave them no peace so they did not linger. Nick's houseboat was closed up and the launch, covered up for the night, bobbed gently on the mooring line.

Carla had not seen Nick since the day before Sophie arrived. She had said nothing about him to Sophie or mentioned him buying her paintings, for she still felt embarrassed by that little episode. Just then, as sometimes happens when thoughts materialise, he came walking towards them with Ranger padding at his side, obviously on his way to check up on his boat. Carla made the introductions.

'Now, *that's* my type,' said Sophie after they went their different ways. 'Where did you meet such a dish?'

'He happens to be my doctor.'

'Your GP? Golly! How's your health these days?'

'Quite adequate, thank you.'

The train that took Sophie back to London passed one that was bringing a weary and disillusioned Milly to Norfolk. She had had no better luck in Scotland than in London. Mrs Mackay, her landlady had been a great help, but even she who knew all the right places for obtaining information had drawn a blank. She did have one disquieting piece of news, however. Some years ago there had been an accident on one of the oil-rigs and among those killed was someone known as Steve. Nothing more was known about him and nobody claimed his body. Milly refused to be dispirited. She harboured a strong and uplifting feeling that Tom was still alive.

'My advice to you, m'dear,' said Mrs Mackay kindly, 'is to go back home and try agen from there. There must be somebody in your ain wee toon who knows what became of him.'

The trouble was, thought Milly, she didn't have her 'ain wee toon'. She didn't have a home of her own, either. She had not had a permanent abode since Fred Lewis had taken her out of her little terraced house in Islington and installed her in a suite of rooms in rented accommodation not a stone's throw from Upper Regent Street, where he had hopes of establishing himself as a couturier.

The train rattled through Manningtree. Milly looked out of the window as they passed the River Stour. The tide was out and a flock of seagulls prodded assiduously at the mudbanks. Boats moored in midstream pulled gently on their anchors. Across the river the Suffolk shore showed greenly through a haze of autumnal sunshine. It was a scene restful to the eyes and Milly felt some of her anxiety drain from her. She was comforted by the thought that she would soon be back in Norfolk. Norfolk, suddenly, stood for home.

Seven

Carisbrooke House at Beckton Market, though nothing to look at outwardly had a very good reputation in that particular corner of Norfolk. In fact, so the rumour had it, one ancient in the town was overheard saying to his elderly daughter, 'Du you put me away, put me away in Carisbrooke, or du you put me down.'

It started life in the nineteenth century as the newly built home of a Norwich solicitor who preferred to live out in the country rather than in the city. After his death it passed through many hands, until just before the First World War it was bought by a father and middle-aged daughter and converted into a private school for girls whose education prepared them for careers as nurses or governesses or failing that, dutiful housewives and mothers. It came downmarket during the Twenties and Thirties in its role as a tenement house and rose again when, after taking in the house adjoining, it blossomed into a popular maternity home.

There was a great demand for such places during the Second World War as most of the maternity wards in voluntary hospitals were reserved for air-raid casualties, and those in the local-authority hospitals were kept for emergencies or difficult labours only. The 1948 National

Health Act, however, put an end to private nursing homes and the building languished on, becoming shabbier and shabbier, housing a variety of small businesses in turn. Then in the Eighties, when the electorate were enjoined to stand on their own two feet, regardless of the fact that some people hadn't the strength to get to their feet, let alone stand on them unaided, and council-run homes for the aged and sick went down like ninepins, the private nursing home came into its own again.

A London-based firm took over Carisbrooke House and enlarged it by taking in the houses on either side, laid out its now two acres of land with lawns and shrubberies, modernised its interior, did what it could to improve its Victorian façade and opened up for business. In no time at all there was a waiting list.

It was to this landmark in an otherwise residential road that Victoria Marsh cycled daily to work. She loved it. She was one of a number of auxiliary carers without whom the nursing home would not have been able to function. She had first gone to work there during her school holidays and at weekends, hoping that might be the first step towards her goal of becoming a qualified nurse. A tussle with her father ensued, for he had wanted her to follow her brothers to university. Her subsequent poor showing in her A-level results resolved that dispute, but it was Irina, with her cool, clear, logical common sense, who clinched the argument.

'My dear Lawrence, which would you rather have – a dedicated and perhaps brilliant nurse, or an unhappy graduate with a third-class degree?' Out of Victoria's hearing she added, 'That girl has a gift for love. She is full of compassion for her fellow man. What is a degree compared with that?'

Larry had capitulated, but reluctantly. 'All right, but only as long as when the time comes for her to train, she trains at a London teaching hospital.'

So they compromised. Victoria was allowed to leave school and continue full time at Carisbrooke as long as she went on with her studies at the evening institute, hopefully to upgrade her A-levels. It made a long day for her, but she was young and healthy, and in spite of her brothers' barbed remarks that she always disappeared to pray whenever there was any washing-up to be done, she thrived on work. She certainly wasn't deprived of that at Carisbrooke.

She tried to love the residents equally but there her compassion was put to the test. Some people, she discovered, were unlovable and it wasn't caused by old age or infirmity either.

One of the older nurses gave her a mild lecture on the subject. 'If a person was a misery when young, it stands to reason that person will still be a misery when old. Old age doesn't automatically endow anyone with sainthood. On the other hand, those who are naturally good-natured remain good-natured all through their lives. On the whole, they're a good bunch here. There are only two or three I'd really like to strangle, but that's nothing to go by. I often feel like strangling my husband.'

The staff were a good bunch too, thought Victoria, working long hours without complaining and always ready to come to her aid when she was in trouble.

There was the time when, having got Mr Metcalf to the lavatory, he obstinately refused to comply. 'I can't do a pee here,' he said. 'I need to face north to pass water and this place doesn't face north.'

Victoria went off to get help and met Sister Sylvia, who stood no nonsense from anybody.

'What's the trouble, Mr Metcalf?'

'I'm in the wrong lavatory. This one faces east. East is for praying. I must face north in order to pee.'

'In that case, Mr Metcalf, I can only suggest that you pray while you pee.'

There was one resident who interested Victoria above all others: a large, bony man who might have been well-covered once but was now just a framework of wasted sinews. His eyes were the liveliest part of him, a faded blue which stared unblinkingly at whoever might be addressing him. His hair was white and scanty, barely covering the scar that ran across his scalp. He had been in a coach crash many years before and suffered multiple injuries, leaving his legs useless and his memory impaired.

He was an unsociable man and kept himself to himself as much as anyone in a wheelchair can. He rarely stayed in the lounge where the television was never switched off, preferring his own room and his own choice of programme on the portable television with which each room was equipped. On fine days, even in winter if there happened to be a brilliant sunset, he would wheel himself out on to the terrace and sit there staring up at the sky. He loved being outdoors but steadfastly refused to join any of the outings put on for the residents in specially adapted coaches and minibuses.

'I think he has a morbid dislike of coaches since his accident,' said Matron.

Sister Sylvia thought he just had a morbid dislike of being with other people and avoided them at all costs.

It took Victoria a considerable time to break through his reserve, but she succeeded in the end through his love of reading. None of the present staff could ever remember him speaking, most believed he had lost his power of speech through the wound to his head. Very little was known about him prior to his accident.

The Norwich-bound coach had ploughed through a hedge and landed on its side in a ditch when the driver had had a heart attack at the wheel. Three passengers had died and many others were injured. There had been no identifying papers on the unconscious man and nothing found among the scattered luggage gave the police any clue as to his name and home address. Unfortunately, many of the cases thrown from the coach had burst open on contact with the ground and their contents had scattered. Matching items to passengers proved an almost impossible task.

The injured man was admitted to the district hospital on the outskirts of Norwich and for the first few months suffered complete loss of memory. Slowly, his memory began to improve, but much of his life prior to the accident was a closed book to him. As far as he knew he had no living relations or a recollection of a home address. He was not completely destitute, however, for a wallet was found on him containing fifty pounds and a single coach ticket to Norwich. He thought his name was Thomas. When he was asked his first name he said he was called Tom, so it was duly recorded that a Tom Thomas of unknown address was admitted to the hospital on 4 August 1987. Because of his name it was assumed he was Welsh, though when he did finally speak it was with a marked Norfolk accent.

When the compensation money from the coach company was eventually paid out he was transferred from the hospital to the newly opened nursing home at Beckton Market and steadily lapsed from being a man of few words to one almost completely silent. One of the more impressionable young nurses said she saw his expression change when he was first wheeled into the lounge where the residents had gathered for afternoon tea. He had looked at the assortment of wheelchairs and walking frames and those residents tucked into easy chairs and anchored in place by shawls and cushions and it seemed, she said, as if shutters had come down over his eyes. He had very little to say for himself after that.

Nurses came and went, some of them never having heard him utter a word. On one occasion young Dr Brooke was appealed to. He was often summoned to Carisbrooke if there was a psychiatric matter to be settled.

'He could speak if he wanted to,' he said. 'There was nothing wrong with his vocal chords the last time he was examined. Perhaps there isn't anything he wants to say. Is there nobody here who has heard him speak?'

'On rare occasions I've heard him say "Shut up". He sometimes shouts in his sleep, too.'

'That's better than shouting during the day, isn't it?'

Matron agreed. The nursing home housed three patients who regularly emitted piercing shrieks like steam engines under pressure. One more would have made life insufferable.

She said hesitantly, 'I've no experience of psychiatric nursing, but I thought if there was some blockage in his mind you might be able to unblock it.'

Dr Brooke smiled faintly. 'I would need to have the patient's co-operation to do that. I don't think I would get very far talking to a silent couch.'

'I do see that. I just wish somebody would hear him say something, even just a little swear word. He doesn't react to anything.'

But Matron was wrong there. Old Tom did react quite violently on one occasion and Victoria was there to hear him. She had just reached the open door of his room with a book from the library in her hand when there came a vocal explosion from within. 'Damn and blast you, God! Why couldn't you have finished me off while you were about it?'

Victoria fled to the washroom in a flood of tears. When

she recovered she thoroughly rinsed her face, then returned, rather subdued, to his room. Old Tom rarely smiled, but there was a semblance of a smile whenever he saw Victoria with a book. He was an avid reader. A library lady visited Carisbrooke once a week but only with a box of light fiction. Tom's taste was for non-fiction, preferably books on country lore. Discovering this, Victoria herself fetched him books from the library. One, entitled *The Poacher's Tale,* proved too successful, for Old Tom wouldn't part with it. When he had finished the last page he went back to the beginning again. She did with difficulty get it away from him eventually and paid the over-due fees herself.

There was one person who could have shed light on Old Tom's identity, if she had had an inkling of where to find him, and she was resting at present on her bed at Thornmere Lodge after another fruitless visit to the records office in Norwich. There were times like this when Milly nearly gave up hope of ever finding Tom alive.

Was there an unmarked grave somewhere, she wondered, containing the remains of her erstwhile husband? Surely she would have come across some news of him before this? But Milly was never one to give up easily. If he's still alive I'll find him, she thought, getting off the bed and straightening her stockings. She still wore a suspender belt and stockings, as she had ever since she was young, though the suspender belt had increased its girth since then. It amused her to learn that stockings and suspender belts were, these days, considered sexy and even seductive.

She saw nothing attractive about gaps of cold, bare flesh between the tops of stockings and the legs of knickers, or panties as they were now called, or the discomfort of sitting on suspender studs. But then, when she was young the sight of a woman smoking a cigarette through a long holder was looked upon as seductive. Times change. Outward appearances change. She sighed, for inwardly she still felt the same young girl with the waist that Tom could span with his outstretched hands.

Looking back over her long life in the rag trade, Milly considered the Fifties the best years of all. The war was over and there was a new spirit of hopefulness in the land. True, rationing still went on for the first few years of the decade but derestriction was on the horizon. It was still safe, as it had been throughout the war, for a woman to be out late at night alone. Children could still go to and from school unaccompanied, and play in streets and parks without their mothers suffering pangs of anxiety. A single murder case could take up pages in the newspapers and some court cases were reported verbatim. There were more jobs than those available to fill them and pleas went out to the young of dependencies to come and fill the vacancies in British factories, railways and hospitals.

It was a lovely time to be young, Milly recalled, regretting the fact that she herself was no longer considered young then. Waists were tiny and skirts were full, bolstered by stiff underslips. Dresses had never been prettier or more flattering, she thought, as she sketched away in her workroom. It was just her luck that she no longer had the figure to show them off at their best.

The dressmaking firm of Lewis and Co. was doing well. Fred had given up his dreams of being in the couture business. Instead he aimed for the middle market, enticing store buyers with lavish lunches before the dress shows that followed. The firm had grown and so had the staff. They employed two part-time girls to model their latest creations. They used out-workers to augment their own seamstresses and soon the Lewis labels were becoming as familiar in the provinces as they were in London.

He owed it mostly to Milly, Fred said magnanimously, for it was her ideas that were behind most of his successful lines. Because she had had no training in the drawing of figures, he sent her off to art classes to improve her technique. It helped, but she lacked the finesse that many fashion designers possessed, so he employed another designer to work alongside her, an older woman who had once worked for a Paris fashion house. She taught Milly much, but she couldn't teach her anything when it came to originality. That was something ingrained, not acquired.

Fred Lewis came from the same background as Milly, another link between them, but though Fred had procured a thin veneer of polish on his way up the social ladder, Milly never quite threw off her humble beginnings. She knew that without Fred she would have stayed for ever in Grant Street, putting her little bit away every week in the post office savings bank. He'd pulled himself up by his bootstraps as the saying went; he had big ideas.

He made money and was generous with it, especially to Milly. His wife knew about their little arrangement and gave it her blessing. She had long since grown tired of that side of married life. Marriage for her meant being able to give up her job and finding somebody else to keep her. Her idea of heaven was a luxury flat with Marks & Spencer one side and a cinema the other. When Fred began to get rich her life-style changed for the better, so much so that she was able now to afford the kind of clothes that Fred had once aspired to manufacture. She did not regret never having had children. They would not have fitted in with her and Fred's way of life.

The Sixties arrived with a flurry of pop culture and flower power, false eyelashes and beehive hair-styles. Backcombing came in and hats went out – and the greatest innovation of all, was the miniskirts. Milly eyed miniskirts askance. Not only because she was too old now to wear them herself, but because they were something she had not envisaged. She was good in her way, but she was no Mary Quant. She had to admit the skirts looked good on the young but wondered what they did for the men on trains and tubes with their daily sight of bared legs that went right up to the erogenous zone. Tights, which came in as a consequence of such skirts, must have greatly minimised their pleasure!

The Seventies. What, she wondered, did she remember of the Seventies? Platform shoes and hot-pants, trouser suits and, for a time, a very short time, ankle-length overcoats. She loved designing trouser suits. She could let her imagination rip, sometimes borrowing from men's fashion wear the latest in waistcoats and jackets and flared trousers. Things seemed duller in the Eighties, a disaster zone for many manufacturers and small businesses. Fred talked about selling up before the bottom fell out of the market. He always knew when it was the right time to buy or sell and he did so now, selling out to a longer established and better known dressmaking business. So their annual pilgrimages to the fashion shows in Paris and Rome, which in their latter years had been made more for pleasure than on business, came to an end.

It always saddened Milly to think that they had no settled home together. They lived mostly in hotels, or she in her flat above the showroom and Fred at his club. He had purchased for Sarah, his wife, the lease of a pretty little house in Chelsea which he visited from time to time, for Sarah and he were still good friends.

Age slowed him down. His sexual appetite, which had always been prodigious, began to wane. Milly smiled whimsically whenever she recalled the last night they had spent together. Suddenly, out of the blue, he'd said, 'D'you remember that scanty little nightie you wore the first time we went to Harrogate?'

'I'm not likely to forget it.'

'You haven't still got it, have you?'

'What do you think!'

'Pity, I would liked to have seen you in that one more time.'

She appeased him by wearing a slip to bed. As he was fond of saying, he 'liked his beauty faintly veiled'.

That was the last time they slept together. He died in her arms, 'going as he was coming' as it were. She hoped wherever he was he was having a good laugh about it. It was the sort of thing that would have appealed to his sense of humour.

She met Sarah at the funeral and went back to the Chelsea house with her later. He had left them both fairly comfortable, neither would have the need to worry about meeting bills in their declining years.

Milly, however, had other things to worry about by then: loneliness and her own state of health. She began to think more and more about Tom. She had never forgotten him, the only man she had ever loved. She had been fond of Fred, extremely fond, but fondness isn't love. When her doctors told her that she had perhaps two years to live, she suddenly realised what she wanted to do. She wanted to make her peace with Tom.

It was autumn and the lawn was strewn with red and gold leaves; the blue tits and great tits returned to the bird table, and blackbirds began stripping the pyracantha of its berries. There were the shrubs to prune and roses to trim and all the hundred and one jobs that a conscientious gardener finds to do in late October. Carla kept her bonfire gently smouldering. There was nobody around to offend, no irate housewife complaining about her ruined washing. That was one advantage of living in isolation.

The nature trail was not so much in use at this tail end of the season. The summer visitors, the schoolchildren on nature hunts, the blackberry and sloe seekers, had come and gone. There was a hiatus now until the flower arrangers came out in force around Christmas time, hunting for attractively shaped bare branches, or anything green or colourful to make up their yuletide decorations.

She was busy too with paintings she intended for the exhibition at the Assembly Rooms in December. She was hoping to double the number of her exhibits. She was going to beg Nicholas to stay away. She wanted to see if they would sell on their own merits rather than because she was known to the purchasers. She worked on them as long as the light lasted. Her need to keep busy bordered on the neurotic: she set herself a target to accomplish by a certain time, and if she didn't she got into a panic. She wanted to tire herself out so much that when she got to bed she would sleep and not lie awake tormented by memories of Tony.

She received little news of him these days. Her one-time informant was now installed in a flat in Clerkenwell, sharing it with four other students, three males and a girl a bit younger than herself. Of the three males, two were in their third year and the third, a mature student, in his first. A week after the new term started Sophie paid her a flying visit, arriving with little warning on a Saturday afternoon. She had cropped her hair and looked younger, and fresh-faced and full of energy. She made Carla feel middle-aged.

'Have you still got your David?' she said, almost before she alighted from the train.

'My Michelangelo? Yes, but it's not unpacked. I didn't think it would go with the cottage. Why?'

'I'd like to borrow him. I'd take great care of him.'

It appeared, as Sophie told her later that day and in between mouthfuls of spaghetti Bolognaise that Carla had conjured up from packets and tins in the store cupboard, that the lads, as she called them, were decorating the walls of their bedrooms and the shared living-room and kitchen with pin-ups of nudes.

'Not just Page Three girls, but torsos from all those magazines from the top shelf of newsagents. Honestly, Carla, wherever we look we're faced with pairs of tits or dimpled cheeks. It's so embarrassing, especially as Della and I can't compete.'

Carla laughed to think of all those bared breasts and bottoms causing Sophie embarrassment. She had never thought of Sophie as easily embarrassed and said so.

'It's when friends drop in. I hate having conversations with people whose eyes keep wandering. They must think I room with a lot of sex maniacs.'

Carla laughed more heartily. 'It sounds as if you do. But of course I'll lend you my David, but only on condition that you take good care of him. Do you think he will embarrass your flatmates in return?'

'I don't think anything would embarrass them. They're just like a lot of kids when they get together, even the one I told you about . . .'

'The serious, scholarly-looking mature student?'

'Yes, even him. He's as bad as the other two when they get going . . .'

'Then what is the point of David?'

'To make them feel small. Della and I are going to hang him in the bathroom and every time they undress they'll see the competition and they won't like it.'

'Sophie, you are as immature as they are.'

'I know, but isn't it fun?'

Carla didn't hear about David's fate for several weeks. Sophie just hadn't the heart to tell her. When she did it was in a letter full of abject apologies. The lads had painted a black bow on David's pride and joy. They had painted in a beard and spectacles, and had given him a handbag.

'Della and I could have wept,' Sophie wrote. 'We worked over poor David all one weekend, trying to get the paint off. Goodness knows what the brutes used, it's indelible. And guess what they have replaced him with? A picture of *The Three Graces*. We just can't win. Carla, I'll get you your David back even if I have to send to Florence for another copy.'

But Carla did not want that. David stood for an epoch of her life that had now vanished. An enriching and enlightening period that had enhanced her perception of art and given her something wonderful to remember all her life. She might, in time, forget Tony, but never would she forget the Florence he had opened out for her.

So David passed out of her life and so, shortly afterwards, did Tony. He sent her a cheque for the balance of the money he owed her. He told her he was now married and working for his father-in-law in his insurance business, not in any important capacity as yet, he said, but he was making himself useful. He found New York an inspiring city and in many ways as cultural, if not more so, as Florence. He admitted he missed the old days. He missed his masterclasses, but he was keeping up with his art and had just finished a painting from memory of the Duomo for his father-in-law's office. He thanked her for her loan, which he was now pleased to be able to return to her, and he finished by saying he was a better man for having known her.

She wished he had not written that coda, it was so patently insincere. She put the letter on her bonfire, then changed her mind and burned her fingers trying to retrieve it. She wrote a polite note by return, thanking him for the cheque and wishing him and his wife a happy future. And that, she thought, was the end of the affair, but the next day she woke up with the first of the migraines that were to plague her regularly that winter.

'So how long have you been having these bad heads?' asked Nicholas.

It was the first time she had approached him professionally; that she had been in his surgery. Her eyes had gone straight to the four water-colours on the opposite wall, bunched together, two above two, and she could not help but feel a little flutter of pride. They looked good there among the various medical notices, the warnings of the dangers of smoking, or reminders of immunisations and the address of the nearest asthma clinic.

So when did she first begin to have such severe headaches? After receiving Tony's last letter, of course, but she would not admit there was any link, even to herself.

'I've been having the occasional headache for several weeks now,' she said, 'but these others – these awful headaches – they're something else again.' She sat awkwardly on the edge of her chair, twisting the strap of her handbag around her fingers, something she did when agitated and which Nick was silently noting. 'This may seem very dramatic, but I'm beginning to fear that I may have a brain tumour.'

Nick's expression did not alter. He questioned her quietly. Had she had any severe vomiting? Progressive deafness? Impaired vision? Paralysis on one side? She shook her head to all enquiries. She had felt sick on occasion but had only brought up a little bile.

'So it's just the headaches.'

She resented that. '*Just* the headaches! They are not just headaches. I feel as if somebody is pounding away inside my head with a hammer. Aspirins are no use. I find the best thing is to lie down in a darkened room and try to sleep them off. The trouble is, I don't sleep very well.'

He took her blood pressure. 'It's up a little but no more than I'd expect from someone who's been worrying herself sick with the thought that she has a brain tumour.'

'You don't think I have?'

'No, I don't think you have, but I'll arrange for you to go into hospital for some tests, just to make sure. In the meantime I'll give you a mild sedative. It will help you sleep. It may allay some of your anxiety too.'

'I didn't think I suffered from anxiety neurosis.'

'Neither do I, but you are as tense as a violin string. What's on your mind, Carla?'

His sudden twist from the impersonal to the personal caught her unawares, and such was her emotional turmoil that tears sprang instantly to her eyes. She had not been addressed in such kindly tones for weeks. Even her father had got impatient with her, putting her moodiness down to loneliness.

'You should get out more,' Larry had admonished her. 'You should mix with people of your own age.'

'I don't know anybody of my own age.'

'And you won't while you shut yourself away here. You should find yourself a job – join a few clubs. Becoming a hermit won't do you any good.'

'I'm not idle. I've got my work – my painting.'

'Yes, and that's not doing you any good either if all you

do is worry about it. You are worrying about the exhibition, aren't you? I can't see why.'

'Supposing I don't sell any paintings, I shall feel such an idiot, especially after the way you've been boosting me up to your friends.'

His eyes flashed with hurt and anger. 'I'd be an unnatural father if I weren't proud of my own daughter. Naturally I boast about you. So what if you don't sell any of your paintings? Just tell yourself that the public don't know a good thing when they see it. Who is it you want to impress, anyway? Who is it you can't bear to see you fail?'

'You, chiefly,' she said.

All the bounce went out of him. His face caved in as it always did when he was deeply moved. For one awful moment she thought he was going to cry.

He put a clumsy arm around her shoulders. 'Oh, my dear . . . I thought – I thought it was that chap in Florence. That's why I was so mad with you, for caring what he thought. Carla – Carla, don't you know yet that I think everything you do is wonderful. Don't you know I envy you the freshness of youth you put in your work. Don't you know you could paint me into the ground?'

He was exaggerating, of course, as he did about most things. Nevertheless she was touched by his concern. 'That chap is no longer in Florence,' she said. 'He lives in New York now and works for an insurance business. And', as if as an afterthought, 'he's married to the boss's daughter.'

His eyes met hers. He studied her for a few moments, not failing to see what that admission had cost her, then he tucked her arm into the crook of his and gave it a gentle squeeze. 'Perhaps it's all for the best, kid. He was no good for you. You're well rid of him. Now let me see what you've done so far. You've been very secretive about it.'

Only three of her paintings were actually completed, the

others were still rough sketches. Of the three she put out for his inspection he pored longest over the one of the Thatched House. He had not seen it before, for Carla always made sure he was out of the way before going there to work.

'This one isn't going up for sale,' he said, tapping it with his finger. 'I'm appropriating this. I'll buy it to give to Irina for Christmas.'

'Actually, she wants to buy it as a Christmas present for you.'

They laughed together. Laughter that cleared the air of any lingering grievance. 'I'm sorry, Dad, for biting your head off,' said Carla contritely. 'I don't know what's the matter with me lately. I'm so jumpy.'

'As I told you before, you don't get out enough – you don't meet enough people. It's not natural, shutting yourself away in this isolated place.'

'I remember you saying something similar to that once before. Do you remember? When you sent me off on my voyage of self-discovery, and where did that lead me?'

'That's all past history now, Carla, and you should profit by your mistakes. Don't ever rely on just one other person for happiness, that's courting disaster. Learn to mix. You've never been a good mixer, have you? As I said, join a club – make yourself go out more. Norwich has a lot to offer, you don't have to stay shut up in this old cottage, brooding . . .'

'I'm not broody,' she broke in indignantly.

He looked at her, his blue eyes thoughtful. 'I said brooding, but I think broody might be more apt. What you need is a family of your own. There's nothing like a family to give you a sense of responsibility. Go out and find yourself a good partner. Someone compatible but not competitive. Someone who loves children and will promise to love, comfort and honour you all the days of your life. You see, I know the marriage service backwards.'

Carla's expression set into one of resignation. 'And so you should after going through it three times. And where shall I find this paragon?'

'Join something. The Norwich Music Appreciation Society or the Singles Club or the Railway Enthusiasts. They're just a few examples. And there's always the College of Art – you're not too old to enrol there . . .'

'Dad! – just go, will you, before I start screaming.'

She had forgotten where she was until looking up she saw her four water-colours on the wall of Nicholas's surgery. His eyes were fixed on her. 'What's on your mind, Carla?'

She wondered what he would say if she actually told him. Just go on gazing at her with those keen, steady eyes of his, she suspected, seeing more than he would ever let on.

She fell back on the excuse her father had suggested to her. 'I think I've got rather worked up about this coming exhibition. I don't think my work is up to scratch.'

His eyes went from her to the water-colours on the wall. 'I don't think you have anything to worry about. Viewers will be queuing up to buy.' Across his desk he smiled at her. 'I promise I'll keep out of the way until your paintings are all sprouting little red stars, but I can't make the same promise for my mother. She's always trying to cadge my paintings for her sitting-room. She'll be at the exhibition as soon as it opens. Remind me about the date.' He wrote it down on his jotting pad. 'She very much wants to meet you,' he said. 'She says that any girl who chooses to live alone in such an isolated spot must be very unusual . . .'

'You mean she thinks I'm a freak?'

He laughed. 'My mother certainly doesn't look on you as

a freak, she wouldn't look on anybody as a freak. As a matter of fact, I think she envies you. She's always complaining that she hardly ever gets any time to herself. Well, it's her fault for being on so many committees. She said she would like to have you to dinner one night. Would you like to please her?'

Put like that Carla felt she had no option but to comply. Nick said he would get his mother to ring her.

He stood up as if to dismiss her. She was the last of his patients that morning and she was sorry it was time to go. She felt so relaxed in his company. It had everything to do with his laid-back personality, she thought, she couldn't imagine him getting worked up over anything. Neither could she imagine him as being other than trustworthy, either as a doctor or a friend.

He walked her to the outer door and they stood awhile, exchanging a few more pleasantries.

'I haven't seen you out with Ranger lately,' she remarked.

A shadow crossed his face. 'Poor old Ranger is in trouble. It's his age, a touch of Anno Domini. He has some difficulty in walking. I hope it's only rheumatism.'

She hoped for his sake it was only that too. Even though he rarely had time to stop and chat, the sight of his broad-shouldered figure coming along the nature trail with Ranger at heel always sent a little tremor of pleasure through her. She put it down to her loneliness. Even the milkman calling for his money or a visit from the postman was quite an event.

Nick stood at the door watching her until she was out of sight. He knew by now he was in love with her; he knew, too, that even if she weren't his patient nothing could come of it. Those beautiful violet eyes, when turned on him, were void of any personal interest. Someone else had preempted his chances of winning her. Damn and blast, he thought, it's all such a holy mess.

Carla had seen Nick's mother about the village on more that one occasion. She was of medium height with a trim figure, and her light-coloured greying hair was cut short and sculptured neatly to her head. She was in her late sixties, Carla guessed, though she could have passed as younger, and her eyes were grey like her son's. Now that autumn had come she wore a lot of tweed, mostly skirts in pretty heather mixtures with high necked sweaters that toned in with them. When not walking, she was out in her yellow Mini. She was an erratic driver and Carla wondered how she had survived the lanes of Thornmere with so little damage to the bodywork.

The call came one morning a few days after her visit to Nick's surgery. 'Hallo. In that Miss Foster? This is Philippa Brooke. I'm so ashamed I haven't been in touch with you before this. Would it be too short a notice if I asked if you could make it for dinner this evening?'

Carla looked at her engagement calendar. Except for the date of the exhibition at the Assembly Rooms it was blank. 'I'm free this evening,' she said.

'Oh, I'm so pleased.' Mrs Brooke had a soft, quite young-sounding voice. 'Nick will come and fetch you – about seven thirty. Will that do?'

'I'll walk. I enjoy a walk in the evening, especially when I've been in all day.'

'Then Nick will walk you. It's dangerous to be out in the lanes at night.'

'Not in Thornmere, surely.'

'I mean without a torch. Only the main street is lamplit. We never go visiting at night without a torch. See you at seven thirty, then.'

Carla dressed carefully that evening. For some reason she wanted to make a good impression on the Brookes. She knew that rumours were rife about her in the village – this strange girl living alone out in the wilds, spending all her time painting. What sort of occupation was that? She should be doing something useful, not idling her life away. What was all this talk of her being the great-granddaughter of Lottie Foster?

There were one or two in the village who remembered Lottie, mostly old ladies, whose ability to recall the past far outmatched their memory of where they had just left their glasses or handbag. Wasn't there some mystery about Lottie? Some thought she had come to a bad end. Others that she had gone to London and made her fortune. Stands to reason she had money, doesn't it, else her great-granddaughter wouldn't be living a life of leisure.

Nicholas came for her early and she was ready for him, wearing a cherry-red dress in wool georgette. Red wasn't her colour, but she had seen the dress in the window of a small dress shop in Norwich and had immediately fallen in love with it. She put on a row of pearls and ear-rings to match, but took them off again. The dress was ideal as it was, it needed no ornamentation.

Nick had Ranger with him. 'You don't mind, do you? He needs the exercise, but he's very slow.'

Carla didn't mind. It was a beautiful evening, and moonlit so there was no need for the torch she saw sticking out of Nick's jacket pocket. They strolled, there was no other word for it, her arm through his and Ranger limping along on his other side, neither making any attempt at conversation until Nick said, apropos of nothing, 'Mum is in a right stew over the dinner.'

'Why? Are there many guests expected?'

'Only you.'

'What have you been telling her about me?'

'She knows you only as a sophisticated young woman who has travelled quite a bit. She thinks you are used to exotic foreign dishes. I'm afraid my mother is what they call a good plain cook.'

Carla thought of the meals she and Sophie had concocted over the gas ring in the flat in the Via Collina, often with leftovers Sophie had brought up from the café below. Looking back now, they were some of the best meals she had ever eaten, but that had more to do with the company than the food. She said, 'I hope your mother hasn't been putting herself out for me.'

'My mother puts herself out for everybody. Here we are.'

He had stopped outside the Queen Anne house Carla often thought of as the prettiest in the village. Its small front garden was completely overshadowed by a huge tree which Nick told her was a walnut.

'Do you get any nuts?'

'We used to, but the tree is very old now. It should come down, it's dangerously near the house, but Mum can't bear the thought of losing it. It would be like killing off an old friend, she says.'

Carla's apprehension at meeting Mrs Brooke suddenly left her. Her only worry now was the thought that perhaps her dress might be too sophisticated for the occasion. But even that worry did not last long once she crossed the threshold of Rodings.

Carla was sensitive to atmosphere. She placed at once, when she entered any house, the type of aura that greeted her, whether offhand, tense, benevolent or welcoming. Rodings radiated nothing but friendliness and hospitality. It was a happy house, she sensed, no undercurrents of dissension here. Warm handshakes and pleasant smiles greeted her. She knew both Dr and Mrs Brooke by sight. Now she was introduced formally.

'Call me Philippa,' said Nick's mother, bearing her away to the downstairs cloakroom situated just off the hall. Here, as in all the the other rooms, were bowls of flowers: sprays of chrysanthemums in autumn colours: dahlias that looked as if they had been cut out of velvet. The house was warm, the central heating supplemented by coal fires in both the dining- and drawing-rooms. The warmth was like a welcome. The gatehouse never got really warm. Her battle against damp was an ongoing campaign.

They sat in the drawing-room drinking sherry. It was a pleasant room, furnished with a mixture of antique and modern pieces which did not clash but melded well together. Carla preferred the modern. There was a great deal of snobbery about antiques which she had never been able to understand. She remembered hearing on the radio someone saying that a stone picked up from the garden was older than anything found at an antique sale. Just because it was old, why did it have to be hallowed? She loved antiques as historical records, but she had no great wish to live with them. Nevertheless, she coveted a beautiful old *chaise longue* upon which at that moment Nick and his father were having a mild disagreement upon the relative ways of treating a particular disease.

She joined Philippa in the kitchen, who was just then donning a blue-and-white apron to protect her embroidered silk blouse.

'Can I do anything to help?' Carla asked.

'Have the men abandoned you?'

'They are discussing a case of irritable bowel syndrome, I thought it best to make a discreet withdrawal.'

'How thoughtless of them, talking shop in front of a visitor, and on such a subject. But it's always the same way when two doctors get together. It's just like that at hospital functions. All the men retire to one end of the room, talking shop and all the wives gather at the other, talking babies, or school fees, or grandchildren, according to age. I feel rather left out of it. I'm past the age for babies and school fees and I have no grandchildren.'

'You'd like grandchildren?'

'I'd give my right arm for a granddaughter. I nearly had a grandchild once – and I've always believed it would have been a girl.'

Carla saw that the other's defences were down and looked away from the ache in her eyes. 'Nick told me,' she said quietly.

'Nick told you about Christine! That's a good sign. For years, he couldn't talk about her.' Philippa sighed. 'Old history now, but one never really forgets.' A slight but poignant pause, then a quick change of subject. 'What do you think of my new Aga?'

Carla, unprepared for such a question, stammered out a banal reply. 'I think it looks great. It suits this lovely old-fashioned kitchen.'

'It's my pride and joy. I had one that was fired by solid fuel, but I was always forgetting to top it up and the blessed thing went out on me. This one is oil-fired and I can't go wrong. Mind you, a gas-fired one would have been better still, but we don't have gas in this way-out part of Thornmere.'

She opened up the door of the slow oven, releasing such a rich and savoury aroma that Carla's mouth watered. She didn't bother cooking much for herself, mostly living on snacks.

'I've cooked steaks. I hope you like steak?'

'I like anything.'

'Nick could live on steaks. Leo used to like his frizzled up and dry, but I did eventually wean him on to the Aga way and that's how he likes them done now.'

'And what's the Aga way.'

'Sealed on both sides in a pan on the hottest of the two hotplates, then cooked slowly in the bottom oven for about thirty to forty minutes. They're ready to serve now. Would you warn the men that there's to be no shop at the table?'

The steaks were delicious, served in their own juices with scalloped potatoes and a crisp salad. The lemon meringue pie that followed tasted as good as it looked. Carla caught Dr Brooke's eye.

'Philippa is an excellent cook,' he said, 'but she won't admit it. She gives all credit to the Aga.'

'It never goes out on one,' said Philippa smugly.

'Unless one forgets to order the oil.'

Philippa clutched at the table. 'Have I forgotten to order the oil again? Oh, don't tell me I've forgotten to order the oil.'

'A load is being delivered tomorrow,' said her husband soothingly. He held out his plate. 'Darling, can you spare another helping of that delicious pie?'

'There's also fresh fruit salad or toffee ice-cream.'

'I'm a pie man, dear.'

They played cards after supper. Carla was a poor card player and their efforts to teach her bridge soon came unstuck, so they played whist instead. She kept to the rules, and as second player always played her lowest card even though she might be holding the only trump. She wasn't to know it was the only trump. She didn't have the knack of counting trumps as they were played and if she had would not have remembered the tally.

'There's many a man walking about without a shirt to his back because he didn't lead trumps,' said Nick teasingly.

She didn't have a clue what he meant, but she smiled back dutifully.

He drove her home when the time came to go. She was reluctant to leave the warmth and comfort of the drawing-room. Never before had she felt so at home in the company of comparative strangers. It wasn't that they put themselves out to make her welcome, for their very attitude was one of welcome. With them, playing cards, chatting, looking through old family albums, she had for a time forgotten her loneliness and the deep-rooted hurt caused by Tony's desertion.

'Your mother and father are very fond of each other,' she said, when Nick drew up at the gatehouse.

'Is it that apparent?'

'To me, it was. It's the way they smiled every time their eyes met. The way they touched hands whenever they passed one another. It seemed to me as if they had to keep reassuring themselves that the other was really there.'

'They were separated for several years during the war, perhaps that's has something to do with it. But you're right, they are sufficient unto one another. Sometimes I feel as if I'm playing gooseberry.'

'You still live with them?'

'No, I have my own little pad over the surgery. Pad. That word dates me, doesn't it. It was a very in word during the Sixties.'

'I was a Sixties baby.'

He grimaced. 'Don't rub it in. I was a student then – makes me feel old to think how long ago it seems.'

He got out of the car, walked round to her side and helped her out. He took the key, and, going ahead of her, opened the kitchen door, entering first to see all was as it should be.

'You should keep a dog,' he said. 'It would be someone to

welcome you every time you came home. There's no welcome like a dog's welcome.'

'I wouldn't know how to deal with a dog. I've never had a pet in my life.'

He couldn't believe this and said so. He had never known his house when there wasn't a pet about. From stick insects to dogs, he had had every kind of pet imaginable.

'Not even a cat?' he queried.

'Especially not a cat – they claw the furniture. Lottie, my great-grandmother, would have given in to me, but my grandmother had the last word. She was also very house proud. That's why there were never any pets.'

'Wasn't there a grandfather to stand up for you?'

'Neither Lottie, nor my grandmother, nor my mother ever married, so there were no men in our house either.'

'No men, no pets, I don't believe this,' he said.

'You're beginning to sound like a gramophone record.' She laughed, but it was a hollow laugh.

He wanted to take her in his arms and kiss the defensive look from her face. He wanted to kiss each of those beautiful but unhappy eyes in turn. He wondered about her childhood and the three women who had moulded her life. 'You must have been a very lonely little girl.'

She had never thought of herself as lonely. Solitary yes – but never lonely, for she always had her imagination to fall back upon. An imagination that as she grew older she channelled into her paintings. But now she realised that that wasn't enough. That loneliness, as her father and Nick well knew, was the root of her troubles. Loneliness, she had discovered, could eat into you like a canker. Loneliness was looking into a glass darkly.

'My mother died when I was still a toddler so I don't remember much about her,' she said wistfully. 'Lottie and my grandmother were my mothers – good mothers they were too, they denied me nothing.'

Nothing except a childhood, Nick pondered. 'When did Larry come into your life?'

'Just over three years ago.'

'And you've been away most of that time. You can't know him all that well.'

'As well as I know myself.'

'But do you know yourself, Carla? Do you really know what you want?'

'You're speaking as a psychiatrist,' she challenged him.

'I'm speaking as a friend,' he corrected her. He took her by her shoulders, drew her nearer and kissed her gently on her cheek. She fought against the impulse to throw her arms around his neck and kiss him back. She wanted the contact of another body. She wanted to feel the reassurance of a man's arms around her. She desperately needed to be needed.

She stood at the kitchen door and watched the rear lights of his car fading into the darkness. What would it take, she wondered, to get him to kiss her on the lips instead of on her cheek? Love? But there was no question of love on her part. She closed the door, going through to the sitting-room and, switching on the fire, knelt in front of it until its warmth began to scorch her arms. Yet it wasn't the same as the warmth of the Queen Anne house. It wasn't warmth that enclosed you like a protective wrapping.

Nick's face rose up like an image before her. Everything about him was large: his frame, his eyes, his nose, his smile – and chiefly his deep-rooted sense of duty. Was that why he wouldn't kiss her on her lips? she wondered.

Eight

Carla survived the exhibition. She survived Christmas and even her twenty-four hours in hospital, undergoing certain tests from which she emerged feeling more of a fraud than ever, since they proved beyond a shadow of doubt that she was not suffering from a brain tumour.

'I'm suffering from hypochondria, which is even worse,' she said ruefully to the young registrar who had given her the good news.

'Your doctor did right to send you to us,' was the reassuring reply.

In some ways the exhibition at the Assembly Rooms was more of an ordeal. She was disappointed not to be sharing a room with Ms Watson and Miss Starling again. She did not find them in either of the other two rooms used for display, so assumed they were too late sending in their applications, or had not bothered. She shared the room instead with a silent young man and several large and studied oils depicting different aspects of family life whose bold lines made, she thought, her dainty little water-colours look rather old-maidish.

She sold three of them very rapidly, two to Philippa Brooke and one to Milly Stevens (a second rendering of the Thornmere Green church) and then was left for several days with no sales, but much interest from casual viewers. She began to feel it was the same story all over again. That only those who knew her personally were really interested in actually buying her work. Her father came to boost her morale on the fourth day.

'You haven't sold Irina's Christmas present, I hope.'

'Irina had a red star stuck on it even before I had a chance to hang it.'

Larry grinned. 'There's loyalty for you, but I must say it looks more imposing here than in your studio.' Indeed *The Thatched House* was Carla's favourite among her exhibits. She was particularly pleased by the way she had caught the exact colour and texture of the thatch. 'I see your companion hasn't had much luck,' her father boomed.

'I don't think people have that kind of money to spare just before Christmas,' Carla said, unlike her father, lowering her voice.

'What angry looking people, Even the baby looks angry – not a smile between them. Is that a breakfast table, do you think? I see a pot of marmalade well to the fore. I must admit it's got something going for it. I think I'll stroll over and have a word with your fellow artist. I like his brushwork, but it could be improved on. Perhaps he would take a word of advice.'

'Oh, Larry – be tactful.'

'When have you known me to be other than tactful?'

While her father was away, Carla sold two more of her paintings, one after the other, very quickly. They were her last sales for the week and she was rather disappointed, though not surprised. They weren't in any way examples of her best work. She hadn't been in the mood to paint for weeks. Throughout, she had been in a vacuum that seemed slowly and painfully to squeeze all stimulus out of her. I'll be better when Christmas is out of the way, she promised herself. I'll make a fresh start after Christmas.

One of the most surprising things to come out of the exhibition was the sight of Larry walking out of the Assembly Rooms with a large oil-painting under one arm. It was the one of the family. Mother, father, and children seated round the breakfast table.

Irina was outraged. 'I am not having that monstrosity in my house,' she declared. 'You know how much I hate modern art. Whatever made you buy it?'

'Mainly because I wanted to encourage a talented young man. I thought of hanging it in the dining-room. It would be quite apt there.'

'Apt! When do we ever breakfast in the dining-room? I will not have that hanging in my dining-room. I will not have it anywhere where I can see it. I can't understand why you bought it. It was very stupid of you.' She pronounced stupid the Norfolk way – stoopid. She had more Hungarian blood in her than she had English. She, unlike Carla, had no ancestral roots going deep into Norfolk soil, yet she had picked up some of the local idiom over the years, often addressing Hannah or Emma as 'my woman' when she felt affectionate.

Carla survived Christmas too. In fact, for a short while over the festive season she even forgot to feel sorry for herself. She was asked to come over to the Thatched House on Christmas Eve to help with the decorations and dressing the tree. She found herself, late that afternoon, sitting at the kitchen table which had been spread with newspapers, helping her two little sisters to spray hydrangea heads with silver or gold paint. Irina, at her work top was rolling pastry for mince pies.

'I had a catastrophe, last year,' she said. 'I have a fluted flan dish with a recipe printed on the base. I made my pastry, as I always do on Christmas Eve, lined my flan dish and put it in the fridge to keep cool until I made the filling on Christmas morning. I went to Communion as usual, and just at the part when I should have been feeling at my holiest I suddenly remembered that I hadn't made a copy of the recipe, and there it was, hidden under the pastry. Do you know what I did – I sniggered. I sniggered, right in the middle of Holy Communion! I was mortified.'

'You can get excommunicated for less than that,' said Larry, making an appearance. He had been in the garden picking holly, and joined them now, ruddy-cheeked and smelling of frost.

'Don't trample mud all over my floor,' said Irina without looking up. 'Go back and wipe your feet.'

'If you would only take the trouble to look, woman, you'd see I'm not wearing my boots, I left them in the utility room along with the holly.'

'Mummy and Daddy are quawwelling. Mummy and Daddy are quawwelling,' sang Emma happily.

'That's not quarrelling, saucepot, that's billing and cooing, with particular emphasis on cooing,' said her father, ruffling her hair. He looked hopefully around the room. 'Any chance of a tired old man getting a cup of coffee?'

'If you could wait just ten minutes, my love, you can have a mince pie with your coffee. Wash your hands first.'

On his way out to the cloakroom Larry passed Carla's end of the table. 'Did you find somewhere to hang the painting?' she said softly.

'In the downstairs loo, somewhere where Irina rarely ventures. That's where the mice got in. I sit and study it. Rumination, I find is a great aid to constipation.'

'Carla and Daddy are whispering secrets,' trilled Emma importantly.

Victoria came in late that evening. She too brought a touch of frost with her and her cheeks were pinched from the cold. She had stayed late at the nursing home helping to hang decorations, but she at once joined Carla and Irina at the table to give a hand stringing tinsel and red ribbon through branches of holly.

'Do they feed you at that home?' said Irina in a tone of voice that suggested she doubted it.

'I'm not hungry. I had a large lunch. Besides I can smell something good on the stove.'

'That's bortsch simmering, and some granary rolls I made earlier, keeping warm in the oven.'

'Did I hear you say you had booze for supper?' said Larry, coming through from the hall.

'Bortsch, Larry, bortsch. You have a one-track mind.'

'There's nothing to stop my having booze with my bortsch, is there? Just to keep up the Christmas spirit.'

Irina raised her large dark eyes ceilingwards. 'If you are going to be like this all over Christmas, Larry, I shall make a point of staying in bed.'

But she didn't. She was up at six to put the twenty-five-pound turkey in the oven. It was the first Christmas that Larry had his complete family all under the roof at the same time, and she intended to make the most of it. Andrew and Tim would both be arriving in time for lunch, and not leaving until Boxing Day. She had enough food to feed an army, she felt. The vegetables were all prepared, the Christmas pudding steaming. Larry's contribution was making the hard sauce. He was an expert on hard sauce, though the word hard was a misnomer. He laced it so generously with brandy it could be poured rather than spooned. Only the two little girls turned up their noses at it. They had golden syrup on their Christmas pudding instead.

Irina went off to church with the feeling that everything

was going well. It vanished, however, when returning home she saw Victoria wheeling her bicycle down the drive of the Thatched House.

'You're not on duty, today,' she wailed. 'You told me weeks ago you weren't on duty over Christmas.'

'I felt I had to offer and I'm only on until after lunch. Most of the single girls volunteered to go in on Christmas Day to give the married, well, those with children, a break. Some are doing the early shift and some the late shift. Don't keep lunch for me, I'll have something when I get in.'

'You know your father likes the traditional Christmas dinner at midday. What time will you be home?'

'Three-ish?'

'It's going to be a long lunch-hour,' said Irina mournfully.

'Then we can skip tea. We always eat too much over Christmas anyway.'

'Speak for yourself, miss. I don't think your brothers or your father would agree with you.'

Carisbrooke House was lit up like a Christmas tree. Every window was illuminated. It was a dark morning and the sky was heavy with snow. Victoria left her bicycle with the others in the shed and let herself in by one of the rear doors. Carisbrooke House, having been extended on three separate occasions, was a labyrinth of passages. She followed her nose to the kitchens where breakfasts were being prepared.

The residents were encouraged to have their meals in the dining-room, except for those confined to their beds. Breakfast was an exception. That was always served in their rooms and there was a choice between a full English breakfast and one euphemistically called Continental, which usually consisted of cereal or porridge, toast and marmalade, tea or coffee.

Victoria put on a plastic apron over her blue uniform dress. Into the pocket she slipped a slim package wrapped in gift paper. 'Is Tom's breakfast ready?'

'Over here.'

This morning it was scrambled egg and bacon, sausage and fried bread and a cup of tea. He ate more at breakfast than the rest of the day's meals put together. One good meal a day seemed to sustain him. He was sitting in his room with a cardigan over his pyjama top when Victoria took it into him. He was not yet washed or shaved, but someone had combed his hair. He greeted her with his usual fierce, though faded, blue gaze.

'Happy Christmas, Tom,' she said.

His look told her what he thought of Christmas.

She put the tray on his bedside table and wheeled that over to his chair, then she took the package from her pocket and placed it beside his plate. Curiosity got the better of him and he opened it. It was the much tattered copy of *The Poacher's Tale*. Persistence on her part and Christmas goodwill on the part of the senior librarian had achieved results. Victoria was at last able to purchase the book for twenty-five pence, not much to pay for a Christmas present, but worth its weight in gold to Old Tom. His eyes slowly filled with tears. 'Thanks,' he said huskily.

He was still in good humour when he was wheeled into the lounge later. The tree occupied one corner of the room – the walls were hung with bunting and evergreens. Everybody except Tom was wearing a paper hat. His was round his neck. His good humour was already showing signs of wearing thin, and when the church choir appeared and took their places in readiness for a carol service he made good his escape. Victoria quickly followed.

'Tom, you must come back to the lounge. They will be giving out presents from the tree soon. You don't want to miss your present, do you?'

'Bugger the present.'

She had not known him so talkative for months. She left him deep in chapter one of *The Poacher's Tale.*

It was nearly five o'clock before the family at the Thatched House exchanged their presents. Most of those from Carla were ones she had bought in Florence with Christmas in mind. She had taken the little girls to a big toy store in Norwich so that they could choose their own, but they had surprised her by saying they preferred something to wear. Children have changed since my day, she thought regretfully, having looked forward to choosing dolls. Instead she found herself in the children's department of one of the main stores and came out with two outfits which would make Hannah and Emma look like demure Victorian misses. She wondered how long it would last, or the dresses either, come to that. The pair went through jeans like termites through leather.

The television was banned on Christmas Day, another of Larry's foibles. 'We have the bally thing on for three hundred and sixty-four days out of three hundred and sixty-five,' he said. 'On this one day we'll make our own amusements.'

So the television was pushed into a corner of the room with its face to the wall, and instead there was Blind Man's Buff and Squeak Piggy Squeak, Hunt the Thimble and any other games that Larry, scraping deep into his childhood memories, could come up with, and most popular of all, Postman's Knock.

Carla was in the hall, waiting to be kissed, her paper hat slightly askew, feeling the effects of a very large gin and tonic Larry had forced on her, when the bell on the outer door rang. She went through the lobby and opened it. It was Nicholas, carrying what was obviously a box of chocolates in one hand and a bottle of something in the other. His shoulders were sprinkled with snow. 'Happy Christmas,' he said. 'I hope you were expecting me. Larry told me to call in if I had the chance.'

She was delighted to see him, if only as an interruption to Postman's Knock which was becoming irksome, as Andrew's kisses became less and less brotherly.

Larry appeared. 'Good to see you, Nick. Glad you could make it. Hope you can stay for supper.'

In the ensuing conversation Carla gathered that Dr and Mrs Brooke had been invited out for the evening to some friends in Norwich, but Nick, being on call, wasn't free to move far from the surgery. The Thatched House being in range of his pager, Larry's invitation was eagerly accepted.

'We're playing Postman's Knock and I haven't never been kissed,' said Emma, thrusting out her botton lip.

'We'll soon remedy that.' Nick swung her up his arms and kissed her under the mistletoe. Over the child's head, his eyes caught those of Carla and the invitation in them was explicit. She smiled faintly and looked away. If she had to rely on a childish game in order to obtain a man's favour she'd rather go without.

The evening passed pleasantly, though with the coming of their guest, the games were forsaken and the television came into its own again. Nick joined Larry and Irina in the dining-room for a game of three-handed bridge. Carla would like to have joined them, if only to sit and watch and learn something. But her father forestalled her.

'You stay and watch telly with the young ones, they're nearer your age than we are. You don't want to spend your time with we oldies.'

It was incredible that that remark should hurt her. She

should have been pleased to be thought of as the same generation as her siblings, yet she liked to think of herself as Irina's contemporary – Nick's too. Her father, being her father and nearly old enough to be her grandfather, was in a different category. So was Andrew. Those bold black eyes were constantly seeking her out, sometimes bestowing a wink in her direction. She felt irritated. What did he mean by flirting with her – a callow youth in his early twenties and her brother to boot, even if she had only come into his life a few months previously? It was hard to believe now that during those last few years in the Wenley house taking care of Lottie, she had been completely unaware that she had a ready-made family just waiting for her to materialise.

Andrew said, 'Don't let's waste time watching this rubbish. I know a good game called Come and Sit on my Lap.'

'I expect it entails kissing?' said Tim wearily.

'Well, yes it does – and a little singing.'

Tim grunted. 'Give it a miss, Andy.'

'I want to play Come and Sit on my Lap,' said Emma, jumping up and down excitedly. 'An' I want Andrew to come and sit on me.'

'I want to watch Walt Disney,' said Hannah decidedly. They all looked at Victoria for her opinion. She was fast asleep.

Poor kid, thought Carla, worn out. Up early to go to Carisbrooke House. Back home helping with the mammoth washing-up after dinner. Missing tea (not that anyone wanted tea) in order to go to Evensong. An example to them all. Then why do I like Tim better than I like Victoria, and Emma better than Hannah? Because I'm not a very nice person, that's why, thought Carla. And certainly not a good Christian.

There was a time in her life when she had considered

herself an ardent Christian, but that had more to do with her crush on the best-looking of the choristers than any marked religious leanings. Michael was just eighteen months older than she and had been in the choir since he was eleven. She hadn't become a regular worshipper until she was fifteen and from then on never missed a service. Sometimes Lottie accompanied her, because, she said, she had reached the age when the afterlife took on a whole new meaning. But Carla had preferred going on her own, sitting just behind the vicarage pew with her eyes constantly straying to the choir stalls, where one fair-haired boy had towered above his fellow choristers. While the vicar's sermon flowed obliviously over her head, she would day-dream, fantasising about eloping to Gretna Green. Whether or not it was still legal to marry in Gretna Green did not worry her. She just loved to dream about it.

They had declared, secretly to each other, their everlasting love. When, however, a few weeks before she was due to go to college her grandmother died suddenly, she had had to give up all ideas of career or marriage and devote herself to the care of her great-grandmother instead. That too was a declaration of love, though she hadn't seen it like that at the time.

But Michael had not been her only reason for attending church. She enjoyed going to church, if one could use the word enjoy in such a context, though a kind of sanctified joy carried her through Communion. Of course there were some services that meant more to her than others. The ante-Communion on Good Friday, Palm Sunday with its concomitant donkey, Easter Day when the church blossomed into flower, christingle with its lingering tang of oranges, and the one she loved best – the Festival of Nine Lessons by candlelight, and they did use real candles, not electric ones, for that service in the pretty little wooden-steepled church at Wenley.

It was Michael who had helped to insert the candles in their sconces and place them at the ends of the pews; and Michael, because of his long reach, snuffed them out again at the close of the service. Some members of the congregation had complained that hot wax dripped on their clothes, others that they could not see to read the hymn sheets by candlelight, but to Carla, in her teens, it was sheer magic – even romantic. She had fallen in love with Michael by candlelight, a love which, by the nature of things, was destined, like the candles, to be snuffed out.

At this point in her ruminations the door opened and her father and Nick came into the room with Irina following. Her father looked put out. 'Just getting into the swing of things,' he said, 'when that bally bleeping thing had to go off.'

'You can't stop the course of nature,' Nick said. 'I have every sympathy with babies who decide to be born on Christmas Day – I was one myself.'

A chorus of 'Happy Birthday's greeted this admission. 'Do you get two presents?' asked Emma anxiously. 'It wouldn't be fair if you didn't get two presents.'

'I get more presents than is good for me. Who's going to see me out, then?'

They all went to the door with him. It was snowing heavily now. The top of his car had a three-inch layer of snow. Larry helped him brush it off.

'Come back and have supper with us,' said Irina. 'I've made a huge pot of soup.'

'Her famous knife-and-fork soup,' said Larry. 'Too thick to eat with a spoon. Just the thing for a cold night like this.'

They waved Nick away. When they trooped back into the house a flurry of snow came with them. Larry put some more logs on the fire, both in the hall and in the drawing-room, then wiped his hands on the seat of his trousers. The dining-room fire was being allowed to die out for they were having supper in the kitchen. The kitchen was the most lived in room in the house.

Nick was back long before they expected him. 'Little girl – six and a half pounds, they're calling her Noelle. I had to stop and wet her head or I would have been back sooner.'

'A toast to little Noelle,' said Larry. 'Irina, let's crack a bottle of champagne.'

Emma's toast was heard easily above the others, a high, off-key singsong trill. 'No-el, No-el, No-el, No-el . . .' She stopped suddenly. 'Who's Ted?' she said.

'Which Ted?'

'The one in the carol. "While shepherds watched their flocks by night, all see Ted on the ground." Who's Ted? That's what I want to know.'

There were shouts of laughter, then Irina said, 'It's time the little ones were in bed. They've had enough excitement for one day,' and to bed they were taken, much to their disgust. Carla promised to come up and read to them, which she did, and whilst reading from a book that had been among their presents, she was struck by the quality of the delightful illustrations, any of which she would have been proud to have executed herself.

When she came back down again she was in a thoughtful mood. The others were already seated at the table and Irina was ladling out her knife-and-fork soup, made from pieces of cold turkey, herbs, vegetables, and split peas. Only Larry and Nick and the boys had room for a plate of cold meats afterwards.

Midnight was tolling when Nick reluctantly tore himself away. He contrived to get Carla to see him to the door. There was not much competition anyway. The three males were anchored to their chairs by their stomachs, and Irina and Victoria were washing-up.

The snow had ceased. The moon had come up. It was just as it should be, a Christmas-card scene.

'I think', Carla said, 'that this has been one of the jolliest Christmases of my life.'

'The latter part was certainly very jolly,' said Nick. His eyes glittered in the moonlight. 'You must learn to play cards, Carla. You could have joined us in a game.'

'I'm no good at cards.'

'You denigrate yourself too easily. As a psychiatrist I would say you were trawling for reassurance.'

'I feel you analyse everything I say.'

He laughed. 'No, I'm not as bad as that.' His tone of voice changed, became more serious. 'Have you noticed anything different about me?'

In the moonlight his features were easily discernible, only his expression was veiled.

'I can't say that I do.'

'My mother was always telling me that her father had a saying about eyes and no-eyes. You come into the latter category, though I suppose it's unfair to expect you to see what isn't there.'

'I wish I knew what you were talking about.'

'My beard. I haven't let it grow in for the winter this year.'

'Oh.' She doubted whether she would have noticed if he had. 'Has anybody commented on it?'

'Irina and Larry, when we were playing cards.'

'What excuses did you make?'

'I said I understood that ladies didn't like being kissed by hairy men.'

'And what makes you think that? I have a friend who thinks beards are very sexy.'

'And you think that too?'

'I do not. I don't like to see hair on the chin or on the chest,' feeling, as she said it, the sensuous pleasure she got when running her fingers through the great mat of black hair on Tony's chest. A shutter came down over her mind. 'Just what are you saying?'

'That I would very much like to kiss you. I've been wanting to kiss you for a very long time.'

'Then why haven't you?'

'Because coming to me as my patient, you put all such possibilities out of my reach.' Yet he did kiss her, drawing her to him and placing his lips lightly on her cheek as he had done once before.

'Tell Larry', he said, 'that this cold air on top of the champagne has rather gone to my head. I think it best if I leave my car in the drive and walk home. I'll be over in the morning to collect it.'

She watched him walking away, crunching into the frozen snow, leaving footprints nearly the size of the yeti's. She put her fingers to the place where he had kissed her cheek, not sure whether she was disappointed or not that it hadn't been on her lips.

Milly spent Christmas on her own. Not that she minded. She liked nothing better on Christmas Day than being alone with the television. She could have on which programme she liked. She could stuff herself with chocolates, or figs, or dates or candied fruits and there was no one to take note, or remind her to leave room for supper later, which was always happening to her as a child.

She could, if she liked, have gone up to the hotel with Jessie, but Milly had spent so many Christmases being alone amid crowds she had jumped at the opportunity to be really on her own. It wasn't for long, anyway. Jessie was coming off duty at six o'clock, then she'd be back at the lodge cooking a brace of pheasants.

'You don't mind pheasants instead of turkey? I always have pheasant at Christmas?' she had asked.

Milly's one experience with pheasant had been a disaster, but she selflessly fell in with Jessie's plans. She even offered to prepare the vegetables to offset her feeling of uselessness, but that was declined. Jessie was bringing what vegetables were needed back from the Hall.

'You can keep an eye on the pheasants for me, they're in the automatic oven and should be just right when I come in. I'll heat the Christmas pudding in the microwave – it won't take a jiffy. If you do want to make yourself useful, you can set the table – with glasses. I'm going to open a bottle of my redcurrent wine.'

Milly would have preferred something from the wine store but would have bitten out her tongue rather than say so. Jessie's taste in alcohol was non-adventurous. Milly had bought her a bottle of advocaat for Christmas, being partial to it herself, but after a sample Jessie had looked at the bottle rather askance and said though she had never been one for custard, she'd keep it for when she was off her food and needed a tonic.

A few last-minute injunctions, then Jessie had taken the long walk up to the Hall, lumbered with gifts of all shapes, presents for the staff, and Milly, not without some relief, settled down with a glass of sherry and the telly.

Within ten minutes she was asleep, and when she came to, couldn't remember for a moment or two where she was. It came back to her in time, but in consequence of a dream it was not so much the living-room of Thornmere Lodge but the living-room of her Uncle Dave's and Aunt Ada's brand-new council house at Whittling Park in Essex.

*

It was a lovely house; it had an indoor lavatory – the first time she had lived in a house with an indoor lavatory – *and* a bathroom. It also had a large garden that backed on to the railway line that went to Liverpool Street. Until the novelty wore off she would run out to watch each train go past, and would often wave to the passengers who would wave back at her unless they were too busy with their newspapers.

Milly loved her Aunt Ada and Uncle Dave best of all her aunts and uncles and was glad they were the first ones to offer her a home after her mother died. They had three sons, all big boys by the time she joined the family and out at work, and they couldn't have made more fuss of her if she had been their own daughter.

Uncle Dave had served with the army in Flanders and, unlike many ex-servicemen, had got a job very soon after demobilisation, and on the strength of having been a farm-worker's son he now worked for a dairy and delivered milk by horse and van to the customers in another part of the town.

Their next-door neighbour was also an ex-serviceman, but there all resemblance ended, for Mr Barker, or Major Barker as he liked to be called, had risen from the ranks to be an officer in the Black and Tans and served most of the war in Ireland.

'Can't see why he's so snotty-nosed,' Milly heard her uncle say to her aunt on one occasion. 'He's only a pen pusher after all, but them that come up from the ranks are the biggest snobs of the lot. Making his kids call him sir. If I had sir-ed my father he would have clouted me for being cheeky.'

Milly disliked and feared Major Barker. He was beetle-browed, had a moustache like the ex-Kaiser's and never smiled. Mrs Barker on the other hand had a soft Irish accent, pretty eyes and a love of fun, except at such times as she lost her temper, then the furniture would come flying out of the back door.

This was excused by the fact that Mrs Barker was Irish. Irish people were inclined to fly off the handle, as Aunt Ada explained to Milly, and Mrs Barker had more reason that most to fly off the handle, being so far from home and her own people, and married to *that* man.

Major Barker had met his wife in Ireland during the war and brought her back to England afterwards. They had two children then. By the time Milly came to live at 6 Heron's Close there were six, which always puzzled Milly, for with six children to run errands for her, why did Mrs Barker bribe Milly with a penny to go up to the Lamb and Flag for a bottle of Guinness?

'Why pick on me?' she complained to Aunt Ada. 'Jimmy and Kathleen and Eddie are all older than me, why can't one of them go?'

'Because they would tell their father and then there would be ructions. You wouldn't want that, would you? Mrs Barker likes you, Milly. She always makes her children share their sweeties with you.'

'And you always make me share my sweets with them. There are six of them and only one of me. It's not fair.'

'Life's not fair, Milly, you'll learn that soon enough, and it's easier to start learning while young.'

Aunt Ada was fairness itself, forever making Milly pretty clothes to wear and dresses for her dolls with the leftover scraps of material. She never lost her temper or threw things at her husband. Mrs Barker had once thrown a dish of cakes at the Major, so Kathleen had confided to Milly in funereal tones. They only had cakes on birthdays and then only a half a one each. On this occasion they didn't have any, the dog got there first.

Another time Mrs Barker came round in hysterics

because Seamus, the youngest, had blown his nose on a ten-shilling note. She had washed it and put it in the oven to dry, then forgot it and it went up in flames. What was she going to put on the table for their Sunday dinner? she sobbed.

Aunt Ada gave her the piece of beef the butcher's boy had delivered that morning intended for their own Sunday dinner.

'We'll have a nice steak and kidney pie for a change,' she told Milly.

With such a kind heart, Milly wondered how her aunt could let her own niece suffer the torments that going for Mrs Barker's Guinness caused her.

It wasn't so much the distance, though it was over a mile, and the first part was through the council estate which was brightly lit. After that came a country road, lampless and skirting some woods. It was here that wild animals lay in wait for her and evil spirits lurked behind trees.

Aunt Ada laughed away the wild animals and evil spirits. 'The only wild animals you'll see at this time of the evening are the rabbits. You're not frightened of rabbits, surely. You enjoy them enough when you meet them in a pie. And as for evil spirits – whoever saw an evil spirit? That's only something out of a fairy-tale.'

Milly had never seen an evil spirit either, but she could imagine one, and hear it too as it panted along behind her on the country road. She would arrive at the jug and bottle department of the Lamb and Flag with ashen cheeks and beating heart. She hadn't the breath to speak, but the barman knew what the shilling wrapped in a screw of paper was for. Sometimes, if he was in a good mood, he gave her an arrowroot biscuit, but even that didn't compensate for the terror of the return journey.

But Aunt Ada had another very valuable asset besides

her flair for dressmaking and a light hand with pastry, she had an aunt – Aunt Mary Ann. She wasn't actually related – Mary Ann had been a close friend of Aunt Ada's mother – but she had always been known as 'aunt'. She was what was called a flower girl, though it seemed strange to Milly that someone with wrinkles and grey hair should be called a girl.

She had her pitch in Leicester Square and sometimes, if Aunt Ada had taken Milly to London to do some 'big' shopping, like buying unbleached cotton sheets from Gamages which Aunt Ada would wash and wash until they turned white, they would, when the shopping was over, take a bus to the West End and surprise Aunt Mary Ann.

Mary Ann loved being surprised by Ada. It usually meant a visit to the public house outside of which she had her pitch where Ada would treat Mary Ann to a double whisky, while she herself daintily sipped a ginger wine. Milly was left in charge of the flowers and the 'takings', kept in a tobacco tin and hidden in the bottom of the basket. Milly's one ambition was to sell some flowers, but she never did, though she looked imploringly at each passer-by. Her reward for her vigil, which sometimes stretched into three-quarters of an hour, was a bunch of violets in season, or a carnation or two that had snapped off short.

'She never gives me any roses,' said Milly on one occasion on their journey home.

'It's her bread and butter, Milly. You can't expect her to give away her bread and butter.'

But Aunt Ada would have done, thought Milly.

Her first Christmas with Aunt Ada opened up a whole new world. Christmas had never been made much of at Carlin Street. Her mother was too busy entertaining the uncles to do much cooking. She would buy a ready-cooked chicken for the two of them and a little Christmas pudding, but she didn't go in for any decorations or sending out cards. She did, however, always buy Milly a good present, usually in the form of clothes, and took her to a big department store so that she could visit Father Christmas in his grotto.

Aunt Ada started preparing for Christmas in October when she made the first of her cakes. This was the big, rich, plummy one that had to have time to mature – and more than that, she let Milly help her. First of all the dried fruit had to be soaked and washed until the rinsing water ran clean. Then it all had to be stoned (Milly's job that, as her fingers were small and nimble). The ingredients had to be weighed out, the eggs beaten – not new-laid eggs, they were too expensive at that time of year, but the slightly cracked ones, that came cheaper – the margarine softened and whipped with the sugar until it turned the colour of cream. The cake-tin had to be greased and sheets of thick brown paper folded and tied round the outside so the cake would not burn.

As all this preparation took an hour or two, and the cake was going to take six hours to bake, it meant that the oven would be out of commission at supper-time, and Uncle Dave would then have to go out for some fish and chips. Milly didn't know what she looked forward to most: the preparations for the cake or the prospects of a fish-and-chip supper.

Making the Christmas puddings followed almost the same routine, except that there was double the amount of preparation. As Aunt Ada's mixing bowl was too small to hold all the ingredients, down from upstairs came the toilet basin that normally graced her washstand. This had to be given a good scour to remove any flavour of soap.

For the Christman puddings, there were the same routine jobs of cleaning and seeding the dried fruit, chopping the crystallised fruit and blanching the almonds. Also there was the task of rendering the dry bread into breadcrumbs and a tedious task it was too, rubbing pieces of bread between the fingertips until the crumbs were the consistency of brown sugar, then grating the suet and nutmegs, squeezing the lemons, beating the eggs and, last but certainly not least according to Uncle Dave, fetching the pint of old ale which was always the last to go in and gave the puddings that particular Christmassy aroma. Mercifully, Milly wasn't expected to trot up to the Lamb and Flag on this occasion. Uncle Dave was always the willing messenger.

On that first, never-to-be-forgotten Christmas at Heron's Close, Aunt Mary Ann came over to visit and to have her customary stir and a wish. Uncle Dave had not yet returned from the ale house and Ada sat her visitor down by the kitchen fire and poured her out a glass of stout, which she warmed for her by inserting in it the business end of a red-hot poker. The liquid in the glass sizzled and foamed. Aunt Mary Ann waited until it had settled down, then took a long draught. 'Ah,' she exclaimed, licking her lips, 'that warmed the cockles of my heart a treat. Just the ticket for a night like this.'

Aunt Ada had just put the kettle on the hob, for she herself preferred a cup of tea, when the strains of 'Good King Wenceslas' in tuneless harmony with an accordian suddenly started up at the back door.

Milly and Aunt Ada exchanged glances. 'That's odd,' she said, 'I've never known carol singers go round to the back before, especially on a dark night like this.'

Mary Ann listened with her head on one side. 'There's one thing for sure, whoever it is can't sing. I can't tell whether it's a man or a woman. I 'spect it's some kids mucking about. Chase them off with the broom, Ada.'

'It sounds like a poor old woman with chest trouble. Find

my purse, Milly, and give whoever it is a penny. Poor soul, she must be desperate coming out on a night like this . . .'

King Wenceslas was by now forging through the 'rude wind's wild lament' . . .

'I don't like to go on my own,' said Milly nervously. 'It could be an evil spirit.'

'You and your evil spirits,' tut-tutted Aunt Ada. 'Come along child, I'll be right behind you.'

Mary Ann eased herself from her chair. 'I'm coming too. I'll give whoever it is a piece of my mind, disturbing us at this time of the evening.'

The light from the kitchen illuminated a bent figure in a shawl that partly obscured her face. The noise from the concertina faded on a dying note.

'It's an old gypsy woman,' declared Mary Ann. Her voice took on a note of compassion. 'Poor old bugger, she's shaking from the cold. Give her a shilling, Ada.'

Milly, who was nearer the ground than the other two, noticed with astonishment that the beggar woman was wearing Mrs Barker's shoes. Another look and she recognised the bottom half of Mrs Barker's skirt. She tugged at her aunt's sleeve but Ada had not been unobservant either.

'She's not shaking – she's laughing! I do declare it's that Mrs Barker.' For the carol singer had straightened up and thrown back her shawl. She was in such a helpless state of laughter that she had to lean against the door jamb for support.

'Took you in nicely, didn't I? Thought I'd just pop across and wish you all greetings of the season . . .'

Mary Ann did not join in the general laughter. She was thoroughly put out by being taken in. She went back to her seat by the fire and pushed the bottle of stout out of sight behind the coal scuttle. She had no intention of sharing the remainder of its contents with someone she knew drank like a fish.

'Come on in before the room freezes over,' Aunt Ada was saying. 'The kettle's just on the boil. I'll have a pot of tea made before you can say Jack Robinson.'

The strains of 'Good King Wenceslas' started up again, this time from the direction of the front door, in a deep bass voice. Ada began to giggle.

'That's my Dave alifting up his voice now. Not much choice of carols we're getting tonight. Go and take the bottle of ale from him, Milly, before he drops it.'

Mary Ann was now even more put out. 'Hope he's left enough for the Christmas puddings,' she muttered.

That Christmas, remembered Milly with nostalgia, had been a yardstick to judge all other Christmases by. None that followed ever came up to it in fun and laughter and industry. When, many years later, she spent another Christmas with her favourite aunt and uncle, Aunt Ada was no longer making her puddings in the tried and trusted method. From then on suet came in packets already shredded; breadcrumbs from the local baker, candied peel came ready chopped, almonds blanched and dried fruit seeded. Nothing ever stays the same, thought Milly.

Nothing did stay the same. Aunt Mary Ann had passed on and Mrs Barker came no more with her shawl and concertina to entertain them. The marriage had broken up. The children were taken in by Dr Barnardos and their mother returned to Ireland. What happened to Major Barker nobody knew, or seemingly cared, he had never been popular with his neighbours. The tenancy of number 7 was taken over by a respectable couple, who turned the neglected garden into a model vegetable plot. Never again was Milly asked to do the Guinness run. In an odd sort of way she missed that too.

And last Christmas, she thought, last Christmas could not have been more different. Whereas that first early Christmas at Heron's Close had been one of unalloyed joy, her last had been one of unalloyed despair. She had spent it with Sarah Lewis at Seaways Lodge, a nursing home on the South Downs.

On Fred's death Sarah had given up her little house in Chelsea and had bought herself a flat on the south coast, if not actually next door to Marks & Spencer at least not a stone's throw away. She and Milly had kept in touch in a desultory fashion, usually around Christmas time when they exchanged cards and up-to-date news. They met occasionally, often when Sarah wanted something new to wear and couldn't rely on her own judgement. Milly had kept her eye in where fashion was concerned and could be relied on to say if something was suitable or not.

Then out of the blue on a November's day she got a call from Sarah's local hospital. Mrs Lewis had been admitted after suffering a severe stroke and as her next of kin, Milly's attendance was required.

Sarah's next of kin! It was the first Milly had heard of it. Then a memory stirred. Once years ago Sarah had mentioned the fact that she had no relations still living and would Milly mind being named as next of kin on an insurance form. Milly saw no reason to mind, overlooking the fact that there was a ten-year difference in their ages and this might mean difficulties in the future.

The difficulties started when she got that summons. Milly took rooms in the town within convenient reach of the hospital and visited Sarah every day. She had changed considerably since Milly last saw her, now actually looking her age. Her stroke had deprived her of her voice and the use of her legs. She made incomprehensible gutteral noises when she tried to speak, which she did constantly. She wasn't a good patient. She frequently lost her temper and was always irritable. So would I be under the same circumstances, thought Milly, trying not to lose patience herself. Nothing could be more frustrating than not being understood.

Finally she was asked by the hospital administrator if she could find alternative accommodation for her friend as her bed was needed. This was no easy matter. Milly had to go through all the business of getting herself power of attorney before she could even start. I'm getting too old to have all this worry, she thought after one particularly gruelling day. She found herself almost envying Sarah, just lying there and being looked after, but was immediately ashamed of such feelings. She was determined to get the best accommodation that money could buy, and it was then she came across the thin dividing line between residential homes and nursing homes.

Residential homes were for those who could still wash and dress themselves, shave and take themselves to the toilet, yet were not fit enough to live alone. They needed someone to take everyday worries from their shoulders; someone to spell out their financial problems. If they were men, they mostly needed someone to wash and cook for them. On the whole, Milly found such places cosy and the atmosphere friendly.

Most of the nursing homes left her hopelessly dejected. Not that care, or kindly attention, or a nurse on call was not available. There was all that – but there was also the knowledge that none of these patients was ever going to get well enough to walk out of there unaided. That all their days were one long unending rehearsal for death. It was too near the bone. It was too mindful of what she herself might have to come to one day. I'd rather cut my throat, she thought.

One of the doctors at the hospital had given her a tip. 'You can always tell a good nursing home from a bad one. If you can smell urine as you enter, don't touch it with a barge pole.'

Using that as some sort of Richter scale, Seaways Lodge hit the jackpot. It smelled of polish and warmth and welcome. A pretty young girl in a maroon uniform came forward and took Milly along to Matron's office. Except for a feeble voice constantly calling 'Ner-erse – ner-erse – ner-erse', like a two-tone alarm system, there was no other sound.

Sarah had a room to herself with a view of the distant sea. It was a pretty room dominated by the colour blue; blue bedspread, blue curtains, blue towels at the hand-basin. Sarah would sit, propped up in bed, giving no sign that she recognised anyone. The expression of despair on her face never changed. The ugly noises that issued from her lips made Milly's blood run cold. I can't put up with this, she thought, yet still she did, going daily to visit her lover's widow.

Sometimes, instead of finding Sarah in bed, Milly found her in a wheelchair in the lounge, one of a dozen of so patients seated in a semicircle round the television set.

None of them seemed to know what was going on, or seemed to be aware of the small screen. Most of them were asleep. Of those awake, one was stroking her hair with her slipper and another was crying silent, helpless tears. Milly wheeled Sarah back to her room.

On Christmas Day, Sarah was not well enough to leave her bedroom for the communal lounge. All afternoon she had sat up in bed making the ugly gutteral noises which

Milly found so distressing. She knew well enough what Sarah was trying to say for her eyes expressed all that was necessary. She was begging Milly to take her away. She plucked at her hands, she clutched her skirt. If looks could shout, she was screaming for help and Milly, nearly at breaking point herself, could do nothing but make promises she knew she couldn't keep.

And when she got back to the suite of rooms in Kensington she called her home, she wasn't at all surprised to receive a telephone call to say that Mrs Lewis had died quite peacefully in her sleep. Peacefully – it was a word she clung to for comfort. She hoped it was true. She felt relieved for Sarah's sake, even more relieved for her own. The experience had left her with a morbid dread and a fear of nursing homes. She gave the one at Beckton Market a wide berth whenever she visited the town. She sometimes saw the residents being wheeled out by the nurses in their neat blue uniforms. Rather than meet one face to face she would cross the road.

Nine

If there was one image which came constantly to Carla's mind it was that of Donatello's statue of St Mary Magdalene in the Baptistery at Florence.

From the day that Tony first took her to see it, it had a disquieting effect on her. From her reading of the Bible she had been prepared for a beautiful and dramatic figure, the one whom Christ had rescued from a frenzied mob and set on the path to redemption. But instead she found herself confronted by an old crone in rags. She was horrified by the apparition and even more horrified at the way Tony laughed at her reaction.

'What do you see?' he teased.

'A travesty,' she answered hesitantly. 'A pitiful and wasted old woman who doesn't look in the least bit saint-like.'

'She was no saint, not when young, anyway. She was a prostitute. Her redemption came through her love of Jesus Christ. What Donatello is trying to express, so we are told, is that she has been reduced to skin and bones because of her repeated self-mortification . . .'

'Scourging herself do you mean, as nuns are supposed to do?'

'Mentally, perhaps . . .'

'And rags? What are her rags suppose to tell us?'

'Sackcloth and ashes? Self-denial? You see here, Carla, a figure of a penitent. See how her hands are clasped in supplication, her eyes plead for forgiveness. Don't you find it moving?'

It moved her but not in the way that Tony meant. She saw here not the ravages of penitence or self-denial, but those of poverty and old age. She found the idea depressing. With careful budgeting she herself could avoid poverty, but old age was unavoidable. 'What could have been in Donatello's mind when he created such a pitiful figure?' she queried.

'We ordinary mortals are not meant to see into the mind of a genius.'

Tony was besotted with Donatello. He had taken her in turn to to the National Museum of the Bargello, to Santa Croce, to San Lorenzo and back to the Duomo – hot on Donatello's trail as he said at the time. Expressions like 'great simplicity', 'delicate images', 'imaginative freedom', 'dramatic quality', fell easily from his lips as they stood before yet another example of the great master's art. By the end of each visit she was so satiated by the very concept of the Renaissance – by the evidence of so much genius – that she began to feel that she was at the apex of a creative whirlpool.

Tony was in one of his euphoric moods. 'You can keep your Michelangelo's David,' he said. 'Wait until you see the one by Donatello.' And that was when he took her to the Bargello Museum where they stood before a nude figure cast in bronze, a slender, girlish youth in thoughtful pose, his face shadowed by the brim of his helmet, the severed head of Goliath at his feet.

'Enough,' said Carla. 'I can't digest any more.' Yet after Tony had taken his leave she voluntarily returned to the

Baptistery to stand before the Magdalene and marvel that a piece of wood could have been fashioned by a human hand into such an unforgettable figure. Idly she wondered why Donatello had chosen wood rather than terracotta or bronze. Was it because Christ had been crucified on a tree? She walked away with hardly a glance at the other works of art all around her. Her own small talent seemed puny by contrast, and not worth worrying about, she felt.

This recollection on a chilly January morning was brought about because of another card she had just received from Sophie. A card depicting the aged Mary Magdalene. It still had the power to depress her. She could not get over the feeling that Tony had taken her to see the Magdalene because it depicted how age and ugliness can replace youth and beauty. She wondered if he had an ulterior motive, for their visit to the Baptistery followed soon after Vanessa's enrolment at the art classes. But she quickly dismissed the idea. It was unworthy of her and unfair to Tony. It was just that she could not throw off a sense of oppression that had been haunting her for days.

How many postcards had Sophie brought out of Florence, she wondered, turning it over in her hands. A whole collection, perhaps, for postcards were Sophie's favourite method of communication when she had little to say. The fridge was festooned with them.

This time Sophie wanted to know if she could come down for a weekend soon and bring Matthew with her. Carla had to think twice before placing anyone called Matthew, then remembered him as the one Sophie referred to as the geriatric student. Carla had no idea that Sophie had anything going with one of her fellow flatmates. Did she prepare the double bed for the two of them in the main bedroom, or a camp bed for Matthew in the small boxroom? The problem was solved by doing both.

It was a crisp morning when she drove into Norwich to meet them off the train. Rime still shimmered on the hedgerows and ice coated the dew ponds in the fields. It wouldn't last. There was warmth enough in the sun to melt it before midday.

The station was busy, as it usually was on a Saturday morning with the influx of travellers meeting those on their way off to the metropolis. Carla spotted Sophie immediately. She stood out like a parakeet among a flock of pigeons. She was fond of bright colours, differing in that from most other students. The man walking beside her looked sombre by contrast.

Carla had imagined Matthew to be much older, but this tall, thin chap looked hardly older than Sophie herself. He had a clever-looking face and a nose like the prow of a windjammer, which gave him rather a hawkish appearance. Later, over lunch in a wine bar in Norwich, she learned that he was in fact thirty-five. He was rather quiet, letting Sophie do all the talking, listening with a faint smile on his lips. Occasionally his gaze caught that of Carla and then the smile spread to his eyes. He looked altogether too pleased with himself for her liking.

'I think it's awful eating out, when rightfully you're my guests,' she said. 'You must let me pay for this.'

'We'll go Dutch. Matt and I always go Dutch, it saves arguments. We wanted to stop off in Norwich to do some shopping. This poor man is going off skiing next month, so he wants to mooch around the sports shops. I'd like to mooch around your market. I've heard a lot about Norwich Market.'

'It doesn't compare with San Lorenzo . . .'

'I could never afford San Lorenzo.'

'Are you after anything in particular?'

'Just a bargain.'

Sophie found her bargain on a junk stall – a lovely old copper ewer that was green with verdigris.

'What on earth can you do with that?' asked Carla.

'Clean it up for one thing, then flog it to a dealer. I bet I get double what I paid for it. Norfolk prices are cheaper than London. Don't look at me like that, Carla. Students like me have to live from hand to mouth, we're not all heiresses.'

'Neither am I at present. I had a letter from my stockbroker the other day which wasn't very encouraging. Your geriatric friend seems well-heeled – going off to Gstaad, I mean.'

'He's as poor as I am, but he's got wealthy cousins. They take him along with them when they go skiing as a kind of tutor-cum-baby sitter to their twin boys, a couple of little horrors by all accounts. Matthew earns every penny of his holiday. All the same I worry about him . . .'

'I don't think you need. He looks the type who can look after himself.'

'It's not that. I worry about all those beautiful and sportive-looking females he'll meet on the nursery slopes. I couldn't trust him not to have an affair if the occasion arose.'

Carla took the opportunity to bring up the matter of sleeping arrangements.

Sophie laughed aloud. 'Has it been worrying you? You look worried. Oh Carla, you dear, old-fashioned duck, Matthew doesn't mind where he sleeps as long as it's with me. The camp bed will be fine. I'd prefer him on the camp bed, he snores like a wart-hog.'

'But . . .'

'He can come up and see me any time, I'll only be across

the landing. Mind you, you're even closer. I hope he doesn't lose his sense of direction. He's inclined to go off course when he sees a pretty girl.'

'Do you love him, Sophie? I mean love as opposed to fancy?'

'Let me put it this way. He means to me what Tony once meant to you.'

A look of despair crossed Carla's face. 'Still means,' she said sadly.

Sophie stopped dead. The crowds in Gentlemen's Walk milled about them. An elderly lady with a shopping basket ran into them, glared and went on.

'Don't tell me you're not over him yet?' Sophie said.

'I don't think I'll ever completely get over him. It seems to be a case of recurring fever. I think I've recovered, then it starts up all over again.'

'Well, how about this for an instant cure. Tony is now a father. Vanessa presented him with a son about a month ago . . .'

Shock went through Carla like an electric current. She went cold, not a shivering, teeth-chattering cold, but a sensation as if all the blood had drained from her body.

Sophie looked alarmed. 'You're not going to faint on me, are you? Carla, please don't faint. Oh, I shouldn't have told you so abruptly – I should have wrapped it up a little.'

'Facts are facts,' said Carla, in a voice that just managed to remain steady. 'Facts are facts no matter how you dress them up. So Tony is a father. Good luck to him.'

She felt dead inside. Her feelings had gone numb. Tony as a husband was still within limits. She could still hang on to a flicker of hope that he might grow weary of his child bride and come back to her. But Tony as a father was a different kettle of fish. She shivered, facing the reality of defeat, then burst into tears.

Sophie hustled her into the wine-bar where earlier they had had lunch. She came back to the table with one black coffee and a small brandy. 'Drink these down. The brandy first, then the coffee.'

'Matthew is waiting for us at the car-park. He'll wonder what's become of us . . .'

'Matthew is old enough and ugly enough to look after himself. Drink these down.'

By the time they caught up with him some thirty minutes later Carla had repaired the ravages her tears had wrought. The brandy had given her a superficial warmth but had not entirely melted the ice about her heart. 'I wonder if it was a shot-gun marriage?' she had queried, as Sophie hurried her along Prince of Wales Road.

'Eh?'

'Tony and Vanessa – I wonder if they had to get married. I can't remember now when the marriage was.'

'Oh Carla, you are so hopelessly old-fashioned, you're like something out of another century. Do people *have* to get married these days? Seems to me they please themselves, not convention.'

'How did you know Tony was a father?' said Carla wearily.

'He sent me a birth announcement card.'

Carla pondered on this. 'How did he know your address?'

'I sent it to him – it was meant as a tease. He considered me a drop-out, he said as much. I was delighted to be able to inform him that I had resumed my university career. He was always a bit sore about the fact that he had no qualifications. In his way, he was a bit of a drop-out too. He wouldn't conform.'

'He's conventional enough now: married, a child, a good position, a wealthy father-in-law. What more could an aspiring businessman want?'

'Let's wish him good luck, Carla, and then forget him.'

'I'll wish him good luck.'

She would never forget him. She had first come alive in his arms, shedding her inhibitions as easily as she had shed her clothes. It was her misfortune that she could not take sex lightly, could not think of it as an exhilarating exercise. For sometimes, latterly, her body betrayed her and cried out for satisfaction. So far she had ignored such cries, knowing that if put to the test, she would fail. Chance would be a fine thing, anyway; whom was she likely to meet in Thornmere? There was always Nicholas Brooke, of course, whom she liked and respected – but he was far too correct to take liberties with.

Matthew was waiting for them, leaning nonchalantly against the car door. His eyes flickered momentarily across her face. She guessed to him it looked mask-like, pallid and red-eyed, but he was not the sort of person to make comments.

'You didn't see anything you liked then,' said Sophie, noting that he was without parcels.

'I saw plenty I liked, but I hadn't that kind of dosh. I'll try that army surplus place when we get back. What's that hideous object you're carrying?'

'Something you are going to get better acquainted with after supper.'

Sophie got them down to it the minute the supper dishes were disposed of. She was in charge. 'I'll need vinegar and salt.' She turned to Carla. 'You have got vinegar, I suppose?'

'Only wine vinegar. Will that do?'

Sophie chuckled. 'It's sounds a bit grand for cleaning copper. Perhaps it will give it an extra-posh gloss.'

She mixed the vinegar and salt into a paste, Carla supplied them all with rags. They set to work and they hadn't been rubbing for long before they came to realise, rather painfully, that the most important ingredient of all was elbow grease.

After an hour they had each cleaned a patch of shining, reddish-gold copper. It encouraged them to go on. Matthew's patch was easily twice the size of theirs. He might be thin but he had staying power. Every now and again he refreshed himself from the bottle of Chianti he had bought for Carla.

'To remind you of Italy,' he had said at the time.

'She doesn't need reminding,' Sophie retorted sharply.

Carla broke up the cleaning party. 'I'm going to bed,' she said. 'I really can't stand another minute of this.' Her intention was to leave the other two alone.

Sophie threw down her cloth as well. 'I'm coming too. I've got a pain between my shoulder blades as if there's a knife sticking in me. What about you, Matt?'

'I think I'll work on for a bit longer. I'll try not to disturb you when I come to bed.'

'It would take an earthquake to disturb me tonight.'

But it was Carla who got disturbed. She wasn't asleep – try as she might, Sophie's revelation had banished all thoughts of sleep. She lay and festered instead, her mind going round in increasing circles. Tony and fatherhood seemed an unlikely combination. He had never shown any interest in children except for the *putti* of the Renaissance, the chubby cherubs as he called them, especially those by Donatello. He would drool over those, but Pia's youngest, a living, delightful, chubby cherub if ever there was one, left him cold.

She heard Matthew coming up the stairs. He made little noise, walking on the balls of his feet like a cat. The footsteps stopped at her door, the knob turned and he entered cautiously.

'Oops . . .' he said. 'Sorry about that. I've come to the wrong room.' He paused. 'I suppose it *is* the wrong room?'

'I'm afraid it is.'

'Pity. Good-night.'

She didn't answer. He went out as deftly and noiselessly as he had come. She listened and heard him go into Sophie's room. A murmur of a sleepy voice, creaking bed springs. The ensuing sounds of rapture left no doubt that Sophie was not in the least upset by being disturbed by an earthquake. Carla turned and buried her head under the pillow.

She was down early the next morning and the first thing that met her eyes was the ewer, shining and proud in the centre of the kitchen table. Matthew had worked hard, staying up until he had finished it. She wished she could feel more charitable towards him but she feared for Sophie's sake. She didn't want Sophie to suffer the way she had.

She made herself a mug of coffee and, wondering if the others would like some also, went up to enquire. They were still asleep, lying in the middle of the bed, their naked limbs exposed and entwined. She pulled the quilt over them, not so much because of the cold but because their nudity embarrassed her.

'You hypocritical old spinster,' she chided herself as she descended the stairs. 'It's only because you're envious.' Knowing that in a way she was.

She was too restless to stay in the house and guessed the other two wouldn't be up for another hour at least. Daylight was breaking and a few birds were beginning to twitter. She fetched her sheepskin coat from upstairs, trying to remember the last time she put it on. She was wary of wearing it in case it aroused strong feelings in the minds of animal rights groups. Not that sheepskin was the same as fur, surely? Lambs weren't killed for their wool – they were killed for food and what would happen to all the fleeces if they weren't made use of?

She was glad of the coat once she got outdoors. Though the sun was attempting a come-back after days of intermittent gloom, the wind was as keen as a razor blade. She was without a hat or scarf and her ears tingled with the cold. She walked head down and only came to a sudden halt when someone said, 'Whoa – there. Where are you going in such a hurry?' It was Nicholas Brooke.

He too was well wrapped up, wearing a fisherman's sweater under a padded jacket. His nose was red and his eyes watered. He steadied her with his hands on her shoulders. He didn't smile in his customary fashion. His face looked drawn and the skin beneath his eyes was white with strain. He was the picture of a man beset with grief and immediately she thought of Ranger; there was no sign of him.

'You've been down to your boat as early as this?' she said, for they had met head-on at the top of the lane that led down to the river.

'I slept there last night. I wasn't good company for myself or anybody else. I was best out of the way.'

'It's Ranger,' she said quietly.

He looked away. 'I took him to the vet's yesterday. It wasn't rheumatism – it wasn't old age, though in one aspect it was – it was a malign tumour in his kidney. It would have been inhuman to allow him to go through all that suffering. I cared for him too much for that.'

She could think of no suitable words of comfort. She had never been that close to an animal. Her deeper feelings had always been confined to people. A sudden gust of wind whipped tears into her eyes – or it could have been from unexpected emotion. She wiped them away with the back of her glove. 'Come back with me,' she said, 'I'll make you a cup of coffee.'

He fell in step beside her and said, looking straight ahead, 'We are not allowed to give the same comfort to human beings. We are not allowed to put them to sleep, when all they want, some of them, is to go to sleep and never wake up again. I have some living dead among my patients, I have seen them in homes. Some, who still have the powers to reason, would welcome release, but it is denied them.'

'You mean euthanasia,' she said, as his voice trailed off. 'You believe in euthanasia?'

'No, I don't believe in euthanasia,' he said, but without much conviction. 'I was trained to save lives, not take them. Nobody has the God-given right to take life. It's a moral issue and I wouldn't like to be the one to have to make a decision. And sometimes life can still be good even to those who are incapable of doing anything for themselves but think and remember. Are we to take that ability from them too?'

'What about those who are in great pain?'

'I don't know the answer to that one. I hope I never have to make such a decision. We can relieve pain up to a point, but in their pain-free moments, do patients still want to die? It's hard to let go, Carla. The will to live is very tenacious.'

This was a side to his nature that was new to her: moralising – introspective. The easygoing, rather laid-back presence he showed to the world was perhaps no more than skin deep. She sensed his sensitivity and saw him suddenly as a man who could be easily hurt.

He stopped suddenly and took her arm. 'Look – look over there.'

She looked towards a newly ploughed field where among its furrows a flock of lapwings were scratching for food, and there in the midst of them, proud in his bright colours, was a cock pheasant. It was February. He was free to roam, no longer a target for the guns. She rejoiced for him.

'Isn't that a good sight to see,' Nick said. 'A moment that makes life worthwhile. There's a subject for a painting for you. How's it coming along, by the way?'

'Very slowly at present. I haven't been in the mood . . .'

'Ah moods. Very soul-destroying at times, moods.'

He himself was in a different mood again over coffee. His voice had lightened, telling her of the revels on New Year's Eve at the home of a colleague. There had not been one dark-haired man among them to take the part of the first-footer. There was one, almost completely bald, who volunteered reluctantly the fact that he had once been dark. His wife vouched for him. She had fallen in love with him on the strength of his thick black hair, she said. So they had supplied him with a bottle of whisky and a piece of coal and pushed him out of the back door so that he would have to walk around the house and come in at the main entrance as the clock struck midnight.

It was the first that Carla had heard of first-footing. 'I'm beginning to realise what a lot I missed in life, not having a man about the house,' she said.

They were interrupted by the sudden appearance of Matthew wearing a towel as a loincloth. 'Sorry about this,' he said. 'But I came to tell you the water has run cold.'

Carla jumped up. 'I'll switch on the emersion heater. It won't take long to heat.'

Nicholas's face closed up. His eyes registered doubt and disappointment. He made to rise. 'I'd better go,' he said stiffly.

'No . . . finish your coffee, please.'

Matthew had not stayed to be introduced. At the sight of Carla's visitor he had done an abrupt right about turn.

Carla explained the situation and noted with wry amusement Nicholas's obvious relief.

'I'd better get back,' he said, with some reluctance. 'There may be an emergency awaiting me . . .'

'I could have given you breakfast. I've got to cook for the other two.'

'I had breakfast on the boat, thank you. Perhaps another time.'

She watched him walk away down the lane, as she had watched many times before when he had Ranger with him. He had walked briskly then, his shoulders squared. Not now. She found it odd that the loss of a pet could cause such pain. But who was she to judge? She had never had a pet. Perhaps in that she was lucky, she thought, one loss less to mourn.

When the renovation of the gatehouse was nearly completed, the question of a bathroom had come up. There was a sizeable walk-in larder leading from the kitchen, but Mr Cartwright, the builder, had pointed out that there was a law preventing a lavatory having access to any place where food was prepared. A small lobby would have solved the problem, but there was not the space for that. The only other alternative was the storage cupboard at the top of the stairs. It wasn't large enough to take a bath but made a fair-sized shower-room, and it was from there that Carla, passing on her way to straighten her bedroom, heard sounds of laughter and much splashing of water. Just like happy carefree children, came her fleeting and somewhat wistful thought.

She insisted on them going out on their own that morning. They begged her to go with them, but she wanted the time at home to prepare lunch. She liked the kitchen to herself when cooking. She gave them directions how to find the river and supplied them with dry bread for the ducks. They ran off like schoolchildren let out of school, all their pent-up energy giving rise to much jostling and pushing and running. Just watching them made her feel that she belonged to an older generation.

She made a stir-fry for lunch, cutting up strips of Norfolk turkey, mixing it with chopped mushrooms, spring onions, red peppers, courgettes and herbs. With it she would serve fried rice and a winter salad. She pondered about a pudding, nothing heavy, and went for the soft option – a tin of tropical fruit served with plain yoghurt.

Her guests were back within two hours, arriving as noisily as they had left. They produced a bottle of white wine. 'Norfolk plonk,' Matthew informed her. 'Straight from the vineyards of north Norfolk. Actually, I can recommend it.'

'Where did you get that? The post office stores aren't licensed. You didn't walk as far as the Ferry Inn?'

'We hitched a lift,' said Sophie, helping herself to a spring onion Carla had left unchopped. 'On a cruiser – a young couple on their honeymoon. They gave us a lift to that riverside pub. We treated them to a beer on the strength of it.'

Carla went quiet, thinking of something Lottie had once told her, of another couple on their honeymoon on the Broads and the consequences of that on her own mother. She shrugged the memory away. 'And you walked back from the Ferry Inn? That's quite a hike.'

'We set out to walk, but your friendly GP overtook us and offered us a lift. He recognised Matt and he remembered me, Carla. Fancy him remembering me. He only saw me once and think of all the different faces he must see in the course of his work. He looked a bit down, I thought. Have you been unkind to him?'

'He was here for breakfast,' Matthew put in. 'He saw me in my dishabille . . .'

'In your what?'

'In your towel, actually. It hardly covered my embarrassment.'

'Will you children please go away and wash your hands,' said Carla impatiently. 'I'm just about to dish up.'

There was no harm in him, really, thought Carla, watching Matthew as he chased Sophie up the stairs. He had enough charm to offset his infantile behaviour. Perhaps he played silly to keep in line with his fellow students. Perhaps the disparity in their ages had a perverse effect on him – and so she went on making excuses for him until it was time to say goodbye at Norwich station.

'It's been a lovely weekend. Come again any time,' she said, and meant it.

'We'll take you up on that. Just expect us when you see us next time. It's been heavenly, a home from home . . .'

'I didn't ask you about your home. Is everything all right?'

'As right as it will ever be. Mum still has her bridge and her car rides and Dad goes along with anything anybody else suggests. He and Mr Hetherington have struck up quite a friendship. Considering all things, everything has panned out very well. Hope it stays that way.' Sophie crossed her fingers. 'Goodbye again, old duck, take care of yourself.' And she gave Carla another, even warmer hug. 'Say goodbye, Matthew. Thank Carla nicely for having you.'

Matthew took Carla's hand. 'Thank you for having me. May I kiss you goodbye?'

It wasn't so much a kiss as a mouthwash with his tongue acting as a wet sponge. Sophie did not witness this, she was busy boarding the train. Carla was too stunned to react. She wished later she had been quick-witted enough to bite his tongue while she had the chance. He stood at the window now, waving goodbye, looking well pleased with himself. Sophie stood beside him, so much in love. Poor Sophie. Carla went off to the Ladies to rinse her mouth, asking herself if there was such a thing as a faithful lover. She decided not.

Milly had come to a momentous decision. She would buy a property in Norfolk. She could not sponge, as she thought of it, on Jessie Stoneham any longer. She did not want to return to her former life, which was little better than living out of a suitcase. She had left it a bit late, but now was the time to put down roots and she might as well plant her roots in Norfolk soil as anywhere else.

Not in Thornmere – it was too quiet in Thornmere – but she had grown to like Beckton, that little town half-way between Norwich and the coast. Beckton had a lot going for it. For one thing it had a market, and there was nothing Milly liked better than poking around in a market. Beckton also had a library and she liked a good read. It had a Corn Exchange which functioned as a community centre and there was always something going on there. It had shops, including a Boots and a Woolworths. It warmed her heart to see two at least of the familiar High Street shop fronts, and last but not least, it had a bus station, with bus services to all parts of Norfolk.

It had everything, she thought, including several desirable residences for sale and she had the means to buy outright. Nothing too big or too modern. She knew what she wanted and she found it in Market Street, a row of Victorian terraced houses, that led from the market place down to the river, a mere stream compared to the wide shallow waters at Thornmere, but a charming backdrop to what was, using modern jargon, a street of gentrified cottages.

Number 22 was not so much gentrified as prettified. She fell in love with it at first sight. 'I don't need to look any further,' she said to the young estate agent accompanying her. 'I can see it doesn't need anything doing to it.'

Stripped of its dainty touches, the valances at the windows, the added coving, the alcoves and shelves, the archway that replaced the door between parlour and living-room, it was very much after the design of the house in Islington where she had lived during the war. Slightly larger and with a garden, but alike in its layout. There all resemblance ended. The house in Islington had been dark, with a boxed-in staircase. This staircase was open tread, rising straight from the front door – plenty of room in which to have a chair-lift fitted. She was busy making plans, following behind the eager young agent who was pointing out aspects she had already noted.

'I would like to buy it as it is, just as it stands with all its fixtures and fittings. It's like a little doll's house,' she said enthusiastically.

The young man bristled with pleasure. Sales were usually poor at this time of year; this could prove a walkover. 'Perhaps that could be arranged,' he said. 'I understand Mr Hind's job is taking him to Canada. They were thinking in terms of an auction.'

'Tell them not to get rid of a thing – not a single object. I'll buy everything going. I could never replace all these little bits and pieces, the frills and flounces, the icing on the cake, as it were. For one thing I haven't got the know-how, and for another I haven't got the patience. How soon before I can move in?'

'That depends on the solicitors. I should say eight weeks at the earliest.'

'Make it sooner than that. I haven't any time to spare – at my age life is short.'

There was no front garden. The doorstep was worn almost flush with the pavement. Milly looked down the narrow street towards the market square, then turned and looked in the other direction towards the river. Two swans paddled slowly upstream. It was ideal she thought; town on the one hand and country on the other.

'It's peaceful here,' she said. 'And I've got to like the peace and the quiet of the countryside. When I was your age I liked the hustle and bustle of the towns. I liked to see lots of other people, I liked the sound of traffic. I've gone off all that now. I like it better as it is here. As quiet as a grave.'

That's the trouble with old people, thought the agent. They have this morbid preoccupation with death.

Ten

Carla woke up one morning to find herself crying. It had never happened to her before. She had often cried in her sleep, but when waking later had assumed it was a dream for there were no tears to confirm it. On this dull February morning, however, her face was wet and so was her pillow. She searched for her handkerchief and found it eventually, down at her feet and screwed up into a damp ball.

She had often woken up depressed before, but never as bad as this – never with this awful sense of unworthiness as if she would be better off dead.

She had felt in low spirits ever since Sophie's and Matthew's visit. Their going had left a void which no amount of work or activity could fill. The paintings she forced herself to finish were a mockery. She hid them rather than destroy them, for destroying them would have been like admitting defeat, and she was determined not to go down whingeing. But now, this morning, even that determination left her. She was finished – useless – robbed, she felt, of her self-esteem.

There seemed no point in getting up – in taking a shower or dressing. What reason had she to get dressed? For whom would she dress? There was nobody. That was the trouble – nobody cared if she got up or not.

She knew that wasn't reasonable, but she wasn't in the right mind to be reasonable. At the moment she hated everybody including herself – mostly herself. 'What good am I?' she said. 'I'm a failure at everything I try to do. Loving – painting – living – I'm useless. I might as well be dead. Who would care if I were dead?'

Her father cared, but only in a transitory way. If she were to quit his life he would get over it. Life would go on for others and eventually she'd be forgotten.

For first time in her life she felt like cursing both her great-grandmother and grandmother. If they had only been like ordinary people with ordinary lives she wouldn't be alone now. She would have had brothers and sisters, aunts and uncles – blood relatives to call upon. But she had nobody – she was all on her own and she was at odds with herself at present.

By eleven o'clock she had summoned up the energy to take a shower, then gone downstairs to make herself a cup of black coffee. There was a card from Sophie on the mat: '. . . Thought you'd like to know I flogged the copper ewer. I won't tell you for how much in case it turns you green, but I won't have to worry about the price of books for the next two terms.'

She flicked the card away from her. It ricocheted against the mantelpiece, then fell at her feet. She couldn't see anything to rejoice about in Sophie's news. They had used her, those two – coming for the weekend to look for bargains and buy skiing equipment – a free bed for the night! A wayward thought that at any other time would have filled her with self-loathing, but this morning she had the devil riding on her shoulder.

By midday, after a stiff dose of brandy, she had recovered sufficently to ring Nicholas Brooke's receptionist to find out if she could make an appointment to see him that day. She said it was an emergency. She had come to the conclusion that it would be better to ask advice than to commit suicide. She had tried to finish herself off once before with a bottle of aspirins, but she had vomited most of them up before they could do any harm. Sophie had come to her aid: had mothered her and got her to bed.

Dear, sweet, understanding Sophie. She picked up the card and read it again, before putting it down on the table. I don't deserve any friends, she thought. I am not *simpatica*. She was thoroughly out of tune with herself.

Her appointment was for three o'clock, but she was so anxious for help she was at the surgery fifteen minutes early. She had tried to scrub her tear-stains away but had only succeeded in making her eyes look redder than ever. Her eyelids had puffed up and the violet-blue of her irises was almost hidden. She was reluctant to face Nick's receptionist, but strangely enough felt no qualms about facing Nick. He was a healer, wasn't he? He would give her something to ease the wormwood in her soul.

He studied her for a long time across his desk before saying, 'You *are* in a sorry state. What have you been doing to yourself?'

'Hating myself. I wish I could go to sleep and never wake up again.'

He reached across and took her hand. 'I normally see my psychiatric patients at the hospital. But I don't want you to think of me as a psychiatrist, or even as a doctor. I want you to think of me as a friend – a friend to whom you could come with your problems . . .'

'I'm desperate enough to talk to anybody who'll listen,' she said, rather ungraciously. 'I think I'll go mad if I have to spend another day just talking to myself.'

'I'm listening and I've got all afternoon. I have no more appointments after this.'

She looked around the room with a disgruntled expression. 'I thought psychiatrists always had a couch. I don't see any couch.'

He permitted himself a faint smile. 'I have a very suitable couch in my rooms at the hospital, but as I said, I am not treating you as a patient but as a friend. Think of me as a listening post. Tell me about your first attack of depression, because this isn't your first, is it? Just talk, Carla. Let it all come out.'

She remembered her first attack very clearly. She had been just eighteen. It was the day of her grandmother's funeral and she had suddenly realised that her tears were not for her grandmother but for herself, for now the care of her great-grandmother fell solely on her shoulders and it was goodbye to her dreams of going to college, goodbye to her career and goodbye to Michael too.

She told Nick that, and of her years of servitude, as she thought of them, caring for Lottie. Seven long years when she had been constantly at her great-grandmother's side, only leaving her for a few days at a time to visit friends.

'I didn't begrudge it,' she said now. 'I loved Lottie – we had a special relationship.'

'Consciously, you didn't begrudge it.' He regarded her thoughtfully with calm grey eyes. 'You suppressed emotions that may have made you feel guilty. But deep in your subconscious you may have felt the loss of your youth and resented it. Depression has deep roots and resentment deeper ones. Tell me how you felt when your great-grandmother died.'

'Relief at first, then guilt for feeling relieved. But then came all the excitement of finding the old gatehouse and discovering I had a father living and so on . . .' She faltered.

'And life was good?'

'It was good,' she admitted. 'It was good for the next few years and then . . .' She hesitated again.

'Tell me, Carla, what happened in Florence.'

She sent him a swift, suspicious look from beneath puffy eyelids. 'I suppose Larry has told you about that – the affair I had?'

'He said there was somebody he would like to flatten. I thought he was playing the role of heavy father and didn't take much notice. So you tell me what happened in Florence.'

She told him, with reservations, something of her experiences in Florence. Some things were too private to share. She did mention, however, her attempt at suicide which left him completely unsurprised, as if he had heard such confidences many times before.

'And your present attack of depression . . . You think that has been triggered off by the latest news you have heard of this – this man?'

She hunched her shoulders defensively. 'Well, I can't say I was over the moon to learn that Tony had become a father. I found it hard enough to imagine him married, he always looked upon marriage as a form of bondage. Now he's fathered a son. That makes it very final. I always kept the small faint hope that we might come together again one day. Now I've given up hope. Without it, there doesn't seem much to live for.'

'I'd say you had everything to live for and I'm speaking now as someone who has been through even more harrowing experiences. I've suffered depression too, or rather a long-lasting despondency, but I got over it. You are still young, young enough to fall in love, perhaps, for the first time in your life.'

He broke off abruptly. Her look brought it home to him that he had fallen into the trap of speaking in platitudes.

Yes, you may well look at me like that, he thought, but what are your experiences? A schoolgirl's crush and an affair with a philanderer. Give yourself a chance, girl, he longed to say. Go out and find somebody who will love you the way you deserve to be loved.

'I could never trust myself to fall in love again,' she said dolefully.

'You say that now because you are in such a low state of despair. Once out of your depression you might have other ideas.'

She picked him up on that. 'That's why I came to see you, hoping you would help me out of this depression.'

'And nothing I have said has helped?'

She looked at her hands because she couldn't bring herself to look at him. 'No,' she said, but added as if as a sop to his self-esteem, 'Perhaps I don't really want any help.'

He stared at her in a baffled way for a moment or two, then got to his feet and began to pace the floor as he was wont to do when struggling with a knotty problem. Finally he came to rest before her. 'I don't think I can do you any good. For one thing, I'm too personally involved and I think you know what I mean by that. I could give you the name of a colleague. A good man. He could help you far more than I could – and . . .' with an attempt at humour, 'he has a very comfortable couch.'

The joke fell flat. Nick was not even sure she had taken it in. She sat there, twisting her hands together. 'I don't think I know what you mean about being too personally involved,' she said.

'I'm talking about our friendship. I'm too closely involved with you to be advising you like this.'

'We're just friends. In a small place like this, you must have other patients who are friends. You don't have problems with that, do you?'

'But I don't want to marry any of them.'

That brought colour to her cheeks. 'That wasn't fair . . . I had no idea . . .'

'I know, I'm sorry. I shouldn't have sprung it on you like that. It just came out . . . I had no intention of saying such a thing, believe me.'

She was silent for a while, and when she spoke again it was in an unhurried and offhand way. 'I have rather a cynical attitude towards marriage. I was bridesmaid to three of my friends. All lavish affairs, no expense spared, you know the sort of thing. None of the marriages lasted. I've often thought since that the exchange of vows mattered far less than the pomp and circumstances. Perhaps my great-grandmother and grandmother had the right idea after all. They never married.'

'From choice?'

'No, not from choice,' she admitted reluctantly.

He came round the desk and helped her to her feet. 'I could prescribe some tablets for you that might help.'

'Tranquilisers?'

'Very mild tranquilisers.'

'No, thank you.' She made a great play of pulling on her gloves, avoiding his eyes, as she had been doing since he had made his oblique proposal. 'No, I don't want any tablets. It was the tablets that kept Lottie alive until well into her ninety-fourth year. She had bottles of them, all stacked along her mantelpiece. I used to feel like gathering them up and throwing them out of the window.'

'You wanted her dead?'

'No, I didn't want her dead . . . I just wanted her at peace.' Her eyes had filled with tears which she quickly blinked away. At last she made herself look at him. 'Thank you for giving me your time.'

'I'm sorry if I wasn't much help.'

'You have been a tremendous help. I was wrong to say you hadn't. Just having someone to talk to has helped. Loneliness is part of my trouble. I should get a job. Victoria tells me they are short-staffed at the nursing home, perhaps I could offer my services there. If there's one thing I have had experience of, it's looking after old people.' Then, as if that struck her as sounding heartless, she quickly amended it by adding, 'Actually I've always got on very well with older people.'

He walked with her to the door. Dusk was rolling back the day. Plaintively, in the distance, a pheasant crowed.

'If it's any comfort to you,' he said, 'creative people are prone to depression. I could cite you many famous people who suffer from or have suffered from it, so don't ever feel ashamed of it. Churchill was a famous victim. He referred to it as his black dog, I believe.'

The clouds parted at that moment, disclosing a slice of moon poised over the tree-tops. 'I don't feel like wishing on a new moon tonight,' said Carla, looking up at it. 'In my present state of mind nothing would go right for me.'

'Then I'll wish for you. Peace of mind and a speedy return to good health, because you are ill, Carla. Depression is an illness.'

She couldn't see his eyes, just the gleam of them in the twilight, but she knew how they would look. Kind and encouraging. Why do I always fall in love with the wrong people? she wondered.

'Why don't you call on my mother?' he said as if the idea had just come to him, though she decided afterwards it had been in his mind all the time. 'She's all on her own as Dad will be tied up in Norwich until this evening. She's the one to talk to, she's a born listener, besides . . .' He paused, as if carefully choosing his words. 'In the past she went through a similar experience to yours. She has never said anything about it – but little things have dropped between her and my father that make me think . . .' His tone changed, became lighter. 'She was baking last night. She made a cherry cake. She makes a great cherry cake – she puts booze in it. It would be a shame to miss a chance of tasting that.'

Philippa answered her ring so promptly that Carla guessed Nick had phoned through to warn his mother. That Philippa appeared not to notice Carla's swollen eyes rather confirmed this. She was shown into a small front room that Philippa called her den. Here, she explained, she shut herself away when she wanted to write letters, or listen to a play on the radio, or to read in peace. She now brought a gate-legged table up to the fire and set it with a drawn threadwork afternoon cloth and china one could see through. Carla exclaimed over the intricacy of the needlework and asked if it were hand done.

'It belonged to a great-aunt and so did the tea service, she left them to me when she died. When she entertained me she used plain starched tablecloths and everyday china – these were always kept for best. Now I find I treat Leo and Nick in the same way. I won't allow either of them to come near them. I do love to drink out of fine bone china, don't you? The tea tastes so much better. I'm so glad you called, I hate eating on my own and I baked a cake last night.'

'Nick told me. He said you'd put booze in it.'

Philippa laughed. 'Nick and his booze. He got that word from his grandfather. My in-laws came and stayed one Christmas when Nick was about seven. My father-in-law made the remark one mealtime that there was booze in the pudding, booze in the sauce, booze in the cake and booze in the trifle. "Is there anything on the table that hasn't got booze in it," he said. That was a new word for Nick and he has never forgotten it. But to put your mind at rest, the only booze in this cake is the sherry I soaked the cherries in. That's why they all sank to the bottom though it shouldn't affect the taste. I made it with free range eggs. They cost twenty pence more a carton than the usual ones, but I didn't mind paying the extra. It eased my conscience over those poor, old, de-beaked hens on the assembly line.'

Philippa's logic might have been a little off course, thought Carla, but her sentiments were in the right place. Her liking for Nick's mother increased enormously.

'Has my son been giving you a hard time?'

Carla reddened. 'My eyes, you mean. Do they look so awful?'

'Not so awful as I imagine they feel. I made up my mind I wouldn't ask, but you look so sad. Has something or somebody made you unhappy, Carla?'

'Not your son, certainly not Nick – he was kindness itself. It's just that I woke up with a crying jag this morning. It's the weather, I expect – these gloomy skies. I think February is the hardest month of the year to get through.'

'Sometimes we get lovely days in February,' said Philippa dreamily. 'The country folk call them weather breeders, or should it be breathers, I can never remember. But it's not just the weather is it, Carla.'

As Nick said, Philippa made a good listener. She listened whilst out it all came – the torrent of pent-up emotion that Carla had found herself unable to unleash on Nick but now, without difficulty, was unleashing on his mother.

'It will be difficult for you to understand,' she said finally. 'You've only had one love in your life. Nick told me that you and Dr Brooke met while at school. You must think I'm very shallow. I ought to have more pride than to hanker after a man who's no longer interested in me. But if I were to see Tony walking down the road right now I'd run to meet him. That's how little pride I've got.'

Philippa was sitting very still, staring into the fire. Carla, fighting against tears herself, was surprised to see that Nick's mother was having trouble with her eyes. 'Excuse me one moment, while I get rid of these things,' Philippa said, rising rather hastily and leaving the room. When she returned, her eyes looked mistier than ever. 'I'll have to look at you through a fog from now on, but never mind, it's better than having my lenses swimming down my cheeks which has happened once when we were entertaining the vicar and his wife. Leo said, "Excuse me, dear, you're losing one of your vital statistics," which didn't help matters. You should have seen the vicar's expression!' And Philippa, remembering, began to laugh in such an infectious way that Carla found herself joining in.

That little interlude sealed their friendship. Carla, in need of a confidante, had found one ready made. So, it appeared subsequently, had Philippa.

It was over their second cup of tea that she broached the subject of her own wartime love affair.

'I was engaged to Nick's father at the time. He was serving overseas, and I loved him dearly, but that didn't stop me having a tempestuous affair with a dashing young airman.'

'It was the war,' Carla broke in as Philippa hesitated. In her time she had heard so many things blamed on the war. Loose morals, lack of principles, ungovernable children, all these incriminations she had heard many times over from Charlotte, her grandmother.

'I can't blame my behaviour on to the war. Other girls remained loyal to their husbands and fiancés. It was something sparked off between Joe and myself which we couldn't resist – didn't try to resist. It was so fervent it would have burned itself out in time, but we didn't have time. He was killed. Later I bore him a daughter.'

Carla looked up and caught an expression on the other's

face that wrung her heart. She felt too unsure of herself to say any more than 'I'm sorry'.

When Philippa presently turned her head, her eyes were unnaturally bright but dry. She said, 'I have a photo taken when she was about two, would you like to see it?'

Carla's mind juggled between curiosity and the wish not to cause this woman more pain. Curiosity won. 'I'd love to see it.'

'I keep it upstairs, I won't be long.'

Philippa returned with a document file from which she took a photograph and handed it to Carla. It was of a winsome-looking little girl with smiling eyes beneath a mass of dark hair. Written across the corner were the words 'Jennifer Anne, July 1945'. Carla could see no likeness in the child either to Nick or his mother.

'If it were in colour you would see that her eyes were a startling blue – just like her father's. She was the image of her father . . .' When Philippa spoke again it was in the form of a recitation. 'I had her adopted. I wasn't in the position to keep her at the time. She went to a good family; I knew she would be loved. They kept the name I chose for her, Jennifer Anne. They emigrated to Kenya after the war and settled there.'

'And you still keep in touch?' The photograph was evidence that they were once.

Philippa bit her lips, looking past Carla as if at some distant horizon. 'She died soon after this photo was taken. They had another child, their own, and they called her Jennifer Anne in memory. I keep in touch with *her*.'

'Is that why you have such a longing for a granddaughter?' said Carla, feeling her way carefully.

Philippa stared at her for a moment or two, blank-eyed, then managed a smile. 'Did Nick tell you that?'

'He said how much you wanted a daughter, and a granddaughter would have been the next-best thing.'

'Yes, it was sad we weren't able to have any more children. I wanted to adopt, but Leo wouldn't even discuss it. You wouldn't think my easygoing husband had such a will of iron, would you? Still, I saw his point. I had given away my own child for adoption and now wanted to adopt another in her place. It didn't seem quite right, did it? I don't want you to get the wrong idea about Leo,' she added. 'He never threw my past misdeeds up in my face. That's all history as far as he is concerned. If ever I feel disloyal, it's to Joe – giving his child away.'

She gave herself a little shrug, as if trying to shake off the past which Carla guessed she would never be able to do. She watched as Philippa took some more documents from the folder on her lap.

'I did the next best thing to adopting,' she said. 'I sponsored a little girl from a deprived country. You must have read about the societies that arrange that sort of thing. It's to help children from the Third World. Foster parents take on an obligation to pay a monthly donation to cover the expenses of sending a child to school and helping with the family's welfare. The money covers such things as supplying seed and other agricultural needs and bringing potable water to the villages. I was given the chance of fostering Jamara, a little eight-year-old from southern Indian. Here is a photo that was enclosed in her first letter to me.'

Carla was handed a photograph of a little dark-skinned, saucer-eyed child, standing stiffly to attention and staring solemnly at the camera.

'The photograph was taken especially for my benefit and I was told particularly to mention the dress when I acknowledged it as the parents go to great trouble to get new clothes for the occasion.'

Carla stared at the little mite with her skimpy white blouse and floral skirt, stick-like legs and bare feet, and tears gathered in her throat. 'She's so painfully thin.'

'The whole family is thin. Mother, father, little brothers and sisters. They work so hard on the land and they never have enough to eat. I feel like sending them great hampers of food and boxes of sweets, but it would never reach them. I'm allowed to send a gift small enough to go in a normal-sized envelope. I used to send hankies and necklaces and things like that, but Jamara never received them, so now, instead of letters I sometimes send picture postcards. She's delighted with those, especially views of London, or pictures of our native flowers and wild animals. She took them to school and they're shown around the class. It gave her a certain cachet, I suppose. It seems so little, I'd like to give her so much more, but I must keep to the rules.'

'Does she write to you?'

'Oh yes, or rather the village scribe does. He gets his information from Jamara then writes it in his own words in the original language. The translation is for my benefit. Here's a typical letter.'

Carla held a flimsy sheet of paper and stared at the unfamiliar writing which looked to her for all the world like embroidery, if embroidery could be transposed into writing. The typewritten translation was more down to earth with several typing errors.

'May I read it?'

'Please do. I have others here if you're really interested. Look a whole bundle of them.'

The typewritten translations were on stiffer paper. Carla picked one at random.

'Dear Foster Parents,
I and my family send our love and regards to you all. We are fine here and hope to hear the same from your end.
I am going to school and studying well. Our teacher teaches very well. We are now having holidays for a week on account of census work.
I received your kind letter and felt glad to hear about you all. We are very much thankful to you for the same.
We celebrated 'Ugandi', our New Year festival, on 17 March in a grand manner. On that day we took bath, wore new clothes, worshipped God, and tasted neem and jaggery, symbolising acceptance of joys and sorrows equally. Jaggery is extracted from sugar cane through simple process. We had three days holidays on account of Ugandi.
Now, we will be having summer and we get too much of hot. The farmers will harvest the crops of finger-millet. My parents will also be doing harvest work. We find the fall of mist in the early morning.
With kind regards,
Your Foster Child,
Jamara.

'It is a very grown up letter for a child of eight,' said Carla, refolding it.

'Jamara was older when I received that and I expect the letter writer or Animator as he sometimes describes himself, helped. Here is another of her letters.'

Dear Foster Parent,
I and my family send our love and regards to you all.
I received your kind letter and card. We felt glad to have them and we are very much thankful to

you for the same. We enjoyed to see on the card. We learn about the type of weather in your place.

We are coming to the end of the rainy season. We will have winter. The weather is pleasant.

We will celebrate 'Gowri and Ganesha' next week. We will instal the idols of Gowri and Ganesha and worship. The idols will be decorated with garments and flowers. The friends and relations will be invited and exchange the oblations. The cultural programme will be held in the evenings.

With regards,
Your Foster Child,
Jamara.

Other letters described the harvesting of jowar and finger-millet. How the fruit of cotton plants burst out in the sun. The effects of the monsoon on the crops. Her delight in the picture postcards of England which her foster-mother had sent her. 'I and my family very happy to see the hills, trees and lake pictures,' she wrote. 'There is a pond in our village, also. I will be writing more in my next letter.'

'Was there a next letter?'

'The letters came right up until she left school and stayed at home to do household chores and look after her younger brothers and sisters, while her parents worked in the fields.'

'So her education was wasted.'

'I wouldn't say that. She must have learned something of her own country during all those years at school. I kid myself I taught her something of our country and customs, too. She certainly taught me something of hers. She's a beautiful young woman now.'

Philippa showed Carla a photograph of a Indian maiden in a sari that fell in graceful folds to her bare feet. Standing straight as a post beside her was a child of about eight, almost identical in appearance, even down to the blouse and skirt, to the one of Jamara when the same age.

'But it can't be Jamara.' Carla voiced her thoughts aloud.

'Image of her, isn't it? No, it's one of her sisters – little Mallamma. It's like starting all over again with Jamara – all those interesting little letters to look forward to.' Philippa sighed. 'I suppose you thinking I'm a foolish, sentimental old woman living out a dream. I'm a fraud, really. I should be doing this for purely altruistic reasons, but I'm doing it for self-gratification. I imagined Jamara and now imagine Mallamma as my grandchild. I dream of going to India and begging her parents to let me adopt her and bringing her back here and lavishing her with beautiful clothes and toys and all the things she'll never have in her own country. I know it's not possible. I know I could ruin her life and break the hearts of her parents. I know what it's like to give up a child. I couldn't inflict that torment on anyone. Oh damn, I'm going to cry again. I think I'll go and replace my lenses – they make good corks. Put some more coal on the fire, Carla. We've let it die down.'

Philippa was away several minutes. Carla stared moodily at the flames that slowly came to life and licked fitfully at the fresh lumps of coal. Pictures emerged, garnered from her mind's eye and thrown in relief on to the black maw of the chimneypiece. Jamara when a child with legs and arms like sticks. Her younger sister, a carbon copy. Jennifer Anne, destined to die young. Philippa and her own particular well of loneliness, and lastly, Nick. He too had suffered loss. He too, like his mother, had been to hell and back again. And I give in to depression, she thought, knowing that she couldn't help herself, but that didn't make her feel any better about it. It wasn't so much giving in to depression as having depression come and take her by the throat – but even as she thought that, she knew she had shaken it off. Not completely, but its grip on her had lessened. Talking to Nick and then to Philippa had done her good.

Philippa came in with two glasses of sherry balanced on a tray. 'I know it's a bit early for happy hour,' she said. 'But I think we deserve a little treat.'

It was a ruse to keep Carla a bit longer. In spite of the unhappy associations, Philippa had enjoyed the time she had spent listening to and exchanging confidences with her visitor. It was a long time since she had had a genuine heart to heart with anybody. Not since Nellie, a wartime friend, had died. It wasn't that she lacked friends, as she would have been the first to admit, but they were in the category of friends to enjoy a gossip with, not confide in. She felt that she had now found a friend in every meaning of the word.

Carla's thoughts ran on the same lines as she picked her way home by the light of the torch. She had left the kitchen porch light on and it twinkled like a beacon as if to welcome her back. Home. She hadn't thought of the cottage as home for a long time. She had thought of it as a prison. All homes can turn into prisons, she told herself. It's the way you look on them.

She looked on it now with a less jaundiced eye and the outcome of that was to go down to the studio, again lighted by the torch. She had once tried it with a lantern, but couldn't get the knack of holding it correctly. She had tried holding it aloft as depicted in a painting of Florence Nightingale, and nearly went ass over collar-stud, as her father delicately put it when she was telling him about it later, tripping over a loose paving stone. Since then, she had concentrated the light on her feet and nearly got garrotted by the washing line she had left out. The outcome of that was her father buying her a torch the size of a milk bottle. But it was certainly an improvement on the lantern.

From the studio she collected a portfolio of her latest sketches. Recently, with the demise of the firm of construction engineers with whom Lottie had invested most of her money in the Sixties when the building trade was booming, Carla's future had become much less secure and she wondered if the time had come to sell her talent in the market-place. Going commercial meant eating humble pie, but better to eat humble pie than to starve.

The paintings were not as bad as she had thought. Some of them were of fairies with translucent wings. She had loved painting fairies when she was young, she had been reared on a diet of fairy-tales but she felt modern children were used to stronger meat. Still, it wouldn't do any harm to browse around the children's sections of the Norwich bookshops. She could pick up ideas, and when she had a portfolio of any size she would seek her father's advice and ask him to put her in touch with a suitable agent. He would have the last laugh, of course, but she didn't mind that. She had grown a second skin against her father.

She went to bed that night in a happier mood than she had for days and slept well and dreamlessly, yet when she woke up in the morning the black dog was back on her shoulder, though in her case the black dog took the form of Donatello's Mary Magdelene.

Eleven

Just when the needy pensioners of Thornmere were congratulating themselves that they had survived another winter and that spring was surely on its way, for weren't the pussy willows in the hedgerows plumping out and the catkins on the hazels turning golden, winter took another deep breath and blew a northerly gale over that bulge of Norfolk which stuck out into the North Sea, causing Thornmere, with other towns and villages in the vicinity, to freeze over.

Carla, reluctant to leave the warmth of her bed, was surprised to see daylight squinting through the curtains, yet her bedside clock said it was only seven o'clock. She was annoyed, too, to find she had awakened so early, for with nothing to get up for, she had fallen into the habit of sleeping late. This morning, however, the light was beckoning and, slipping into her dressing-gown, she padded over to the window and drew back the curtains.

The artist in her thrilled with delight at the scene that met her eyes: a winter wonderland of silver and white that glittered like tinsel in the pale winter sun. Not snow as such, but rime as thick as snow that coated even the tiniest sprig and thinnest blade of grass. Nothing had escaped that frost.

Yet the housewife in her silently moaned. More frozen pipes. More going round with her hair-dryer thawing out inaccessible bends. More crouching over the electric fire, scorching her legs while her back froze. More counting the cost as the figures on the electricity meter reached dizzy heights. She had never had to worry about money before. It was a new sensation for her and she hated it, but in the end the artist got the better of the housewife trying to make ends meet and she hurriedly showered and dressed and got out her sketch-book.

After rooting around the children's book departments in the city stores she had changed her mind about the suitability of fairy-tales for children. Things had altered considerably since her day. Fairy-tales were out. Aliens from outer space were very much in, though to her mind there was very little basic difference. Anthropomorphous animals were also out and humans very much in, especially the younger breed of humans with their implausible but entertaining adventures. She could see how they appealed to young readers and returned home with ideas aplenty in her mind, but when she tried to get them down on paper she found it a different matter. Words failed her.

'You can't expect to be good at everything,' her father said. 'You can paint. Be satisfied with that.'

'Beatrix Potter did both.'

'You are not, my dear, Beatrix Potter.'

Larry hadn't been up to form that winter. He had a cold which he nourished with such loving care it was reluctant to go. He wouldn't stay in bed but preferred to crouch over the fire in the drawing-room so that the family could all share his bouts of coughing and ear-splitting sneezes. As Irina said on one of her escapes to Carla, 'When your father is ill we all suffer. Come and see him soon, Carla. He misses you.'

'Just lately, I haven't been fit company for anyone.'

'It's only the winter blues. We all get run down this time of year.'

'I don't feel so much run down as wrung out. As if some great giant has taken hold of me and squeezed me dry. I don't have emotions any more. I'm a nobody.'

Irina shrugged into her coat with every sign of impatience. 'Sometimes, Carla, you exasperate me even more than your father does, and I wouldn't have thought that possible. Do you know what I do when I'm fed up? I scrub the kitchen floor. Just at present it's cleaner than the table.'

'I'd never feel depressed enough to want to scrub a kitchen floor.'

But today, under the influence of the winter scenario, Carla felt inspired to work – work more in keeping with her inclinations. She would paint the scene from her bedroom window. She was struggling to get the jewel-like texture of the frost on to paper when the telephone rang.

It was Nick. 'You didn't follow up your visit of last week,' he said.

'I didn't see the point.' And because that sounded somewhat ungracious, she added in a more placating tone, 'I realise I have to work out my own problems.'

'And how do you intend to do that?'

'I've made a start. I'm writing a book. Well, illustrating it, actually. I'll add the text later. It keeps me from brooding, so even if it comes to nothing it's not a wasted effort.'

'I have an alternative, if you're interested.'

'Alternative to what?'

'A means of combating depression,' he said, and she stood, listening quietly, while he explained.

He had a patient – an ex-patient rather – an accountant, with every prospect of being taken on as a partner in his firm until, that was, his wife left him; then his whole life had fallen apart. His subsequent depression made Carla's seem like a mild aberration.

'You *cured* him?' said Carla questioningly.

'I wish I could claim the credit. He is cured, but I had nothing to do with it. He took up meditation – studied it seriously – now he practises it full-time. He gave up his job in order to preach his own particular gospel. "Peace through meditation." He's a changed man, Carla. He used to have swings of mood, up in the heights, down in the depths – perhaps that's why his wife left him – now he's one of the most unruffled people I know. Believe me, Carla, I think he could do more for you with his meditation than I could with my couch. Anyway, it's worth a try.'

'Why didn't you mention him when I saw you the other day?'

'Because I hadn't given him a thought in months, then yesterday afternoon, in Norwich, I ran into him. He's got a recruiting office just off Mayberry Street in Bargate.'

Bargate was a part of Norwich Carla knew little about and rarely visited. There were no shops there, only wharves and warehouses some of which had fallen into disrepair.

'What do you mean by recruiting office?'

He laughed. 'I was being too clever by half. He wouldn't like to hear me calling it that. It's where he interviews prospective members. I made an appointment for you to see him tomorrow morning at ten o'clock.'

She was so taken aback by his presumption that for a moment she was bereft of speech. 'Nick, are you trying to get me to join a cult?'

'No, I just want you to go and see Oliver Peel. He wanted you to confirm the appointment personally, so give him a ring first. Have you got pen and paper at the ready?' He gave her the details. 'Good luck, Carla. Give it a go.'

Give it a go. Who did Nick think she was? She tried to

remember all she had heard or read about meditation. Transcendental meditation. Peace through meditation. Pictures of hirsute gurus came to her mind. Visions of yellow-robed apostles flashed across her inner eye. She found it hard to believe that such a sane and practical person as Nick could suggest such a thing. It *was* a cult. She had always been suspicious of cults. They hadn't had a very good press lately. She had no intention of joining a cult.

She paced the room, the piece of paper with Oliver Peel's telephone number between her fingers, with half a mind to throw it in the waste bin. Was Nick playing a joke on her? Testing her to see whether she would take him seriously? What she couldn't take seriously was the idea that meditation could cure her depression. Then her thoughts took a sudden swing in the opposite direction. Why not call Nick's bluff? Have the laugh on him? In any case, he had aroused her interest in this Oliver Peel. She really wanted to see this moody soul turned peacemaker. She rang the number.

It is not always easy to tell a person's character from their voice alone. Fat people, she had found, sounded quite thin on the radio, and vice versa. Oliver Peel sounded friendly but somewhat reserved. He didn't gush at her. She could have been making an appointment with her bank manager or dentist. It wasn't until he said, 'There are certain rituals to go through before the initiation. I think you should be prepared,' that a few hairs began to rise on the back of her neck.

'What kind of rituals?' she said tersely.

'Not rituals as such, but you must bring some fruit as an offering. Something bland. No citrus fruit. Nothing like a lemon or an orange or a lime – the acid would sour the relationship.'

She was sure by now that she was having her leg pulled.

This was something that Nick and this Oliver had thought up between them. 'A pineapple?' she suggested.

Hesitation, then just a hint of amusement in his voice. 'No, I think not.'

Too prickly, no doubt. I'll take a melon, she thought, that will fox him. But when she wandered around the fruit and vegetable stalls in Norwich market the following morning she changed her mind. She didn't want to start off on the wrong foot, she didn't want Oliver Peel to think she was taking the mickey and she felt he was perceptive enough to see through such a gesture. Bananas were bland enough. She couldn't go wrong with bananas, so she bought the largest bunch she could find and with these made her way to Finney's Passage.

The premises looked like a house converted into a shop, a very dull-looking shop with net curtains at the windows. A small notice on the door gave the only clue as to its identity. 'Peace through Meditation' it proclaimed. The door was locked.

She waited for what seemed hours, but it was only ten minutes by her watch. She had just decided for the umpteenth time to give up when she saw a cyclist approaching, bumptity-bump over the cobbles, with a supermarket carrier bag dangling from the handlebars. He had obviously been out to buy his groceries. Carla wondered idly if he lived above the 'shop'. He dismounted and came across holding out one ungloved hand.

'Miss Foster? Oliver Peel. Sorry I wasn't here to let you in. I meant to get the place warmed up, ready for you, but I was held up at the supermarket – very busy there this morning. Then I was waylaid by one of my clients. She wanted to know more about a course that's on the agenda. Well, I see you found your way all right. Most people are unfamiliar with this part of Norwich.'

He looked so ordinary, so normal, no outward sign of anything touching on the paranormal, that her suspicions that this might be an elaborate joke on Nick's part resurfaced. She quickly dismissed that idea. The expression in Oliver's eyes was too patently honest.

The office he ushered her into was dark and musty and also practically bare. He lit an ancient gas fire that seemed reluctant to hand back any heat. There was a large poster on the wall showing people in white robes levitating in a lotus position. Only a few inches of daylight showed between them and the mattress on the ground, but they were flying nevertheless. She was fascinated. 'Can people really do that?' she asked.

'If their faith is strong enough.

'I'll go through a few facts of meditation,' he said, as he relieved her of her coat, something she was sorry he had to do. They sat on either side of the popping gas fire. It was like sitting round a candle. The only other pieces of furniture in the room were an office desk (very ink-stained) and a metal filing cabinet, both so well used she suspected they were second-hand. A door separated these two items. She shivered – not entirely from the cold. She always got goose-pimples when dealing with the unexpected.

She closed her mind to her discomfort and gave him her attention. He was feeding her information, the words coming out like a recitative. '. . . Until the seventeenth century there was no doubt of the link between mind and body. Only in this more let us call it sophisticated age has that doubt been questioned. It's a question of mind over matter. Now the belief has gone full cycle and even the medical profession are coming to realise the strength of the mind's healing power. Although meditation is considered a means of developing the spiritual life of a religious person, it is used by many to obtain peace of mind. With peace of mind our physical health improves. Would you accept that?'

'I certainly would,' agreed Carla, recalling how she felt when she was in the depths of depression. Cold, clammy even, too weary to take any trouble with her appearance, indifferent to her own welfare. And when not depressed? How long ago was it when she had last felt on top of the world? She couldn't remember, but she could remember how she had felt then – that nothing was beyond her.

'If meditation can cure my depression,' she said, 'I'm willing to try it. I'll try anything.'

But when he led her through the door into the adjoining room she instinctively drew back. It was like entering an Eastern temple. There was an altar draped with foreign silks on which stood a small statue of the Buddha, and above the altar a large portrait of a chubby, bearded Asian with little rounded cheeks and large twinkling eyes, as if he were enjoying some private joke. The smell of incense was in the air and flowers were arranged picturesquely in a bowl on the table. There was a carpet on the floor and altogether it looked far more imposing than the outer office, though it didn't take much to do that. Still Carla felt uneasy. 'I'm Church of England,' she said stoutly. 'I don't intend to change my religion.'

'There is no question of you changing your religion. Transcendental meditation is non-denominational. It transcends all religions. Is this your offering?'

She couldn't be sure but she thought she saw a tightening of his lips, as if he were trying not to smile when she handed over the span of bananas. He placed the fruit on the altar. Enough to keep him in puddings for a week, she thought mischievously. She rather expected him to chant some kind of prayer, but he did not. He led her to a red-plush-upholstered chair and took another beside her.

'Before I instruct you in the method of meditation,' he said, 'I'll run through what effects it should have; that is, if you are meditating correctly. Some people, I'm afraid, never achieve absolute meditation because they either can't, or won't, give themselves up to it. The important thing is to prepare yourself in the correct manner. Never lie down to meditate – always sit – but chose a comfortable chair. Sit at ease, your hands in your lap, eyes closed. Relax. You can't meditate properly unless you are relaxed. I will give you a word to repeat over and over to yourself while you are doing this. We call it a mantra. A mantra is a sacred word believed to have peculiar power for the one who uses it. It is short and syllabic.' He took her by surprise when he leaned towards her and said a word in her ear. 'Did you get that?' And when she nodded, 'You must never reveal it to anybody. That is your own personal mantra and to tell anyone else about it will break the trust.'

Then and there, Carla decided that everybody who had elected to be instructed in meditation was given the same word with its peculiar power. For if not, how could all the tens of thousands of followers all over the world have a different mantra? There couldn't be enough significant words to go round, and if someone died, would they take the secret of their mantra with them? She was still in a slightly sceptical mode. And then something most weird began to happen.

She was sitting as she had been instructed, her eyes closed, relaxed and repeating the mantra to herself.

'Twenty minutes', said Oliver, 'for meditation. It takes five minutes or so to compose yourself sufficently to fall into a deep level of consciousness and another five to come out again. Ignore all external noises or interruptions. When you do this in your home alone – and to get any benefit from it must be practised morning and evening – ignore the telephone or the doorbell. Let nothing interrupt your meditating. You must give yourself up to it completely . . .'

His voice drifted away and she heard it from a distance, coming hollowly as through a funnel. Darkness descended against her eyelids, split now and again by brilliant lights like shooting stars. She felt as if she were drifting in soft, warm darkness where there was no pain or worry or tension, just this lovely sensation of being a feather blown along by a friendly wind.

A tremendous sigh shook her, then another. The dark beyond her eyes began to lighten. Something or someone was trying to prise her eyelids open. She gave another unyielding sigh. She was still silently repeating her mantra when Oliver said, 'Your twenty minutes is up.'

She couldn't believe him. She had closed her eyes for no more than a few minutes. And yet, this feeling of well-being? This terrible urge to go across and kiss the Buddha on the top of his head?

'I fell asleep,' she said defensively.

Oliver smiled. 'You weren't asleep. I always know those who fall asleep. Some even snore. You kept sighing. Well, how do you feel now?'

'Relaxed,' she said. 'Really relaxed, as if I've had a good, long rest.'

'That's the after-effects of peace.'

He stood up and broke off one of the bananas and handed it back to her.

'What do I do with this?'

'Eat it if you like. We always give back part of the offering. It symbolises the strengthening of the bond.' Still feeling as if she were sleep-walking, she followed him to the outer door of the office.

'Would you like to join my group in a weekend retreat?' he asked. 'Next weekend, actually. We're meeting up at an old house in Arlington, west Norfolk, which is being used as a convent now. The sisters are quite willing to have us as their guests. Would you like to come? If so, I'll send you all the details about it – fees etc. Have you got transport?'

She had transport, but what about him? He couldn't afford to run a car any longer, Nick had told her. Since giving up all his worldly goods, including his job and his lovely house in Eaton, he had been living on a tithe of his former salary as a full-time counsellor in meditation. And happier with it, said Nick, such was his faith.

'Do you take guests – I mean at this weekend retreat at Arlington. I was thinking of Nick – Dr Brooke. If it weren't for him I wouldn't be here now. I know he's not a member of your sect, but if you could stretch a point? I won't know anybody there. I would rather like someone to hold my hand.'

So she was vulnerable, this seemingly self-assured young woman, he thought. 'I'm sure it could be arranged,' he said kindly. 'I have a great regard for Dr Brooke.'

She didn't know what to do with the banana. It was quite a responsibility, as if suddenly she had been put in charge of a holy relic. It didn't seem right to eat it, or throw it away either. She decided in the end to put it out for the birds. Weren't they God's creatures, too?

She was still in the afterglow of meditation when she reached the gatehouse. She walked around, admiring her different possessions as if seeing them for the first time, as in a way she was, for they all had a patina of freshness about them she had never noticed before. I'm looking at the world through rose-coloured spectacles, she thought. Well, it made a change from looking through a glass darkly.

But of course it wore off, this feeling of light-headedness

and light-heartedness. She was back to earth by the evening. Even meditating did not revive the euphoria of the morning's session. For one thing, she kept opening her eyes to see what the time was. The twenty minutes crawled like hours. The statue in the Baptistery was no longer perched on her shoulder, but she was hovering close.

Nick called for her at ten o'clock on Saturday morning, driving his old Volvo, a car as sturdy and reliable as its driver, she considered. He had made no bones about joining her for the weekend. He said he was looking forward to it. He came dressed as if preparing for a walk to the South Pole. 'It's always cold in west Norfolk,' he said.

It was cold here in Thornmere. There had been another sharp frost in the night and again the landscape glittered like silver. The difference today was a brilliant blue sky from which the sun shone down through skein-like clouds. It was the last weekend of February and there were signs of spring everywhere. Blackbirds were squaring up to rivals. Thrushes were marking out their territorial rights with song, bulbs were sprouting in every nook and cranny of the garden and the camellia had put out a few hardy buds.

'All this frost seems out of place,' said Carla.

'I suggest you pack a hot-water bottle.'

She had done more that that, she had packed an extra jogging suit, to use as pyjamas if the need arose. She didn't think satin would be warm enough.

It was a pleasant drive. Most of the countryside was new to Carla, as she'd kept mostly to the east or north in her explorations. This was truly rural Norfolk, bordering on to the Fens. The villages were villages still, many had not yet been 'discovered' by incomers. Nearly every village had its duck pond, which was rare in her part of Norfolk, though today the ducks skidded, rather than paddled, on the frozen surfaces. On one occasion Carla saw an elderly lady in apron and slippers pouring a kettle of boiling water on to the ice. 'It will be frozen over again before she gets back to her cottage,' Nick commented.

'She won't give up. She looks the determined sort and the sun's on her side.'

They stopped once for coffee at an inn they came to at the side of the road. Its main attraction was the open log fire in the grate. Never mind the fumes or the sudden bursts of smoke that came gusting down the chimney, it was giving out warmth. They were the only customers, though a few tables at the back were laid for lunch.

'It's another twenty minutes' drive,' said Nick, coming back with the coffee. 'We can't miss it, the landlord says. Past the lake and then the church and it's on the left-hand side. A stone house with turrets and a wild garden.'

'Sounds interesting,' said Carla, hoping that it too had open fires and a good stock of logs.

'Did Oliver mention that it will be all vegetarian food?'

'No, he didn't.' It didn't matter to Carla. She suddenly smiled. 'But how are you going to get on without meat for a whole weekend?'

'I think I'll survive, unless they offer me nut cutlets. It might be a good idea to recce the village. Some of these way out places have damn fine little restaurants and there's sure to be a pub. I won't starve.'

'It's good of you to come with me when this really isn't your scene.'

'I put you on to it. I feel responsible. In any case, it's all experience. I never shut the door on experience.'

'Have you got a mantra?'

'A what?'

'Never mind.'

The door was opened to them by a nun in a short veil and

smart navy-blue suit with a small crucifix pinned to one lapel. She welcomed them in with a warm smile. 'You're the first of our guests to arrive. Would you like to go through to the drawing-room? Lunch is at one o'clock.'

She opened the door of one of the rooms that led out of the hall and ushered them in. The oak-block flooring in the hall and drawing-room shone like glass. Rugs were few and stragetically placed. Nick took care to step over them rather than on to them, seeing himself taking off like a sleigh. The drawing-room was furnished mostly with chairs of the dining-room variety, two large sofas and a television set. The nun had vanished.

The silence was awe-inspiring. Nick broke it. 'There's no fire,' he said. 'There's no bloody heating at all.' His breath turned to vapour that drifted on the air.

Outside, the sun beckoned. The french doors were unlocked. 'Let's get our circulation moving,' he suggested. 'We'll freeze if we stay in here.'

The grounds were expansive, surrounding the house on all sides. A large area was given over to the growing of vegetables, which seemed feasible, said Nick, if all they lived on were bally vegetables. Beyond was the orchard and carpeting the ground between the trees was a vast spread of gold and white: aconites and snowdrops, growing in harmony.

Carla forgot her qualms, even, for a moment, forgot the cold, her inner self was feasting on a more gentle face of nature. She had never seen anything lovelier, she thought, than that spread of yellow and white. She wished she had brought her sketch-book and that she had her camera. She was distracted by a pair of fieldfares who were stripping a pyracantha hedge of the last of its berries. They were an extra bonus.

'I feel exuberant,' she cried. 'I feel carefree. I honestly think my depression has left me.'

'Or else gone off to find somewhere warmer,' said Nick. His nose glowed red. 'Come, let's have a run round the grounds. Work up an appetite for our cabbage soup.'

It wasn't cabbage soup but lentil, and before that they were taken up to be shown their rooms and introduced to their fellow guests. Carla was delighted to find that she overlooked the gardens. Viewed from a height, the gold and white carpet looked even more effective. The bedroom itself was like an ice-box, colder than it had been in the grounds. The nuns, she had discovered already, lived in the one-time servants wing, behind the green baize door. Carla imagined them sitting round a kitchen range the size of a bus.

She eyed her fellow guests with interest during luncheon. Oliver Peel wasn't among them, he wasn't arriving until the first session in the afternoon, so there was no one to make introductions. Nobody felt like talking much to start with. Some of them (the younger ones) fell on their food as if they hadn't eaten since the day before. The soup was followed by great bowls of winter salad served with home-made granary bread and what passed for butter. The guests were not shy about second helpings, even third and fourth by those with hearty appetites. One woman of her own age, plump and pretty with curly hair, exchanged smiles with her. She was with two others of the same age. Women outnumbered men though there were two sets of husbands and wives. One girl stood out because of her magenta hair and dead-white face. She smoked incessantly until one of the men reminded her that smoking was not allowed, then she flounced out of the room and they didn't see her again until Oliver put in an appearance and they assembled in the drawing-room for their first hour of instruction.

'Well, what did you make of that?' Carla asked Nick when, the session over, they returned to the dining-room to find that cups of hot strong tea and a plate of biscuits had arrived on the table. They had sat (or shivered) through a tape of an evangelist guru who had made a tour of Europe and America preaching his philosophy of meditation. The tape was so old and had been played so often it was like watching figures in a snowstorm. The sound was almost indecipherable.

'I didn't hear too well – there was too much competition from chattering teeth. They sounded like castanets. Did you notice that girl with the odd-coloured hair? What on earth was she wearing?'

'Her sleeping bag.'

Nick grinned. 'Well, full marks to her for ingenuity.' His grin didn't last. It was replaced by one of his serious looks. 'Did you realise she's a junkie?'

'I've never met a drug addict. How can you tell?'

'I didn't say she's an addict, but she's heavily into drugs. I've treated too many of them not to see the signs. I reckon half the young ones here this weekend are on drugs, but give them their due. They're trying to kick the habit or they wouldn't be here. Let's hope Oliver Peel can do something for them.'

'He did something for me,' said Carla. 'The day I enrolled. I went full of scepticism and came away converted.'

'And nothing you have experienced here has changed your mind?'

'On the contrary.'

'Good.'

They found another opportunity to walk in the grounds before it got too dark to see, this time in company with the couple who had given a lift to their instructor. The man, Mr Cooper, knew a lot about plants and gave them their biological names when pointing them out. Only later did they discover that he ran a nursery garden. They seemed such a well-adjusted couple, Carla wondered why they thought they needed meditation.

She asked the name of a delightful flowering shrub that had taken her eye that morning. Its scent alone made it a must for her garden.

'Viburnum farreri. An old favourite and one of the earliest viburnums to flower. Is your garden exposed?'

'Very.'

'The flowers can stand up to about ten degrees of frost. If it can grow here I should think it would grow anywhere.'

Mrs Cooper was walking behind them with Nick. Like her husband, she spoke with a soft Norfolk burr. 'Don't let him con you into buying anything,' she said. 'He can't forget business even for a weekend.'

'What I find so surprising', said Nick, 'is that a couple like you should be here at all.'

'I was thinking the same about you,' said Mrs Cooper, smiling shyly.

'He came to hold my hand,' said Carla over her shoulder.

Mr Cooper gave what sounded like a grunt. 'You could say we're here for the same purpose. Holding our daughter's hand. That's what we came for.'

'She's the one who was anxious to join the group,' put in Mrs Cooper hastily. They had come to a halt by the flowering carpet which now, in the last light of the day, began to lose its colour but not its subtle mossy fragrance. By unspoken consent they did not walk on any further, but turned and headed back towards the house. The air began to bite.

Mrs Cooper seemed compelled to tell Carla more about her daughter. 'It isn't that, you know, there's anything wrong with her, but she does get so much help from transcendental meditation. She persuaded me to join and then I persuaded Edward, because you wouldn't get him to come to anything like this normally. Then at the last minute,' here, Mrs Cooper's voice faltered a bit, 'she wasn't able to come . . .'

'You mean that wretched little toe-rag wouldn't let her.' Her husband's voice was full of irritation. 'Keep to the truth, woman. That's what we're here for, isn't it – to seek the path of truth.' He turned to Nick. 'He's the reason her nerves are in such a state. He's the reason we're on this transcending lark, or whatever they call it, this weekend. The bastard hadn't even crawled out of the woodwork when we called for her this morning. We could have whisked her away without him knowing, but she said he had threatened to leave her if she went. Good riddance to bad rubbish is what I say to that, but she wouldn't go against him.'

Mrs Cooper looked uncomfortable. 'I think it's time for our next session, dear,' she said, taking her husband's arm.

She hurried him on. Carla and Nick lingered behind, reluctant to leave the peace and solitude of the garden.

'I think if you were to borrow one of the couches and set up shop in one of the spare rooms, you'd do a marvellous trade,' said Carla flippantly.

But Nick wasn't in the mood for flippancy. 'There's a hell of a lot of unhappiness among this group,' he said. 'I'm going to have a whack at this meditation business. I might need it before the weekend is over. Tell me your mantra, Carla.'

'I can't – it's a secret.'

'Then think one up for me. Short and syllabic, I think you described it.'

'Ba-na-na?' she suggested.

Supper was much like lunch, but with a greater variety of

salads. Coffee was left out for them in the drawing-room. An electric fire had made a welcome appearance in the hearth. The girl with magenta hair and a youth with acne took full possession of it, squatting in front of it in the lotus position. Carla found herself a place on one of the couches, wedged between the plumpish girl with the natural curls and a twitchy woman who sniffed continuously. Many had followed the magenta-haired girl's dodge for keeping warm and were wearing their sleeping bags. Some just had their faces showing. Carla, looking round the room, bit her lip to preserve her sobriety. They looked, she thought, like a lot of shapeless Russian dolls. All the same, she wished she had thought to bring *her* sleeping bag. A jogging suit was a poor substitute.

The woman with the curls introduced herself as Karen. 'How long have you and your partner been practising meditation?'

'He isn't my partner, he's just a friend. He hasn't practised it at all. I've been doing it a week.'

'A *week*! Oh heavens, I've been doing it for six months and I'm not half as relaxed as you. I can't get the hang of meditation. I keep opening my eyes to see the time by my watch – it always seems such a long twenty minutes. I really come to these weekend meetings for the food anyway. I adore vegetarian food.'

'Can't you have vegetarian food at home?'

'It's not easy. You see my husband is a butcher. He thinks I'm daft.'

After good-nights all round and an exchange of glances with Nick, Carla, going to her room, found to her extreme delight a hot water bottle in her bed. She sent her blessings winging to the heads of the holy sisters. They were similar, she fancied, to the invisible servants that waited on Beauty in the Beast's castle. Never seen. Moving noiselessly and effortlessly in the service of their cold and ever hungry guests. They had visited every bedroom and left a warm offering in the bed. Now she had two hot water bottles, one to cuddle and one for her feet that for the past two hours had been like blocks of ice.

It had been an interesting evening, with much discussion on the merits of meditation. Most there, Carla included, agreed they got benefit from it. Others were more sceptical. Some, like the Coopers, could not make up their mind one way or the other.

Oliver tried his best to convince them. He told them, and he was whole-heartedly sincere in this, that if enough believers could come together and encircle any part of the world where fighting was taking place and sit there in one huge unbroken circle, silently meditating, the fighting would stop. 'Meditation on such a scale', he explained, 'would be powerful enough to reach out and negate the aggression. Peace would break out.

'Such a feeling of love for one's neighbour would come over the protagonists that war, eventually, would cease altogether,' he added to a mostly doubtful audience. Carla thought him brave to come out with such ideas in the face of so much disbelief. She could feel cynicism coming in waves towards her, though nobody voiced their doubts. They might think Oliver something of a simpleton, but a decent and sincere type who kept firm to his beliefs, so they kept their doubts to themselves. Nobody wanted to hurt his feelings.

For herself, much as she wanted to believe in such a miracle she found it impossible. How could it be arranged anyway? How about the sheer logistics of bringing millions of believers together? And if that could not be achieved, how could their philosophy be proved or disproved? Still, it was a thought-provoking idea and sent her off to bed with her faith in the essential goodness of human nature deepening.

She wasn't ready for sleep. The day's events rolled before her inner eye like a kaleidoscope of images. She had made a warm enfolding dent in the middle of the bed which she was loath to lose, otherwise she would have been tossing and turning. She remembered something Oliver had said about using the mantra to woo sleep, the only time it was deemed advisable to meditate lying down. She tried it and almost before she had said her password to peace a half-dozen times she had fallen into a dreamless sleep from which she was awakened by a scratching at the door. Light was streaming through the curtains. She squinted at her travelling clock. Breakfast was at eight thirty. She had an hour.

The scratching came again, so she hadn't imagined it. She padded to the door in the sports socks she was wearing in lieu of bedsocks. Nick was standing there, wearing a fisherman's sweater over his pyjamas and holding two steaming mugs.

'I hope that's tea you're carrying,' she said.

He thought he had never seen her so desirable as now, with her chestnut hair all tangled, her beautiful violet eyes full of sleep and her jogging suit crumpled.

They sat on the side of her bed and took large, appreciative gulps. He smelled of pine bath salts and aftershave, though the day before he had bewailed the fact that he was minus his beard.

'Did you go down to the forbidden zone behind the green baize door?'

'I wouldn't dare. I've already heard preparations going on down there. I found what at college we called a gippy cupboard, a recess with tea- and coffee-making materials just along the corridor, next to the bathroom. There's lashings of hot water, by the way. I've had my bath.'

She finished her tea and handed him back the empty mug. 'I didn't see you to say good-night properly. What happened to you?'

'I sat up talking to Oliver. He's a funny chap. So utterly sold on this idea. I mean, creating peace in the world by world-wide meditation. I ask you.'

'You think it bosh.'

'I don't think it bosh – I just think it's a pipe-dream. Nice idea, though.' He looked at her. 'You're shivering. Better go and have your bath.'

Other men would have suggested getting into bed with her and warming her up that way, but Nick was a stickler for the rules, she thought, as later she wallowed in hot water up to her chin until someone in a hurry banged on the door. As she passed the staircase on the way back to her room she thought she felt heat coming up from downstairs. Perhaps the sisters had lit a real fire. Wishful thinking, she discovered, for when she went down not even the one-bar electric fire was on. Yet it seemed milder. There had been no frost in the night. Drops of what had been frost now hung from every branch and twig, glinting like jewels in the sun. She felt amazingly fit.

Breakfast was a huge tureen of porridge from which they helped themselves. There were also muesli and prunes, baskets of bread cut into doorsteps and stacks of toast. Latecomers, and there were many, scraped round the porridge pot and ate cold toast.

'What a time to get up on a Sunday,' said the magenta-haired girl moodily.

Carla and Nick had their last walk in the grounds before the morning session started. Mr and Mrs Cooper joined them.

'My husband wants to apologise for the way he carried on yesterday,' said Mrs Cooper, pushing her husband forward like some recalcitrant child. 'It's not like him to go off the handle like that. He should keep calm because of his high blood pressure. That's why we joined the group in the first place.'

'We joined the group because of Rosie,' retorted her husband, shrugging her off. 'She asked us to. She didn't like going on her own, she said. She used not to be like that. She was always a hail-fellow-well-met sort of girl until she married that bastard.'

'Ted!' wailed Mrs Cooper in panic. 'You promised.'

'Let him say it, if it makes him feel better,' said Nick. 'A swear word now and again gets the poison out of the system – and lowers the blood pressure,' he added helpfully.

Mrs Cooper didn't seem to appreciate that kind of help. Her tone was hostile. 'In that case my husband should have the lowest blood pressure on record. If you'll excuse us, we have some packing to do. We're not staying for lunch. We're anxious to get home.'

'I somehow don't think they're getting much benefit from their TM,' said Nick, once the Coopers were out of earshot.

'They're not the only ones. Half of them here fall asleep instead.'

'I must admit I'm in that catagory myself.'

Lunch was put on early that day and the group dispersed after one last communal session of meditation. Oliver came round to say goodbye to each member personally. He asked Carla if she would like to attend the monthly meetings they held at the TM centre in Norwich. She said she would. She still felt she needed all the help she could get. They were approached by the magenta-haired girl and the pimply youth who had now become inseparable, to ask if they were going anywhere near Norwich.

'We bypass it.'

'Could you give us a lift to the bus station?'

Nick, who had been looking forward to having Carla to himself, agreed reluctantly.

'They haven't spoken to us all the weekend,' said Carla heatedly. 'As a matter of fact, the girl's been giving me some very dirty looks as if she despises all that I stand for. Now that they want something from us, they've come over all smarmy.'

'They're just a couple of kids.'

The 'couple of kids' kept them waiting twenty minutes in the car. When they eventually arrived the youth asked if they could wait another 'sec', as he had something to collect. They waited ten minutes. He returned, breathless, clutching a fistful of snowdrops and aconites. 'I nearly had a close encounter of an embarrassing kind,' he informed them.

Nick raised his eyebrows. 'Did you have permission to pick those?' he asked.

'Aw, they won't miss them – there are masses of them. They're for my landlady to soften her up. I forgot to tell her I'd be away for the weekend.'

All four gave a collective sigh of relief when they reached Norwich bus station. It had been an uncomfortable journey, silent for the most part because the two in the back were not conversationalists and though she tried her best, Carla was unable to make contact with them on any point, not even transcendentally speaking. The last time she looked back at them they were both fast asleep propping each other up. She couldn't see the posy anywhere, she hoped it wasn't squashed between them – they were sitting that close.

At the bus station they both got out without a word, without saying thank you either, thought Carla, but at the last moment the girl turned back. 'Thank you for the lift,' she said, somewhat grudgingly.

She looked ill. Her face had an unhealthy pallor, smudges underlined her eyes. Pity took the place of Carla's indignation. 'Take care of yourself,' she heard herself saying, like some fussy old aunt.

The girl coloured up. 'I know how to look after number one,' she said. She caught up with the boy and said something to him and they both laughed. Yet at the bus-stop she turned and waved.

'You've made a conquest there,' said Nick.

'Is she a drug addict?'

'She was. Oliver was telling me about her. He admires her; she's trying so hard to kick the habit. He said that's why she comes to these meetings. I thought she came to eat.'

They drove in silence for a while, then Nick said, 'Did you really get any benefit from the weekend?'

Had she got any benefit from the weekend? More than she realised at the time, perhaps. It suddenly dawned on her that she hadn't given Tony a thought in the past two days. Had he been frozen out of existence – the man who had shown her the delights of Florence and had instilled in her his obsession with Renaissance art? She would always be grateful to him for that, but gratitude wasn't undying love. She could learn to live with gratitude. Yes, she had benefited. She had more confidence in the future now.

'You're very quiet,' said Nick. 'Are you meditating?'

'In a way, but it has just struck me that the gatehouse will strike as cold as that convent when I first go into it.'

'I thought of that. I intend to unload you at Rodings first and let Mum thaw you out, while I nip up the lane and switch on your heating. Then I'll come and join you round the fire and indulge in my Sunday afternoon pastime – tea and crumpets, with the butter oozing out of all the holes.'

'How do you know your mother will have any crumpets?'

'Because I arranged it all before we left.'

On the same Saturday that Carla was walking around the grounds of Arlington House with Nick, admiring the snowdrops and aconites, Milly was wandering round the market at Beckton, as she had done every Saturday since she decided to buy the little house in Market Street.

Completion day was 16 March, so she hadn't long to wait before she moved into her own home. Not that she could complain about the one she shared with Jessie, who made her feel not so much a lodger as a long-time friend, but she was anxious to have her own bits and pieces around her again and to be mistress of her own domain.

Once she was settled, she'd be able to pick up the threads in her search for Tom. Not a day went past without her thinking of him. Not a night passed without her praying for his welfare. All the time she had been negotiating for the purchase of the house in Market Street she had imagined what it would be like if he were moving in with her. She got it into her head that she was preparing a home for him too. She knew it was a foolish notion that might only bring her grief in the long run, but it didn't hurt to fantasise and she got such pleasure from doing so.

She'd learn how to make him rabbit stew and how to make a steak and kidney pudding, which was even more ambitious. They'd go for long, slow walks together when the evenings drew out, either down to the river or round the empty market square. They'd pop into the King's Head for a snifter, before returning to the comfort of their cottage home – not that Tom had been a drinker, not compared to Fred Lewis, but he had liked an occasional glass of bitter. And she would enjoy anything in Tom's company, she knew that now. She forgot in her fancies that he was now a man in his seventies. When she conjured up his image it was always as she had last seen him, blue eyes blazing, expression grim, shutting the door in her face.

He'd have forgotten that, she thought. He wasn't one to nurse a grievance. She was the one for that.

She had stopped at a stall that sold remnants of household linen and her eye was caught by a piece at the bottom of a pile. She pulled it out. It was satin chintz, patterned with a design of ferns in autumn colours. She rooted around and found another piece to match. Enough here for two cushions. Just what she wanted to set off the sandy coloured two-seater sofa she had bought from the young Hinds. It would be good to have some sewing to do again, to feel a needle between her fingers. She could, she knew, at any time borrow Jessie Stoneham's sewing machine, but it would be a challenge to get back to sewing by hand. She had been idle for too long.

As she was paying for her purchases Victoria, pushing Tom in his wheelchair, was heading for the public library, housed in part of the old Corn Exchange. She was negotiating her way between the market stalls when a stout little person, stepping back without looking behind her, collided with the chair and was nearly projected into the old man's lap.

'Look where you're going, can't you?' growled Tom.

'Oh, I'm so sorry,' cried Victoria.

'Oh, my God,' exclaimed Milly. She was staring at Tom as if she were a rabbit hypnotised by a snake.

'Are you hurt. I did rather ram into you,' said Victoria, blushing with confusion.

'No, I'm not hurt. It's just that I . . . I thought I saw a ghost, that's all.' Milly drew her tongue over dry lips. 'You're from Carisbrooke House, aren't you? This is Mr – er – Mr?'

'Thomas. Tom Thomas. Are you sure you're not hurt? You've gone very pale.'

'Just cold, dearie. Someone just walked over my grave. Well, it's too chilly to keep you here talking, you'll both get cold. I think I'll get myself a cup of tea . . .'

She needed something stronger than tea. She made for the King's Head rather than Anne's Pantry. Being market day it was crowded, not a seat to be had, except at the counter. She hated sitting at the bar, it made her feel like a barfly, but she had no choice – either sit down or fall down.

Tom. It couldn't be Tom – and yet she'd know those furious blue eyes anywhere, though the rest of him had changed out of recognition. It seemed inconceivable that while she had been chasing around London or Aberdeen, he had been safe all the time in a nursing home in this obscure little market town.

'You've got a sense of humour, haven't you, Lord,' she said, taking another sip of her brandy. 'But thank you all the same for finding him for me in the end. I always hoped you would.'

She finished off the rest of the brandy in one go, went into the Ladies to tidy up and dab her nose with powder, then looked at her watch. She had half an hour before young Kevin Smithson was due to pick her up. Half an hour was more than ample to introduce herself to the matron of Carisbrooke Nursing Home and exchange some information.

February frost had given gave way to March sunshine, which in turn had given way to April showers. The garden of the gatehouse was transferred into a bower to which Carla and Philippa, both working industriously in the studio, would turn their attention from time to time. Well, they had to get inspiration from somewhere, said Philippa, and one didn't get it by staring at a brick wall.

They were collaborating on a children's book, with Philippa providing the text. Carla had learnt from Nick that his mother in her younger days had written articles and short stories for children which were published in various annuals, and had once embarked on a book but had never finished it. Carla, struggling unsuccessfully with an unfamiliar medium, turned to Philippa for help which culminated in the Big Idea – that they would produce a children's picture book between them.

They sometimes worked up at Rodings, but as the weather got warmer, more often in Carla's studio. Philippa's unfinished book came out of mothballs. It was a simple but delightful tale of two children spending a holiday on their grandparents' farm and befriending an old chap, or Mr Chap as they called him, who lived in a caravan. It was a flying caravan. It had adventures. Not in outer space but just a short way up in the sky – about the same height as a witch's broomstick, high enough to clear the church steeple. They became so engrossed, their imaginations ran riot. Carla, who firmly believed she couldn't paint figures, got carried away with her caricatures of the farmer and his wife and little dumplings of children; and Philippa thought Mr Chap himself, with his rosy cheeks and halo of silver hair, was a masterpiece. Both Leo and Nick were anxious to see this masterpiece, but the women were keeping their work under wraps until it was finished,

Larry, however, would not be put off. He said he would have to see a sample of their work before he could approach an agent. His verdict was to keep at it. 'I think you're on to something here, girls,' he said. 'I can see this has great commercial possibilities.'

'I don't like that word "commercial",' said Carla doubtfully.

'It pays the bills, kiddo. Some works of art don't begin to make money until long after the creator's death. I presume you don't want to wait until then? With all this industry, do you still find time to do your stint at Carisbrooke House?'

It was only once a week. She had taken over the duties of the library lady who had suddenly found herself a full-time job. The work wasn't demanding, but the circumstances were. At times Carla had to steel herself to venture into this domain of wasted bodies and atrophied minds. But the residents' uncomplaining acceptance of their lot, their stoicism in the face of adversity (with minor exceptions) was an example to her, as were the patience and good humour of the staff. More than ever she felt ashamed of her recent depression, which now seemed so trivial in comparison.

Never did the transcendental meditation seem more beneficial than after a morning or afternoon at Carisbrooke House. She would arise refreshed and eager to get on with her painting. She had never felt such enthusiasm for work since her early days in Florence, and her enthusiasm in turn infected Philippa.

Philippa took her by surprise one day by breaking a prolonged but busy silence with the remark, 'I wish you could bring yourself to love my son. That way I would gain a daughter.'

Carla took a moment or two to recover. 'I like him tremendously, but . . . I just can't fall in love to order,' she said defensively.

'I didn't ask you to fall in love with him – just to love him.'

'I wouldn't know the difference.'

'One falls in and out of love indiscriminately, but love can last for ever and what's more grow stronger with time.'

Carla raised her eyes and met those of the woman opposite. Smoky grey, like her son's, and just as direct. 'Are you trying to tell me that you weren't in love with Nick's father?'

'Not when I married him – that came later. Now I am more than ever in love with him.'

They worked on again in silence, a silence that throbbed with possibilities and which this time Carla broke. 'I'd do anything for you, Philippa, you know that, but I can't promise to fall in love with your son.'

'To like tremendously is a good foundation to build on.'

Towards the end of April, Sophie came down on a flying visit on her own. Carla met her at Norwich, picking her out of crowds at the station by her attire. She was wearing a long black-and-white cotten skirt and over that a hand-knitted purple lambswool sweater which came nearly to her knees. Each time Carla saw her she looked more and more like the conventional student. She was letting her hair grow again and wore it scooped back in a large purple hair-slide.

'No Matthew this time,' said Carla, successfully hiding her relief.

'No Matthew,' said Sophie without any trace of regret.

'May I know why?'

'I outgrew him, Carla, as simple as that. He's ten years older than I am, yet he'll never be an adult, not in some ways. He's one of the Peter Pans of this world.'

'Is there anyone else to take his place?'

'No, and I don't intend that there will be until I've got my degree – that's the most important thing in my life now. I'm moving back home, it will be cheaper than paying rent and the journey isn't too far. Old Mr Hetherington died, did I tell you? I can have his room now. Dad has taken his place at the bridge table. He's not a very good player, but he's improving with pactice. Yes, things have worked out quite well at Maple Avenue. How are things with you?'

Carla couldn't wait to get Sophie back to the gatehouse to show her the intended book. It was all in loose pages as yet, her sketches and Philippa's text. She put them in order.

Sophie was impressed. 'Well, I'd buy it for one,' she said, when she had read it through a second time. 'I wouldn't hesitate to buy a copy. How much will it cost?'

'The first thing we have to do is to find a publisher and that's a lot harder than actually writing a book, so I've been told. But this is only the rough copy, it will be months before it's ready to be sent out.'

Sophie insisted on walking down to the river that evening. She said if Carla had lived looking on to the Clerkenwell Road, she'd want to rest her eyes on something fresh and green for a change. They were in a giggly mood, like a couple of girls let out of school shaking off, for the time being, the restraints of adulthood. There was no sign of Nick. The tarpaulin was lashed over the cockpit of his boat, the launch made fast to the mooring-line. Carla tried not to show her disappointment. She hadn't seen him for a couple of weeks and wondered if he were avoiding her.

Sophie, fascinated, was watching a frog amongst the reeds with a smaller frog clinging to its back. 'There's a mummy frog taking her youngster for a swim,' she said delightedly.

'They are actually in the act of mating. The smaller one is the male.'

'What fascinating things go on in the country.'

Two ducks waddled past them, slipped into the river and started to copulate. 'They can only do it in water,' Carla explained.

'Ye Gods, they're all at it.'

'It's that time of year.'

'It's putting ideas in my head. Let's get back and have something to drink. I need some lime-juice. Have you got any lime-juice?'

'Yes, I have lime-juice. But why lime-juice?'

'It's a passion-killer. My grandfather told me it was issued to the troops in France during the First World War.'

'Did it kill his passion?'

'He didn't say.'

Sophie brought up the subject of Tony that evening. She had received a long letter from Signora Offredi giving her the latest news of their one-time acquaintances. Tony was back, renting an apartment near the Boboli Gardens and at present looking for a studio, as he wanted to start taking his masterclasses again. Signorina Angelica was in partnership with him.

'Partnership. Is that what they call it now?' said Carla, surprising herself by her lack of interest. 'Does that mean his marriage is all washed-up?'

'I never did see Tony as a married man, did you? He's only really had one love in his life and that's Florence. I'm surprised he left his baby son, though.'

'He never did seem to have any interest in babies,' said Carla harshly. 'Unless they had been sculptured by Donatello.' Her expression softened. 'Still, I wish him luck. I don't bear him any grudges.'

'You're more forbearing than I could ever be.'

'No, just grateful. He opened my eyes to a lot of things.'

'Meaning Florence?'

'Meaning Florence among much else.'

When next morning, she returned to the gatehouse after seeing Sophie off at Norwich, she found a letter bearing an Italian stamp on the mat. Even before she stooped to pick it up she recognised the handwriting Her heart began to hammer.

Dear Carla, [Tony wrote],

You no doubt will hear, or perhaps already have heard, many stories about me – what a rotter I am, etc., etc. I make no excuses. I wasn't cut out to be a husband, let alone a father, but I would have stayed and tried to make a go of it if I had been given the chance. I wasn't given the chance and I'm not blaming that on my father-in-law. He acted in what he considered was the best way for his daughter. He was right – I could never have made her happy and there's somebody else in the wings waiting for that opportunity. It's his now. I parted from Vanessa amicably and I shall be welcomed back on visits. Naturally I want to keep in touch with my son.

But I wanted you to know the truth, Carla. I know the stories that you hear from others will be garbled. I'm not making excuses for my behaviour, but I have my regrets – bitter regrets, for the most part. I could not let you go on thinking you had no talent for water-colours. You have a refreshing talent. I could not tell you so because I was jealous. You know I couldn't bear competition. Forgive me, Carla, and God bless you.

He had not signed it. She read it through again and wiped her tears away with the back of her hand. She felt as if she had been given a reprieve. She would be able to think of him in future without pain. It was all in the past now and though it had caused her many a sleepless night at times, her relationship with Tony had enriched her in other ways.

She bent down and thrust the letter between the bars of the kitchen boiler. There was no point in keeping it. The words were etched on her mind.

Philippa called on a social visit a day later. They did no work, just idled, mostly in the garden, listening to the birdsong and breathing in the heavy fragrance of the wallflowers that Carla had planted beneath the kitchen window.

Nick, Carla discovered for the first time, had gone to America for a conference and had stayed on to visit his in-laws and old colleagues. Philippa and Leo had taken advantage of his absence to make a quick visit to Edinburgh. While there, Philippa had bought herself a pleated skirt in Royal Stuart tartan and was wearing it today with a black silk top. She said she and Leo tried to get to Edinburgh at least once a year, twice if they could manage it. They had a special affinity with Auld Reekie, she said, they went there whenever their batteries needed recharging. She had come to ask Carla a special favour.

'It's this little dog I have to collect from the dogs' home – I picked it out before I went away. No, it's not for me; I bought it on impulse for Nicholas. The old, old story, bought when a puppy as a Christmas present for some children, but as soon as it got too big the parents didn't want to know . . .'

'I thought you said it was little?'

'I meant it was still young. It's not fully grown yet. It's adorable. Seven-eighths border collie and one-eighth fox, if its eyes are anything to go by. They are beautiful, the loveliest golden eyes you ever saw. I would love to keep him for myself, but Leo says it's too late at our age to embark on another pet as it could easily outlive us.'

Philippa looked appealingly at the younger woman. 'Nick will love it when he sees it, but he always said he wouldn't have another dog after Ranger. He might not take it kindly from me, his interfering old mum. He doesn't like a *fait accompli,* he likes to think things over very carefully before he makes a move. And he wouldn't buy a dog from a pet shop anyway. He'd go to a breeder.'

'But I thought you said this came from a dogs' home?'

'It did, but before that it was in a pet shop. I spotted him when I went over the dogs' home with the WI and fell in love with him straight away.' Again Philippa looked beseechingly at her companion. 'What I am trying to do, in my roundabout fashion, is to ask you if you would deliver the dog for me. Nick wouldn't refuse you anything.'

And that was how Sam became Carla's lodger for the next day or two, much against her inclination at first. She was soon won over, even though he was not fully house-trained, and even worse, chewed through the main stem of her Nellie Moser which was just breaking out into fresh leaf.

He did more damage to her lawn than the moles. He used it as a trampoline until he had softened it up, then dug lumps out of it with his sharp nose. She forgave him everything. When Philippa rang her to say that Nick was home again and was spending the next few days on his boat, her spirits plummeted. Her honeymoon with Sam was over.

She walked him to the river, or rather, he walked her, straining and choking at the end of the leash until he was nearly on the point of throttling himself. She doubted whether she would be able to contain him when he was fully grown, but it wouldn't be her problem then. She nearly turned back.

Nick spotted her from the deck of his old cruiser and came to meet her. He looked well and bronzed from his short sojourn in California and he looked from her to Sam, who was greeting him as hysterically as he greeted all newcomers, with a quizzical smile. 'So this is Sam,' he said.

'You know about him!'

'Dad told me. He thought I should be forewarned. Friendly little chap, isn't he? Yes, I think I could get quite attached to him in time.'

'I've got quite attached to him in a very short time.'

The smile slowly faded from his eyes to be replaced by an expression of such earnestness that it slightly unnerved her. 'I've missed you,' he said. 'All I could think of while I was away was coming home to you. You know I can't offer you anything but marriage, and I do know what love is all about. I read that once on a piece of a charred letter that had blown over into the lane from your garden.'

But she had forgotten about the bonfire in the garden. She had even forgotten about the so-called dream letters she had once written but never posted to Tony.

'I know nothing about marriage,' she said warily.

'I do and its good. I can highly recommend it.'

She was still so unsure. He wanted to take her in his arms and kiss the troubled look from her eyes, but one false move now could put him back months. 'Have you no feelings for me at all?'

'Oh yes.' Her smile was encouraging. 'When with you I always feel that I have come into a safe harbour.'

'If that isn't a sound basis for marriage, I don't know what is,' he said softly.

They had forgotten Sam. He had whimpered around them

for a while, then, not getting any attention, had trotted down the gangplank to explore the strange and tempting smells of the river bank. There, he had put up a water-vole and his howls of triumph had sent a covey of ducks on the wing. When he had extricated himself from the reeds and shaken the muddy water out of his coat he found his way back to the cockpit. He could hear voices and laughter from below. Contented, he stretched out in the warm spring sunshine and fell asleep. All was well with his world.

Milly had settled happily in the little house in Market Street and several weeks had passed before one afternoon, answering the door to an unexpected knock, she came face to face with Carla. Her smile broke out like a sunburst. 'I was just thinking about you,' she said. 'I've been hearing such very nice things about you – you're going to be married.'

'And I've been hearing the most extraordinary things about you,' Carla answered. 'You've found your husband.' She was carrying a huge bunch of cottage garden flowers and a small parcel done up in pink tissue paper. 'Just a small house-warming present, and my apologies for taking so long about it. I've been meaning to call so many times, but you know what they say about good intentions. Actually, I've been busy with my painting and other things, but that's no excuse. I should have called on you long before this.'

Milly brushed aside her excuses. 'I'm never in nowadays – I'm usually up at Carisbrooke. I looked for you every time I visited, but you had either just left or hadn't arrived, or it wasn't your day for calling. I suppose Victoria told you.'

'About finding your husband? Everybody's talking about it. It's unbelievable. Oh, Milly, I'm so happy for you. Do tell me how it all came about.'

It was over tea in the little parlour that overlooked the street, decorated in autumn tones and with hardly room for a pin between the porcelain and crystal figurines on the mantelpiece and shelves, that Carla was given the details. The astonishing revelation that Old Tom was the missing husband. The tedious interviews with officials until the matter was finally cleared up. The nursing home's bewildered acceptance that their mystery resident wasn't Welsh at all but Norfolk born and from Thornmere Green, of all places. Thomas Stevens, would you believe, not Tom Thomas. Then the flurry of excitement blowing over, things settling down and going on much as before except that now Milly was a daily visitor and took it upon herself to take sole charge of her husband while she was there. To the staff and residents he was still Old Tom, except that he was even more quiet these days, if that was at all possible, than he had been before.

Carla was taken to see over the cottage. It seemed to her like a Wendy house – a life-sized doll's house. Not one for frills and flounces and lace trimmings herself, here they looked as if they belonged. All the same, it was difficult to imagine the lugubrious Tom in such a setting. Not that there was any likelihood of that. Milly had given up all such hopes within a few days of being reunited with her husband, she said. He needed expert attention. He needed twenty-four-hour professional care. If she had been younger she wouldn't have hesitated, but she knew her limits. She salved her conscience, she told Carla, by visiting him as often as she could.

Later she walked with Carla to the top of the street. 'Thank you for coming. I've enjoyed our little natter. And thank you for my house-warming present.'

'It's rather like bringing coals to Newcastle,' Carla answered with a laugh. She had given Milly an alabaster statuette of a small cherub holding a fish nearly as big as himself. 'I got it in Florence,' she said. 'I couldn't resist buying it. He has such an angelic smile.'

Carla's smile, if not angelic, had something other-worldly about it, Milly thought, looking fondly up at the girl. It was over a year now since chance had thrown them together on the Norwich-bound train. Then, Carla had had a sad and listless way about her, now she was vibrant with happiness.

Milly squeezed her hand. 'I love my present from Florence. It will have pride of place on my mantelpiece,' she said.

Market Street being so narrow, Carla had left her car parked in the square. It wasn't until she was fitting the key into the lock that she remembered she hadn't given Milly the date of her wedding. It didn't matter. Milly's name would be heading the wedding guest list.

Every time Milly entered her little house a feeling of well-being swept over her. Even now, returning from seeing Carla off, a matter of only a few yards or so, she felt the assurance of a safe home-coming to a traveller. Perhaps it was because she had never had a home of her own before, except for a time the rented house in Islington? That had also been number 22. She thought of it as a happy coincidence. She had had many a good time in that little house near Islington Green.

But when she shut the street door behind her, her mind reverted, as it always did, to Tom. At first he had ignored her, as he did all those he didn't trust or didn't know, but gradually he listened more and more to her chatter. She spent all her time, when she wasn't pushing him, talking to him. She had a prodigious memory and she treated him to a blow-by-blow account of the events of their short married life. She took him step by step through her subsequent career, referring to Fred Lewis when she had to as her boss.

Whether Tom took it in or not she didn't know, whenever he looked at her it was with a faded but unrelenting stare. It was like trying to converse with a tailor's dummy, she thought, except that Tom was no tailor's dummy, just the reverse, but still she persisted.

And one day she was rewarded. He actually responded, the first time he had uttered a word in her presence. 'You're not my Milly,' he said.

'What do you mean, I'm not your Milly? Of course I'm your Milly. How would I know so much about the two of us if I wasn't?'

'You're not my Milly,' he insisted. 'I could lift my Milly single-handed. It'ud take a fork-lift truck to get you off the ground.'

Well, it was a start, she thought, wiping her eyes. She was hurt of course, but she had to laugh.

Matters had improved since then. He even threw her an odd word now and again, like a crust to a hungry dog. Once, she thought she saw recognition flicker in and out of his eyes. It was a milestone in their relationship. After that, she found she didn't have to talk so much. They could sit for long periods in silent communion, often out on the veranda, for she remembered that Tom was at his happiest when out of doors.

It was a glorious day in early June when they had sat out together for the last time. The wistaria climbing up the wall of the house drooped late-flowering fronds of blossom all about them. Bumble-bees tumbled among the lavender and rival blackbirds tried to outdo each other in song. Milly dozed and dreamed of Carla's wedding. August wasn't all that long to wait. She was making herself a cornflower-blue blouse to go with her navy-blue suit. It was to be a quiet wedding, she had been warned, only the family and a few friends. She felt honoured to have been asked. Of all things, they were honeymooning in Nick's old boat. They could only spare a few days anyway, as Nick had already used up his annual leave. They would take a real honeymoon later. And they weren't even moving into a new home, but using the flat over the surgery and the gatehouse down the lane as the fancy took them. A funny arrangement to Milly's tidy mind, but she expected they would inherit that lovely old Queen Anne house at the other end of the village when the time came.

She was pulled back from the brink of sleep by something scrabbling at her arm. It was Tom, trying to reach for her hand. She gave it to him, small, soft and dimpled, and his, large, horny, and emaciated, closed over it.

'I scoured London for you, Milly,' he said. His voice was little more than a breathless whisper, but quite comprehensible. 'I never gave up hope of finding you.'

Her eyes brimmed over. 'I know that, dear,' she said.

'I couldn't come before. There was the old man to look after and my job to do.' The effort to talk left him out of breath, but he struggled on. 'I went to the house in Grant Street, but it had been pulled down. The whole bloody street had gone. It's a block of flats now.'

'I know, dear, but don't let that upset you, it all happened a long time ago. We've found each other again. That's all that matters.'

She longed to know more about those years that were lost to both of them, but that little forage into the past had exhausted him. She knew by the slackening of his grasp that he had fallen asleep again. His breathing became less laboured. She was not quite fully awake herself, but the blackbirds kept her from drifting off. She wasn't sentimental about birds and wished they would shut up. Still, it was pleasant sitting here with Tom. Romantic in a way, to be united in their old age. She didn't regret the past, all in all she'd had a good life and the quest for Tom and finding him had given her something to live for, for she refused to accept that she had nothing to live for. She dozed and awoke again. Tom had fallen into a deep sleep, his head lolling, his mouth slightly open. He looked peaceful. Her mouth was dry. She could murder a cup of tea and as if in answer to her prayer Victoria appeared with the tea trolley.

'Cup of tea, Mrs Stevens? Tom's asleep. What shall I do about his tea?'

'He won't like being missed out.'

But they couldn't wake him up. First Victoria tried on her own. Then Milly, getting desperate, shook him violently.

Victoria gently intervened. 'Don't do that, Mrs Stevens, it won't do any good and you're only upsetting yourself. I'll go and fetch Sister Sylvia.'

Milly took Tom's hand and put it to her lips. Tears rained heedlessly down her cheeks. 'You could've waited for me, Tom. We could have got to the pearly gates together,' she said.

The little house in Market Street seemed quieter than ever when she returned to it in the cool of the evening. The hours she had spent in Matron's room, trying to get through the endless cups of tea that came at regular intervals, while the necessary but irksome tasks following a death had to be fulfilled. They let her go at last, but with reluctance. A bed had been made up for her in one of the rooms, but she wanted the solace of her own little house. Finally, someone brought her home.

'Are you sure you'll be all right?' she was asked. 'You don't want anybody to stay the night with you?'

Yes, she would be all right. No, she didn't want anybody to stay the night. She knew just what she had to do. It was something she had planned when she first received her own death sentence. Secreted away in an old handbag was a cache of sleeping tablets she had been adding to for months. They were her way out when the pain got too much. Well the pain was too much now, a different pain, a kind of empty, nagging pain, but unbearable just the same She couldn't go on without Tom. What had she to live for now?

But those long ago years in Aunt Ada's care had left their mark. She had attended Sunday school regularly, she had been made to learn the Ten Commandants by heart. She had been taught that it was as sinful to kill oneself as one's fellow man. In her lifetime it had even been a criminal offence. For her punishment she might never see Tom again and she was a firm believer in the afterlife.

So she put the sleeping tablets back in their hiding place until they were really needed and made herself a cup of tea, for the ones at the nursing home had been left untouched. Then she fetched her sewing from her bedroom cupboard. She had one more buttonhole to do on the cornflower-blue blouse and she liked to do her buttonholes by hand.

'Our first honeymoon was heaven, Tom,' she said aloud, needing to hear a human voice, if only her own, in this empty void. 'Perhaps our second honeymoon will be in heaven too.' A short pause for reflection, a tearful smile. 'Or, more likely, the other place.'

Also by Elizabeth Tettmar
and available in Mandarin Paperbacks

THE YEARS BETWEEN

Elizabeth Tettmar

Sometimes love is worth waiting for . . .

When Helena Roseberry, living in the sleepy Norfolk village of Thornmere meets radical journalist Paul Berkeley just after the Great War, her life is transformed. Passionately in love, she runs away with Paul to London.

Daniel Harker, a millionaire war profiteer and owner of Thornmere Hall, has long wanted the one thing his money can't buy: the love of Helena. Even though, along with the rest of Thornmere, she despises him. He knows that one day she will return to the village, no longer a young, innocent girl. And he has never been one to accept defeat gracefully . . .

THE SCARLET LANDSCAPE

Elizabeth Tettmar

On Saturday 7th 1940, the day she had fondly hoped would see her married, Philippa Byrd was having her first permanent wave. Since Leo had left for Aldershot without further discussion of their future state of rebellion.

Philippa lives in Essex and works in a London bank. She falls in love with the cautious Leo at a Boy Scouts dance and has dreamt of marriage ever since. Leo is not one to show his feelings, but Philippa knows that 'still waters run deep' and when war breaks out she is sure it will galvanise him into action. But Leo, ever the pessimist, decides it would be best to wait, and the wedding bells ringing in Philippa's ears jangle to a halt.

Leo is suddenly posted overseas, and Philippa, now working in a Norwich bank and resigned to awaiting his return, meets dashing young pilot Joe Gilbert, stationed near Thornmere. It is then she discovers the real meaning of love and her life is turned upside down.

HOUSE OF BIRDS

Elizabeth Tettmar

Foster women don't marry, you'll learn that soon enough . . .

All tall, all beautiful, all born out of wedlock:

Lottie – Daughter of Norfolkshire signalman, violated in the first bloom of her womanhood – never to return to the gatehouse of her childhood;

Charlotte – The child of a man she believed a war hero, embittered by life until she discovers the love of an American airman;

Charley – Born in an air-raid shelter, brought up by her mother and grandmother, the beauty who falls for the artist who must paint her into his life;

Carla – The happy-go-lucky girl who cares for her great-grandmother, rediscovers the gatehouse of so long ago and finally pieces together the buried secrets of four generations of Foster women.